The Spirit of Troy

Arleen McFadden Anderson

Dear Kelly
Hope you enjoy the
Happy reading
stay. Merry Christmas
Arleen

ISBN-13: 978-1542773515
ISBN-10: 1542773512

DEDICATION

This story was written for all the hardworking, intrepid school bus drivers of the world, to dog lovers everywhere, and for those who are intrigued by the mysteries of the spirit.

TABLE OF CONTENTS

ACKNOWLEDGMENTS

Thanks to my unforgettable co-workers at Krise Bus Service in Harborcreek, Pennsylvania for their friendship, help, and understanding as I learned what it takes to be a school bus driver and for their encouragement as I was writing my first novel, Cliodhna's Wave.

Special thanks to my brother, Frank McFadden, for his encouragement, and answering my incessant questions, and for sharing his knowledge in mortuary science which proved to be such a help in writing The Spirit of Troy.

1

EMPTY NEST

Cathy Pantona's heart ached as she waited on the back deck for her husband, Paul, to arrive home from work to put the family's beloved sheltie, Sadie, to rest with the other family pets that had passed on through the years. Their children, Julia, Anthony, and Alexandra, who had grown up with Sadie, were there for the occasion, somber faced and subdued. Cathy was especially emotional about Sadie's passing because in two months Alexandra would be graduating from high school and leaving home to begin her freshman year at Carnegie Mellon University, College of Fine Arts, in Pittsburgh, Pennsylvania. Two years ago, Cathy had felt anxious and sad when Anthony began his studies in Forensic Science and Archaeology at Mercyhurst University in Erie but, because it was only a half-hour drive to Mercyhurst and she saw him quite often, she had adjusted to his leaving. With Sadie's passing and Alexandra soon fledging, Cathy was now feeling a panicky desperation mixed with her grief.

The Pantona's had adopted Sadie when the kids were eleven, seven, and five; and, although the girls adored Sadie and vice versa, seven-year-old Tony had developed a special bond with the pup. Anthony tagged along when Cathy took Sadie to veterinarian appointments, the groomer, and to puppy and obedience classes where he was eager to learn how to handle Sadie. Much to Cathy's and Paul's surprise, Tony took on the responsibilities of feeding, walking, and bathing Sadie. He loved roughhousing with her, teaching her tricks, and taking her to explore the woods that

1

separated their back yard from St. Margaret's Cemetery. Cathy smiled remembering her mixture of displeasure and amusement when Anthony and Sadie would arrive home from their adventures completely filthy then sending him off to bathe Sadie in the back yard. She closed her eyes a moment and could almost hear their cheerful duet of laughter and barking as the two got soaked in the process. Cathy had been concerned about how Anthony would handle the loss. When he first heard the news, he had broken down, but now he appeared to be holding up fairly well. When he arrived, he seemed stoically sad and Cathy's eyes had welled up immediately, knowing he was hiding his sorrow.

Julia was seated in the wrought iron bench in the midst of Cathy's perennial garden to the side of the pet graves. Julia was Cathy's and Paul's girly-girl daughter who had graduated from cosmetology school and was making such a nice income working at Trendy Tresses Hair Salon she was able to purchase her own little cottage style house that had a white picket fence in front and small fenced-in back yard near the salon. Ever since Cathy could remember, Julia had been interested in clothing, makeup, and hairstyles, and was constantly experimenting with new ways to wear her hair. It was difficult for Cathy to picture the natural light brown tone of Julia's hair anymore. After Julia's relentless nagging to be allowed to dye her hair blonde for her sixteenth birthday, Cathy had finally surrendered. Since then, Julia had tried every hair color of the rainbow at one time or another. Lately, Julia had her hair styled in a smooth asymmetrical cut, colored very dark, with fine subtle streaks of purple intermingled. As much as Cathy questioned Julia's adventurous hair color experiments, she had to admit the slight hint of purple enhanced how beautiful Julia looked surrounded by blue wild indigo, pink dicentra, foamflower, and dwarf iris against the green backdrop of the woods.

Alexandra and Anthony were strolling and talking among the pet graves, no doubt reminiscing. Despite being six inches shorter than Tony, Alexandra so resembled him they looked like twins. They both had dark, straight, brunette hair, dark eyes, and an olive complexion that tanned easily. Appearance, however, was where their similarity ended. Alexandra tended to be brutally honest and outspoken, and dressed in a devil-may-care style, putting together outlandish outfits with finds from garage sales, estate sales, thrift stores, and consignment shops. Somehow, though, she always looked put together, the colors and patterns blending together pleasingly. Today she wore black jeans that were splotched with light sky blue paint, combined with a blouse straight out of the 1940's that had flowers the same blue as the paint splotches. To top off her ensemble, she wore a floppy, black, straw hat that she had dressed up by creating a hatband using a wide, sky blue ribbon tied around the crown leaving the ends trailing down her back. On the right side of the ribbon, she had pinned a small bouquet of blue iris and baby's breath.

Tony's personality was much more reserved than Alexandra's. He was an excellent listener, did not jump to conclusions, was more self-controlled, and thought before he spoke. He would definitely speak his mind, but was more diplomatic, seldom blurting things out abruptly. He tended to be a conciliator who often rescued his sister from jams when she expressed herself in her uncensored fashion. He was amused by things Alexandra said and did, and she appreciated his support.

The loss of Sadie exaggerated Cathy's desire to hold onto her children, which conflicted with the pride she felt in them for the fine young adults they had become. Looking at Anthony wistfully, she wanted to move an errant lock of his dark, straight hair that hung before his left eye. She would have to tell him to let Julia trim his hair while they were both here together.

Paul pulled into the driveway and Cathy got up to kiss him hello. "Hi, Hon. Just going to go in and change," Paul told her.

"Okay. I'll go and wait with the kids." Cathy picked up a small wreath leaning against the wall behind her chair and walked to the Pantona Pet Cemetery. She placed the wreath against the white pet coffin which sat where Paul would dig her grave after dinner when it was cooler. Cathy glanced to the right of Sadie's coffin at Suzy's grave. Suzy was a black and white, fifty pound, pit bull terrier/Labrador retriever/boxer mix that Cathy had adopted from the animal shelter a year before she and Paul married. When Suzy died, all three children had been inconsolable. The household had plodded along in a fog of depression for several months until Paul came home from work one day with six-week-old Sadie and joy was restored to the family.

To Suzy's right lay Big Sammy. Cathy fondly remembered the large grey feral cat who had wandered into their lives from the woods that separated their property from St. Margaret Cemetery to

3

retire from his wild ways and allow the Pantona family the privilege of his company. When Sammy moved in, Sadie had just turned one and Cathy was still amusedly amazed remembering how the old tomcat tolerated the rambunctious Sadie, and how the two eventually became great playmates and companions.

Cathy smiled when she looked at the large round rock with a goldfish painted on it that sat front and center of all the graves. Julia, being the oldest, had been the first of the children to be given the responsibility of her very own pet--a goldfish she named Goldilocks. When Goldilocks died and Paul and Cathy had intended to provide a fish funeral down the toilet, Julia had been mortified and insisted Goldie be buried with due respect and reverence. Cathy shook her head wondering how many fish fertilized the ground around that stone along with Goldilocks. She glanced at the remaining graves--a lawn statue of a rabbit marking the resting spot for Alexandra's black and white rabbit, Elmer; and four garden stepping stones engraved with images of birds memorializing parakeets, Buttercup and Petey, Caruso the canary, and Bella the lovebird. Overlooking all of the Pantona pets was a four-foot statue of Saint Francis with a bird on his shoulder, a lamb at his feet, and a bowl in his hands that Cathy tried to keep filled with birdseed.

Paul came jogging across the lawn to the gathering place and, as if on cue, the sun's rays burst from behind a fluffy cloud. When he reached them, Cathy, Julia, Anthony, and Alexandra were lined up by Sadie's grave. Paul bowed his head. "Another one of our loving family members, Sadie, has left us and she will wait for our spirits to join her on the other side," he said softly. "The strong bonds between all of us and Sadie can never be broken and we need only remember her to reestablish the connection we shared. As we recall the joy of living with her, we can be comforted that we will reunite with her at our passing. Sadie was a loyal, loving, vital part of our family, and she will be sorely missed until we see her again." Following that, Paul recited The Rainbow Bridge Prayer and The Twenty-Third Psalm.

With misty eyes, everyone placed a red rose on Sadie's coffin and Paul, Cathy, and Julia headed back to the house. Alexandra stayed back to talk with Tony. "I guess that's it."

"Yeah," Tony said softly. "It's not going to be the same without Sadie around here."

"I know," Alexandra replied dismally, glancing at her mother walking hand in hand with her father toward the house. "I think it's actually going to be the worst for Mom. After I leave in September, she's going to feel really lonesome. You know how she is."

"Yeah, Mom and Dad are going to have to get another pet or she's going to have to start a hobby to keep busy. Wonder if we could get her interested in something. Maybe for her birthday we could chip in and get her a membership at a fitness club or something."

"I don't know. I don't recall her ever complaining that she's not exercising enough, but you never know. I'll feel her out. Between you, me, and Julia, we ought to come up with something."

Alexandra and Tony joined their parents and Julia inside, and after reminiscing about Sadie, and touching upon what was going on in each of their lives, conversation eventually rolled around to Alexandra's schoolwork and graduation. "I've got to get busy on my research paper for history. Everyone's got to trace their ancestry back to 1800, pick one favorite relative, then describe what life may have been like for him or her," she bemoaned wearily.

"Oh my gosh, Alexandra! Don't tell me you haven't even started on that yet," Cathy reprimanded.

Alexandra grimaced, regretting that she opened the subject. "Oh, I've started, but it's a long project. It's hard to track down information about non-descript, every-day people. It's not exactly my favorite thing to do."

"Unfortunately, honey, there are many things in life that won't be your favorites, but you'll have to do them anyway," Paul told her.

"Yes," Cathy agreed, "And remember, you never know how something might benefit you in the future."

"I'm not planning on being a historian, genealogist, writer, or anything like that. So, this project is just a waste of my time," Allie insisted.

"I'm sure your history teacher knows you're an art student. Why don't you do some illustrations with your report. You have an interest in vintage clothing. Maybe it would be fun for you to add sketches of the dress of the day. In fact, you could possibly do a street scene of what it might have looked like in the eighteen hundreds. I don't know if you'd be able to use that with your report, but you certainly could add it to the portfolio you have to compile for the art department," Cathy suggested.

"Maybe," Alexandra began considering the idea.

"How about if I help you with your report?" Cathy offered enthusiastically.

"Mom!" Although actually wanting some help, Alexandra bristled at the suggestion she needed help. "I'm supposed to do this myself."

"I know that. I'm not going to do it for you. I'll just help you with the research. I'll see if I can find some good websites to use and we can go to the Courthouse, Vital Records Office, maybe the library to see if we can locate information about our ancestors. I've wanted to research our family tree anyway."

Alexandra's mixed feelings about her mother helping with the project disintegrated when it dawned on her that this might be exactly the thing her mother needed. Her mother's zeal was obvious. Allie could rationalize accepting the much needed help because it was beneficial to her mother as well. "Sure then, thanks! That would be awesome. Mr. Harris already gave us a couple of websites to look at to get everyone started."

"Great, honey. Right after dinner you can show me what you've gotten done so far and we'll get this project moving."

Alexandra stiffened. She had nothing to show her mother that she'd accomplished. "O-okay," she stammered.

Everyone lingered around the table after they finished eating until Paul announced, "Might as well get out there and prepare Sadie's final resting place next to Suzy. I know Suzy will make her feel welcome." Paul smiled slightly.

"I'll go out and help you, Dad," Tony said. The two left the house to retrieve their shovels from the shed and then headed to the pet cemetery.

After Julia, Alexandra, and Cathy cleaned up the kitchen, Julia said, "I'll be on my way, Mom. I've got a couple errands to run on the way home and work week starts again tomorrow, you know. Got to get my beauty rest."

"Okay, dear. Thanks for coming over."

"Jeez, Mom. You don't have to thank me for that! Thank you for cooking dinner for all of us." Julia hugged Cathy and kissed her cheek goodbye. "Bye, Allie," she said as exited the back door.

"Bye, sis," Allie responded. "See you soon."

Cathy looked out the back window and saw that Paul and Tony were making headway in their digging. They were leaning on their shovels looking sweaty and dirty. "Let's bring your brother and father something to drink."

"Good idea," said Allie who immediately got up and retrieved a couple of large insulated tumblers with tops on them while Cathy got out the large pitcher of lemonade from the fridge. "I want to say a final farewell to Sadie, anyway," she said while putting ice in the tumblers.

"You carry the glasses and I'll bring the pitcher to refill for them," Cathy replied and the two left the kitchen.

When Allie and Cathy joined the boys, it appeared the grave was deep enough to accommodate the coffin. "Looks like you're just about done," Cathy said.

"I want to go just a little bit deeper," Paul said. "Thanks for the lemonade, ladies." He took a long drink. "Boy, that's good. Lucky, the ground back here is softened up a little from the rain yesterday."

"Yeah, and not too many rocks, although there were a couple big ones," Tony said pointing to a round boulder close to two-foot in diameter.

"It's good that you were helping me, Tony. I wouldn't have been able to get that out by myself."

"Gee, it's kind of pretty," Cathy said walking over to inspect the rock closer. "I can see some pinks in that stone that are set off by black. It'll make a nice landscaping rock."

Paul laughed. "If you're going to use it for landscaping, I'd appreciate it if you found a place for it back here. I don't even want to try and get it on the cart. I think it will look fine right where it is now between Sadie and Suzie's headstones."

"Mm, we'll see," Cathy replied.

"Well, if you've got an idea where you want it, tell me now while your son's here so he can help me move it," Paul rolled his eyes, handed his glass to Allie, and went back to digging as did Tony.

Allie held their glasses while Cathy refilled them. "We'll put your drinks down over here on the table by the bench."

"Okay, thanks girls," Paul shouted from the hole.

Tony thrust his shovel in again and hit something solid. He tried a couple more times, with the same result. "Dad, I think I might have hit a big tree root or something."

Paul turned around and tried his luck, then started digging a little less deeply to see what they were hitting. Cathy and Allie returned to the gravesite to observe. After a few minutes, Tony bent over and began removing dirt with his gloved hands. "I don't know, Dad. Here's some splintering wood, but it doesn't look like a tree root. And this is soft. There's something hard down there, too." Everyone peered into the hole, but the light was waning so it was impossible to see what was buried where they were digging.

"Do you want to dig down further?" Tony asked his father.

Paul considered a moment. "It's probably tree roots is all, son. Maybe some rocks, too." He glanced at Cathy and Allie who were staring wide-eyed into the grave. "I don't think it's some buried treasure chest, if that's what you're hoping. I think we should just stop digging here, place Sadie in her resting spot, and cover her up."

"But Dad, don't you want to see if there is something buried there?" Tony asked.

"What in the world do you think is under here, son? I think your studies might be feeding your imagination a little," Paul laughed.

"Your father's right, Tony. You've dug down far enough. Sadie needs to be laid to rest," Cathy said, then turned to Alexandra, "Now, you wanted to start on your history paper, didn't you? Let's get started."

Allie had hoped her mother had forgotten their conversation about her term paper and was braced for a quarrel when they got up to her room. Surprisingly, though, instead of being angry about the lack of progress on the report, Cathy seemed gratified to feel so needed by her daughter and dove into the project wholeheartedly.

With her mother helping with the research, the part Allie disliked the most, Allie was able to concentrate on the creative end and, as her mother suggested, added sketches of clothing and household objects of the 1800's. She also took her mother's advice and painted a street scene inspired from what she had learned from their research. She depicted the sidewalks made of wood, the streets hard-packed dirt, and store signs made from simple pieces of wood with hand-painted lettering. Women walked on the sidewalks wearing tight-bodiced, full-skirted dresses carrying parasols. She painted a couple of men sitting in chairs on the sidewalk, one leaning against a storefront lighting a pipe. She painted a beautiful woman wearing a dark blue, flower-printed dress walking on the sidewalk holding the hand of a young lad with blonde hair wearing overalls, with an Australian shepherd dog following them. A large, dark bay horse was harnessed to a buckboard wagon in front of a general store, its reins tied to the hitching rail. Mr. Harris gave Allie the highest grade possible for her term paper and added extra credit for her artwork.

Alexandra had been right. Helping with her history paper was the start of a new passion for her mother who became consumed with researching the Pantona family tree. One website, in particular, Find-A-Grave.com, had particularly fascinated Cathy. Not only was it helpful with Allie's project, but Cathy developed friendships online with the Find-A-Grave community. Cathy signed up as a volunteer to help locate and photograph graves in the Erie County area for people looking for graves of relatives through Find-A-Grave and she developed a close friendship with the secretary at St. Margaret Cemetery, Sharon Mitchell.

2

THE MISSING MOTHER

By August, Find-A-Grave volunteering had become part of Cathy's daily routine. She enjoyed satisfying the requests of people who were trying to find long lost relatives and friends. If she was asked to find and photograph a gravesite, she oftentimes found the grave unkempt and would take it upon herself to tidy it up. On a couple of occasions, relatives had ordered flowers at a local florist and requested that the bouquets be placed on the grave of their loved ones, a service Cathy very much enjoyed providing.

It was a balmy August morning, and Cathy was again assisting an individual looking for a relative believed to be buried in St. Margaret Cemetery. This was the fourth time she was responding to an inquiry at St. Margaret and, because of the proximity to her home, she was thrilled to accept the assignment. She always enjoyed the stroll through the patch of woods that separated the cemetery from their property.

When she and Paul moved into their home, Paul had cleared a path to enable her to visit her mother's grave in St. Margaret Cemetery whenever she wished. Cathy and her mother, Grace, shared an extremely close relationship grown from the fact that Cathy's father had abandoned the family shortly after Cathy was born. From then on Grace and Cathy were a team, strong together in their love and support of one another. When Grace passed after an unsuccessful battle against cancer shortly after Paul and Cathy married, Cathy felt devastated, lost, and frightened.

That was, in fact, the reason they purchased their home so close to the cemetery--so Cathy could remain close to her mother.

Cathy said hello to the deceased family pets as she passed through the Pantona Pet Cemetery and began her walk to St. Margaret Cemetery. The sun was glittering through the rustling leaves while chipmunks, squirrels, and birds skittered about. As she walked, she squinted through the foliage hoping to get a glimpse of the deer that often visited her yard at dusk and dawn. In only fifteen minutes, she was entering the manicured solemnity of the cemetery grounds. She planned to visit her mother's grave, and along the way, she acknowledged the now familiar names on headstones as if they were her mother's friends and neighbors. One day, she would try to learn a little more about their lives, too.

She arrived at her mother's plot and carefully brushed off the few stray leaves and bits of debris from the top of the gravestone and swept away some grass clippings off its base. "Hi, Mom," she said in a very quiet voice. "Thanks for watching out for me. I feel you with me constantly." She continued talking as she yanked out a few weeds that did not require a tool to pull. "Oh my, I'm going to have to remember to come back with my weed digger and a bucket. Some of these weeds are toughies." A fleeting feeling of chagrin caused Cathy to look around to see if anyone was within earshot. Seeing no one, she continued talking. "We really miss you, Mom. You know, Allie's almost ready to leave for school. The house is going to seem awfully empty without her. She's grown up way too fast, but we'll get through it. Going to look for a neighbor of yours today. He's been here for a long time--looks like he died in the Civil War. Wonder if you've had occasion to meet him." Cathy smiled. "Name's Sergeant Jeffrey Powell. If you see him around, tell him I'm looking for him on behalf of one of his descendants, okay?" Cathy got up. "Bye for now. I'm going to see what I can do about finding Sergeant Powell. Love you, Mom."

On her way to the cemetery office, she smiled, thinking how ridiculous she probably sounded. However, what did it matter, she felt a sense of communication with her mother. Another five minutes and Cathy was entering the cemetery office.

"Hi Sharon. Here to bother you again today," Cathy said with a smile.

"Oh, you're no bother. I'm always happy to see you when you drop by. How are you today?"

"I'm great. Enjoying the beautiful weather."

"I envy you for that. Of course, as much as I'd like summers off, I don't know that I'd want to be a school bus driver. The people I'm responsible for never cause trouble."

"No, you never have to yell at them to stay in their seat, or to quiet down, do you," Cathy agreed with a little laugh.

"No, we've got a pretty peaceful bunch here," Sharon smirked. "So, what're you up to today? Looking for another lost relative for someone?"

"Mm-hm, yes I am. This gentleman will probably be in the oldest part of the cemetery. His name is Sergeant Jeffrey Powell and he died during the Civil War."

"Oh, yes, he'd be among the first people buried here. St. Margaret Cemetery was established during the Civil War--1862. His grave won't be very far from the office. Having died that long ago, I hope his headstone will still be legible. A lot of the old memorials are so eroded by the elements that the engravings have been reduced to mere dimples in the stones." Sharon sat down at her computer and began typing. "Let's see if we can find him. I'm glad we've loaded all of our residents in the computer. It's quicker and easier to look people up and we have access to much more information about them." A couple more pecks at her keyboard and, "Uh-huh, here he is--Sergeant Jeffrey James Powell, died July 2, 1863. He's in Section A, Lot Number 1, Grave Number 44. At the St. Margaret Statue, take the road to the left. All roads converge upon the centerpiece and the sections are shaped like pie pieces from there, but you know that by now." Sharon jotted the information on a piece of scratch paper and handed it to Cathy. "I'll pull up the map for you." Sharon hit a few keys and turned her computer screen for Cathy to see.

"Just like you thought," Cathy said. "His grave isn't too far from here at all."

"No, it's not," Sharon turned her screen back. "I'll print out this section for you and note some of the names of the people around Sergeant Powell. That way, if you can't read his stone, you might be able to identify it by the others around it."

"Wonderful! Thanks, Sharon. You're such a help. You know, you should consider becoming a member of Find-A-Grave, too. We could go and look for people together."

"If I had more time, I would."

"Maybe one day. Until then, you can be my official technical helper," Cathy grinned. "Better let you get back to work."

"Don't do me any favors," Sharon smiled. "Stop back before you go home and let me know what you find."

"Okay, I'll be back." Cathy exited the air-conditioned office, glad to be back in the warm summer air. She turned to the left and saw the marker for Section A. Looking for the lot, she glanced at the names and dates on the headstones as she walked. As Sharon had thought, some engravings had been reduced to illegible soft indentations in white stone markers.

Cathy stopped and studied the printout in her hand. She walked in eight rows and counted the number of graves from the edge of the section. As she walked, she looked for any of the names Sharon had jotted down. With satisfaction, she discovered the Flynn memorial and saw a large bush next to it where Sergeant Powell's grave should have been. She walked to the headstone on the other side of the bush, which was in poor but legible shape, and saw it did not belong to Sergeant Powell. She found the stones for several other names that Sharon noted on the map, and squinted suspiciously at the large bush. Was that a glimpse of stone crying out for discovery within the overgrown bush?

Separating the branches, Cathy discovered it was not one large bush, it was two bushes, grown together to form one mass, concealing a thin tablet-style grave marker within it. Pulling the tangled foliage and intertwined branches apart a little further and peering in, she was thrilled to see the name, "Powell," clearly legible on the stone. She did her best to take a photograph of the headstone and the current state of the gravesite. Once she showed the photo to Sharon, Cathy knew the groundskeepers would be put to work to clean up Sergeant Powell's little piece of real estate right away.

Being such a beautiful day, Cathy strolled a little longer through Section A, glancing at the names of Sergeant Powell's neighbors. She found it interesting, if not downright intriguing, to read headstones, especially the older ones that occasionally had a poetic note inscribed in honor of the deceased. Drawn to the flowers

13

adorning the graves in the bordering lot, she came upon several block type monuments bearing the name, Anatoli. In the center was a black-stained obelisk decorated with carved grapevines with the inscription, Virgilio Crudele Anatoli, Father, June 19, 1817 to May 14, 1895. 'Wonder if he's the first of the Anatolis to live in Harborcreek,' Cathy mused as she walked around the obelisk looking for Mrs. Anatoli's inscription. Not seeing a name for the matriarch, Cathy frowned and read the names on the stones surrounding Virgilio's obelisk carefully. The four Anatoli memorials in closest proximity to Virgilio's marked the resting spot for one teenaged boy and three men born from 1844 to 1854, all with "Son" inscribed above their names.

'Hmm, what a close-knit family to be still placing flowers at the graves of decedents that died that long ago,' Cathy mused. She wandered a little more but saw no sign of a memorial for Virgilio's wife, presumably the mother of his sons, and she headed back to the cemetery office.

"Find him?" Sharon asked when Cathy walked in.

"Mm-hm, he was hiding behind some bushes, but I found him." Cathy took her phone from her pocket and showed Sharon the photos of Sergeant Powell's gravesite and marker.

"Oh my! I'll tell the groundskeepers to clean that up. We need to cut those bushes way back or pull them out altogether. We can't have our Civil War heroes hidden away in the bushes."

"Yes, I'm glad someone contacted us. Do you think Sergeant Powell put a bug in his great-great-great grandson's ear that someone needed to tend to his grave?" Cathy giggled.

"You never know," Sharon smiled with a raised eyebrow.

"Sure looks like no one has been around to watch over his grave for a long time. I didn't see any other Powell graves around his, either. Do you think he was the first and last of his line around here?"

"Could be. The U.S. was changing rapidly in Civil War times, adding territories and all. Maybe his family heeded the call to go west and seek their fortune. Where does the person who sent the inquiry live?"

"Idaho, so you're probably right. That's when the west was being settled, the Transcontinental Railroad was being constructed, and all that. Perhaps the family was having a hard time making ends meet after Sergeant Powell died and thought they'd try and make it out west." Cathy put her phone back in her pocket. "I'll send the photos to the family and let them know Sergeant Powell's resting place will be cleaned up and once it is, I'll send photos of the makeover to them."

"I'm sure they'll be comforted to know the Sergeant was found and his plot will be looked after from now on."

"I'm sure they will and they'll be glad that a piece of their family history has been found. I saw that he's buried near a number of the members of the Anatoli family. I didn't realize how long that family had been living in Harborcreek."

"Mm-hm, from what I understand, the Anatolis were one of the first families to settle here. I think most of the Anatolis are interred at St. Margaret, but they're not all in that particular section. You'll find them here and there throughout the cemetery. You know, don't you, that St. Margaret Cemetery was once part of their land that they donated to the church for use as a cemetery."

"No, I didn't know that," Cathy replied with interest.

"Yes, if you think they own a large farm now, you should look up the records at the Historical Society. It was immense in the eighteen hundreds. I don't know how they could've taken care of it. Of course, they had a number of children. Do you know they're the first family to grow grapes around here? I think grapes were more or less an experiment for Mr. Anatoli and he grew a variety of other crops and had livestock, too. But, like I said, they donated a large parcel to the church, sold some parcels, then gave sections to their children, until what's left is the farm they own today with the main family home on Depot Road, many times remodeled. Still a nice piece of land, but nothing like it was to begin with. In fact, I'm pretty sure your property was once part of their farm, too. Might be interesting to research it."

"Hmm. I might just do that when I go downtown again," Cathy hesitated a moment. "And I may be going very soon. I noticed something strange about the Anatoli graves that's aroused my curiosity."

"Oh? What's that?"

"On the obelisk, there's no inscription next to Virgilio's for his wife, and I didn't see a separate marker for her anywhere else in that section either. Do you know if she's buried in another section of St. Margaret?

"Not off hand, but I can look it up. I'll have to look at Virgilio's record to find out her name and cross reference. You're right, that's unusual."

"I thought so, too."

"I wonder if she outlived Mr. Anatoli and remarried. Maybe she's with her new husband's family."

"Virgilio died in his eighties, so that seems unlikely," said Cathy. "But you never know. She could've been a very young woman when they married."

"She might even be buried with her own mother and father. I'll do some checking to see if there's a record of her interment here."

"Maybe I'll take a drive to the courthouse tomorrow and see if I can find out anything more about her. Do you want to go to lunch tomorrow and compare notes?"

"Sure, I'd love to." Sharon snickered. "I like this--I kind of feel like a detective."

"Me, too," Cathy laughed. "Guess that's why I like Find-A-Grave. You're always trying to find someone, but one good thing, your quarry always stays put. How about if I swing by here around noon tomorrow?"

"Sounds good."

"Thanks again for your help. See you tomorrow."

"It's my pleasure, Cathy. It's always a treat when you come by. You give me a little break from my routine."

"I'm sure things can get a little dead around here," Cathy winked and walked to the door with a little wave.

Sharon groaned and shook her head, smiling. "See you tomorrow."

Cathy shared her mystery with Paul and Allie during supper. "I came upon something strange while I was at the cemetery today."

"Uh-oh," Paul laughed. "You're not going to tell us you're seeing ghosts, are you?"

"Tch, no," Cathy responded, amused but slightly irritated by his sarcasm. "Actually, what I didn't see is the strange thing. I had just located a Civil War veteran's grave today for a Find-A-Grave client and the veteran happened to be in the same section as the Anatoli family. Sharon says that the Anatolis buried in St. Margaret were one of the first families to settle in Harborcreek. I saw graves for the father, Virgilio, and four of his sons, but there's no grave for the mother. Don't you think that's odd?"

Alexandra looked up but did not display the same interest as Cathy.

"What are you talking about?" Paul asked.

"I looked all around and there's a grave for the founding father and his offspring, but no mother. Wonder what became of her?"

"Maybe she's buried in her folks' plot," Paul suggested.

"That's what we were wondering. Sharon's going to see if she can find out her name in the cemetery records and see if that's the case. It just seems strange, though."

"When you consider the Anatolis are a little strange, guess you should figure their ancestors might be, too," Allie said with a chuckle.

"I wouldn't say they're strange, dear. They just keep to themselves a little more than other people," Cathy said.

"Oh, Mom, you're being nice. They're not strange or quiet, they're just stuck up," Alexandra said matter-of-factly.

"Now, Alexandra, you don't know that for certain. I don't recall you having much contact with any of them."

"That's why. She didn't want to associate with commoners like me. Don't forget, Amelia Anatoli was one year ahead of me in school and she lived so close by. I remember how she was and the things the other kids said about her."

"Allie, Amelia didn't even go to the same school as you, so you don't really know her. Maybe she's just shy. You can't decide on a person's character simply by hearsay."

"It's not just hearsay, Mom. Even though she's always gone to private schools, I've seen her in action at football games. Of course, she was a cheerleader but I could just see how she was with the other girls and guys for that matter. Evie told me…"

Paul cut off his daughter's gossip by returning to the subject of the missing Mrs. Anatoli, prompting a dirty look from Allie. "Maybe Mrs. Anatoli left the old man, hon."

"In those days? Cathy said. "Not likely."

"So what do you think happened to her?" Paul asked.

"It's not so much that I think something happened to her. I'm just curious about where she might be buried and why she's not lying next to Mr. Anatoli, but, now that you put it that way . . ."

"Oh, no. Don't concoct some sordid story and start acting like you think you're a cold case detective. The Anatolis might not appreciate you searching for skeletons in their family closet," Paul advised. "Why don't you forget about them and finish your work on our own family tree."

"Oh, I'm working on ours, but this intrigued me today."

"Being intrigued is fine, but the history of the Anatoli family isn't your concern." A line of disapproval appeared between Paul's eyebrows. "I can't wait until school starts and you get back on your bus route. You have a little too much time on your hands and I think you're getting over-involved with this Find-A-Grave stuff."

"I'm going to ignore that. It's just a hobby and I enjoy it. I find it interesting. And I'm helping people out," Cathy said with a touch of smugness. "I've found that the people I've helped through Find-A-Grave have been very grateful and the Anatolis might end up feeling the same way."

Paul rolled his eyes, shook his head, and skewed his pursed lips into a crooked line which Cathy interpreted as disapproval, disgust, and disrespect. She now wished she hadn't brought up her Anatoli mystery and was certainly glad she didn't mention her plan to go to the Courthouse to do further research.

Although the subject was dropped for the rest of the night, Cathy went to bed still wondering why there was no Mrs. Anatoli buried by Virgilio Anatoli and his sons in St. Margaret Cemetery.

3

MISS MARPLE

Paul jumped out of bed to turn the alarm off so as not to disturb Cathy, but he wasn't quick enough. Cathy had awakened and was now sitting up in bed, yawning, and rubbing her eyes.

"I'm sorry, hon. Go back to sleep," he whispered.

"No, I want to get up early today."

"What on earth for?" Paul laughed. "I'd give my eye teeth to have summers off and sleep in."

"The thing is, I want to get the most out of my time off, and I've got a lot to do today."

"Oh? What's on your agenda?"

"For one thing, I'm going to lunch with Sharon." Cathy stretched and hopped out of bed.

"That's not going to be until around noon. What've you got, another Find-A-Grave project?"

"Mm-hm." Cathy put on her robe and hoped he would leave it at that.

"I didn't even know you got on the computer last night. Who's the dear departed this time?"

"I'm not even sure of the full name, honey. I'm going to have to do some research downtown." Cathy saw the light turn on in Paul's head and cringed.

"Don't tell me you're actually going to look into the whereabouts of the missing Mrs. Anatoli." Paul put his hands on his hips and looked at Cathy with reproach.

"Don't look at me like that! I'm not your child. I'm curious, and it doesn't hurt anyone to look at public records."

"Oh, honey, I really don't think you should be snooping into the past of someone else's family."

"Good Lord, Paul. It's not my big plan to drag a skeleton out of the closet and wave it around town to humiliate anyone. I'm just satisfying my own curiosity. Besides, how would someone from the Anatoli family find out I'm researching their ancestors?"

"You never know, Cath. One of the clerks might know one of the Anatolis." Paul sighed loudly, turned, and walked into the bathroom. "But, suit yourself. I know you're going to do it anyway."

"That's right," Cathy said in a singsong voice. "Since I'm up, do you want me to make a nice breakfast for you for a change?"

"No thanks. I'll just have my usual cup of coffee. My stomach might not know what to do with a full belly before I go to work."

Cathy shrugged. "Okay, I'll go start a fresh pot of coffee while you take your shower. How about a bagel with cream cheese?"

"That sounds good."

As Cathy walked downstairs, bits and pieces of the dreams she'd had during the night flitted through her thoughts. She poured water in the coffeemaker and shivered remembering the last dream she'd had. It was the kind of dream everyone experiences now and then, but the kind she especially hated. She dreamt she was falling, but as hard as she tried, she couldn't picture from what she was falling, why she was falling, or how far she was falling. All she knew was that she was falling, arms flailing, with that weightless, helpless feeling of plummeting to the ground, with butterflies in her stomach, and the spine-tingling terror dreading the inevitable collision with the earth. She had awakened with a start while still in mid-air, and returned to a light sleep before the alarm went off.

Cathy took a couple of bagels and the cream cheese out of the refrigerator, put the bagels in the toaster oven, and got the morning newspaper from the tube holder next to the mailbox. It was another beautiful day. She smiled at the golden glow of the sun just coming up over the lush green waves of the grapevines across the road and inhaled the delicious aroma of the Concords that were plump on the vine, almost ready for harvest. Soon, Mr. Hackenburg would be telling her and Paul to go ahead and pick a bunch for themselves now and then. The thought of those fresh-picked, juicy, tender, purple balls made her mouth water. She went back in the house looking over the headlines.

By the time Paul entered the kitchen, Cathy was already enjoying her bagel and a cup of coffee. "You sleep okay?" he asked kissing her forehead. "You seemed a little restless last night." Paul poured coffee into his tall Pittsburgh Steelers travel mug.

"I don't feel tired but I was restless--had a lot of dreams. My personal theatre was open last night."

"Do you think your dwelling on Mrs. Anatoli and your plans for today might have had anything to do with that?" Paul raised an eyebrow.

"You're making way too big a deal out of this," Cathy said, putting her cup down and staring at him. "So what if one of the Anatolis finds out I'm researching their family? Maybe they'll even be flattered."

"Really?" Paul laughed a little. "Put yourself in their place. How would you feel if someone was investigating your ancestors?"

"I'd be grateful, ask them what they'd found, and join them."

Paul shook his head. "Okay, honey. That's fine, but I don't think everyone would feel that way. Myself, I'd be very curious about why some neighbor I didn't know very well was so interested in my family's history."

"Let's just drop it, all right? If any problem arises because of what I'm doing, I'll cross that bridge when I come to it."

"Okay, Miss Marple, you go ahead and do your thing." Paul wrapped his bagel in a napkin and patted her back on his way to the door. "I've got to run. Big meeting this morning about a new client we picked up. I'll see you later. And stay out of trouble!"

Cathy laughed. "See you tonight. And, hey, I've got a ways to go before I'm as old as Miss Marple."

"But you're just as nosy."

"Thanks. I love you, too, honey."

After taking her shower and straightening up the house, Cathy headed to the Erie County Courthouse. At the Marriage License Bureau in Room 123, she found out that Virgilio Anatoli had married Lavinia Evelina Rosetti on July 13, 1843 when Virgilio was twenty-five and Lavinia was sixteen, but saw no other marriage record for Lavinia. Armed with Lavinia's maiden name and birth date of April 13, 1827, Cathy went next door to the Register of Wills to ask if their office could provide a date of death for Lavinia. Unable to help, the Register of Wills sent her to the basement to search records in the courthouse computer system.

On her way downstairs, Cathy's cellphone rang. "Hi, Sharon," she answered. "I'm at the courthouse right now and I found their marriage record. I'm on my way downstairs right now to do a search on the computer to see if I can find a date of death for Mrs. Anatoli. If I can't, I might drive to Vital Statistics or just do some poking around on my computer at home. We still on for lunch?"

"Yes, I'm looking forward to it," Sharon said. "I'm afraid I ran into a problem on my end. I wasn't even able to learn her name. It was weird. Her name was once listed with Virgilio's on the information for the burial site, but it was inked out so I couldn't read it. Let me have her name. Maybe she is buried here with her parents."

"Sure, it's Lavinia Evelina Rosetti." Cathy spelled it out for Sharon.

"Great. I'll see what I can find."

"Okay, I'll see you in a while."

Cathy was at the cemetery office a little before noon. Sharon was straightening up her desk when Cathy walked in. "Ready?" Cathy asked.

"Yep, just want to put the phones on voicemail till I'm back. Mr. Burns is at an appointment and won't be back until two-ish." Sharon pressed a couple buttons on her phone, took her purse from under her desk, and locked the door on their way out. "I'm afraid what I've found out makes everything all the more thought-provoking. I don't see any record for Lavinia at St. Margaret under Anatoli or Rosetti, even though her parents, brothers, and sisters are here. I even did a search just using her first name, but found nothing."

"Mmm, the plot thickens," Cathy said in a low voice and giggled. "Now that I've got her name, I can't wait until I can look her up on Find-A-Grave. If I don't see her, I'll try and get some advice from my on-line friends there."

"I'll talk to Mr. Burns when he gets back, too," Sharon said. "Maybe he'll have an idea how we can locate her."

"Gosh, poor Lavinia, lost for almost two hundred years."

"I wouldn't say she's lost. She might be lying peacefully where she should be for a perfectly logical reason. We just don't know where she is and why, yet. We'll find her," Sharon said with certainty.

"I hope so; my curious mind wants to know." Cathy opened her car and the two women got in.

"Did you look into the history of your property at all?"

"No, I didn't have enough time. I'm sure I'll be going back plenty of times after this, though. So where do you want to go? What're you hungry for?" Cathy asked as she pulled out of her parking spot. "I kind of have a taste for Panera Bread food."

"All right with me. I love Panera Bread and haven't been there in a while. Just keep me away from the bakery."

"You're no fun."

"No, I think I'm too much fun. I've got about twenty pounds to show for it that I'd like to get rid of." Sharon laughed and patted her stomach.

"Oh, come on. You look fine. Treat yourself. It's not like we go out to lunch together every day. I know I'm going to indulge."

"You're wicked," Sharon laughed again.

"I'm not wicked; it's their bakery that's wicked!"

The two batted around ideas about Lavinia's whereabouts and the possible reasons she was not at St. Margaret Cemetery throughout lunch, intermixed with discussions about their families, and idle chit-chat, without coming up with any new ideas, until Sharon asked Cathy if she had seen the marriage photo and write-up of a mutual acquaintance's daughter in the newspaper recently.

"That's it!" Cathy said louder than she intended and struck the table with her hand.

Sharon jumped, startled.

They both laughed and Cathy explained, "There might be something about her in an old newspaper. If the Anatolis were big landowners at that time, they were newsworthy people. Maybe there's a story about them getting divorced, or her dying, or leaving him, or going missing--something in the paper. Instead of going home after dropping you off, I think I'll take a trip to the library and see what I can find in the old Times News archives, if it was the Times News then, and if the library has records that go back that far."

"That's a great idea," Sharon said. "I'd love to go with you. If you still need any help looking through papers this weekend, let me know."

"I probably will," Cathy replied. "I'm not sure how often they would've published the paper back then, but there's sure to be a good number of issues that I'll have to go through. I think the most logical thing would be to start with the date of the last son's birth which we can find from his gravestone."

"That is, if Lavinia is the wife who gave birth to him. Maybe she didn't stay with Virgilio that long."

"Well, we could learn that if there's a birth announcement in the paper. I imagine they would announce births in those days for large landowners like Virgilio must have been. Vital Records in Erie County only goes back so far."

"Remember, I'll be available if you need me to help you this weekend."

When they returned to the cemetery, Cathy got out of the car with Sharon and walked to the Anatoli graves. She found the last-born son at rest by Virgilio's obelisk was Michael, born September 19, 1854. She jotted the information down on her purse notepad and left for the Blasco Library.

The woman at the information desk directed her to the Heritage Room where a middle-aged woman with chin length, dark, fluffy hair was working on a computer at a centrally located desk. She saw Cathy approaching, adjusted the reading glasses perched on her nose, and softly greeted her with a friendly smile. "Hello, I'm Karen. Is there anything I can help you with today, miss?"

Cathy explained what she was researching and Karen walked from behind the information desk to lead her to the microfilm files and readers. "That's an intriguing little project. In those days, the paper that eventually became the Erie Times was called the Erie Dispatch and was a weekly publication until 1864 when it became a daily. Another paper, the Erie Herald, which started up in 1878, merged with the Dispatch and the paper eventually changed its name to the Erie Dispatch Herald. The Times wasn't known as the Erie Daily Times until 1888. You can put your things down on any of the desks here," Karen told her and showed her where the issues of the Erie Dispatch were located. After explaining the organization of the microfilm, she pulled out the reel that would contain the September 19, 1854 birth announcement for Michael Anatoli and handed it to Cathy. "If you don't find anything in the Dispatch, you might want to look at The Erie Gazette which ran from 1820 through 1882 or the Erie Observer which began in 1829 and continued until 1888." Karen showed Cathy the location of those reels of microfilm. "Also, if you exhaust the microfilm records, I can show you where the obituary index is. Those records go back to 1822, so, those might be of help to you, too."

"Looks like I've got my work cut out for me. Let's hope I find something. Thanks for your help." Cathy said.

"Certainly. There are other materials that might be of interest to you, also. We have collections on family histories, county, and local histories, so just let me know and I'll be glad to show you where those are. Now, do you know how to use the microfilm readers?"

"Oh, yes. I'm an old hand at it. I just had a refresher course when I helped my daughter with a project recently."

"Okay, then. Good luck."

"Thank you. You've been a great help." Cathy smiled and sat down at the reader where she had deposited her purse and notebook. Because the Dispatch was printed weekly in 1854, it didn't take long to locate the birth announcement. Sure enough, Lavinia was listed as Michael Anatoli's mother, so she was very much alive on that date.

It occurred to Cathy that perhaps Lavinia could have died when she gave birth to Michael or shortly thereafter because of complications from the birth. At that time, St. Margaret Cemetery didn't exist because the land for the cemetery hadn't yet been donated to the church by Virgilio. Perhaps he donated the parcel because Lavinia was buried there and maybe Lavinia's grave was one of the unreadable graves in the oldest part of the cemetery. Of course, no record would exist of her burial site simply because the cemetery didn't exist when she was buried. On this premise, Cathy searched for a mention of Lavinia having passed away in childbirth in the next few issues, but saw nothing.

Next, Cathy requested the librarian to direct her to the obituary index. She scanned the data for the years 1854 through 1930 and found no record of Lavinia's death under Anatoli or Rosetti. She went back to the microfilm and scanned issues of The Dispatch, the Gazette, and the Observer for Death Notices.

Going on five o'clock, Cathy sighed heavily and decided to call it a day. She felt a headache starting from eyestrain and mental exhaustion, and was eager to relax and get some fresh air. When she got to her car, she phoned in an order for Chinese food, and then called Sharon to fill her in on the results of her sleuthing.

"If we look over the newspapers a little more carefully than I did today, and maybe the family histories, I'm hoping we'll find out what happened to Lavinia. It could be a long, tedious process. Are you sure you have enough time to help me with this on Saturday?"

"Sure I'm sure. If I didn't, I'd make the time. You've got me curious about this, too."

"I'm glad to hear that. Paul's got me thinking there's something wrong with me for wondering about this so much." Cathy laughed. "Probably a man-woman thing."

Sharon joined Cathy's laughter. "Yes, that Mars-Venus misunderstanding. But we Venetians can't stop now."

4

TROY

Cathy was putting the takeout Chinese food on the counter when she heard the garage door open. Pleased with the good timing, she began setting the table. "Hi Hon," she greeted Paul with a smile when he walked in. "How was work today?"

"Fine, but it's not over yet. I've got some homework tonight, probably Thursday, Friday, and, depending on how things go, through the weekend and Monday. We've got to get an ad campaign ready to go by the beginning of next week for our new client. Plan is to present it to them next Tuesday."

"What's the rush?"

"Oh, I don't know. That's the way things are nowadays. Everyone wants things done with the snap of a finger. And, of course, you know how Harry is, the customer is always right and he expects us to get it done."

"I'm sorry, dear." Cathy dished out the rice, topped it off with chicken with cashew nuts, and put a plate of eggrolls in the center of the table with packets of sauces.

"Where's Allie?"

"She went to the beach today. I bet she'll stay there till the sun goes down like we used to. Whatever time she gets home, there'll be leftovers."

"So, how'd your day go? Did you have a nice lunch with Sharon? You crack the case about Mrs. Anatoli?" He needled with a slight sneer.

Cathy grinned back defensively. "Yes, we had a nice lunch, but, no, I did not *crack the case about Mrs. Anatoli*, thank you. It gets more mysterious the more I look into it. Did you know that the Anatoli family donated the St. Margaret cemetery property? Sharon didn't tell me the specific date, but my latest theory about Mrs. Anatoli is that when she died she was buried on the property Virgilio donated, and that's exactly why he donated the property. Her grave might even be right there marked by one of the stones that have been eroded to illegibility."

Paul mulled over the possibility. "That could be, but how do you know she didn't outlive him, leave him, or divorce him, and might be buried somewhere, maybe not even around here, with a different husband?"

"I don't, so there's still some work to do on this."

"Work to do?" Paul burst out a laugh. "If it's work, why in the world are you doing it?"

"Work is not always a four letter word, honey." Cathy felt like she was talking to a child. "If you like what you're doing, you're putting forth effort, it is work, but it's rewarding. I know you enjoy what you're doing, don't you?"

"Yes, to a certain extent, but . . ."

"But what? You went to school for what you're doing and you've got a job in your field. Not everyone can say that."

"You forget, my field was fine art. What I'm doing can't be considered fine art. I've twisted it into marketing/advertising so I can make a living." Paul sounded downhearted.

"Oh, honey, you're making a living with your creativity and art talent and you do a great job. You know you're proud of what you do. I've seen how involved you get with your projects, and you have done some wonderful canvases and drawings in your spare time, so . . ."

"I haven't touched a paintbrush and done anything just to do it in years. I just wish I didn't have to be rushed through things by other people and had a little more free time."

"What I think is, you need to relax a little. It's a beautiful night. How about going for a walk with me after we're done eating."

"I'm sorry babe, I can't," Paul looked at her apologetically. "Told you, I have homework tonight. Actually, I'm not going to have much free time until this presentation is done. If our proposal is a go on Tuesday, Harry wants everything in place to start the campaign by Friday next week."

"Oh, come on, hon. A little fresh air and exercise will clear your mind and refresh you. You'll probably be one hundred percent more productive."

"No, really, Cath, I've got to work on this tonight so I'm ready for the brainstorming session we're having first thing tomorrow morning." Tom pushed his chair back and stood up, put his hand on her back, and kissed her on the top of the head. "Maybe tomorrow night or Friday I'll go with you since I'm planning on going into the office over the weekend. Maybe we'll be able to do something together Sunday. But right now, I really need to hunker down on this."

"Okay," Cathy sighed, disappointed.

"I'm really sorry, hon. I'd love to go with you, but tomorrow's going to be here sooner than you think. Got to put my nose to the grindstone." Paul felt guilty seeing the glum look on Cathy's face. "Why don't you give one of your girlfriends a call?

"No, it's getting a little late. By the time I find someone who wants to go with me, the sun will be going down. I'll just take a short walk by myself and come back and relax on the deck while you slave away upstairs."

"Sorry, sweetie." Tom kissed her again. "I'll be up in my hole."

"Okay, dear. I might try and wrestle you away to take a break a little later." Cathy was almost done cleaning up the kitchen when she heard a car in the driveway followed by a car door slamming. She hurried to the back door and stopped Allie before she came in. "Now brush off all that sand, and hang your blankets and towels on the line before you come in."

Alexandra rolled her eyes and motioned to the clothesline. "Look," she said.

"Oh, good for you," Cathy smiled, used to her daughter's occasional smartass attitude. "Okay, you may enter. I trust you now."

"Thanks, Mommy Dearest," Allie said walking by.

Cathy's back stiffened a little, but let the snarky comment slide. "We just finished eating, hon," Cathy told her. "I just put Cashew Chicken and eggrolls from New China in the fridge. It's probably still warm."

"Sounds good, but I had a bite at Sara's already," Allie replied. "Besides, I've got to jump in the shower. Doug's picking me up at seven-thirty to go to an eight o'clock movie."

Cathy was happy to hear Allie had gotten something to eat. Slender as Allie was, she was perpetually on a diet, especially in summer when she wanted to look good in her bathing suit, and when she went to the beach, she often wouldn't eat anything all day long. "Well, if you're hungry when you get home, it's in there," Cathy told her, "And, don't forget, young lady, we want you in by one a.m."

"Oh, Mom," Allie sighed, and then stared, wide-eyed at Cathy. "Don't worry. I'm tired after being out in the sun all day. We're just going to the show and he's going to bring me home. I'll be back way before one."

"Just wanted to remind you, dear." Cathy said as Allie breezed by. Cathy felt queasy thinking how soon it would be when she would have no idea what Allie would be doing or how late she'd be staying out. She was so consumed by this disturbing thought, she hardly knew she had gotten her walking sneakers and put them on. She smiled at the knowledge she needed to go for a refreshing walk as much as Paul did.

Cathy grabbed a couple of carrots from the fridge and put them in her pocket for the horses that were often in the pasture at the end of Davison Road. Stepping onto the front porch, Cathy savored the scent of the grapes and walked to the side of the road. 'He doesn't know what he's missing,' she thought, savoring the soft early twilight breeze, and the colors starting to appear in the sky.

After about fifteen minutes, she arrived at the horse pasture and, as she had hoped, several horses were grazing, including her favorite, a large, bay stallion that was so dark he almost looked black. He'd been the one who initiated the friendship with Cathy a few years ago by coming to the fence one day and walking along with her. When Cathy stopped, the stallion did as well. He turned to face her, and bobbed his head as if inviting her to come over and chat. Then he put his head over the fence to allow her to stroke his cheek. At the time, Cathy wondered if he acted that way to everyone but preferred to think he had taken a special fancy to her. Today, as usual, her equine friend sauntered over to the fence to say hello. Cathy rewarded him with a carrot and a pat on the cheek. "Here you go, my beautiful boy," she told him. A pretty chestnut mare was walking over slowly. "Oh, I see you have a sweetheart here," she smiled and treated the mare with a carrot, too. The other two horses in the pasture kept their distance and continued grazing.

After a little more silly talk with her horse friends, Cathy said farewell, looped around Dougan Road, to Backus Road, to McGill Road, and then headed back home. She took a quick shower, poured herself a tall glass of green ice tea, and sat in her favorite chair on the back deck. Relaxing and looking over her back yard, she noticed some weeds getting out of hand, and thought she should have delayed her shower so she could have gotten a little gardening done.

"Oh well, it's too late now," she thought, leaning back, sipping her tea, and watching for signs of deer in the woods. Something moved just inside the tree line beyond the Pantona pet cemetery. She squinted trying to figure out what it was. The animal wasn't big enough to be a deer and it appeared to be larger than a fox. She wondered if it could possibly be a young coyote. She got up from her chair, leaned over the deck rail when it emerged from the woods, and saw it wasn't a coyote, it was a scraggly, multi-colored dog sniffing and scratching at Sadie's grave. From this distance, it didn't look like any of the neighbors' dogs. She walked slowly down the steps of the deck to get a closer look.

The dog noticed her, and stood very tall with its ears plastered back, growling. Cathy stopped a moment, then started inching forward while talking soothingly to the dog. It ran back into the woods, but not so far that it was out of sight. Cathy stopped again, hoping it would not bolt away altogether. Soon, the dog was sneaking toward her. It appeared to be an Australian Shepherd, with dark ears and coppery cheeks. Its back was a dark combination of greys and black. Its legs and belly were probably white but looked grey because of the dog's unkempt, dirty condition.

Cathy crouched down among her departed pets, and with a calm, soft voice, encouraged the dog to come to her. The Aussie watched her warily, panting, occasionally darting farther into the woods, but eventually he walked tentatively toward her. She noticed he was limping, favoring his left back leg. Cathy sat cross-legged next to her St. Francis statue with her side to the dog, casting furtive glances toward him, continuing her gentle coaxing.

31

Finally, she heard him approaching from behind, sniffing. She let him investigate her with his nose, until he started smelling her hand. Finally, he allowed her to gently caress his shoulder. This was the first time she noticed he had one brown eye and one startlingly ice blue eye. She looked directly in his eyes, he looked in hers, and their mutual trust was sealed.

He put his front paws on Cathy's thigh and stretched to lick her cheek. After the dog kiss, he was all over her. As dirty and smelly as he was, Cathy was overjoyed with the show of affection, and equally disturbed by his emaciated condition. When he threw himself onto his back to allow her to rub his meager belly, the name Troy popped into her head. "Okay, little Troy," she said cheerfully, pushing herself to her feet, "Why don't you come along with me."

Troy limped happily along, sometimes beside her, sometimes in front, sometimes lingering behind to sniff something on their way to the house. Cathy played with him along the way. He appeared to be between one and two years old and in need of a good meal as well as some TLC. She still had some of Sadie's food in the pantry, and had a collection of leashes, collars, toys, and other dog necessities stored in the hall closet awaiting the next canine family member when the time was right. She smiled at Troy, knowing that time had arrived.

She let Troy to his own devices to investigate the yard while she decided what to do next. It was too late to call the vet, but she'd read that if a dog hadn't eaten in a very long time, it could become very sick if it ate a large amount of food all of a sudden. She wasn't sure how long it had been since Troy had eaten a proper meal, so she decided she'd provide only small portions of food in intervals a few hours apart with clean water until Dr. Warner could look him over. If it appeared he was doing well after a couple small meals, she'd increase the amount later.

Working on the assumption that Troy had fleas, Cathy retrieved Sadie's plastic toddler pool from the shed, placed it near the deck steps, turned on the outside spigot, unwound the hose, and started filling the pool for a flea bath. She then placed the flea comb, brush, flea shampoo, rags, collar, leash, toys, a muzzle (which she hoped she wouldn't need), and the dreaded cone of shame within grabbing distance on the deck steps.

Cathy found Troy digging at Sadie's grave again. She bribed him away with a tennis ball to chase and once his energy seemed depleted, she got to work. At first, the grooming tools frightened him, but with only some mild grumbling, he tolerated the procedure. When she wet him down to begin the bath, he hung his head and curled in on himself, but did not struggle. She tenderly handled his back left leg as she washed it and noticed it was swollen. Troy yelped, growled, and attempted to nip her, but Cathy managed to get it clean. Since the flea shampoo had to soak in his coat for a full ten minutes, Cathy had to put the cone on him to prevent him from licking the shampoo. Troy whined, barked, and rubbed the cone against anything he could find, even though Cathy tried to distract him by walking him around the yard and presenting toys to him. Once she rinsed him, took the cone off, and played with him in some clean water in the pool, Troy forgot all about the previous torture she'd put him through.

It was pandemonium trying to dry him, Troy preferring to play tug with the towels rather than be patted dry with them. Cathy was dripping wet by the time she was done and was thrilled to see what a beautiful little guy Troy was. His chest was a bright cottony white as were his front legs, paws, and belly. His back was a saddle of light grey with contrasting black splotches. The inside of his back legs were a coppery brown and the outside grey with black spots. Cathy was in love and knew a family somewhere had to be missing this sweet-tempered cutie.

After eating, being bathed, playing, and getting a little love, Troy flopped down on the deck and fell asleep next to Cathy's chair. He was in a deep sleep immediately, his little paws twitching and legs moving as if he were running. Cathy looked at Troy fondly, feeling herself becoming emotionally attached to him already. The sky was now a fiery red with the sun setting. She got up as quietly as she could and went upstairs to share her new treasure with Paul.

Cathy knocked and entered the office. "How you coming, hon?"

"Pretty good. Think I'll be able to wrap up here in an hour or so."

"The sun's almost gone. Why don't you take a quick break and take a look. It's a gorgeous sight tonight."

"Good idea. Watching a pretty sunset might rev up my creative juices." As they walked through the kitchen, Paul grabbed a can of beer from the refrigerator and, as he opened the door to the deck, laughed when the little Aussie Shepherd jumped on him in greeting.

"Who's this?" Paul crouched down to pet and play with Troy, still laughing.

"I'm calling him Troy," Cathy said with a broad smile. "I noticed him in the woods and managed to get him to come to me. I've been busy cleaning him up ever since. I don't know who he belongs to, but I'll see what I can do about that tomorrow. I'll take him to the vet to check him out and they'll see if he's microchipped."

"Are you going to drop him off at the ANNA Shelter?"

"I don't know. I'd really like to take care of him myself. Maybe they'll let me post his picture on their website, though."

"Uh-oh. I can see what's coming." Paul smiled at Cathy.

"You've got to admit, he's pretty darn cute. If no one claims him, he may be just what we need around here. I do miss Sadie awfully and I know you do, too."

"You're right, I do, but we better not get our hopes up too high, honey. I have a feeling this little boy has a family that's looking for him."

"We'll find out."

Troy slept on Sadie's old dog bed that Cathy placed on the floor next to her side of the bed. He woke Cathy up in the middle of the night by jumping up and snuggling next to her. She cuddled the soft pup and drifted off to sleep thinking about Troy's eyes. She thought to herself how much she liked the name Troy and that if she would have had another son, she might have named him Troy.

As her mind freed itself from the bonds of consciousness, visions of the day, her distant past, and her present, mixed with her hopes and fears of what the future might hold. She had a sense of timelessness, weightlessness, and, like the night before, she was falling, tumbling down, unable to grab anything to stop her descent. There was blackness, and suddenly she was watching Troy playing on a sunny day in a grassy field at the edge of the woods. He was barking excitedly and bounding about in long, straw-colored grass. Jumping and diving into the grass like a fox, he intermittently sniffed around as if he were hunting something.

One big pounce and the giggling of a child could be heard mixed with Troy's playful barks. The head of a young boy peeked out of the grass, his blonde hair shining almost white in the sun, blending in with the wild grass. The boy's glittering sapphire blue eyes, rimmed in dark blue, stared directly, icily through Cathy's eyes touching her soul, making her shiver. She awoke abruptly, full of terror and a profound sadness. She attributed the terror to the feeling of falling at the beginning of the dream, but the underlying intense grief confused her.

Troy licked her face. Comforted by his presence, she petted him and fell back to sleep, Troy curled up next to her for the remainder of the night.

5

PUPPY LOVE

Cathy and Paul were startled awake by Troy's barking at the alarm followed by him nuzzling them, play digging at the bedsheets and then wrestling with them. 'If his family shows up and claims him, I'm going to be devastated,' Cathy thought woefully.

"Good morning, little guy. How are you?" Paul chuckled pulling Troy on top of him. Troy licked his face, jumped over Cathy to the floor, and stood at the doorway looking at them expectantly.

"I think he needs to go out," said Cathy.

"Or he wants breakfast," Paul laughed. "And you do know what that means, don't you Cath?"

"That he's smart?" Cathy asked, ignoring the implication.

"That he's house-trained and used to living with people, so don't get too wrapped up in him," Paul warned, getting out of bed. "Someone, somewhere is sure to be looking for him."

"Tch, I know," Cathy said and sighed. "Let's just enjoy him while we've got him, okay?"

"How can we not?" Paul went into the bathroom, and Troy wandered down the hall stopping to sniff at the bottom of Allie's closed bedroom door.

"Troy!" Cathy whispered, and he hopped to her holding his left back leg in the air. She intended to carry him down the stairs, but before she could grab him, he was halfway down completely at ease using three legs. He accompanied her outside when she got the newspaper and did his duty for which Cathy praised him with a,

36

"Good Boy." She picked up his morning constitutional using the bag the paper came in, thinking, 'Like old times,' remembering the routine with Sadie and Suzy.

While she prepared a pot of coffee, she decided toast and an orange would do for her breakfast this morning since she hoped to join Allie in her morning run. She heard Paul hurrying down the stairs. "Would you like a bagel again this morning to take with you?" she asked loudly, starting for the refrigerator.

Paul rushed into the kitchen and leaned his laptop case against the cabinets while he poured his coffee. "No, babe, not today, thanks. They'll probably have doughnuts or something at the meeting today."

Troy had his front paws on the counter edge to see what Paul was doing. "Off," Paul said and Troy obediently pushed himself away from the counter, sat down, and looked at Paul alertly as if showing what a good boy he was.

Cathy watched Troy and Paul interacting, feeling that twinge of sadness again, and recalled her dream. 'I bet I felt sad at the end of my dream because I'm worried about his family taking him back. Wouldn't that be funny if there was a little blonde boy with bright blue eyes in Troy's family?'

Seeing Cathy staring lovingly at Troy, Paul affirmed her feelings. "You're right, hon, he's irresistible. I'm more than half-hoping he's not chipped and we end up being able to keep him."

"Me, too." Cathy turned her face up to accept Paul's goodbye peck.

"Call you later."

"Okay. I'll let you know what's going on. Good luck this morning."

"Thanks, hon."

Troy made a beeline to the door when Paul opened it and barked as he watched his new master head to the garage. Moments later, Allie wandered into the kitchen rubbing her eyes. "Was that a dog I heard?"

In answer to her question, Troy was at Allie's feet, smelling her.

"What the . . . ?" Allie bent over and reached toward Troy, who, at first, shied away. "Hey, it's okay. Come here boy," she said softly, crouching to Troy's level. Troy obliged, put his paws on her knee and stretched while yawning. "Where'd he come from?" Allie chuckled, concentrating her attention on Troy.

"I saw him last night in the woods, behind our pet cemetery. Isn't he a doll?" Cathy walked over to the two of them. "No ID on him, so I'm going to get him in to see Dr. Warner today to check him out and see if he's microchipped."

"And if he's not?"

"I'll just have to see what I can do to locate his owners. Until then, I'll take care of him. I decided to call him Troy for now, and he seems to be answering to it. He probably would answer to anything since he was hungry and hurt."

"Troy? Why Troy?"

"I don't know. It just occurred to me when I was looking at him." Cathy scratched Troy's head.

"Did you tell Tony or Julia about him?"

"Not yet. I was too busy cleaning him up last night. I'll get in touch with them today some time. Maybe I'll ask them if they want to come over for dinner Saturday."

"They're going to love him."

"I already do and that's a problem. It already pains me to think of losing him," Cathy sighed. "Looks like you're ready to go for your run. Did you want something light to eat first?"

"No, I ate too much at Sara's yesterday. Had a milkshake, and then had buttered popcorn at the show. I think I can do without. I'll have an apple or something when I get back."

"I'll join you if you want some company."

"Sure, and we can bring Troy along with us. Aussie Shepherds need a lot of exercise."

"I think we're going to have to leave Troy at home. He's got a limp and until the vet looks at his leg, I think he should take it easy."

"He does? I didn't notice it."

"You haven't seen him walking yet. Watch." Cathy got up and started walking to the treat bowl on the counter. "Come here, Troy."

Troy was hesitant to leave the attention he was getting from Allie, but when Cathy held a treat out to him, he hurried over.

"Oh, poor boy," Allie cooed. "Tch, I guess you're right. How come you're taking him to the Vet? Why don't you wait. It should be up to his owners to take care of that."

"Who knows how long that might be. The longer you wait, the worse it could get. If his owners do show up, they'll hopefully reimburse us. If not, at least I'll know I did right by Troy. Why don't you get acquainted with him while I change. Then, when I get down, can you help me get the large dog kennel from the garage?"

"Ah, Mom, do you really think we need to put him in the kennel?" Allie whined.

"Honey, he's got that bad leg and we don't know how he'll be left alone in a strange house. He'll feel much more secure in the kennel," Cathy said as she headed upstairs avoiding the disapproving look she knew Allie was sending her way.

Troy was apparently kennel trained as he entered the dog crate with no hesitation and made himself comfortable on the fluffy dog bed Cathy provided for him along with a chew toy, water, and food.

"Look how good he's being, Mom. Do you really want him caged up like that?"

Cathy snorted a little laugh at her daughter's over-concern. "Yes, he's being good and he's relaxed. He'll be perfectly fine until we get back. Now come on, let's go."

They warmed up with a brisk walk, progressing to a jog. Allie took it easy on her mother by running intermittently with jogging and walking.

"Can't beat this sunrise," Allie remarked admiring the golden glow the rising sun cast on the grape fields.

"I heard it's going to be a hot one today," Cathy told her.

"Yeah, might be another beach day for me."

"I'm going to have to see what I can do about finding Troy's family. I'll probably make up some flyers and post some info online about him."

"He's so cute. I sure wish we could keep him." Allie was walking next to Cathy and looked her in the eye. "He'd be great company for you, too."

"He sure would." Cathy put her arm across Allie's shoulders and gave her a squeeze. "He'd sure keep me from getting too lonely once you're off to school."

"I'm only going to be a couple hours away, Mom. You can always take a day trip and come visit me."

"They jogged in silence for about a mile until they were approaching the entrance to St. Margaret Cemetery."

"I think I've had enough, hon," Cathy said through her huffing and puffing. "Why don't we cut through the cemetery. I'll show you the Anatoli graves I was talking about the other night."

Allie agreed perfunctorily. "Sure," she said, shrugging her shoulders.

They walked through the gate, past the caretaker's house and office building, toward the Anatoli plot. "Oh, first I'll show you Sergeant Powell's grave. He's the Civil War veteran whose grave I found for the family that contacted Find-A-Grave."

Cathy was excited to see Sergeant Powell's grave all cleaned up. The two large overgrown bushes had been removed and new sod had been placed around his stone. A small flag was flying with a gold medallion on the pole honoring him for his service in the Civil War, and a pop-up vase had been installed that now held a small bouquet of white carnations.

"Wow!" Cathy exclaimed. "I'm going to have to thank Sharon for this. I wonder if she knows what a beautiful job they did." Cathy grabbed her phone and snapped a couple of pictures, texting Sharon and attaching the photos. "Here's what it looked like before, Allie."

"My gosh, they sure did fix it up!" Allie exclaimed.

"His family ought to be thrilled." Her phone pinged announcing a text, and Cathy smiled. "How thoughtful. It was Sharon who supplied the carnations," she told Allie.

Cathy crouched down and rubbed her hand over the date on the stone. "Hmm, think of the changes from then till now. If Sergeant Powell only knew."

She got up and slowly walked with Allie noting any interesting gravestones on the way to the Anatoli plot. "Here are the Anatoli graves I told you about," Cathy told her. "Look at how someone is still placing flowers at the graves. The flowers looked a little better when I saw them the other day. They're a little wilted now. But I think it's pretty nice that someone is taking the time to remember relatives they couldn't have possible met."

"Mm-hm," Allie murmured. "And the colorful flowers make the cemetery look prettier, too."

Neither of them noticed an elderly woman dressed in a long black dress, black stockings, black orthopedic shoes, and a black lace scarf over her head watching them two to three hundred yards away. She was balancing herself with the use of a carved wooden

40

cane and cradled fresh white, red, and purple cut flowers in her other arm.

"See, there's no grave for Lavinia here," Cathy remarked. "You know, I saw a couple of headstones that are illegible around here. I'm wondering if one of them might be hers."

"Could be," Allie agreed, now showing a bit more interest than she had the other night. "It's too bad they used stone that eroded so easily in those days. I'm sure they had no idea their loved ones' markers would one day be reduced to a blank slate."

"No, I'm sure they didn't. I, think I'll text Sharon the locations of these unidentified graves that are around the Anatoli plot and see if she has a record of the occupants." Cathy began her search for unreadable headstones and finally noticed the woman in black and waved. The woman didn't reciprocate, her gaze remained unwavering.

"Do you know her?" asked Allie.

"No, I was just trying to be friendly. I noticed her looking at us."

A middle-aged woman wearing shorts and a golf shirt joined the older woman and started talking to her. "Uh-oh, Mom. Do you know who that younger woman is?"

"No, I don't. Do you?"

"Yes, that's Amelia's mother--Mrs. Anatoli. She's probably wondering what the hell we're doing hanging around their family plot."

"Alexandra. Watch your tongue in the cemetery."

"Oh, please, Mother." Alexandra rolled her eyes.

"Uh, let's not tell your father about this unless we have to, okay? He seems paranoid about me checking into Lavinia Anatoli's whereabouts as it is. If they make a stink of us being here, I'll take care of it."

"Okay, Mom, but you do realize I can use this information to my advantage, don't you?" Allie said with a sly smile.

"Why you little blackmailer! As your mother, I believe I've got a little more leverage on you than you've got on me, so don't get any ideas."

"Just saying," Allie laughed.

Cathy found two illegible stones fairly close to the Anatoli brothers' gravesites and texted the locations to Sharon. Cathy and Allie passed by Cathy's mother's resting place, then the family's departed pets' graves, bidding all of them their best wishes as they walked by.

Troy barked excitedly as soon as he heard them on the back deck.

"I hope he wasn't barking the entire time we were gone," Allie said with a mixture of sympathy and accusation. "I wish you wouldn't have caged him."

"You should know by now that it's good for dogs to be kennel trained. There are plenty of times dogs need to be confined, so it's important they get comfortable with being kenneled. It's not cruelty. In fact, a lot of dogs like their kennels. It feels like a den to them."

"But Mom," she insisted. "He's brand new to our house and you just threw him in there."

"Oh my God, Allie. Listen to yourself," Cathy laughed. "You're totally exaggerating. He went in there fine and he's got all the comforts of home; a blanket, water, food, a toy." Cathy chuckled, shaking her head as she opened the back door.

Allie hurried over to the kennel to release Troy who jumped on her and licked her face.

"Okay, I guess you've reached hero status for breaking him out of prison," Cathy laughed.

"I guess so," Allie giggled, wrestling with Troy. "It's nice to have a dog around again."

"I agree," said Cathy, smiling as she watched Allie and Troy playing. "Troy's made me realize just how much I need a dog or cat to complete our family."

"Well, if his owners do turn up, we're going to have to take a trip to the pound. I'd love it if you'd keep Troy, though. He's perfect." Allie headed for the staircase. "I'm going to get ready to go. I'd take Troy with me if he didn't have to see the vet."

"Don't worry; there'll be time for you to take him to Presque Isle before you leave for school. If he gets the okay from the vet, you can even take him tomorrow if you're going again. Oh, by the way, why don't you take a couple pictures of Troy to show your friends. Maybe one of them has heard of someone missing a dog meeting his description."

"Good idea," said Allie, grabbing her phone and snapped a couple pictures. "Come on, Troy. Keep me company while I get ready for the beach."

"I'm going to call Dr. Warner's office and do some things to try to locate Troy's folks. Remember, if you talk to your brother and sister, don't let them know. I want to surprise them."

Dr. Warner's staff squeezed Troy in at eleven a.m. giving Cathy plenty of time to post pictures of him on Facebook and other social media sites and to create a handful of flyers about Troy to pin on bulletin boards around town. Shortly into her project, she received a text from Sharon. Disappointingly, Sharon had identified the mystery graves as belonging to other people.

Dr. Warner's receptionist, Maureen, and vet tech, Vicki, were tickled to meet Troy. "Great to see you, Cathy," Maureen greeted as she checked in their new patient.

"We knew it wouldn't be long before you'd adopt a new dog or cat," Vicki remarked while squatting down to get acquainted with Troy."

"Well he's not officially mine yet, but if it doesn't work out that we can adopt Troy, he's made us realize it is time we fill the void left by Sadie." Cathy related how Troy wandered out of the woods. "You haven't heard of anyone losing a dog like Troy, have you?" she asked, hoping they hadn't.

"No," they agreed, shaking their heads. "But if we find he doesn't have a chip, we'll ask around."

"I'll put one of my flyers on your bulletin board, if you don't mind," said Cathy.

"Why don't you just let me hold onto one until we see if he's chipped or not. If he's not, I'll put it up for you," Maureen told her.

"Thanks, Maureen," Cathy said, following Vicki into the examination area. "You're going to be proud of me," she said smiling.

"Oh, other than having another dog with you, why?"

"I brought you a present. A stool sample," Cathy said laughing while removing a small sealed plastic container from her purse.

A hearty laugh burst out of Vicki. "Why yes, I am proud of you. So many people forget about that. You get a gold star. Thank you."

They put Troy on the scale, Vicki noting his weight to be thirty-eight pounds. "The weight of Aussies can vary quite a bit, so it's hard to say just how underweight he is. He just might be on the small side, but it's obvious he needs to put on some weight. Of course, you knew that. That'll be a task Troy will be sure to enjoy, won't you, boy?" Vicki gave Troy a pat. "What has he eaten since you've had him?"

"We still had some of Sadie's food tucked away in the pantry so I gave him a couple of small meals of that last night. He seemed to have done fine, so I increased it a little this morning."

"That was smart. If you'd have let him gorge himself, he could've gotten very sick."

Once in the exam room, Vicki scanned Troy for a microchip while Cathy held her breath. "Well, no chip."

Cathy was thrilled but quickly quashed her joy, knowing his owners still might be found.

Vicki took Troy's temperature, listened to his heart and examined him physically. "Well, one thing, he's hasn't been neutered yet." She looked at his ears, eyes, and teeth, then recorded the information in the computer. "With the exception of his weight and lame back left leg, Troy seems pretty healthy. We'll see what Dr. Warner has to say. It won't be a minute. I'll take a good look at the present you brought us," she chuckled.

"Thanks, Vicki."

When Dr. Warner entered, Troy hid under the bench where Cathy was perched. Cathy stood and Dr. Warner gave her a hug. "Got a new patient for you, Doctor."

"I see! What a handsome boy, too!" Dr. Warner crouched down and charmed Troy from his safe spot. "So, I hear he dropped by and said hello last night, eh?" she asked letting Troy became comfortable with her.

"Yes, and I've fallen for him already. I've half a notion not to even try to find his owners, but I wouldn't feel right about that. I'd feel like a kidnapper. I'm going to try my best to find them and hope he's been lost from a good home." Cathy got down on the floor with Dr. Warner and Troy. "I gave Maureen a flyer I made to put on your bulletin board. If we find his family, I think it's time my family and I find ourselves our own Troy."

"Definitely the best way to recover from a loss is to throw yourself into a new love. There are so many pets out there needing a good home." Dr. Warner ran a flea comb here and there through Troy's hair, and checked the results. "That's good, no sign of fleas."

Cathy described the flea bath fun of the previous night, getting a laugh out of Dr. Warner who continued her more thorough physical exam of Troy, palpating his belly, feeling around for any bumps, lumps, or ticks, and scrutinizing his eyes, ears, mouth, and teeth. "I'm very pleased. He seems very healthy, especially considering he had an adventure out in the woods all by himself for a little while. Judging by his condition, I don't think he was camping out for very long. We'll put him on a prescription diet for a couple of weeks and then ease him back into a regular diet. I'll want to coordinate with his regular vet if we find his family. Now let's take a look at that leg."

She studied Troy's gait, then felt and manipulated his leg. "If you were his rightful owner, I'd recommend an x-ray to try to see what's going on."

"Go ahead and take the x-ray. He'll stay with us if we can't find his owners and, if we do find them, we'll be able to tell them what's wrong." Dr. Warner leashed Troy and took him out of the exam room.

As Cathy waited for their return, she visualized the jubilant reunion between Troy and his family. She pictured a blonde, blue-eyed, sevenish-year-old boy, a twelvish-year-old girl with straight, light brown hair, and two youngish parents greeting Troy with hugs and kisses, then taking him away forever. She felt like crying.

It wasn't long before Dr. Warner returned with Troy. She darkened the room a little and pulled the x-rays up on the computer. "Hmm. Well, there's no evidence of a break, healed or otherwise. His joints and bones all look normal. Definitely no dislocation." She examined Troy's leg gently again. "He might have a bad muscle sprain or strain. I'll give you some anti-inflammatory medication. You can give him one tablet every twelve hours and you should ice his leg ten minutes at a time as he tolerates it to get that swelling down. Try to minimize his activity as much as possible. We'll call you in a couple days to see how he's doing."

Before she went home, Cathy stopped at several other area veterinarians, Giant Eagle, My Dad's Pizza, and Walmart to post informational flyers about Troy. She would try to think of other places that had bulletin boards; but, for now, she was satisfied she was putting forth an honest effort in trying to locate Troy's family.

Troy was keeping Cathy company in the kitchen as she prepared dinner when the phone rang. At first, she thought it was Paul calling, but a woman's voice, so quiet Cathy could barely hear her, said, "Hello, I'm calling about the dog."

Someone could have punched Cathy in the gut. She looked at Troy and couldn't respond.

"Hello, hello," the voice persisted. "Is anyone there?"

Tears welled in Cathy's eyes. 'How could it be so soon?' she wondered. "Oh, um, yes. I'm sorry. I'm here. H-how did you find out about him?"

"Facebook. I recognized him immediately. His name is Blueboy because of his blue eye. I miss him terribly. When can I come get him? Where do you live?"

Cathy wasn't ready for this. She had to make sure this woman was the rightful owner and she hadn't even had time to think of pertinent questions to ask. "Um, of course you realize I want to make sure you are his real family. What can you tell me about the dog, Miss?"

"Oh, it's Mrs. Mrs. Vugsta. It's me and my husband," she responded. "My little boy Blue just turned one year old. I have his birth record. He's not fixed yet and we've had him since he was a pup. He tends to be a little timid and shy at first, but once he knows someone, he's playful and lovable."

Cathy's heart sank when the woman continued describing Troy and his behavior to a T. When she talked about Troy's lameness, a fact Cathy intentionally withheld from her internet posts and flyers, Cathy was sure Troy was not Troy, but Blueboy, but she could not bring herself to think of him with that name. She also was now aware that Troy's leg problem predated his becoming lost. "What did your vet say regarding his leg?"

"Blueboy got around fine, so we didn't worry about it."

Mrs. Vugsta's answer concerned Cathy making her wonder just how much veterinarian care Troy had ever received. "Who's your vet?"

The woman's voice broke and she sounded on the verge of hysteria. "What difference does it make? He's my dog, his name's Blueboy, and I want him back."

"How did Blueboy become lost? Where do you live?" Cathy heard Mrs. Vugsta crying.

"We live in Girard and I have no idea how he got lost."

"But, ma'am, we're in Harborcreek, at least thirty miles away from you. How did he get way out here?"

"I don't know. All's I know is I want him back," Mrs. Vugsta sobbed. "Why are you being so difficult? I thought you wanted to fiind his owners. I'm his owner. I want him back!"

Cathy heard an angry male voice yelling in the background. "Who are you talking to?"

"Just Mom, dear." Although muffled Cathy could hear Mrs. Vugsta's barely controlled crying.

"Mother, hell! I know what you're doing. Who is this?" he said gruffly into the phone.

Cathy didn't know what to do. "I-I was talking to your wife about a stray dog."

"I knew it," she heard the man yell before he disconnected the call.

Cathy's emotions were a mix of sorrow for Troy's past, and jubilation for his present and future, which, without question, would now be in the Pantona household. She knew the kids and Paul would definitely feel the same way. Upon reflection, though, Cathy thought it might be best not to reveal the phone conversation to everyone immediately. She would first wait to see if Mrs. Vugsta called again.

Cathy lay in bed that night wondering about Troy's former family as he cuddled up to her side. After her phone conversation with Mrs. Vugsta, she would fight to keep Troy. His former mistress might genuinely love him and want to have him back, but, clearly, her husband did not, and it seemed evident to Cathy that Mr. Vugsta was responsible for Troy ending up in Harborcreek. Cathy hoped she would not hear from them again. She also wondered if Mr. Vugsta punished Mrs. Vugsta after the phone call. Cathy held Troy close and sighed, happy he was now safe and he would receive the love he deserved for the rest of his life. Feeling certain Troy was there to stay, Cathy drifted off into slumberland.

She was watching Troy and the blonde boy playing in the field again. The two tussled and wrestled in the grass, tumbling over each other, the boy giggling gleefully, and the dog reciprocating in yips and barks. The boy ran, calling his dog to follow. "Toby," he shouted, "Come get me." The boy stood at the edge of the woods and his frailty was obvious. He was very thin and pale, his left arm appeared to be much shorter than his right, and he had a four inch block of wood attached to the bottom of his left shoe. He attempted to run with Toby, but stumbled and fell into the soft grass. Toby jumped on top of him, then more wrestling and giggling ensued.

Like a thunderclap, an angry male voice yelled, "Troy!" Cathy woke up confused.

6

THE FLIM FLAM MAN

Julia knew it was sure to be another busy Friday at Trendy Tresses. This Friday, in particular, was going to be a busier and longer day than usual for her because she was filling in for her good friend and fellow stylist, Anita, who was on her honeymoon. Julia's appointments were scheduled back to back and double-booked, with trims squeezed between perms or colors all day from eight a.m. to eight p.m. with only a couple of small breaks to grab quick bites to eat. A good number of the appointments were for students wanting to look their best for their return to school mixed in with the regulars. The only way Julia would be able to accommodate any walk-ins today would be if she had a no-show or a cancellation.

Julia had just started a cup of coffee when, at ten minutes to eight, the door buzzer announced her first appointment had arrived. On a day like today, an early start was better than a late one. She greeted her customer with a smile and her marathon day began.

By eleven o'clock, Julia's feet were aching and she was glad all had gone well thus far so she could catch her breath during the fifteen-minute break she'd allotted for herself. She settled into the couch in the break room with yogurt, a power bar, and a cup of coffee, resting her feet on Bonnie's yard sale find steamer trunk, which served both as a storage box and a coffee table. Julia checked her phone and saw a text to both her and Tony from their mother that had arrived twenty minutes ago. "Hope both of you are having a good day. Would you like to come over for supper tomorrow?"

"Great, what time?" Julia responded.

"Eating @ 6 - but come over any time. I've got some exciting news."

"You're a big tease."

"I know. Hee Hee. You'll see tomorrow. Don't work too hard. Love you."

"Love you, too."

Julia shook her head, smiling. Her mother knew well that she would go crazy wondering about what was going on. She was just finishing her yogurt when Nora, the receptionist, buzzed her. "Mrs. Anatoli is here."

"Thanks, Nora," Julia told her. "I'll be right there." She put the magazine she had been flipping through on the steamer trunk, disposed of her refuse, and thought to herself, 'Round two,' and she rejoined the hive of activity in the salon.

"Hi, Luella. How are you today?" Julia greeted Mrs. Anatoli cheerfully. "I really appreciate you coming in a little early this week."

"Oh, that's quite all right, Julia. It doesn't happen that often," Luella responded returning Julia's smile. "Are you ready for me or should I have a seat for a moment?"

"We're all set, dear. Come on over here to the sinks and we'll get your hair washed." Julia placed the white neck strip and styling cape on Luella. "So, are we going to do anything different today?"

"Oh, no. Just want a little shape-up again, get the split ends cut off," Luella chuckled. "One day I'm going to surprise you, though, and say I want a change."

"Your style suits you, but if you ever do want to try something different, you certainly have the length to do it." Now that Luella was getting a little older and the years of processing had taken their toll on Luella's hair, Julia wished she could get Luella into a more up-to-date cut. It would make her hair healthier and she'd look years younger.

"No, Gino doesn't like short hair on women. He likes me to keep it this way, the way I wore it when we first started dating. If he gets a notion he's tired of it, that'll be the time I can try a new style." Luella shrugged her shoulders and half-smiled. "Until then, I'll keep him happy."

This wasn't the first time Julia felt sorry for Luella and wondered just how much and how harshly Gino controlled his household. Luella never overtly complained, but Julia read between the lines and behind Luella's smile. A fleeting scowl of concern crossed Julia's brow. Today, she would try to draw Luella out a little. "My gosh, Luella, you don't really think Gino would care if you changed things up a bit, do you?" Julia asked as she massaged Luella's scalp working the shampoo into a nice lather. "Sometimes a little change like that can spice a relationship up a bit. He might like it."

Luella's face scrunched as if she felt a sharp stomach pain and she shook her head. "Um, I don't think so. Gino has a notion of how he likes things and, you know, I'm his wife. I like him to be happy."

"I'm sure he likes you to be happy, too, doesn't he?"

"Of course." There was a defensive edge to Luella's voice, so Julia told herself to be careful about how much further she pushed. "And, you know," Luella softly and slowly pondered, "I am very happy. I really don't care that much about my hairstyle. He provides for us and it's up to me to take care of him, the kids, and the house. I don't know what I'd do without him. We did get married right out of high school and I've never worked . . ." Luella abruptly stopped talking.

Julia surmised that Luella must have contemplated the prospect of leaving Gino on occasion, but, like many women, she felt trapped in her situation. Luella truly needed a friend and Julia wondered if she was filling that slot. Never had Luella ever talked about doing anything with anyone other than her family. Julia could only assume that Gino preferred not to share Luella with anyone else, female friends included. "As long as you're happy, hon." Julia rinsed Luella's hair and wrapped her head in a towel. "Working out of the home or in the home, it's all work. If it's satisfying to the one who's doing the work, it's all good." Julia smiled reassuringly at Luella and patted her back. "Now come on over here and I'll shape you up."

They walked to Julia's chair. "So how are your kids doing? Amelia should be starting back to school soon, shouldn't she? My sister's leaving for Carnegie Mellon in a week or so."

"Oh, yes, Amelia's just about ready. She's studying Psychology at Behrend and seems to love it and Adam will be graduating with his BS in Electrical Engineering this year.. They both really wanted to go away to school, but Gino said, 'I know what goes on in college. You're going to commute and pay attention to your studies.' And he was right. They're both doing great at Behrend. Then I'll have my later two for a while longer yet, Vincent and Nico, who are quite a bit younger. Vincent's eight and Nico just six."

"Alexandra is the youngest in our family and my mother and father are sure going to miss her."

"I can understand that," Luella agreed. "Once all my kids are on their own, our house is going to feel pretty empty. Of course, I may still have Gino's grandmother, Celia, to take care of. She's actually pretty healthy, so . . ."

"You'd have made a terrific nurse," Julia told her. "You're such a good caregiver."

Luella smiled. "It's easy when it's family."

"So Celia is doing well?"

"Mm-hm. She still gets around and her mind is as sharp as a tack. She still wears her mourning clothes for Grampa Anatoli. I take her to the cemetery to visit his grave quite often. Actually, that's about the only place she likes to go anymore."

There was silence between Julia and Luella for a few moments, Luella's brow furrowed into a puzzled expression. "The strangest thing happened yesterday. I took Celia out to the cemetery and while we were visiting my Grandpa's grave, a couple of people were hanging around the older Anatoli graves; two women, one about my age and one late teens or early twenties. It upset Celia quite a bit. I wasn't going to tell Gino, but Celia told him, and he went through the roof. I have no idea why they were there or why Gino should have been so upset. Of course, he always has been a rather private man, even with me. He keeps me in the dark about a lot of things and he really never talks about his ancestors. I don't think the people at the cemetery were relation, so I don't know why they'd be paying so much attention to the Anatoli graves."

"What exactly were they doing? Did they bring flowers or disturb the graves?" Julia asked.

"No, they were just looking at the graves and talking. I didn't see a car parked anywhere and they were dressed in jogging clothes."

"Maybe they were just cooling down after a run and were just remarking about the dates on the stones."

"It seemed more than just a passing interest. They actually looked as if they were searching for something or someone--a name."

"Could be they were shirttail relation that you'd never met before from out of town and they just decided to check out the family graves."

"I'd think Celia might have recognized them if that were the case, or at least she'd have an idea who they were."

"If they were way out on some twig of the family tree she might not have an idea. A lot of people these days are interested in researching their ancestry and," Julia stopped suddenly remembering her mother's new obsession and proximity to the cemetery, "if they discovered that one of your husband's forefathers was somehow linked to their family, they may have used Find-A-Grave.com, and that's how they ended up in the cemetery that day. Have you ever heard of Find-A-Grave?"

"No, I'm afraid I don't do too much on the computer with the exception of looking at the kids' school schedules and all. Gino always helps me with it."

Julia pictured Mr. Anatoli hovering over Luella making sure she only looked at the websites he wanted her to look at. "Well, Find-A-Grave.com is a website where you can find where just about anyone is laid to rest. A lot of people use it to assist in researching their family history, some like to look up gravesites of celebrities, historic figures, heroes, villains, or just to look at unusual graves."

Luella laughed. "I think we can rule out celebrity seekers being interested in the Anatoli plot, but, who knows, you could be right. They could be some shirttail relation, although, you'd be going way out on a limb there." They both laughed. "I might talk about it to Grandma. She'd know better than Gino."

"It might be fun to meet a new relative. If you see them again, you'll have to speak to them."

"That's for sure. Gino was so angry we didn't question them this time about what they were up to, I can't imagine how he'd blow up if we see them again and don't talk to them." Luella shrugged and shook her head a little. "If I see them again, I'll definitely find out who they are."

"I wouldn't think it's anything to be concerned about, Luella. When I visit the cemetery, I often find myself looking at gravesites of strangers if the people died a long time ago. I think a lot of people do. It's just a natural curiosity about the past."

"I suppose."

Trimming done, Julia turned on her blow drier and styled Luella's hair. After the finishing touches and a little spray, she gave Luella a hand mirror and spun the chair slowly so Luella could see all sides. "Okay?"

"Mm-hm. Looks great. Thanks, Julia." Luella paid and set up her next appointment.

Cathy slapped a sandwich together. The house, silent and still, gave her a feeling of isolation and emptiness. 'So this is how it's going to be once Allie's off to school. Of course, I'll be back to work, and there's Troy.' She now regretted allowing Allie to take Troy to the beach today. 'Anything could happen out there; he could get lost again, he could get hurt, he could get ticks, he could drown . . .' Cathy realized she was letting her imagination get the best of her. Her phone binged with a response text from Tony saying he'd be there for dinner on Saturday, extricating her from her negative thoughts.

"What kind of surprise? Animal - vegetable - or mineral?" he asked about her tease.

"You'll just have to see," Cathy wrote with a winky face emoji. Then she sent, "Love you. See you Saturday."

Tony texted a thumbs-up.

Then she immediately texted Sharon. "Got some free time," she wrote. "Going to library to start reading newspapers. Will let you know if I find anything." Having given herself a feeling of purpose, she wolfed down her sandwich and drink, tidied up the kitchen and left.

Just beating the lunch hour traffic downtown, Cathy made it to the Blasco Library in fifteen minutes. On her way to the microfilm files, Cathy greeted Karen with a nod and a smile. She located the microfilm for the Erie Dispatch that contained the birth announcement for Michael Anatoli, sat down at the nearest available reader, and commenced her meticulous search for any news relating to the Anatoli family.

Cathy wound the microfilm quickly to Michael's birth announcement and began reading each issue of the Dispatch, hoping to find some clue to Lavinia's fate and final resting place. 'If nothing else, I'm getting a taste of the times,' she realized as she felt herself becoming emotionally involved in the arguments of the day as the Civil War was brewing. Despite knowing how severe the bigotry and hatred in society must have been at that time, the blatant racist rhetoric published still caught her by surprise. Even articles written by abolitionists revealed that the poison of prejudice tainted their thinking as well--some of the articles pondered problems, such as, what to do with the slaves once they were freed. She scowled and shook her head trying to wrap her head around the mindset of the era, and even though racism, prejudice, and hate are far from being eradicated today, she was thoroughly glad she was not living in the eighteen hundreds.

The place of women and men in society was also disturbingly well defined in those days as evidenced in articles and editorials. The attitudes of the day not only came through news reports and editorials, but also through jokes published which showed a blasé acceptance of domestic violence, corporal punishment for children, and drunkenness as normal parts of life.

What Cathy read in the Dispatch also made it apparent that Erie County was still part of a developing frontier. Available farmland for sale was abundant as were items homesteaders and startup farmers would need; i.e. building materials, livestock, farming equipment, tools, seed, and feed, etc.

She was amused to find ads in almost every issue touting "elixir preparations of unusual excellence" for treating "incipient cholera to ordinary diarrhea" and other unbelievable, all-inclusive ranges of diseases. It was easy to envision a snake-oil salesman hawking his miracle cure on the street.

Cathy pictured herself walking over wooden sidewalks wearing the fashions described or depicted in advertisements. She could see horses clomping along pulling rickety carts over State Street, which was probably hard-packed dirt or cobblestone in those days. She could hear the clatter of wagons, the occasional slap of reins on a snorting horse's behind, the clopping of horses' hooves, and the chatter of people on the street making small talk and discussing the issues of the day.

Cathy already had an idea what times must have been like in the eighteen hundreds from movies she had seen, novels she had read, and history courses she had taken, but she felt she was time traveling as she read page after page of the Dispatch. She was becoming as familiar with the names of people and places of the eighteen hundreds as she was with those in the news today.

Her heart skipped a beat when she came upon an ad for produce from the Anatoli Family Farm. The woodcut illustration, bordered with grape vines, showed a man and a woman standing centered behind a table that was heaped with all manner of fresh fruits and vegetables. "Oh my gosh! It's them! This is Lavinia and her family and there are four more children than I thought they had--two girls and two boys!" she whispered aloud. Lavinia wore a bonnet tied in a large bow under her chin. What could be seen of her hair appeared to be dark. She wore a dark dress with a tight bodice. Lavinia stood next to a broad-shouldered, tall, balding gentleman with an unkempt Elliott mustache. He wore a bowtie, suspenders holding up his drawers, and a somewhat wrinkled-looking white shirt. Lavinia's right hand rested on the shoulders of a thin boy next to her who so resembled the blonde boy appearing in her dreams of late, Cathy's skin constricted in goosebumps.

Centered at the bottom of the ad, was written, "The Anatoli Family." A line in print too small to read was underneath that. Cathy zoomed in and felt as if she were being introduced to each member of the Anatoli family. All of the individuals were identified by name under their image. She caught her breath and shuddered when she saw the name, Troy, identifying the small boy standing next to Lavinia! "You've got to be kidding," Cathy whispered to herself as she stared at the name in disbelief.

She took note of the girls' names, Christina and Lydia, and the name of the other son missing from the Anatoli plot, Leonardo, but she could not get over the coincidence surrounding the boy, Troy, for seemingly having appeared in her dreams and for her having thought of the name, Troy, for their adopted stray dog. Cathy couldn't take her eyes off of Troy and Lavinia, feeling an odd sense of communication with them, as if they were coming to life and trying to tell her something. 'Wait till I tell Sharon,' she mused. 'Wonder what she'll think.' She printed out a copy of the ad to show Sharon.

Cathy continued reading the microfilmed papers until her eyes burned. She leaned back in her chair, rubbed her eyes, and squinted, adjusted her vision from the bright screen she'd been staring at, and looked at the wall clock. Seeing it was almost three-thirty, she decided to call it a day, and jotted down the date of the next issue to review, March 1, 1860. After placing the microfilm back in its proper place, she was reaching for her phone to text Sharon when it binged with a text from Sharon. "Find anything interesting?" followed by, "FYI - Rcvd call this AM from Mr. Anatoli re people looking at family plot. Advised it is permitted as long as no one is vandalizing."

"Thanks for the heads-up," Cathy texted back. "Mystery not solved yet, but I know what Lavinia & whole family looks like! Saw an ad - whole family in picture! There are 2 girls and 2 boys we didn't know about. Printed it out. Eager to show you. Got to the 3-1-60 edition but lots more papers to go."

"I still can help," Sharon responded.

"How about breakfast tomorrow and then here?"

"Ok. 8:30 at Perkins?"

"Perfect."

"Ok. See you in the AM"

Cathy sent Sharon a thumbs-up, pushed in her chair and left.

The house was still empty when Cathy got home, but she was pleasantly surprised when Alexandra came home with Troy shortly after four-thirty. Troy skipped over to Cathy on his three good legs and greeted her with happy enthusiasm, warming her heart. He was full of sand and not completely dry, but romping with him was such a delight, she didn't care about the mess being made.

"Everybody loved him, Mom," Allie told Cathy, "but nobody recognized him. I think he belongs with us. He was meant to be for you." She smiled and tussled Troy's hair.

Cathy held herself back from telling Allie about the phone call from the Vugsta's, and instead asked, "How'd he do with the water?"

"He was afraid of it at first, but once he got over that, he had a blast. He was chasing his Frisbee and bringing it back. He's going to be a tired puppy tonight."

"I'm sure you're right. Did his leg seem to be bothering him?"

"Not really--just favoring it, limping like always, and when I was getting him used to the water, he was kicking it, so I don't know what to make of that. Do you think he's faking a sore leg to get sympathy?" Allie laughed.

Cathy chuckled at the thought. "That'd certainly be a first, but I don't think so, hon. Swimming is used as rehab a lot because it's so gentle on the joints. Maybe it only hurts when he puts pressure on it. Are you hungry?"

"Not famished, but I could eat. What are we having?"

"I wasn't exactly sure what to fix since it's Friday. I didn't know if you would be eating at home or not. What are you hungry for?"

"You know what I like, anything quick and light."

"I've got a whole wheat pizza crust. How about if I throw together a pizza with some mushrooms, sweet peppers, tomatoes, spinach, and cheese. Shrimp might be good on it, too. How does that sound?"

"Mmm. Yummy. I'll help you cut up the veggies."

"Okay, but first I want to rinse the sand out of Troy before our house turns into a sandbox."

"I'll jump into the shower while you're doing that. Doug's picking me up a little later to go out tonight."

"You're not planning to drive to New York to go drinking, are you?"

"Mom," Allie groaned, avoiding a direct answer.

Cathy recognized the deflection. "Allie, you know the rules around here." Not wanting to hear a blatant lie from Allie about where she was going, Cathy said sternly, "We don't want you drinking or in a car with someone who's drinking and driving, so remember, if you need a ride for any reason--call!"

"Tch," Allie clucked and made a sour face. "I know! I know!" Allie turned to go upstairs.

"And curfew is still one a.m.," Cathy added. She wished she didn't have to create friction between them so close to the day Allie would be leaving, but, all the same, felt it was her parental duty to keep reminding her. If it did any good to keep her safe, it was well worth it. "Now don't just go running out to the car when Doug gets here. I'd like to have a word with him."

"Oh my God!" Allie said in utter frustration walking through the living room.

"Thank you, dear," Cathy half-smiled, hoping to cool the tension.

Allie mime-mocked her mother's 'Thank you, dear,' as she went upstairs.

"C'mon Troy," Cathy called, clapping her hands, the image of little Troy Anatoli flashing in her head. "Let's go play in the water!"

When Paul arrived home he heard Cathy's laughter and Troy's barking from the backyard, and he walked around to investigate. "What's going on here? Another bath already?" he laughed.

Troy burst out of Cathy's arms and jumped on Paul sharing his wetness. Cathy ran after Troy, "Sorry hon. He's a slippery little devil. He came home with half the beach on him, so I'm just rinsing him off."

"By the look of it, you're getting a shower, too."

"Do you think?" she laughed, shaking water off her arms, her hair dripping and clothes soaked. "What have you got there?" she asked noticing a white plastic grocery bag in his hand.

"I had a taste for peaches and stopped by Finnell Farms on the way home."

"Perfect. I'll make a pie for dessert tomorrow night." Cathy threw a towel at Paul. "Give me a hand here, would you?"

Paul grabbed Troy's collar to control him, while Cathy sprayed the water through the dog's coat. "So how'd you spend your day today, hon?"

"After getting done around here, I went to the library."

Paul gave her a troubled look. "Oh no, still trying to find out about Mrs. Anatoli?"

"Yes I am, and I'm finding it very interesting." Cathy hesitated, unsure how much she wanted to tell Paul. "I saw a picture of the whole family in an ad in an old paper today."

"Really? Well, then, there you are. She did exist. Case closed."

"No, it's becoming even more intriguing. There are two girls and two more boys in the family that I didn't know about, too; none of whom are buried with the other sons."

"Obviously, they're gone and resting in peace somewhere. Let them rest in peace for heaven's sake! You have nothing to do with them."

Cathy decided now was not the time to tell Paul about the one boy's name and his resemblance to the boy in her dreams, if ever there would be a time to tell him. "Even if I never discover anything about the whereabouts of Lavinia and her other four children, I'm enjoying reading the old newspapers."

"Just remember what I said, okay? Your interest may not be appreciated by the Anatoli family."

Cathy felt her face flush, remembering Sharon's last text. "Oh, don't worry, everything will be fine."

An August thunderstorm thwarted Paul's and Cathy's plans for an evening walk, but it was just as well. Paul dozed off on the couch while Cathy was cleaning up the kitchen. She woke him and they retired early, Troy sprawled out at the foot of the bed on Cathy's feet. Cathy's personal private cinema began playing immediately after she drifted off.

A horse-drawn buckboard wagon jiggled over a hard-packed dirt road. It was driven by a woman in an ultramarine blue dress flecked with small light yellow flowers who Cathy recognized as Lavinia. On her head was a cream-colored bonnet trimmed with dark blue eyelet and adorned with a small bouquet of blue iris and baby's breath. A sky blue ribbon tied in a large bow under her chin affixed the bonnet to her head. The ends of the ribbon fluttered in the breeze as her wagon rattled along. The dark blue of her dress accentuated her sapphire eyes that matched the blue eyes of the thin blonde youngster perched beside her who Cathy knew as Troy. The Aussie Shepherd that had appeared with the boy in Cathy's recent dreams was barking and running back and forth in the back of the wagon.

"Whoa, Bruno." Lavinia said, pulling on the reins, "Whoa," she said again in a low, soothing tone elongating the word, as she maneuvered the large bay stallion to stop in front of the general store.

Tying a cream-colored shawl over her shoulders, she anxiously watched slender little Troy jump down, holding his wide-brimmed straw hat. When his knees buckled on landing, Lavinia scolded, "Careful!" and was relieved when he caught his balance and stood up.

Troy smiled at her, "I'm okay, Ma. Don't worry."

Lavinia promptly handed the reins to the boy. "Here, Troy, tie him up, please." Troy took the reins and looked to the back of the wagon while tying the horse to the rail. "C'mon Toby," the boy yelled and the dog jumped from the back of the wagon and joined Troy on the wooden sidewalk.

Troy hurried to the side of the wagon and held his right hand up to help his mother step down.

"Thank you darlin'," she said with a loving smile.

The sound of Troy's uneven gait intermittently clomping with his mother's balanced footsteps along with Toby's paw patter, made it sound like there were more than just three of them walking toward the door. When the bell over the door jingled as they entered, a chunky but solidly built short man with white muttonchops and adjoining mustache looked up from the counter on which sat several large glass jars of hard candy. "Hello, Lavinia," he said cheerily, reaching in for a piece of candy which he held out to Troy. "And how are you, Master Troy?"

"Go ahead, honey," Lavinia said to Troy who took the piece of candy.

"I'm fine. Thank you Mr. Kraus," Troy said, as he unwrapped the candy and popped it into his mouth.

"You're welcome, son."

"Good morning, Quentin," Lavinia stroked the back of Troy's head and smiled. "We're here to pick up our order. I trust everything is in?"

"Yes, ma'am. It is, indeed." Mr. Kraus turned to an open double doorway and shouted, "Isaac! Come out here, would you, boy?" He then walked around the counter to join Lavinia and Troy. "I just received some very nice fabric from Boston. Come, let me show you." Gently taking her elbow, he led her down an aisle, Troy and Toby following, Troy touching every item that caught his interest.

Hurried footsteps could be heard and a sandy-haired young man caught up to the small group, panting. "Yes, Mr. Kraus?"

"Need you to load the Anatoli's order onto their wagon, please."

"Sure thing, Mr. Kraus. Right away." Isaac walked back to the double door entrance and disappeared.

"Ah, here we are." Mr. Kraus stopped at a table covered with bolts of fabric, three to four high and ten long. "These cotton prints would make lovely dresses for you and your girls," he said as he slid his hand under a striking floral pattern on a magenta background.

Lavinia felt the material. "Oh, yes. You're right. I could make some beautiful dresses with any of these cottons."

"And over here, we've received some extremely durable cotton canvas which would be wonderful for your husband's and boys' clothing."

Lavinia glanced sadly at Troy in his worn tan overalls she had put together from a pair of Virgilio's old workpants, knowing Virgilio might approve of material for a new pair of work pants for himself, but for all the rest of the boys, probably not.

Reading her face, Quentin offered some hope. "It's just about harvest time for grapes. Perhaps we can work something out when Virgilio brings in his grapes."

A faint light of hope brightened her face. "Why thank you, Quentin. I'll mention that to him."

"Good. You do that," Mr. Kraus said. "It's the least I can do for fine customers and friends like you folks. Now let's see how Isaac is doing with your order."

Isaac was half-way through the door and supplied the answer, "Just a couple things left to load up, Ma'am," he said, tipping his cap to her.

"Guess we'll settle up, then," Lavinia said to Mr. Kraus, untying the ribbon of her small, embroidered reticule handbag, handing him thirty dollars.

Mr. Kraus placed the money in his cash register. "Two dollars change," he said handing her the difference.

"This is it," Isaac announced as he moved a couple large sacks of chicken feed and flour across the floor on a handcart.

"Thank you, Isaac," Lavinia told him.

"You're welcome, Ma'am," he replied. Troy hurried to the door and held it open for Isaac, then followed him out with Toby at his heels.

"Thank you, Mrs. Anatoli," Mr. Kraus said with a quick nod of his head. "It's always a pleasure to see you."

"You as well," Lavinia smiled. "I'll be sure to tell Virgilio about the fabric. He should be coming in to see you very soon about his grapes."

"I'll be looking forward to seeing him." Quentin started around the counter to hold the door for her, but Troy beat him to it as he reentered the store.

"Bye, Mr. Kraus," Troy said cheerily.

"Bye, son. You be good, now."

Lavinia noticed a small crowd was formed down the street around a man standing on a small stage in front of a black, horse-drawn carriage that had a sign affixed to its top proclaiming, "Dr. B. Goodbody's Miracle Health Restorative." The man, presumably Dr. Goodbody, was dressed up in a top hat, a double-breasted tailcoat, a bright white pleated shirt, and a cravat at his neck. Dr. Goodbody held an amber, square-shaped bottle in his left hand above his head, and in his right, he held a cane, which he waved around, pointing to people, to his sign, or to a table of the amber bottles next to him, sometimes using the cane to tap something for emphasis. His voice boomed down the street, "This miracle elixir, if taken as prescribed, will cure what ails you from head to toe, from arthritis to paralysis. Come one, come all. We all have conditions, some little, some small. The secret recipe for this potion, known only to the natives who live deep in the Amazon jungle, was divulged to me by them in gratitude for bringing Christianity to them during my missionary expedition in that region. Therefore, you could say this miracle medicine is brought to you by Jesus Christ himself! Derived from exotic plants and ingredients only found in the impenetrable Amazon jungle, this potion will cure sickness as simple as the common cold to one as deadly as cancer. No matter what your problem may be--low spirits, diarrhea, consumption, indigestion, constipation, liver disease, scurvy, syphilis, side pains, bad breath, stunted growth-- this miracle mixture will mend your malady. Only two dollars a bottle. A small price to pay for the restoration of your health."

An individual in the front of the crowd held two dollars out to Dr. Goodbody, who gave him a bottle in return. "You're a wise man, sir," Dr. Goodbody said with a toothy smile, then he looked back at the crowd. "Who else needs to end their suffering?"

While listening to Dr. Goodbody's sales pitch, Lavinia took Troy's hand and made her way to the gathering. Seeing her approach with her limping boy at her side, Dr. Goodbody boomed out. "And you, Madam. I see you have a handsome young man with you who may benefit from this elixir of life. I assure you, if you start giving your son this potion, he'll be right as rain and grow strong as an ox. His infirmity will go away and one day will be but a bad memory of his past. Only two dollars, Madam, which is certainly a small price to pay to restore strength and health to your fine boy. You won't be sorry, I assure you." He held a bottle out to her. The label depicted a healthy, buff South American native standing with his arms outstretched, the sun shining down through the trees behind him.

Lavinia untied the ribbon of her small embroidered purse, removed the two dollars change she'd received from Mr. Kraus, and handed it to Dr. Goodbody, her stomach turning, fully aware how Virgilio would react to her purchase.

Cathy woke up with a churning stomach, feeling panicky and guilty, as if she were sharing Lavinia's unease. In three minutes, the alarm would sound, so Cathy sat up to shake off her dream and join the real world.

When Paul awoke, Cathy was doing deep breathing exercises. He laughed and asked, "What in the world are you doing?"

"Oh, just trying to wake up," she lied.

"Mm-hm. Another dream?"

"If you must know, yes. It really wasn't a bad dream, just . . ."

"Just what? You look worried as hell."

"I guess I'm just empathizing with one of the people in my dreams." Cathy closed her eyes and continued her deep breathing.

"Don't tell me. Lavinia?" Paul smiled. "You better watch out. You might just be inviting her ghost to visit."

"Hmm, you know what? I wouldn't mind that at all. I'd be able to ask her all my questions and we'd find out where she and her children were resting," Cathy smiled.

"Okay, my dear. If she does happen to contact you, don't forget to introduce me, will you? I'll want to apologize to her for being disturbed by you."

Cathy threw her pillow at Paul, who ducked into the bathroom.

7

THE ANGEL

Like every other morning since Troy joined the family, he announced the clock alarm was sounding by barking, jumping on the bed, and nuzzling Cathy and Paul. The morning routine continued with Paul getting in the shower and Cathy letting Troy out while she got the paper.

"Sure wish you didn't have to head off to work today," Cathy told Paul when he came into the kitchen.

"You and me, both." Paul filled a travel mug with coffee. "I'd regret it if I didn't though. I'd always think I could've done just a little bit better if I'd put the time in."

"You're harder on yourself than Harry could ever be," Cathy said. "I doubt he wants you to work at the office all through the weekend."

"I'm just going in for a little while. I'll probably even make it home before you do."

"We'll see. I've got to get home to cook dinner. I want to make that pie for tonight, too."

"I don't know why you don't just meet Sharon and come home. You're putting an awful lot of time and effort into something that's none of your business."

Cathy glared at Paul. "I'm perfectly aware of your opinion about this, dear, and I'm pursuing it regardless. I'm interested and I don't know why it should bother you so much."

"It doesn't really bother me," Paul responded.

"Well it obviously does and I wish you'd just quit being so critical of what I'm doing."

"Let's just drop it, okay?" Paul raised his hands in surrender. "I won't say another word." He bent down to give her a kiss.

Cathy didn't believe him, but kissed him back. "I'll see you later, then."

"Have a good time with Sharon."

"I will."

Cathy finished her cup of coffee and got herself ready to meet Sharon for breakfast. When she got upstairs, Troy again went to Allie's door and began sniffing. Cathy opened Allie's door and let Troy in. He jumped on Allie's bed and curled up next to her feet.

Cathy and Sharon met at Perkins at eight-thirty as arranged. After greeting each other and exchanging the normal niceties, they began discussing Lavinia and the Anatoli clan. Cathy took the printout from her purse and handed it to Sharon with a magnifying glass for her to read the names.

"Wow! It's strange to see these people we've been so curious about. I've been eager to see the picture ever since you texted me the other day."

Cathy was unsure if she should tell Sharon about her recent dreams and said quietly, "And there's something very strange - almost spooky strange to me."

Sharon opened her eyes wide, her curiosity now piqued to the max, "Oh?"

"Now, I know this will sound incredible, but the little boy named Troy next to Lavinia there . . ." Cathy waited.

"Yes, I'm listening," Sharon said.

"Well, he looks exactly like the boy that's been in my dreams lately."

"What dreams? You haven't mentioned any dreams you've been having."

"I guess I've always written dreams off as reflections of what was going on in my life, and the dreams I've had lately didn't seem interesting enough to talk about until now." Cathy spoke a little slower, a little quieter, and looked at Sharon wondering if she should continue. "I've just been dreaming about a little boy of the eighteen hundreds that seems to have grown up on a farm. And then I come upon this family photo and find Troy is the boy in my dreams, or he looks just like him -- well, it's very weird. And there's something else that's stranger yet."

Sharon squinted a moment. "And what's that?"

"Um, let's see, how do I start. For one thing, we have a new addition in our household."

"New addition?" Sharon's eyes grew wide in happy surprise and anticipation. "What are you talking about?"

"We found a dog, actually he found us, and we've adopted him."

"When did all this happen?"

"Just this week. It was the day after all this started with Lavinia." Cathy stopped a moment to think. "What was it? Just Tuesday, I guess, and Wednesday the dog showed up in the woods behind our house." Cathy now wanted to tell Sharon everything and began talking quickly. "I was relaxing on the back deck and saw him and finagled him to come to me. Then I cleaned him up and took him in. I tried to find his owners by placing his photo on Facebook and putting up some flyers and they saw his picture and contacted me the same day. But, in talking to them it seemed apparent the husband didn't want the dog and he must have driven him from Girard to Harborcreek and abandoned him near our house. But the strangest part of everything is what I named him."

"What?"

"Troy!"

"For the little Anatoli boy?"

"Not really. I didn't even know about Troy Anatoli until I saw the photo yesterday. The name occurred to me on Wednesday when the dog appeared in the woods." Cathy shook her head. "I don't know. These coincidences just seem so strange. So what do you think?"

Sharon didn't want Cathy to think she was questioning her credulity. "Well, you know how dreams are. It's hard to remember them clearly once you're awake and the day has gone by. Maybe the boy in your dreams did resemble Troy Anatoli a little, but, because the ad is a concrete image, compared to a fuzzy dream image, you think he looked more like Troy than he really did. And now that you've seen the photo, and it struck you so vividly, you probably will see Troy Anatoli in your dreams. You know, you could have actually seen the ad when you were skimming papers and his image just stuck in your subconscious and Troy's name might even have been in the birth announcement for Michael but you didn't pay attention. You were just basically looking for info on Lavinia, remember?" Sharon handed the printout of the ad back to Cathy.

"Well, maybe," Cathy said trying to convince herself and shook her head as if trying to shake out the troublesome thoughts. "So, let's change the subject. Tell me more about Mr. Anatoli's call to you."

"His call surprised me. I've never gotten a call complaining that people were looking at their relatives' graves before," Sharon laughed. "Once in a while, if some vandalism has been occurring in the cemetery, someone might call, but we don't get complaints regarding people simply looking at gravesites. First Mr. Anatoli asked that we take a look at the old Anatoli graves to see if they were okay and to make sure the flowers were still there. He said people were snooping around and he was worried the graves might be desecrated. I told him I'd be sure to have someone check them out. Then he requested we make sure no one was hanging around their family plot that didn't belong there. I told him there was really no practical way to do that. He wasn't too pleased with that response. I told him the best we could do would be to advise our groundskeepers to keep an eye out and check the graves when they were working in that area."

"Did that satisfy him?"

"I'm not sure. He still wasn't especially happy when we hung up, but, for heaven's sake, what did he expect--us to put guards around the Anatoli graves?"

"Guess I better make myself scarce around that area now," Cathy said, somewhat disappointed. "I probably won't have to look at the stones again, anyway."

"Oh, it's certainly up to you. There's no law saying you can't look at the graves of other peoples' ancestors and you're certainly not doing anything harmful. But, if you're uncomfortable and there's anything you need to know, you know I'll help you." Sharon noticed their waitress at another table and put on her reading glasses. "We better decide what we want to eat."

After contemplating the selections and deciding on their breakfast, Sharon asked, "So, what are we going to search for in the old newspapers? Anything specific?"

"Not really--just any mention of the family, or really anything that might give even a hint of what could have become of Lavinia and the rest of the children. The kids could've grown up, moved away, and died in other parts of the country. Even Lavinia could have. So, anything interesting about the times or what was happening in the area might relate to what happened to them. We're going to have to try and read between the lines. I've gotten to the year before the Civil War began. Leonardo looked to be a teenager in the picture so maybe he joined the service.

The newspapers make very interesting reading, to tell you the truth I like getting a real feel for the times. I didn't want to spend a lot of time reading articles that obviously didn't have much to do with the Anatolis, but when you think of it, almost anything and everything could have had an impact on their lives. So, who knows what will be important."

"You're right. Even reports of severe weather, not just in Harborcreek, but in, say, New York. It's possible they could have traveled there and gotten caught in a horrible winter storm. You know how bad it can get between here and New York. It was probably even more treacherous to travel that route in those days."

"That's for sure," Cathy agreed. "We could watch out for that. Their disappearance in a storm might be mentioned in the news, but maybe not. Who knows. Maybe Virgilio didn't want it reported or didn't tell anyone for some reason. We'll just have to see what occurs to us--use our imagination a bit. In fact, after we go through all the relevant issues of the Dispatch, I might even review them again quickly to make sure I thought everything through. So, it's going to be a long process. Unfortunately," Cathy made a pouty face, "I'm not going to have as much time as I thought I'd have to work on this today. I have to get home to prepare for a nice dinner tonight. Anthony and Julia are coming over for dinner tonight. They don't know about Troy yet, so I'm going to surprise them and I wanted to make sure we all have a nice family dinner before we take Alexandra to Pittsburgh next Saturday."

The fact that her last offspring was leaving made her stomach do a flip-flop and a feeling of sadness infected her mood. The feeling was fleeting, however, when she pictured Troy bounding around the house. "One thing, even though it's strange I named him Troy, I like that it reminds me there are things in life that you just can't explain. Who knows why he came into my life just when it was a perfect time to adopt a dog. Who knows why I thought to name him Troy." Cathy took her phone from her purse and found the photos she'd already taken of Troy. "Here he is. He's not blonde like little boy Troy, but he's cute as a button."

Sharon took Cathy's phone and chuckled. "Oh my gosh, he's darling!"

"I know he'll help prevent me from having the blues when Paul and I will be empty nesters. I love him already."

"Pets do a great job of brightening spirits. I think there'd be a lot less people on antidepressants if they adopted a pet." Sharon handed the phone back to Cathy.

Cathy chattered about Troy like a proud new mother, which led to talk about both of their families during breakfast. They lingered, talking, having several cups of coffee after their table was cleared until Cathy said, "We'd better get going or we won't get anything done at the library."

Cathy introduced Sharon to Karen in the research room, then Cathy and Sharon headed for the microfilm files. They sat down at microfilm readers next to each other and loaded their respective machines. It didn't take long before Sharon remarked, "I see what you mean. I'm getting a vivid picture of how things were back then--the way everyone lived, dressed, the tension of the times, and even the way people talked to each other. At least in print, the language is so formal!"

"I've become so engrossed in this, it's no wonder I'm having dreams, I suppose." Cathy chuckled.

Sharon laughed. "At least your dreams are more interesting than, say, dreaming about work. Your imagination is almost letting you experience a different time period. I'd almost be looking forward to my next night's dream if I were you."

"I kind of do," Cathy smiled. "It seems that everything I see in the papers turns up in a dream in one way or another. Of course, seeing Lavinia's picture in the ad, impressed me, so naturally she'd show up in a dream. And, of course, since she was appearing in the ads section, I think of her in a store, and those outrageous elixir ads are in each paper, so those had to appear in a dream. I almost can predict the plot of my dreams by what I read at the library."

"Oh my gosh," Cathy exclaimed. "Here's another copy of their ad. Maybe you're right and I did skim over their ad before and it somehow registered in my subconscious. Do you want me to print it out for you?"

"Yes, please. I'll show it to Mr. Burns. I think he'll enjoy seeing a picture of some of our long-time residents."

The two women got back to work, silently engrossed in reading the Erie Dispatch of the 1800's. After a little while, Sharon chuckled. "There certainly were a lot of charlatans claiming to be doctors selling medicine in those days," she remarked. "I thought the potion pushing salesman was a Hollywood exaggeration, but looks like they were real and rather commonplace."

"I was surprised, too. Did you read the cure claims? Hard to believe people bought into that."

"I guess medicine was so unsophisticated, people were willing to try anything to cure what ailed them. Thank God we're living today."

When two o'clock rolled around, Cathy sat back. "That's about all the time I've got today. Better get home to get dinner going and straighten up the house a little."

"I'm disappointed," Sharon said. "I was hoping today would be the day, that maybe I'd bring you some luck." The two microfilm readers whirred as Cathy and Sharon rewound the films in their readers.

"Don't worry, we'll hit pay dirt sooner or later," Cathy said as she put her microfilm back into its box. "The longer it takes, the more exciting it will be when we do discover something."

"Since you're going to be gone next Saturday, maybe I'll come down here again to continue our research if you don't solve our mystery during the week. Unless you'd prefer that I wait until you can be here, too."

"Oh, no. That would be wonderful if you could help out if you've got the time."

"Oh, I'll make the time." Sharon lowered the tone of her voice and said dramatically, "Going to stay on it until we crack the case, Sherlock."

Cathy was pleased to see Paul's car in the driveway but somewhat dismayed that Tony was already there. She had wanted to see his face when he met Troy. Troy was at the front door to greet her with excited barks and a full body wag when she walked in. She crouched to receive his sloppy dog kisses. "Happy to see you, too, sweetie," she giggled and smiled at Tony. "Well I guess you've already been introduced."

"Hi, Mom," Tony got off the couch and gave Cathy a hug. "Yes we have. So he's your big surprise, huh?" Tony laughed.

"Mm-hm. At least I'll be able to see Julia's reaction. She's been so busy lately at work, she might not get her till dinner's almost ready and I don't think Allie spilled the beans." Cathy smiled. "So, what made you come so early? I didn't expect you for a couple of hours."

"I thought I'd watch some of the Northern Trust Open with Dad."

"Who's winning?"

"Nice battle between Dustin Johnson and Jordan Spieth. They're tied for the lead right now," Tony told her.

"How's my boy, Matt Kuchar, doing?" she asked, perching herself on the end of the seat of the easy chair next to them.

"He's had some great shots. Not far off the lead," Paul said.

"That's good. I've always liked him. Glad to see you managed to keep it to a half day, hon. Did you get a lot done?" she asked Paul.

"Yeah, it's coming along pretty well, I'd say. Thought if I gave it a rest and look at it with fresh eyes tomorrow, I'll be able to finish 'er up."

"Oh, Paul, tomorrow, too?" Cathy slumped. "I thought maybe we could do something together."

"We might still have time to do something later on tomorrow afternoon."

"Oh, you'll be too tired," Cathy sighed.

"We're doing something together right now, aren't we?" Paul opened his arms wide as if encircling the three of them and the TV.

Cathy laughed. "You're technically right."

"And if you hadn't been at the library on your project, you'd have been enjoying the pleasure of our company for a lot longer."

"Oh darn. Yes, I guess I missed a super good time."

"What project, Mom? You still working on our family tree?" Tony asked.

"Not our family tree, son," Paul interjected. "Someone else's. She's developed an unhealthy curiosity about the Anatoli family."

"What?" he asked, puzzled.

Cathy gave Tony as much information as she dared in front of Paul, going into detail about Lavinia and leaving out mention of her dreams and Troy's name, while Paul cast disapproving glances her way. "I'd really like to find out what became of Lavinia and her other four children. There's something very wrong. I feel it in my bones."

"That's really interesting, Mom," Tony said.

"I guess you come by it honestly," Paul said to Tony with a smirk.

"It makes me curious, too, Dad. I frankly find it intriguing." Tony winked at his mother.

Cathy beamed with love and gratitude at her son. The affirmation that this was not merely some quixotic pursuit, that it had some merit, was all she needed to see it through.

"It'd be great if you can find out what the story is, Mom. You'll have to keep me informed."

"I definitely will, son." Cathy walked over and kissed Tony's forehead. "Better get that pie going and the roast ready for the oven." As she passed Paul she gave him a raised eyebrow with a sidelong glance.

Paul shrugged his shoulders. "I still say it's none of your business."

Troy followed Cathy to the kitchen and put his paws on the counter, enticed by the roast. When she told him to get down, he pushed himself off the counter and hurried to the front door with a demanding bark.

Cathy followed. "Have to go out? Good boy, Troy."

"I'll get him, Mom," Tony offered.

"Thanks, hon."

Tony clicked on Troy's leash. "Think I'll take him for a little walk after he does his business.

Troy scratched the ground when he was done and tried to tear off toward the cemetery. "Hold on Troy," Tony said sharply. "You almost tore my arm out of its socket. I've got to pick this up, you know." He laughed and tugged at the leash to get Troy to settle down.

"Okay, boy. Now we can go," Tony told him after he disposed of the doggee-do bag. Troy once again darted toward the cemetery. Curious now about the Anatolis, Tony thought he may as well walk through the cemetery with Troy. Further attempts to get Troy under control were successful only sporadically as they walked. If squirrels or chipmunks were not stimulating Troy's prey response, Troy was pulling toward the cemetery. Once there, Troy stopped, looked around, and sniffed the air. Tony laughed. "That was quite the walk you took me on. You going to calm down now?"

Troy looked at Tony, panting, tongue out, a dog smile on his face. As they worked their way through the cemetery, Troy sniffed everything he could sniff, his concentration only occasionally being interrupted by a squirrel. All of a sudden, Troy sniffed the air again then tore in a beeline toward the Anatoli obelisk that was a few hundred yards away, the leash slipping from Tony's hand. When Tony caught up to Troy, Troy was standing in attack mode, hackles up, growling at the obelisk. Tony was surprised to see he was in the middle of the Anatoli family graves and staring at Virgilio's marker.

"Calm down, boy," Tony said to Troy as he took the leash again. "What's this all about?" He gave the leash a couple quick tugs and looked at the graves his mother had just told him about.

Tony looked around, trying to decide which way to go next, and noticed a lifesize statue of an angel in Lot 4 of Section A. As he neared the statue, its details became clear. It was actually a statue of two angels, a female and a small boy, and the statue was not a monument. The female angel stood about five feet tall. Its plump round face looked lovingly down upon the boy angel who returned her gaze. Her arm rested softly upon the boy angel's shoulders. Two purple hyacinths bound together with a purple ribbon lay at the base of the statue. Tony picked them up to sniff their sweet scent.

Naturally, Troy busily sniffed the statue and the ground around it. After appreciating the sculpture and the hyacinths for a few minutes, Tony leaned the hyacinths against the statue, then looked at the surrounding headstones. He was stunned to find that he was standing in the midst of markers bearing the surname, Rosetti. Remembering his mother had told him Rosetti was Lavinia's maiden name, he began searching for a stone reading Lavinia Rosetti Anatoli. Failing that, he noted the location of two illegible headstones in the vicinity of the Rosetti plot for his mother, then turned to continue his walk with Troy. Troy, however, had other idea and braced his front paws pulling against the leash, refusing to move. A little encouragement along with treats and Troy changed his mind and trotted alongside Tony.

Paul went into the kitchen during a commercial break to get another beer and remarked, "Did you have to drag our son into your little mystery?"

Annoyed, Cathy stopped peeling potatoes to look at Paul. "Have you been sitting there stewing about that all this time?"

"Not really stewing, but I just don't want him getting wrapped up in this, too."

"You know, I'm really sick of your paranoia about this." Cathy continued her peeling with a little more zeal than before. "What horrible consequence are you expecting to result from my interest? No matter what I find out, I'm certainly not intending to publicize anything. I just find it interesting. That's all there is to it."

"And it's not just that. It's also the time you're putting into this thing. You say you want to spend more time with me, but today you're off at the library all morning. If you're going to be doing something why don't you put your energy into bringing some money into this household? We've got two kids in school now, a mortgage, bills, and what do you do all day but run around putting your nose in everyone's business but our own. It's all on me--on my shoulders! Then you bring this dog into the family. Another mouth to feed and care for. How much did that vet bill cost us the other day?"

Taken aback, tears sprang to her eyes. Cathy was not ready for Paul's tongue-lashing. Defensive, hurt, and angry, she slammed down the potato peeler and shouted back, "I do bring money into this house and, on top of that, I do everything else around here to keep this house running without you bending one little finger. If you think I'm some kind of gold digger, I sure as hell would've found someone with more gold than you've got." Cathy was breathing hard and wondered what in the world happened to make this day erupt into such a ugly storm. Tears began flowing down her cheeks and she tore off a paper towel from the holder to dry them.

Paul came up behind her and put his arms around her waist. She tried to shake him off of her, but he held her tight and kissed the back of her head. "I'm sorry hon," he said softly. "I guess I'm pushing myself too much lately and I'm taking it out on you. I'm so sorry. What I just said isn't how I truly feel at all. I'm sorry."

Cathy turned around in his arms, her eyes glittery with tears that still leaked out. "I'm sorry, too. We should both think before we speak." They hugged each other for a long minute, the side of Cathy's face against Paul's chest. "Go on back to your golf. I only have a little bit left to do here."

It was on the tip of Paul's tongue to perpetuate the argument but kept his thoughts to himself and got comfortable on the couch again.

About ten minutes later, Tony and Troy burst through the front door. As Tony detached Troy's leash, he called to Cathy, "Hey, Mom, guess what! I found the Rosetti graves. You did say that was Lavinia Anatoli's maiden name, didn't you?"

Cathy cringed and looked over the counter at Tony. "You did?" she asked with a mixture of curiosity, excitement, and distress over Paul's reaction.

Paul turned from the television set to scowl at Cathy. Cathy gave Paul a quick return scowl. "Where are they located?" she asked Tony.

"Lot 4 of Section A. Here, I wrote down the location of a couple of stones I couldn't read that you might want to check out."

"Thanks, son!" Cathy kissed his cheek.

Tony laughed. "Troy, here, took me to the Anatoli graves first. He made a beeline there and for some reason does not like the obelisk monument." Tony chuckled. "I'm not sure what he didn't like about it, but he was just standing there, growling at it. Maybe a coyote or fox sprayed on the stone. Who knows. And when you look for the Rosetti graves, just look for the angel statue. You can see it from the Anatoli graves. The statue stands right in the middle of the Rosetti plot."

"I don't suppose you saw a stone for Lavinia, did you?" Cathy asked.

"Afraid not. All the graves were dated in the eighteen hundreds around the angel statue, but I didn't see one for her."

"That doesn't really surprise me. Sharon didn't find any record for Lavinia Rosetti in the computer, but I'll ask her about the two graves you couldn't identify anyway, and we'll just keep on searching."

"You know, I'm wondering about the angel statue. There's was no name on its base, and there were two purple hyacinths lying at the base. Someone definitely put them there. So it's something to ask Sharon about."

"Mm-hm, you never know. Especially when you consider that the land for the cemetery was donated by Virgilio Anatoli. I'd speculated that he donated it because maybe he buried Lavinia there. I wonder if he simply marked the spot where she's buried with the statue. We don't know when she died and what kind of record-keeping they had way back then, so maybe . . ." Cathy could tell Paul had heard enough of this discussion. "I've got to talk to Sharon about this!"

"Be sure to let me know what she says," Tony said with excited interest.

"I definitely will. Thanks, son"

Paul refused to look at them and stared coldly at the television set.

8

SATURDAY DINNER

It wasn't long before Alexandra arrived home weighed down with her purchases from a shopping trip with one of her girlfriends.

"Looks like you did well," Cathy remarked with a smile. "Think you have everything you need now?"

"Yeah, I think so. If I don't, there are plenty of places to shop in Pittsburgh."

"That's definitely true. And you better keep in mind that you'll have a spending limit. You have more important expenses while you're in school."

Allie laughed. "You're worried about me spending too much? You know the places I like to shop." Allie stood before her mother, arms and hands out to each side, and she spun around. "Look at me. I'm definitely a second hand Rose."

"Okay, Rosie, show me your bargains."

Allie proceeded to display her purchases, some clothing, a couple decorative items, and some normal school necessities. From a large bag she removed a plastic grocery store bag. "And look what I found at Oregon Antiques. She only charged me five dollars."

Cathy caught her breath looking at the beaded purse with a shoulder strap that reminded her of the embroidered reticule handbag carried by Lavinia in her recent dream.

"Great for going out, don't you think? "Just missing a little beading but I can fix that." Allie said admiring the purse. She noticed her mother's face. "What's wrong?"

"Nothing's wrong, dear." Cathy laughed at herself. "It just reminds me of a purse in one of my dreams."

"You had a dream about a purse?"

"No, but a woman in one of my dreams was carrying a similar looking purse, but the one in my dream wasn't beaded."

Allie smiled and stuck her head in the refrigerator. "Don't tell me--Lavinia Anatoli?"

"If you must know, yes," Cathy admitted. "Now don't spoil your appetite. It won't be too long before we eat."

"I'm only going to grab an apple," Allie said a trifle irritated. "What are you making tonight, anyway?"

"Thought I'd get fancy and make prime rib," Cathy replied as she took the peach pie out of the oven to cool.

"Mmm. Peach pie, too? Do we have any vanilla ice cream?"

"Yes, dear." Cathy chuckled. "What about your diet?"

"Oh, I'll make an exception tonight. Besides, I didn't eat much to leave room for tonight's dinner." Allie took a bite of her apple. "What time is Jules going to be here?"

"Not till close to suppertime. The salon closes at five today and I think she was coming here right after."

"If I'm not downstairs when she pulls up, holler for me, okay? I want to see her face when Troy greets her."

"Ok, hon. I'll let you know," Cathy agreed as Allie gathered her things and headed to her room.

Cathy checked the roast and started straightening up the house, gathering newspapers, magazines and other odds and ends that were out of place downstairs.

"Good God, Cathy. Sit down. It's just our kids," Paul laughed.

"Gee, thanks, Dad," Tony laughed as well.

"What I'm saying is, you don't have to get the house in pristine condition for them. They've seen it before in much worse shape than this," he laughed again and reached out for Cathy. "Sit down and relax a few minutes with me, will you?"

Cathy put the papers in a neat pile on the coffee table placing the magazines on top, took two empty soda cans to the kitchen, then sat down next to Paul, leaning against him. He held her close with his arm over her shoulders.

Cathy was taking the roast out of the oven to rest when she heard a car door slam. She hurried into the living room where Allie, Tony, Paul, and Troy were lounging. "I think Julia just got here."

There was a quick knock at the door and Julia was entering, startling Troy out of Allie's grasp. Troy bounded to the door barking loudly with Allie chasing after him, catching him by the collar before he could jump on Julia.

"Oh my God," shrieked Julia. "Are you trying to give me a heart attack? Guess I'm lucky he's not vicious."

"Sorry, Julia. He doesn't know you. Of course, he actually doesn't know us or the house that much yet either." Allie said while holding Troy's collar and scratching his wagging butt. "Mom named him Troy,"

Julia crouched down to pet her new fur brother and glanced at Cathy, smiling. "I take it Troy is your big secret?"

"Yes, isn't he a doll?" Cathy said coming over to the door. Julia got up and they hugged and gave each other a kiss on the cheek. "How'd your day go, dear?" The three women walked back into the living room and sat down.

"It's been hectic since I've been covering for Anita, but she'll be back in a week. After three days of it, I'm beat, but she'd do the same for me."

"Aren't any of the other girls helping out?"

"Yes, but I'm taking the lion's share of her clients and it's been hard to juggle appointments with my regular customers. Most of my regulars have been very understanding and accommodating, but there have been a few . . ." Julia shook her head and sighed. "I think I managed to keep everybody happy, though."

"Oh, I'm sure you have, hon," Cathy told her, putting her hand on Julia's forearm. "Don't you even think about it."

"I was a little worried about asking Luella Anatoli to come in earlier than normal, but she was fine about it."

Cathy closed her eyes, and avoided looking at Paul. She was going to change the subject quickly, but before she could get out the words, 'That's good,' Julia continued talking.

"Just wondering, Mom, were you working for Find-A-Grave at St. Margaret on Thursday?"

Feeling Paul's piercing gaze, Cathy stood up, motioning for Julia. "Yes, dear. They're keeping me pretty busy and I'm really enjoying it. Why don't you come out and help me in the kitchen and tell me more about Anita's honeymoon. Where did she go? Have you heard from her?" Cathy hurried toward the kitchen.

Paul snorted his breath out hard through his nose, shaking his head, a look of disapproval on his face as he watched Cathy and Julia leave the room.

"Oh, they went to Maui and no one's heard from her with the exception of her mother who stopped in the shop the other day and told us she's having a wonderful time. She's in love with the place, of course. Maybe one of these days I'll get there, too," said Julia as she trailed Cathy to the stove.

Cathy's and Julia's abrupt move to the kitchen startled Troy again, who accompanied them barking all the way. Cathy smiled and thought, 'Good boy, drown us out.' She didn't attempt to quiet Troy and said loudly to Julia, "Can you get out some bowls for the mashed potatoes, gravy, and vegetables, hon?"

"Sure, Mom. Oh, and what I wanted to ask you is, when you were at the cemetery, were you around the Anatoli graves?"

Cathy put her finger to her lips and whispered, "Ssh, yes, I was there with your sister. Didn't you know I was researching one of the Anatoli ancestors?"

Julia shook her head and whispered back, "No, I didn't. Who contacted you to do that and who are you trying to find? And why are we whispering? Is the roast not supposed to know?" Julia laughed.

"No, I'd rather not talk about it in front of your father." Cathy looked up from dishing the mashed potatoes into a bowl and glanced toward the living room to see if Paul might be listening. "He doesn't approve. He thinks I'm spending too much time on it and considers it none of my business."

"Well, you're responding to a request to Find-A-Grave so . . ."

That's just it. No one asked for the research. I'm just satisfying my own curiosity. When I was there this week, I happened to notice that one of the granddames of the Anatoli family didn't seem to be buried where you'd think she'd be buried and, well, I wondered why and where she is and decided to look into it. So now your father thinks I'm snooping and that if the Anatolis get wind of my interest it might lead to trouble."

"Sorry to say this, Mom, but Dad might be right," said Julia. "Mrs. Anatoli said her grandmother-in-law and Mr. Anatoli were pretty upset that strangers were so interested in their family plot.."

Cathy and Julia had not noticed Paul at the entrance to the kitchen. "Uh-huh," he said. "I told you, Cathy! You're going to end up having the Anatolis slapping some invasion of privacy suit on us or something."

"Oh, come on, Paul. That's ridiculous. I'm not invading anyone's privacy. I can't be sued for looking at graves in the cemetery and researching public records."

"Who knows. People are sue-happy these days. Even if they don't sue us, why would you want to antagonize them? You didn't know if they'd be upset before, but you do now, so I want you to stop."

Julia mouthed the word, 'Sorry,' to her mother.

Cathy sighed and placed her hand on Julia's forearm. "That's okay dear," then she looked at Paul and said, somewhat disgusted and discouraged. "Okay, you might be right. If seeing people just looking at their old family gravesites gets them in an uproar, heaven knows how they'd react if they found out someone was looking at their family records at the library and courthouse."

"That's right. I'm glad to hear you're coming to your senses about this," Paul said with satisfaction. "I have no idea what made you think this is any of your concern."

"All right, already. I was just curious, that's all. Besides, I probably won't have that much time anymore now that school will be back in session. So you won't have to worry about some Hatfield and McCoy drama starting here in Harborcreek because of me."

"Good. I'm glad to hear it," Paul said, pleased to hear Cathy now saw reason and agreed with him. "Now what do you want done with this roast? Do you want me to carve it?"

"Yes, that would be great. Just put the slices on this platter," she said placing one next to the roast. "We'll get everything else on the table in the dining room while you're doing that."

While eating, conversation centered on Troy's antics, Tony's studies, and Allie starting at Carnegie Mellon next weekend. Everyone forgot about the Anatolis and their missing family members, with the exception of Cathy, who was unable to purge thoughts of Lavinia and Troy from her mind.

Cathy, all keyed up from the evening and unable to sleep, decided to have a glass of wine while sitting on the deck and listening to the night sounds. She felt her eyelids getting heavy and returned to bed. The wine had helped and she quickly drifted into a deep sleep.

She slept through the alarm and when Paul left the house for work, Cathy woke up. The sun was brightening her bedroom and she sat up feeling quite refreshed. Washing her face in the bathroom, she attempted to relieve the allergy itchiness in her eyes by rubbing them. She rubbed harder than she should have, causing her vision to blur when she looked in the mirror. Lavinia looked back at her with eyes red from crying. It was a mere moment. Cathy blinked and it was over. It was, as usual, her face reflected in the mirror. Cathy turned on the spigot to brush her teeth recalling the dream she'd had that evening.

A loaded buckboard was traveling slowly over a dry dirt road leaving a cloud of dust behind. Lavinia, in her blue dress, was driving with Troy and Toby next to her. In the distance was a farmhouse with a large front porch and a barn. All of a sudden, they were in front of the house and Lavinia was saying, "Whoa, Bruno," in a low voice. She engaged the brake lever once the wagon stopped.

"Here, Mom," Troy said handing her the bottle of Dr. Goodbody's Miracle Health Restorative that he'd been safeguarding for the ride home, and he then climbed down from the wagon, Toby jumping off after him. As before, Troy hurried around to take his mother's hand while she stepped down to the ground.

Cathy brushed out her hair and got dressed, then headed downstairs. She made a pot of coffee and put an English muffin in the toaster, her actions on autopilot as her mind drifted back to the dream she'd had that night.

Virgilio was making his way from the barn to the wagon and two teenaged girls were standing on the porch of the farmhouse.

"What take you so long?" Virgilio boomed angrily. "You have change for me?" He held out his hand to Lavinia.

"I'm sorry, Virgilio," Lavinia said in a soft tone she hoped would appease him. "I don't have any change."

"Kraus is a thief! Stronzo ladro,"[1] Virgilio yelled. "He shoulda give you two dollars back!" Virgilio's face was beet red. "Stupida! You no ask? I told you how much it was."

"It wasn't Mr. Kraus, Virgilio. I used the money to buy something." Lavinia had been preparing herself for Virgilio's ferocious anger for the entire trip home. "Go inside, Troy," she said. "And have your sisters go inside with you, too."

Instead of obeying, Troy positioned himself between Lavinia and his father.

"Troy, do as I say," Lavinia said firmly, pointing at the house. "Go inside right now."

Troy reluctantly walked toward the house and looked back just in time to see his father slap Lavinia hard across her face. "Sei una sporca ladra puttana!"[2] he shouted. "You have no right to spend my money without asking," Virgilio growled menacingly scowling down upon her.

"I bought medicine for Troy," she responded defensively, bringing her free hand to her stinging cheek and holding the bottle for Virgilio to see.

Troy started running back toward the commotion, but Lavinia saw him. "Do as I said, Troy."

"What is this?" Virgilio grabbed the bottle from her hand and slowly sounded out the name of the elixir. "Stupida puttana,[3] you steal for your regazzo senza valore![4] He's good for nothing--inutile[5].

You throw away my money on him. He's never going to be no good. Madonna mia!" Virgilio looked at the bottle then shoved it back at Lavinia, laughing derisively. "So you think this grow a new leg and arm for him, eh? Che fesso!"[6]

---

[1] Assohole thief
[2] You're a dirty whore thief
[3] Stupid whore
[4] Worthless boy
[5] Useless
[6] What a fool

Cathy was mindlessly buttering her English muffin when she became flabbergasted at the realization her dream was peppered with Italian, a language she'd never studied. She opened her junk drawer, grabbed a pencil and piece of paper and jotted down the words she could remember, spelling them phonetically to the best of her ability to see if she could translate them online.

9

SCOTT HOLLOW

Cathy was stunned when she discovered the Italian words were legitimate and they made sense in the context of what Virgilio had said. She put her laptop on the coffee table, sipping her coffee and staring at the television screen, not paying a bit of attention to what was being said on Meet the Press.

Allie broke her out of her stupor by greeting her, "Good morning."

"Oh, morning dear," Cathy responded.

"What're they talking about today on Meet the Press?" Allie asked, sitting down next to her mother.

"Hmm, oh, I'm afraid I wasn't paying much attention to the show. Of course, they're talking about Hurricane Harvey in Texas, but that's about all I know."

Allie glanced at the computer screen. "Are you trying to learn Italian?"

"No, I just needed to look up a couple terms I came across."

"Really?" Allie laughed. "What in the world have you been reading?"

"Never mind," Cathy said and closed the laptop. "So what have you got on your agenda today?"

"Kelsea and I wanted to take Troy and her dog for a hike at Scott Hollow today. Ever since I met her this past summer, she's been telling me how pretty it is there. She takes her dog there all the time since it almost borders her back yard."

"I don't know, hon. You know Troy isn't exactly steady on his feet. Do you know what the trails are like there, if there are any trails at all?"

"I know there're trails, but I'm not really sure what they're like. But Kelsea does. She'll make sure we don't go anywhere that's not safe and I'm sure she'll be especially careful since Troy limps."

Cathy was shaking her head. "I don't think it's a good idea."

"How about if you come with us. You can keep a close eye on Troy and, besides, it'll be nice to spend some time with you since I'm leaving next weekend."

"Uh-huh," Cathy smirked. "I think it's more like you wanting to spend some time with Troy, isn't it?"

"No, really, Mom. I did think it'd be fun for the two dogs and Kelsea and me to go, but it'd be fun with you, too. I know you like to go for walks and hikes, right?"

Still skeptical, Cathy raised her eyebrows and shrugged.

"Well, then, come with us. You'll enjoy it and I can introduce you to her folks. You haven't met them yet."

Cathy was convinced Allie's invitation was genuine and it warmed her heart. It had been a long time since she'd felt that she was more than just an annoyance to her daughter. A rush of love for her daughter flowed through Cathy. "Okay, then. Just let me know when you want to go."

Kelsea was walking her American Water Spaniel, Gilda, in front of her house when Cathy and Allie pulled in the driveway. This was the first introduction of Troy to Gilda, so everyone was pleased when the two dogs were friendly with each other after their initial get-acquainted sniffing.

"Okay," said Kelsea, "I suggest we go east if you want to get a workout. It's a pretty steady uphill climb. We can rest at the top and then we can take it easy on the way back. Gilda, here, loves it. Don't you girl?" Kelsea ruffled Gilda's curly coat and the two began walking toward the tree line, with Allie, Cathy and Troy following.

"The paths here aren't as easy to navigate as a park, of course, since not many people come up here. I hardly ever run into anyone when I hike with Gilda and I always try to keep her close.

If she decides to chase a chipmunk or squirrel or something, I don't want her sliding over the edge or surprising a coyote."

"We're going to have to watch Troy extra carefully because of his lame back leg," Cathy said. "So, don't you go running off, pretty boy," she said to Troy.

Once in the wooded area, the three women walked quietly together, occasionally calling the dogs back to them if they ventured too far away investigating the area or treeing squirrels. "There are so many trees around here, the dogs don't get to chase the squirrels too far. There's always an escape route up a tree a few feet away for the squirrel," Kelsea laughed. "But, it's still fun for the dogs."

"But is it fun for the squirrels?" snickered Allie.

"Of course it is! I really think squirrels love to tease dogs," Kelsea laughed. "Once we get to the top of the hill, there's a magnificent view. You can see all the way down to Lake Erie," she told them. "The best vantage point is a little plateau at the top overlooking a rocky drop of maybe two hundred feet straight down. It's not as impressive as Wintergreen Gorge, but it's deep enough to give you a nice dose of vertigo looking down."

"So what you're saying is, 'If you're bothered by heights, don't get too near the edge," said Allie.

"Mm-hm. I think that would be wise," Kelsea smiled. "There are no guardrails up there."

With each step, Allie exercised her artist's eye conceptualizing compositions and snapping photos with her cellphone as a visual note.

They pointed out things that caught their attention and stopped to watch a pileated woodpecker hammering on a large tree. By the time they reached Kelsea's plateau, everyone badly needed to catch their breath.

The three approached the edge of the cliff and took in the view. "You're right," Cathy said, "This is a mini Wintergreen Gorge."

"I don't think we should get too close to the edge," Kelsea cautioned. "Since I've been coming up here, I've noticed the change in the gorge from erosion. Some areas were much steeper and after winter or severe storms, I've noticed chunks and rocks at the top that looked immovable have broken off and tumbled down to the bottom. The trees that somehow took root and grew from a seed wedged in a crevice in the side of the hill, too, sometimes just break loose taking part of the hill with them."

"It's always amazing to see how trees can grow like that. It just appears they've got their feet stuck in the side of the hill to keep them upright," Allie remarked and sat down cross-legged to enjoy the view. "I noticed what look to be footpaths that lead down to the creek. Have you taken them down?"

"I have, but they're pretty precarious. Some parts of the paths have completely eroded away, so I wouldn't recommend it, especially with the dogs. You have to be a little creative to keep going down."

"I think this is enough adventure for me, and I hope you're not getting any idea of climbing down there some day, Allie." Cathy said firmly, then checked the ground for ants and other bugs before she sat down.

Allie rolled her eyes, shook her head and looked at Kelsea and smiled.

"This is a great place to relax and think," Cathy said, "Solitude, great view, nice breeze. Once the leaves start changing color, it must be spectacular."

"Oh, it is. I've taken a ton of photos in the fall from up here." Kelsea took her phone from her pocket and found some snapshots. "When we get back to my house, I'll show you some of the photos I've taken with my good camera."

"Are you going to concentrate on landscape photography?" asked Allie.

"Not really. I do enjoy representational photography, taking landscapes and all that, but I want to explore all subjects, macro to micro to portrait, action, and fine art. I'm interested in all of it. I particularly want to learn techniques that can turn a photo into something other than simply a recording of reality. You ought to dabble in photography, Allie. With your creativity, I'll bet you could do a lot with it."

"I've been thinking about it. There are probably plenty of ways I could incorporate photography into what I already do."

Troy got up from his resting position next to the three women and began sniffing his way toward a narrow foot path that led down to the right. "Troy!" Cathy called. He did not turn around and she saw that the spindly path widened to a flat ledge supporting an outcropping of rocks. It appeared the rocks might have piled up there from a landslide years ago. Just beyond and above the rocks was an eastern white oak, grasping the side of the hill for dear life with its strong roots. Perched atop the pile of rocks was a red-tailed hawk alert for its next meal.

"Look at that!" Cathy exclaimed to Allie and Kelsea. Both girls grabbed their phones and took pictures of the hawk. Troy began barking, disturbing the hawk into flying off.

"Rats," said Kelsea. "I wish I had my other camera. I've already gotten some nice shots of the hawk sitting there and a few of it flying, but always dream of that one perfect shot. I can experiment with these cellphone shots on Photoshop, though. I've wondered if it's always the same hawk up here. I think it could be. From what I've read, red-tailed hawks like to stay in the same area for their entire lives. I've got one photo I particularly like of the hawk just taking off from those rocks that I'll have to show you. I printed it out and framed it for my dad for Father's Day this year."

"It looks like the top might have crumbled and a rock slide occurred a long time ago," Allie remarked.

"That's what I think, too. If you look at the top edge of the cliff there, it dips in, like a chunk is missing," Kelsea responded.

Troy continued picking his way toward the rocks in question, followed by Gilda. Cathy whistled for the dogs and called for Troy again. When Kelsea called Gilda's name, Gilda stopped and looked back, but Troy continued on his adventurous quest.

"Do you think there's a nest in the rocks?" Cathy speculated aloud as she started after Troy. Another call from Kelsea for Gilda and Gilda came racing back. Cathy sighed, "It would have been nice if Troy would have followed Gilda back, but guess I can't get too upset for him not listening. He hasn't even been with us a full week yet and heaven knows how much training he's had. I better go after him."

"Be careful, Mom," Allie said.

"Yes, Mrs. Pantona. Look before you step. Part of that path is pretty loose footing. Some of the path is okay, but not all of it."

"Don't worry, I'll be fine."

Troy had only managed to cover about fifteen yards along the path. He now stood on a spot wide enough for him to turn around and was looking for a way to go farther.

Cathy inched her way to Troy, trying not to look down, but occasionally peeking, causing her to immediately feel dizzy and her stomach to turn. Troy seemed to be deciding whether to hop to a ledge below or to continue on the short, precarious ribbon of the path leading from where he stood to a wider section of the path.

Cathy finally reached Troy and clicked his leash onto his collar. "Come on, Troy," she urged, jerking his leash a couple times. Troy pulled back. "Troy! Come! Let's go!" she said, jerking the leash again. Troy refused again with a growl.

Thinking he might be frightened, Cathy tried another tack. "You're okay, boy. Follow me. Everything's fine." She offered him a treat from her pocket, which he pushed away with his nose. Finally, she used her Master voice, and shortened the leash. Troy begrudgingly accompanied Cathy up the narrow, unstable path, to Allie, Kelsea, and Gilda.

"Phew, not a fan of heights," Cathy said with relief.

"You know what they say," Allie said.

"What's that, dear?"

"You've got to face your fears. It was probably good for you."

"Maybe, but I'm not one to want to tempt fate. I'm getting too old for that kind of thing."

"Oh, I don't think so. You're pretty spry old girl," Allie teased with a laugh. "How about we try rock climbing one of these days?"

"Hiking from Kelsea's to here was enough of a rock climb for me."

After a little more rest, they made their way back to Kelsea's house. "Come on in. I'll show you the photos I've taken of Scott Hollow." Kelsea opened the entry door off the cement patio to the downstairs family room. The dogs bounded in, Gilda leading the way through the family room and up a wide staircase of six steps to a more formal living room   Kelsea called for Gilda, and Cathy and Allie hollered for Troy. Kelsea's mother and father appeared at the head of the stairs.

"You and your entourage certainly make a grand entrance," laughed her mother.

"Mom and Dad, this is Allie's mom, Cathy Pantona."

Kelsea's parents continued down the staircase extending their hands to Cathy. "Hi, Cathy. Tom and Amanda. Pleased to meet you," Mr. Kendrick said. "We're so glad Allie and Kelsea connected and are starting their freshman year at Carnegie Mellon together. Having a friend to pal around with will make their transition to college life a lot nicer for both of them."

"I agree," Cathy said, shaking their hands. "A lot safer, too. They can look out for each other."

Both Troy and Gilda were pestering Tom and Amanda for attention. "I guess this is the new addition to your household that Allie's told us so much about."

"That he is. We're already so attached to him, it seems like he's been with us for years," Cathy smiled. "Come here, Troy." This time, Troy came to Cathy immediately. "Where was that a little while ago, you stinker?" she laughed and gave him a treat from her pocket. Cathy told the Kendricks about Troy's expedition at the top of Scott Hollow.

"A little explorer, eh?"

"You'd think he'd have that out of his system since he was lost in the woods, wouldn't you?" Allie noted.

"I'm afraid he wasn't as much lost as he was dumped, poor boy?"

"How do you know that?" Allie asked, taken aback.

Cathy revealed the disturbing phone conversation she'd had with the Vugsta's on Thursday.

"Why didn't you tell us?"

"For one thing, I wanted to see if they called again, and they haven't. I wasn't sure if your father would feel obligated to return Troy to the couple even though the husband, obviously, did not want to keep him. Since they haven't phoned back, I'm sure your father would agree that Troy's much better off with us. I'll probably get a license for him tomorrow when I go downtown and I'm going to make an appointment to get Troy neutered as soon as I can, so I'll probably tell your dad this week."

"What if the woman divorces her husband and demands Troy back? What then?"

Cathy marveled that Allie could be so like her father, worrying about a situation that likely would never happen. "We'll cross that bridge if and when we come to it. I doubt that will happen, though."

Kelsea had turned on their sixty-inch television and made herself comfortable on the couch with her laptop. "The photos will look so much better on the bigger screen," she said as she scrolled through her photo gallery for the folder for Scott Hollow.

"I won't bore you with all the photos I've taken there--I'll just try to show you the best ones."

The first of Kelsea's photos was a panorama on a sparkling day from the top of the hill, followed by the same shot taken in different seasons. She showed dozens of colorful fall photos along the route to the top, down the other side, some including wildlife she was lucky enough to encounter and capture on film, receiving admiring comments from her small audience. She had a few pictures of views straight down the most severe drops to the creek. "I tried to take shots at different times of day with different weather and light conditions, playing with filters and, of course, editing with Photoshop. I've even got a few cool night shots. For those, I had to talk Mom and Dad into letting me go up there at night. Of course, Dad insisted on going up with me." Kelsea raised an eyebrow and turned around to stare at her father who was standing in back of the couch directly behind her.

Her father laughed. "Sorry, dear. I sure as heck wasn't going to let you climb up there all by yourself at night. Your mother and I would've been worried sick. In fact, it would be downright negligent for us to let you go up there alone at night."

"Oh my gosh! I had a flashlight so I could see where I was going. I know the paths up there like the back of my hand. Plus, Gilda was with me."

"And I didn't want her to get lost or hurt either."

"Oh, Dad. I guess it's your job to worry, isn't it," Kelsea laughed."

"Afraid so. You're stuck with me. But I have to admit, it was well worth the trip going up there. You managed to get some beautiful photos that night." Tom said and patted Kelsea's shoulder.

Kelsea turned around to continue showing her photos. "Now, last, but not least, I've got some pictures that highlight the rocky ledge where Troy was headed and the hawk we saw perched there today."

"Oh, you saw your hawk up there again today?" Amanda asked. "That reminds me, Kelsea took a fantastic shot of that area with the hawk on the ledge just ready to take off. She matted and framed a print of it and gave it to Tom for Father's Day last year. I'll go get it to show you."

"Oh, don't get up, hon, sit tight. I'll go get it." Tom left the family room.

Kelsea continued going through the photos with the hawk in them. "You decide--same hawk or not? I'm saying, same, and I think he deserves a name if he's a full-time neighbor."

"Oh, that's a beautiful picture, Kelsea!" Allie exclaimed about a close-up of the hawk with the natural background blurred, blended, and muted making the hawk look even more striking.

"Yes, it is," Cathy said in awe. "I think you're going to go far with your photography, Kelsea. You're very talented."

Kelsea loved the praise but felt shy about it at the same time. "Thanks, Mrs. Pantona. I have a lot to learn, though."

"Well, you certainly have a great start."

"So what do you think about christening our resident hawk?" Kelsea asked.

"Since we don't know if the hawk is a male or a female, we'll have to give it a unisex name," said Allie.

"I think I've read the females are bigger than the males," said Amanda. "Do you think that's a large hawk?"

Kelsea laughed a little. "I don't know. I'm not any expert on hawks, so I can't say if this hawk is big compared to other hawks," Kelsea mused.

Tom came down the steps into the family room again with the framed photo in hand. "Why don't you just call him Red, for now."

"Or her . . ." Kelsea smiled. "But Red would still work."

"Oh my goodness!" Cathy exclaimed.

Allie concurred with, "Wow."

The vertical photo showed the depth of the gorge with trees and bushes clinging by their roots to its rugged sides. Rays of sun shot down from behind bright white cumulous clouds floating in a deep ultramarine blue sky giving a brilliant, almost religious look to the rocks and the hawk.

10

LAVINIA'S BROTHER

Monday, Cathy woke up with a start before the alarm went off. After the hike and looking at the photos of Scott Hollow, she had known she'd probably have a dream about falling. As predicted, she did, but this time she was aware that she was falling over the cliff at Scott Hollow, not from some unknown elevated place. She sat up, clearing her eyes and head of her dizziness and then shuffled into the bathroom.

The alarm woke Paul who was surprised to find that Cathy was already out of bed. He squinted toward the bathroom, the light from the vanity shining in his eyes. "I thought we agreed," he said loudly in his gravely morning voice. "You were going to give up this Anatoli nonsense."

"Good morning to you, too," Cathy said, irritated, as she came back into the bedroom. "Why is that the first thing out of your mouth this morning?"

"Well, you're up already, even before the alarm. What else has managed to get you up this early all summer long?"

"I've gotten up early plenty of times this summer. If you must know, the startup meeting for driving is today at nine a.m., so I thought I'd get up now and get something done around here before I go, if that's all right with you. And, I'll probably do my dry run right after the meeting so I can get it out of the way."

Paul just scowled, pursed his lips, and went into the bathroom.

Now that both Cathy and Paul were in foul moods, they fed their Monday morning bad attitude with silence save for the

95

exasperating news on television, which left them both feeling ineffective and depressed combining with their testiness. "Do what you want," Paul sighed in resignation as he got up to leave. "We could all be dead tomorrow the way things are going in this world." Paul barely gave Cathy a goodbye peck on her cheek.

Cathy just looked at Paul as he turned and walked out of the house. As cynical as Paul's comment was, Cathy felt the same way. She sighed and felt a soft chin on her knee. Troy looked up at her soulfully with his bi-colored eyes. Cathy stroked his head. "Yes," she said aloud to him. "Nothing at all I can do about it but take care of those I love including you, of course, sweet boy, and enjoy life while I've still got it."

Cathy got up and carried her coffee cup to the coffee maker. "Speaking of enjoying life, do you want to go for a walk before I leave for my meeting?" Troy did a spin and ran to the hook by the back door where the leashes were hung. "I guess you do," Cathy laughed. "Well, come upstairs with me. I've got to change, first."

Mulling over Paul's good morning greeting made Cathy feeling rebellious and defiant. She decided to heed her own advice about enjoying life and do what she wanted. She'd go to the cemetery to look at the Rosetti graves and the statue Tony had described seeing. After that, she'd go talk to Sharon. 'I don't care what our lord and master says,' she thought. 'I'm enjoying this little mystery of mine which is certainly a harmless distraction.' She threw a bottle of water, her phone, notepad, and a pen in her backpack and in a few minutes she was leaving the house with Troy.

As they walked over the path to the cemetery, Cathy brooded over Paul's negative attitude regarding her amateur investigation and wondered if he was changing, and if he was going to turn into a controlling SOB like some of the boyfriends she'd had when she was a teenager. 'Twenty years,' she thought to herself. 'Had he always been like this but I never noticed? Or, am I the one who is changing? Am I becoming more independent-minded? Is it because both kids will be gone to school and Paul is used to bossing them around and now he feels he needs to boss me around?'

She began thinking about Ken who she had dated and fantasized about marrying at one point in her life, but what happened? She wondered what life would have been like if she had married Ken. Their relationship was free and loose It was exciting, but one that was totally uncommitted. She never knew when she would hear from him, even if she would hear from him, after they went out. They never discussed fidelity. It was understood they both could date others if they were so inclined, although Cathy seldom did while she was seeing Ken. She never questioned him about other girls and he never questioned her about going out with other guys. When they saw each other, they enjoyed themselves and she never asked and he never offered a commitment that he would even call her again.

It was wonderful, but it was awful--more awful than wonderful; and then she met Paul, who was the exact opposite of Ken with regard to stability--a relief for Cathy. After dating Paul, she wondered if her relationship with Ken had actually been driving her crazy. She felt she could finally breathe and relax with Paul. Dating Paul, she didn't have to fight to suppress all her anxiety, jealousy, doubt, and longing as she did with Ken, because there was none. 'Still,' she wondered, 'Would I appreciate the freedom now?' Feeling physically ill remembering her relationship with Ken, 'Nah,' she concluded. 'The insecurity would've gotten to me. We'd have been divorced in a year or two, or I'd have gone completely off my rocker.'

Troy had been happily treeing squirrels as Cathy pondered the possibilities of the past. As they entered the cemetery grounds, Troy ran up to her. "Now what section was it that Tony said he found the Rosetti graves?" she wondered out loud. As they walked further she said to Troy, "Let's hope Grandma Anatoli isn't visiting right now. She'd probably have a fit if she saw you walking on the graves of her ancestors."

Cathy continued along the narrow cemetery path while Troy weaved his way among the tombstones. She spotted Virgilio's obelisk and looked around for Luella or Grandma Anatoli. Troy saw the monument at the same time, and tore ahead of Cathy, barking as he ran. Cathy figured he was after a squirrel or maybe a rabbit. When she caught up to him, she found him snarling and barking at the obelisk.

"Ssh, quiet now," Cathy instructed reaching in her pocket for some dog bribery. The treat ignored, she grabbed Troy's collar. He was so worked up he turned and snapped at her, receiving an instant correction from Cathy. "No," she said firmly and quickly attached his leash. "Leave it," she said jerking at the leash and making him follow her away from the Anatoli graves. "Now calm down, boy. What in the world has gotten into you? Did you find a rabbit den over there?" Hearing the word rabbit, Troy became excited again. "Okay, so that's it. You chased him and found his home, huh boy?" She patted his head. "I forgive you, then. Guess we'll have to work on you letting someone grab your collar. Have to work on a lot of things. I think you'll be going to school pretty soon, little boy, just like my other two kids. Come on, let's find the Rosettis. Do you remember where they are?"

Cathy looked around in search of the statue, again checking to see if Luella and Grandma Anatoli were in the vicinity. Relieved to see that she and Troy seemed to have the cemetery to themselves, she turned toward Lot 4 of Section A and saw the head of the statue not far away peeking above the other headstones. "I think we've found it. Let's go, Troy."

"Sure enough, here they are," Cathy whispered excitedly to Troy, petting his head and giving him a treat. "You were here with Tony, huh, boy?" Troy sniffed all around the statue while Cathy admired it, thinking, 'Tony was right--very beautiful and touching.' As did her son, Cathy picked up the purple hyacinths and smelled them picturing Grandma Anatoli staring at her holding red, white, and purple cut flowers in her arm.

Cathy looked at all of the gravestones in the area, but as she suspected, none of them belonged to Lavinia. She took out the note Tony had written and found the two grave markers that were so worn the names were illegible. She approximated how close those graves were to the angel statue and jotted down the names on the surrounding gravestones to make it easier for Sharon to identify the deceased buried under the unreadable stones. "Okay, Bud, let's go," Cathy said putting the note in her pocket.

Sharon looked up from her work when Cathy and Troy walked in. "Hey Cathy, you didn't tell me you were coming. And who's this with you? Troy Anatoli's namesake?" Sharon came around to the front of the reception counter and crouched to say hello to Troy. At the same time, Troy bolted to her, yanking the leash from Cathy's hand.

"Troy, no!" Cathy yelled but she was too late. Troy already had his paws on Sharon and was licking her face. "Sorry, we're going to have to go to puppy school to learn some manners."

"He's all right," Sharon assured Cathy.

Just then, Mr. Burns walked out of his office with some papers in his hand. Hearing the voices in the reception area, he came around the counter to see who was in the office. "Oh, hello Mrs. Pantona. Here to get information for another Find-A-Grave client?" he asked cheerfully in his deep voice.

Mr. Burns was tall, lean, and gaunt whose appearance belied the open and easy-going, jovial optimist that he actually was. "By the way, I'm glad you had to find Sergeant Powell's grave. I would've guessed he would have been transferred some time ago to Arlington National Cemetery or another military cemetery like many other Civil War veterans. Now that his grave's been found again, we'll be able to honor him by keeping it tidy."

"Yes, your crew certainly did a nice job on his grave. I sent photos to the family and they were very grateful."

"Speaking of photos, Sharon showed me the printout of the Anatoli Farm ad you found in the archived newspapers. So very interesting to see. I, myself, find it curious about Lavinia Anatoli. Her children not buried there is not that unusual, but the mother missing is. Sharon asked me if I had any information that may shed some light on her whereabouts, but, unfortunately, I haven't any. The only thing I know is what you and Sharon here have thus far uncovered. As for other sources for your research, I really can't think of any," he told Cathy while also giving Troy a bit of attention.

"I hope you don't mind me contacting Sharon about this and Find-A-Grave clients, or me stopping by for that matter," Cathy said, slightly embarrassed. "If you do, I'll restrict contacting her to after work.

"No, no. Sharon's been with me for quite some time and I know she wouldn't shortchange her work here. I trust her to manage her time responsibly and she hasn't disappointed me yet." Mr. Burns put his papers on the counter patted his hand on them and turned to Sharon. "Speaking of responsibilities, this is a contract for prearrangements, Sharon. If you could prepare it for signature tomorrow, I'd appreciate it. The clients will be here at two."

"Sure, Mr. Burns. That's no problem."

When Mr. Burns turned to go back into his office, Sharon got up from greeting Troy. "I can see why you fell for Troy. He's adorable. So what's brought you in today? Did you find out something new?"

"Yes, a little bit. Tony found the Rosetti plot this past Saturday and came upon something."

"He didn't find a marker for Lavinia, did he?"

"No, afraid not. He found a couple of illegible stones and a large statue of two angels, one of which appears to be a female angel and one an angel that is a young boy. It doesn't appear to be a monument because there are no names on it although it appears someone is placing cut flowers next to it. One thing I found especially fascinating is that the statue so resembles Lavinia and Troy in the Anatoli ad that it's uncanny. The stance is the same, the female angel's arm is on the boy's shoulders, and the only difference is that the two are looking at each other, not face forward like in the ad."

"Now that you mention it, I do recall seeing that statue. I'd forgotten all about it. I don't walk around the grounds very often."

Cathy retrieved the note from her pocket. "Here's information regarding the location of the statue and blank headstones. Do you think you could see if the angel statue might actually be a grave marker, and who the two unknown graves belong to?"

"Sure, let's see what I can find out." Sharon took the piece of paper and sat down at her desk.

"If no one is buried under the statue, I wonder if it sits atop a spot that was meant to be a grave."

"We'll see," said Sharon starting a search on her computer. "I actually doubt if Lavinia's and/or any of the children's names were ever on the statue or mystery graves because, if that were so, we'd have a record of their names at St. Margaret. As far as the possibility the spot under the statue was meant to be a grave. . ." Sharon's voice trailed off as she continued to peck at her keyboard. "Ah, here we are." The survey of the cemetery now appeared on her screen and she zoomed in on the Rosetti plot. "Now, let's see." Sharon studied her computer screen, zooming in and out and moving to different graves. "Okay, you know what?" she said in surprise. "It looks like there's nothing under the statue but it appears there's enough room there for a gravesite. All of Section A of the cemetery has been marked completely filled for years but I would suppose someone could conceivably purchase that spot if they wanted it. Apparently, no one has in all these years, though, and the statue is not owned by the cemetery."

"Hm, do you find that strange, or no?" Cathy asked.

"Yes, somewhat. Decorative areas are generally owned by the cemetery and no one is buried there. I think I'll talk to Mr. Burns about this when he has a second. I never really thought about it before."

"Yes, Sharon, please do. I'd be extremely interested in what he has to say."

"Now, let's check into the two graves with illegible headstones." Sharon slid the screen around and enlarged another area, then clicked to another screen. "Okay, this one is between Rodolfo and Carmine Rosetti and Julius and his wife, Ruth."

"It was a very small stone. I was thinking it could have been for a child."

"It is. And, I've got a copy of the old Burial Permit scanned in. The old Permits allowed much more information than we allow today because as time went on, privacy laws became more stringent. It says, 'Baby boy Rosetti, son of Rodolfo and Carmine Rosetti,' and gives his age as zero. Date of death is February 8, 1856 and says the cause of death is shock." Sharon shook her head. "Tch, poor thing. I wonder . . ." and she found Carmine's burial record. "Yep. It's so sad. Both Carmine and Baby Rosetti died on the same day. Her cause of death is listed as hemorrhage."

"It'd be downright scary to be pregnant in those days. Dying in childbirth was all too common."

"That's right," agreed Sharon. "And to top it off, families were always huge in those days. Having a baby was almost like playing Russian Roulette." Sharon clicked back to the plot map. "Now, let's see who is in this other mystery grave." She zoomed in on the grave in question. "Name is Ernest Rosetti. He died April 13, 1877; born October 20, 1824, was fifty-two years old. I wonder what was the cause of his death." Sharon looked at the Burial Permit listings page and clicked on Ernest's name. "Oh my! This is interesting. He died of a gunshot wound."

"A gunshot wound? Wow! I wonder what the story is behind that." Cathy jotted down the information about Ernest Rosetti.

"There's got to be an article or two about Ernest being shot to death in the Dispatch. Going to be looking for that info."

"Here's something else, Cathy. He's one of Lavinia's brothers. Look at the name of Ernest's mother and father." Sharon looked at Cathy.

Cathy looked back at Sharon, her eyebrows raised in surprise. "Wow! Wonder what kind of trouble he got into?"

"You've got to remember this area hadn't been open for settlement for very long. It was still kind of lawless. I'd think it would have made the papers, though."

"Oh my God, Sharon. The deeper we look into this, the more questions we've got, and if Paul thinks I'm going to quit now, he's sadly mistaken." Cathy was eager to text Tony, but didn't want to distract him from his schoolwork. She'd talk to him later.

Troy was lying on his side almost asleep next to Sharon's chair. "Okay," Cathy said to him. "Get up lazy bones."

Troy rolled over onto his back and stretched his legs, then flopped on his other side, causing Sharon and Cathy to laugh.

Cathy made kissing noises and called Troy to her. Troy stood up, yawned, stretched again and shook himself before walking over to her. "Okay. Awake now?" Cathy chuckled. "Need a cup of coffee?" she laughed again.

"Let's give him a little water before you go. It's pretty hot and humid out there today." Sharon filled a little dish with water from the kitchenette and put it on the floor, which Troy quickly lapped up.

"Ready now?" Cathy asked Troy. "We'll take the long way home around the cemetery. Then I have to go to my meeting."

On their way out, Sharon said, "Keep in touch."

"You know I will and thanks again," Cathy said.

Cathy walked some and jogged some with Troy, showered quickly, and made it to the high school just in time for the startup meeting. The safety director did a presentation regarding school shootings and the part the bus drivers might have to play in the event of an incident at one of the schools or on the bus. This year, drivers and aides would be required to pass a first aid course geared toward such an event. Other than that, the meeting was routine. Cathy would be driving the same route as always and went over to the bus garage break room to review her route for the new year. She highlighted the new students and changes on her route sheet, started a time sheet, grabbed a pre-trip inspection checklist, and left for her dry run.

A handful of other drivers were taking care of their dry runs that morning, too, and Cathy walked to the back right corner of the parking lot with Sandy, whose parking spot was opposite Cathy's. "Could you help me with my lights? After, I'll help you with yours." Cathy said to Sandy.

"Sure. Give me a holler or a honk when you're ready."

Cathy patted the hood of Bus 35 and asked it out loud, "How are you Betsy? Have a good summer?" She smiled as she started circling the bus doing her outside inspection. "Mm-hm, had your spa bath to begin the school year and, oooh, new shoes, too! Super." Cathy laughed. The outside done, Cathy entered the bus. "Whew! Let's cool you down while I check the seats and windows." Cathy opened the bus windows as she walked down the bus then went back to the driver's seat to set her mirrors, do her brake test, check the gauges, radio, then the alarms, exits, etc. and then walked over to Sandy's bus. "Are you ready for your lights?" she asked.

"Yep. Just finished my brake test," said Sandy.

Cathy walked behind Sandy's bus to the driver's side so Sandy could see her in her driver's mirror, and gave her thumbs up as Sandy went through the sequence of her lights and eight-ways. Sandy reciprocated with Cathy and both were ready to go.

"Looks like you pass your physical, Betsy," Cathy said as she slowly pulled from her parking spot to begin the route. Cathy took her time and practiced using her reds at a few houses when there was no traffic on the road that would be disturbed. She made quick notes on her route sheet of something distinctive about any new house or new turn added to her route. When she passed the lichgate to St. Margaret Cemetery, she was reminded of the information unearthed today and of Lavinia and Troy. Her mind began to wander and she almost missed a new stop--a house right past the cemetery. She had to force her thoughts of the Anatolis to the back of her mind and considered it a warning to avoid thinking about Lavinia and Troy when passing the cemetery while she was driving her route with kids on board. She made a mental note that the driveway for this new stop was lined by large maple trees, making the driveway easy to miss.

She turned onto Depot Road from Davison Road. The uphill climb on Depot Road to Station Road had twists and turns that were treacherous in winter. There was not much of a berm and a guardrail was the only protection from a steep drop-off. She took note of another new stop before she had to make a left turn onto Station Road, another dangerous part of her route in winter. It was a steady decline then all of a sudden turned uphill following a long, curving steep slope, the top of which was part of Scott Hollow. Because the hill and trees on one side blocked the sun for a good part of the day, in winter this section of Station Road often was icy while most other roads were simply wet. Cathy glanced at the Kendrick's house sitting back from the road and fondly remembered yesterday's hike. As she started up the hill, Bus 35 began to hesitate. It continued to lose power and chugged along as it struggled up the hill. Cathy urged the bus forward, saying, "Come on old girl. You can do it," but just over the crest, the bus stalled.

"Argh!" groaned Cathy. "Sorry, babe, going to have to write you up and you're going to have to see the doctor. Can't have you doing that when I've got kids riding." She set her emergency brake, shut everything down, put on her four-ways, and thought she'd try to restart in a few minutes. She got up from her seat to get her emergency triangles and flares and almost jumped out of her skin when the emergency buzzer started blasting, her reds flashed, the bus arm extended, and the passenger door opened.

She sat down quickly to turn everything off glancing down the road to check for traffic, getting blinded by the bright sunshine in the process, then glancing in her rearview mirror, blinking to get the sunspots out of her eyes. There was something yellow in the back. She squinted. It looked like blonde hair, a blurred, ephemeral image of a blonde boy--Troy? Her eyes cleared and she realized the yellow child check sign attached by magnet in the back of the bus must have mixed in with her sun-spotted vision. She couldn't get any of the lights or alarms to turn off.

"Good God!" Cathy exclaimed. "What the devil is going on?" I'm so glad I did my dry run good and early. The mechanics might need a lot of time to figure out what's wrong.'

With the bus not powered up, the only thing Cathy could think to do was to start it again. As soon as she turned the key to the on position, the buzzers and lights stopped, the arm swung back in position, the passenger door closed, and the bus was quiet. Confused, Cathy waited for the gauges to settle and the wait-to-start light to go out, then turned the engine over. Bus 35 started with no problem and was purring like a kitten.

The rest of the dry run went without a hitch. She did her post-trip inspection and filled out a Maintenance Request to attach to her Inspection Report. She hoped this would not turn into some illusive problem that was not identifiable until it was actually occurring.

"I hope to God they find out what's wrong," she told Jessi, the Dispatcher. "Otherwise, I'm going to be worried about this happening every time I take the wheel."

"I hope so, too," Jessi replied. "You don't want to stall out in a car, let alone a bus."

"That's for sure," Cathy agreed. "Oh, guess what? We've adopted a new dog," Cathy told Jessi who also was an animal enthusiast.

"Really? What does he look like?"

Cathy showed Jessi a photo of Troy and told her how his adoption came about. "I'll pop by with him some time if you want to meet him."

"You know I would." Jessi smiled.

"I'm on my way to the library or I'd run home right now and get him."

"That's all right--I'm swamped getting ready for the new school year."

"Yeah. I guess you would be, but, when things settle down, I'll bring him around. See you on the twenty-ninth."

It was close to two o'clock by the time Cathy left for the library. Her eagerness to learn something about Ernest Rosetti's death in the Dispatch made it hard to drive in the slow-going traffic. Cathy's patience was further tested as she navigating the congestion of the downtown streets from the late lunch bunch. When she found the main parking lot of the library completely filled, she wanted to scream. She parked on the unpaved area on the west side of the building and hurried to the Heritage Room. Cathy quickly grabbed the reel containing the April 13, 1877 issue of The Dispatch. She threaded the film into the machine and whirred through the issues, stopped, saw where she was in the reel, then whirred again, repeating until she was near April thirteenth.

Finally, she found the issue and scoured the paper. Seeing nothing, she continued on to the Saturday and Sunday papers. In the Monday issue she finally spotted an article headlined, *Shooting Death*, and began reading.

On Friday, last, Mr. Ernest Rosetti of the Village of Harbour Creek was shot dead by Mr. Virgilio Anatoli in front of Kraus Mercantile on State Street in Erie after Mr. Rosetti took his leave of O'Shaughnessy's Saloon. Being in a state of intoxication and intense excitement Mr. Rosetti hailed Mr. Anatoli from across the street and assailed Mr. Anatoli and applied to him such opprobrious epithets and defamatory accusations that Mr. Anatoli did take umbrage to the libelous obscenities and confronted Mr. Rosetti in the street demanding to settle the matter. Mr. Rosetti drew a pistol and fired three times at Mr. Anatoli without effect due to his state of inebriation when the latter returned fire. Mr. Rosetti was mortally wounded by a shot to the head, the ball exiting the back of his skull. The shooting having occurred during the height of the business day there were many passersby who witnessed the atrocity. Mr. Anatoli surrendered to the Sheriff without incident and is incarcerated at the Erie County Jail under suspicion of murder pending further investigation into the matter.

In the next week's paper Cathy found only a small report about the shooting entitled, *The Rosetti Murder*, tucked in the middle of a string of one-paragraph articles:

The Coroner's inquiry into the circumstances relating to the death of Ernest Rosetti from a gunshot wound to the head resulted in the release of Mr. Virgilio Anatoli on the grounds the shooting was in self-defense.

Cathy printed out both articles.

11

DREAM ON

Cathy felt she would burst if she couldn't tell someone about Ernest Rosetti and texted Sharon immediately with her news.

Sharon texted back, "Holy cow! P.S. Mr. Burns had no idea about the potential for a gravesite under the angels. He's going to look into it."

Cathy saw the time was ten minutes after four. She guessed that Tony might be returning to his room after class and quickly texted him. "R U Busy?" she asked.

"Hi Mom - No - Just got in. What's up?"

"Found out about angels & 2 unmarked graves."

"?"

"Enough space for grave under Angels. Small stone for infant died in childbirth with mother Carmine buried next to him. Other grave Lavinia's brother, Ernest, shot by Virgilio on April 13, 1877!"

"What?!"

"Yes-shot on State Street, Erie. I'm still at library - had to tell you. Didn't want to discuss on phone with Dad around."

"Understand. Interesting."

"Will fill you in more later?"

"Okay."

"Love you."

"Love you too."

Cathy put away the microfilm and headed home. On the way, she picked up some fresh tomatoes and sweet corn to have with hamburgers on the grill.

Troy, having been cooped up in the house since she left for the bus startup meeting in the morning, greeted her with exuberance when she arrived home.

"All right, all right," Cathy laughed, receiving his, 'Welcome home, I thought you left me forever,' greeting.

"Come on out. I know you have to pee," she told him. After watering the grass, he trailed her about while she got the grill cleaned and ready to cook the burgers.

Paul got home as Cathy was filling her large stockpot with water for the corn. His suit jacket hung over his computer case, his tie hung around his neck, and the top two buttons of his shirt were undone.

"Hi honey. How was your day? You look tired," Cathy said as he walked toward her. Troy ran to him and jumped on him looking for attention. Paul petted Troy's head lethargically.

"I am, and I'm not done yet." Paul came over to Cathy and they kissed hello. "What's for dinner tonight?"

"Just burgers on the grill, fresh tomatoes, and sweet corn."

Paul's face turned hard and a fleeting frown crossed his brow. "You don't want me to cook the burgers, do you?" He tried to sound like he was offering, but Cathy knew better.

"No, no. I think I can handle it," she said, trying to sound cheerful.

"Good," Paul said walking out of the kitchen. "I'm beat." He flopped down on the couch, kicked off his shoes, and turned the television on.

"Are you ready to eat? This won't take long," Cathy called to Paul from the kitchen.

"I don't care. I guess," Paul replied.

"Why don't you get out of your work clothes and put on some shorts so you can be comfortable. I'll get supper going."

Paul didn't reply but got up and went to the bedroom to do just that. Although Cathy hated to see Paul so bedraggled, she was relieved he didn't want to find out how she spent her afternoon. It was inevitable he would ask her sometime this evening, so she pondered what to say. Lately almost anything seemed to set him off, and knowing that she had, according to him, spent the day being a busybody, he'd probably have a fit. He probably would resent it just because she had a perfectly peachy day when, apparently, he'd had a rough day today.

She heard Paul coming down the stairs and sit back down on the couch with a sigh. "Would you like a beer, dear?"

"Sure, thanks."

Cathy got the can out of the fridge and poured the beer into a pilsner glass. "Here you go, dear," she said, handing the glass and can to him.

"Thanks, hon." When Cathy turned to go back into the kitchen, Paul put his glass and the can on the coffee table and grabbed her hand. "You don't have to cook right this second. Why don't you sit down with me to relax a little."

"Well, I've got the water heating for the corn already and the grill is on, too."

"So, it'll take a while for the water to boil, and hamburgers don't take that long to cook. Besides, Allie's not home yet. Just sit down for a second."

Cathy sat down and asked preemptively, "So how was your day? Everything go all right?"

"Oh, could've gone better." Paul's mouth twisted into an unhappy grimace. "Apparently, our new client had some brainstorms over the weekend which is requiring everyone to rework what they've already done." Paul took a long drink of his beer. "So, now we're all scrambling around figuring out how to fit his ideas with ours. Lots of discussions--loud discussions, if you know what I mean. Then IT problems! God! If the client wants to have his own campaign, then he should go ahead and do it. He can't just get us going on something and then throw a wrench into it the day before we're supposed to present it to him! And now my whole night is going to be upstairs in front of my computer screen. Look, I'd like some free time to just sit on the deck and relax for a change."

"It'll be all over tomorrow, won't it? Why don't you go outside with Troy and forget about it for now. I'll let you know when everything is ready."

Troy was sitting up with his tongue hanging out looking expectantly at Paul.

Paul poured the remainder of the can of beer into his glass and stood up, glass in hand. "Come on, Troy," he said flatly. Troy stood up, backed out between the coffee table and couch, then ran to the back door.

Cathy took the patted out burgers out of the fridge and grabbed the bag containing the corn, watching Paul and Troy walk into the back yard. Paul picked up a tennis ball from the basket of toys that sat on the deck and started playing fetch with Troy.

'Hope Allie comes home soon to deflect conversation to her. Don't want him to start asking about my day,' Cathy thought. She went out to the steps of the deck to shuck the corn.

Cathy felt someone was granting her wish as Allie pulled into the driveway. Troy abandoned his game to run to her car, with Paul walking after him. Paul's posture was much more natural now, his shoulders no longer bunched up around his neck and he had a smile on his face. 'Thank God for Troy,' Cathy thought.

"Hi kid," Paul shouted to his daughter. "Where have you been all day?"

Cathy cringed, wondering if Allie spending another day at the beach with her friends would put Paul right back in his bad mood.

"Don't you remember?" Allie reminded him, getting out of her car. "I told you that everyone was meeting at Beach 10 today. Last day when most of us could get together before going off to school. The only ones that weren't there were Tony and a couple other kids. It was a blast."

"Your mother's just getting dinner ready. Did you eat?"

"No, no one brought food," Allie said. She popped her trunk open and grabbed her blanket and beach gear. Troy started attacking the blanket. "Come on, Troy. Cut it out," Allie laughed. "We figured if anyone got hungry, we could just grab something at the snack bar."

"Well, did you?"

"What, eat? No, I wasn't hungry," she continued to struggle with Troy, who was now trying to play tug with the blanket.

"Troy, no, leave it!" Paul yelled more harshly than necessary, stunning the dog and Allie. "Here, give me that," he impatiently instructed Allie.

"Jeez, Dad. He's just playing," Allie said relinquishing the blanket and rolling her eyes.

Cathy saw Paul's back stiffen as he glared at his daughter walking away from him. 'Good God, this is going to be a great evening,' Cathy thought.

"Okay, guys. How many burgers do you want?" Cathy yelled over to them.

"Just one for me," Allie replied.

"I'll take two," said Paul.

"There'll be more if you want," Cathy advised.

"So Mom, did you get Troy a dog license today? You did go downtown, didn't you?" Allie asked as she started up the stairs of the deck.

Cathy looked for any indication from Paul that he had heard Allie's question. The slight turn of his head her way let her know he had. She turned quickly to retreat to the kitchen. "No, afraid not," Cathy replied in a normal speaking voice as she walked through the doorway. She hoped she was far enough away from Paul so he could not hear her.

Allie followed Cathy inside. "You didn't what, go downtown, or get Troy a license?"

"I happened to think that Dr. Warner will be able to issue a license once we make sure he has all his shots and get him neutered. They're going to need proof he has gotten his shots, you know." Cathy grabbed the plate of patted-out burgers and the bag of buns.

"I'm going to take a quick shower before dinner," Allie announced.

"Okay, but I'm putting the burgers on right now, so it won't be long at all." Cathy headed back outside and hurriedly put the hamburgers and the buns on the grill. She caught Paul looking at her as if he were going to ask her something so avoided looking at him, then returned to the kitchen to slice tomatoes and some onion for the hamburgers.

Between checking on the burgers, getting the table ready for dinner, and cooking the corn, Cathy kept herself bustling around so that Paul didn't bother her. Everything was just about ready and Allie hadn't come downstairs. "What do you want to drink, Allie?" Cathy shouted upstairs.

"Lemonade," Allie yelled back.

Paul came in the back door. "I'll just have another beer." He sat down at his traditional place at the table.

Troy lapped up half a dish of water, slopping some on the floor and leaving a trail to where he decided to plop down under the kitchen table. He was panting heavily, tongue hanging out to the side, bright eyed, perky eared, with a happy smile on his face.

"You sure did a good job of wearing him out," Cathy smiled.

"Yeah. For being lame, he sure doesn't let it slow him down," Paul chuckled. "This dog's got a lot of spunk." Paul took a swig of his beer. "So what's this about getting a license for him? You better wait a while. His rightful owners may still show up. I'm not sure what the law is about assuming ownership of a dog, but he hasn't been with us for a full week yet."

"I actually did hear from his owners."

"You did?" Paul's anger flared immediately. "Why didn't you tell me? Why haven't you returned him to them? What's the matter with you?"

As much as Cathy did not like Paul's chastisement, she much preferred friction about Troy rather than him finding out she hadn't given up on her inquiry about the Anatolis. Cathy described her conversation with the Vugsta's as accurately as she could remember. "I wanted to see if they called back before I told anyone or did anything further," she explained.

"So, I take it they haven't contacted you again."

"No, they haven't, and I'm glad. I'd be worried sick about Troy the way Mr. Vugsta seemed on the phone. I'm sure he'd drop him off somewhere else or find a different owner for him. Maybe he'd even take him to a shelter. Who knows. I'm just glad Troy found us instead of anyone else. I think he was meant to be ours."

"He is a great dog. You know the vet bill is going to be pretty big if he needs all his shots and needs to be neutered, don't you."

"I know, but with adoption, comes responsibility. We probably would have adopted a dog anyway if Troy hadn't come along, so those expenses come with the territory."

"Depends if you find a rescue, or get a puppy from a breeder."

"Well, we've got a rescue that rescued us, and I think he's worth it." Cathy hurried to the bottom of the staircase to avoid arguing with Paul about money and yelled again to Allie, "I'm getting the burgers off the grill. Hurry up or the corn and sandwiches will get cold," then she quickly exited to get the hamburgers.

When she returned to the table, Allie was sitting in her chair, buttering a cob of corn, as was Paul. "How was the beach?" She asked Allie.

"It was wonderful, as always. Wish that's all I had to do was lay around at the beach all my life," Allie smiled.

"You and me, both," Paul agreed.

"Boy, that Mr. Vugsta must be a real jerk. How could anyone just abandon a pet? There must be a law against that," Allie said.

"If nothing else, there's probably a sizable fine for abandoning a pet. Of course, they'd have to know who the owner is," Paul said.

"We know the guy's name. Maybe we should report him," Allie replied.

"I don't know about that, hon. Who knows what complications could arise. Troy might have to be given back to them, or given up to a shelter," Cathy said. "It would be a big mess when we want to end up adopting him anyway."

"One thing you haven't considered, dear," Paul looked at Cathy. "Mr. Vugsta's got our phone number. Right now, he could be waiting, hoping, we'll get Troy to the vet and take care of all his healthcare. He could call back in a month or two, say they've changed their minds and want him back. If we don't give Troy back to him, he could accuse us of dognapping. Maybe you should hold off on calling the vet, Cathy."

"What? Now you're really fantasizing, Paul. That's a little farfetched, don't you think?" Cathy wondered where he got his ideas. "Troy needs his shots, he needs to be neutered, they're not going to call back, and I'm going to contact Dr. Warner tomorrow."

Paul frowned and his mouth hardened. They ate in strained silence for a few long minutes until Paul asked, "If you didn't go downtown today, what did you do all afternoon?"

Cathy counted to ten so she wouldn't escalate the tension in the room. She took a deep breath, closed her eyes for a moment, then stared hard at Paul and said, "I wasn't done with my dry run until after two. There wasn't too much time after that, so I just ran to Fennell Farms and got the corn and tomatoes, and after that I just spent some time with Troy."

"Mmm," Paul grunted, then said under his breath, "Must be nice."

"Paul, are you trying to start a fight? Because it sure sounds like you are. If you're frustrated with work, I'm sorry, but I'd appreciate it if you'd leave your frustrations at the office." She looked away from him and quickly added, "I got in touch with Tony for a few minutes today."

"Oh? How are things going for him?" Paul asked.

"Fine. Nothing new. I just wanted to say hello."

No one spoke for a few minutes until Allie said, "Doug's coming over around seven. Not sure if we'll be going out anywhere or if we'll just hang out here."

"That's fine, dear. You and Doug can amuse Mr. Troy if you want."

"That's what I was thinking. I'll see what Doug wants to do."

Paul wadded up his napkin and tossed it in the middle of his plate. "Well, better get up to the office. See you again, who knows when tonight."

The strain of not being able to share the story she had uncovered about Ernest Rosetti made Cathy feel tense, and the reason she had to hold it in depressed her. With Allie and Doug busy with Troy outside and Paul working, Cathy got the articles she printed out and phoned Tony. It was a relief being able to toss about ideas and sharing information with him, who seemed as interested as she was.

She poured a glass of wine for herself, grabbed the novel she was currently reading, and headed upstairs. She knocked quietly on the office door and opened it slightly. "Do you know how long you're going to stay up?" she asked Paul.

"No, afraid not," Paul said unhappily. "I hope it's not past midnight."

"I hope not, too. If there was something I could do to help you, I would," Cathy sympathized. "I'm going to go soak in a tub and read a little before I go to sleep. Maybe I'll still be awake when you come to bed."

"Don't stay awake on my account. I really don't know what time I'll be done."

"Okay. Try not to stay up too late."

"Yeah," Paul grunted.

Cathy fell asleep with her book open over her chest. Between the murder mystery she was reading and the information she discovered about Ernest Rosetti, the stage was set in her unconscious to dream about Virgilio's and Ernest's confrontation on State Street.

Virgilio was loading provisions onto his wagon with the help of Isaac. Mr. Kraus was standing at the entrance to his store, chatting with Virgilio. State Street was busy with carriages, wagons, and horses going up and down the street and people walking on the sidewalks.

Not far from Virgilio's wagon, a commotion was occurring. Two large, muscular men were dragging a man, who was shouting obscenities, out of O'Shaughnessy's Saloon. He was tossed off the boardwalk and landed in a heap on the dirt road. Cathy's dreaming mind understood this man to be Ernest Rosetti.

Ernest had difficulty getting up, then struggled to keep his balance as he dusted off his dirty khaki overalls, the whole time mumbling to himself. He stumbled in a weaving path toward a horse tied up on the opposite side of the street from Virgilio's wagon. Virgilio stood at the back of his wagon watching Ernest approach.

Squinting, Ernest bent over, almost falling, and yelled, pointing at Virgilio, "Murderer!"

"Go home and sleep it off you miserable drunk," Virgilio said with disgust and turned back to his wagon.

Ernest fumbled with his right hand to get his gun from its holster. "You fucking, murdering bastard! You better make your amends right now."

Virgilio turned around and laughed. "Look at you. You can't even walk."

"Lavinia," Ernest yelled, his gun now in his hand but just hanging by his side. "My beautiful sister. She should be here celebrating her fiftieth birthday today with her children." Ernest lifted his hand and pointed the gun at Virgilio, trying to hold it steady with both hands. "Tell me what you did to her and my nephew or I'll blow your brains out."

"You know that was all sorted out long ago. It was her own fault. I tell her not to go off with that man, but she did not listen to me. He promised to take her and Troy to St. James School in Hagerstown, Maryland. I tell her the war make it too dangerous to travel. But she, like the rest of you, stupido. She kill herself and my son. Be mad at your stubborn sister, not me."

"Liar!" Ernest screamed, continuing to walk unsteadily toward Virgilio. "I was going to take her to the train station to get there. Don't you remember? I was the one who got the papers for her. There was no stranger taking her anywhere! You killed her. I know you killed her. I know how you treated her. And you finally went too far. I know you killed her and I want to know what you did to her and where she is."

"Idiota! You're so drunk you can't even hold that gun steady. Put it down before you hurt yourself." Virgilio laughed derisively.

"No. I've got a birthday present for my sister today. I'm going to send you to her to apologize and then our good Lord will be sending you to Hell!" Ernest fired at Virgilio, the kick of the gun knocking him on his rear.

Virgilio pulled his gun and walked over to Ernest. Ernest fired at Virgilio while trying to get up and missed again. Ernest's arms were flailing around as he tried to get his balance and he accidentally fired his gun into the air.

"Drop your gun," Virgilio demanded.

"You're going to pay for what you've done," Ernest growled and tried to position his gun to shoot Virgilio.

Virgilio placed the end of the barrel of his gun in the middle of Ernest's forehead and fired. Ernest's head exploded with the shot that exited the back of his head. Ernest fell to the street, dead.

Mr. Kraus, Isaac, other shopkeepers and people on the sidewalks and street ran to Ernest. "Get the sheriff," someone yelled.

"You all saw," Virgilio proclaimed. "He was shooting at me. I had to shoot."

"Yes, yes, Virgilio. We saw it all." Mr. Kraus lay his hand on Virgilio's back. "Better come with me and wait for the sheriff. He'll sort everything out. It was self-defense. So sad. Everyone knows Ernest has never accepted the disappearance of Lavinia and poor little Troy. Once the sheriff talks to everyone, I'm sure he'll let you go."

Virgilio and Mr. Kraus sat in chairs in front of the store. "Take Mr. Anatoli's horse and wagon around back, will you, Isaac. When Virg is let out, he'll get them."

Paul didn't get to bed until after two a.m. and disturbed Cathy from her dream.

"What time is it?" she asked.

"Late. I'm going to be dead tomorrow," Paul said. "Go back to sleep." Paul moaned as he relaxed into the mattress.

Cathy got up to use the bathroom then went over to her backpack that was on the chair in the corner of the room. She felt in the pockets for her notepad to jot down a few things from her dream to research.

"What are you doing?" Paul asked, annoyed. "Come back to bed."

"I'll be back in a second. I need to find something from my backpack."

"Now? What can you need from your backpack now?" Paul whined.

"Just my notepad."

"For what? Get it in the morning."

"No. I might forget what I want to write down."

"Tch," Paul clucked and punched his pillow. "What's so urgent to write down this second?" His question was so muffled from his face in his pillow, Cathy could barely understand him.

"Just a couple details from a dream I was having."

Paul turned over and flipped on his bedlight and sat up, scowling at her, a sour look on his face.

"I don't need the light, honey. Lie down. Get some sleep," Cathy told him, almost as irritated with Paul as he was with her. "See. I've got my notepad and I can go into the bathroom to do this."

"I've got to go in there, too," Paul said getting up and stomping into the bathroom.

"Suit yourself," Cathy whispered and went over to Paul's bedside table and wrote down under her phonetically spelled Italian words, St. James School and Hagerstown, Maryland.

Paul came back and glanced at her notepad. "What's this? Learning Italian? Thought you were jotting down something from a dream."

"I am. Those words were from a dream I had a few days ago and these two are places from the dream I just had."

"Don't tell me. I don't think I want to know."

"Yes, I think we're both better off if you don't ask and I don't tell."

"All right. You done now?" Paul asked exasperated.

"Yes."

"Then put that away and lay down so I can get some sleep."

"Jeez, yes sir!" Cathy got comfortable in bed and soon she was back in Lavinia's world again. This was a different Lavinia in her dream, though. She was a very young Lavinia in this dream--a teenager. Lavinia was dancing with a young man at a celebration--a barn dance. Her dance partner was not Virgilio and resembled a young version of Paul with lighter hair.

Virgilio lurked along the sides of the room walking slowly behind the people who were conversing and watching the dancers. He carried a glass of punch, his eyes glued on Lavinia. She and her dance partner seemed oblivious to Virgilio's stare.

When the music stopped, Lavinia walked off the dance floor, her hand in the crook of her escort's arm. She sat down on one of the chairs along the perimeter of the room and her young man walked to the refreshment table. The small band began playing another song and Virgilio put his glass on a windowsill and strode over to Lavinia, facing her dancing partner as they both arrived in front of Lavinia at the same time.

Before the sandy-haired young man could utter a word, Virgilio bowed slightly and held out his right hand to Lavinia. "May I dance with questa bellissima signiorina?"[7] he asked in his thick Italian accent looking Lavinia's beau dead in the eye. Without waiting for an answer, Virgilio yanked Lavinia onto the dance floor leaving her boyfriend on the sidelines holding two glasses of punch and boiling with anger.

Lavinia was flattered at having so much attention paid to her when she'd only turned sixteen recently. She was drawn to Virgilio's dark good looks and his forceful approach. She knew that Virgilio was ten years older than she and also knew he had established himself in the area having purchased a large parcel of land and erected an attractive home on the property with the help of the neighbors. As Virgilio whirled Lavinia around the dancefloor, she saw her mother and father smiling approvingly, young Ernest sitting on a bale of hay looking bored, and her two older brothers and sister on the dance floor smiling as she passed them. She saw her previous partner looking dejected and angry, still holding two glasses of punch, waiting for the end of the song.

Instead of going to the side of the room when the music stopped, Virgilio led her outside, lust for Lavinia almost making him salivate. She accompanied him blindly, in a daze.

Virgilio's accent was so thick, Lavinia had to strain to understand what he was saying. The Rosettis were striving to

---

[7] This beautiful young lady

speak mostly English in their home, therefore, Lavinia only knew a smattering of Italian. However, between her smattering of Italian and his mixture of English and Italian she and Virgilio managed to communicate.

Virgilio walked with her away from the barn telling her, "I have been watching you. You are most beautiful. I like beautiful things. Come over here, I will show you my magnifico Calabrese, Bruno. You like horses, yes?"

They walked to Bruno, a magnificent dark bay stallion standing over sixteen hands high. "He's beautiful," Lavinia said in awe and stroked Bruno's shoulder, to which Bruno snorted, shook his head and looked at her.

"You like to go for ride?" Virgilio asked. "Just for little bit. Bellisimo evening. I take you to my house, show you how beautiful it is. I bring you back right away." Virgilio held out his hand. Lavinia accepted with a smile and a blush and stepped into his buggy.

It took only ten minutes to arrive in front of Virgilio's home. "I remember when everyone pitched in to help you build your house, but I was so young then, I can't remember what the inside was like."

"Come. I show you."

Virgilio put his hand on her back, ushering her in, and closed the door with his other hand. She saw the house was very roomy, tidy, spartanly furnished, and definitely needed a woman's touch. His hand still on her back, he moved in front of her and pushed her against him. He enclosed her with his arms, lowered her down to the floor, and hiked up her skirt. Lavinia struggled, was stunned and shocked, and didn't realize what was happening or what to do. He kissed her on the mouth hard and she tried to turn her head away, but could not. He brought down her pantaloons and assaulted her. Lavinia was confused and scared, but her attraction to him and her excitement from their dancing allowed him to penetrate her easily. Tears of humiliation, rage, fear, disappointment, and terror rolled down her face.

"Don't cry. You're mine now. I marry you. I need to have a wife. " As he ejaculated, he uttered, "I love you," which phrase Lavinia would never again hear from Virgilio's lips.

When he was spent he told her, "Clean yourself up. We go back to dance and you don't tell your familia. I court you, we will marry. Now you cannot marry anyone else."

Cathy woke up, horrified and exhausted.

12

LIMBO

Mere moments later, the alarm went off startling Cathy from her stunned stupor, as scenes from her dream appeared and disappeared from her consciousness. She blinked and Troy was licking her face, tromping and stumbling over her to greet Paul, who was none too pleased with Troy's morning cheer.

Paul pushed Troy away and groaned. "Give me another half hour, would you?" he managed to grumble before putting his pillow over his head in an attempt to hide from the day.

"Come on, Troy, let Daddy sleep a little. He had a long night." Cathy and Troy went downstairs for their morning routine then Cathy made some extra strong coffee. When she went upstairs to wake Paul, she took her notepad downstairs with her. She took her coffee into the living room and opened her laptop on the coffee table.

As soon as her browser was open, she searched Civil War, Hagerstown, Maryland and found that the Battle of Antietam occurred only fifteen miles away from Hagerstown. Consequently, it was conceivable that a woman and child traveling could be abducted and never heard from again if they were traveling in that area when the Battle of Antietam was being fought. If that was the case, Cathy had a possible date of death for Lavinia and Troy; September 17, 1862, or thereabouts. Then she looked up St. James School and found that, yes, indeed, there was a St. James Boarding School open at that time in Hagerstown, Maryland.

Cathy's mouth dropped open. She took her cup of coffee and leaned back into the sofa. How could this be? Was there a logical reason for her to dream these things that she didn't consciously remember from history classes or learning from the old newspapers she'd been reading? Had she heard the Italian words in movies, perhaps? Was her mind digging out things tucked away in her memory from American history classes? Certainly far-fetched possibilities, but what about St. James School? There was absolutely no reason to have known about St. James School before. It was impossible to understand.

Paul walked into the living room. "Oh, there you are. I'm leaving. Wanted to give you a kiss goodbye." He leaned down, they kissed, and he glanced at her computer screen. "What're you looking at? Oh, so you found your St. James School?"

"Yes. It's a school in Maryland." Cathy paused, not knowing how much more to say. "I, uh, you know, I dreamt about it, sort of."

Paul smirked and laughed a little. "Hon, either you did or you didn't dream about it."

"I didn't exactly dream about the school specifically. I dreamt about someone mentioning the school in my dream. I wanted to see if it actually existed and it does and it has--since 1842 in Hagerstown, Maryland." She looked at Paul trying to discern his reaction. "I think it's pretty freaky. What do you think?"

"Did you dream of it as a school in Maryland?"

"Yes! So it just astounds me. I'm speechless and don't know what to think."

"It is strange, but my advice would be to remain speechless, to not think about it, and forget it." Paul stroked Cathy's head. "Your dream world is not the real world. I think you should concentrate on the real world. Right now, I'm in the real world, saying goodbye to my real wife, leaving my real house, trying to keep my real dog from ripping my real pants, and I'm going to drive my real car to my real job." Paul started walking to the door, Troy right beside him.

"I just don't understand where all this is coming from."

"How about your head? Dreams are just that. They're nothing you can touch. They're out there, floating around." Paul put his free hand above his head wiggling his fingers. "They're nothing."

"Or everything! Without dreams, where would anyone be?"

"We'd all be dealing with reality the best we can, that's where." Paul pursed his lips into a twisted smile. "You're thinking too much. Put that computer away and go somewhere with Troy.

He'll keep you tethered to reality." Troy barked at Paul. "Go on, go to your mother," Paul told him. "By the way, I might be home early if all goes well today."

"Hope so. You need some time off."

Paul smiled. "Stay out of trouble," he said as he walked out, closing the door behind him.

Troy jumped up on the door and whined and barked watching Paul walk away. When he got down, he looked at Cathy as if to ask desperately, "Where's he going?"

"It's okay kid, he'll be back," Cathy laughed. "Come here." Troy limped over and stared at her searchingly.

"I need a refill." Cathy got up and went to the kitchen for another cup of coffee with Troy following.

A little after eight o'clock, Cathy called Dr. Warner's office and scheduled Troy for his shots and neutering for the following Monday. Afterward, she texted Sharon to invite her to come over for lunch, then she grabbed a cookie and began planning her day. She would only have the morning hours to review any newspapers at the library, so she hurriedly finished her cookie and got ready to go, leaving Allie a message that she would be home around eleven o'clock to make lunch and that Sharon would be joining them.

Instead of picking up where she left off, armed with a possible date that Lavinia and Troy might have gone missing, Cathy pulled out the roll of microfilm containing the Dispatch issues from September through December 1862. She finally came across what she had been looking for in the November 7, 1862 issue of The Dispatch.

WIFE AND SON DISAPPEARS

November 7, 1862: Little progress is being made toward solving the mystery of the disappearance of Mrs. Lavinia Anatoli and ten-year-old Troy Anatoli from the Village of Harbour Creek. When Erie County Sheriff John Swalley visited the Anatoli home, he found all of Mrs. Anatoli's wearing apparel missing.

Mr. Anatoli declares that Mrs. Anatoli absconded with a traveling salesman who made assurances he would provide for Mrs. Anatoli and her son and that young Troy Anatoli would be enrolled in St. James School in Hagerstown, Maryland to make something of himself. Mr. Anatoli further stated that he has now disowned both wife and child and has no interest in searching for them.

Virgilio Anatoli is a farmer living on a large parcel of land with his seven other children. Many believe he killed his wife and son and is being closely watched.

Cathy printed out the article and went home. When she pulled in, she found Allie on the phone trying to watch Troy in the back yard at the same time. Troy raced over to greet Cathy and followed her inside. As it was almost eleven, Cathy got busy making pasta salad for lunch.

After she finished her phone conversation, Allie joined Cathy and Troy in the kitchen. "Are you going to join Sharon and me for lunch today, hon? Cathy asked her.

"Mm-hm, yes, I thought I might," Allie replied. "I don't have any plans until later, plus I wanted to say goodbye to Sharon. Need any help?"

"Yes, thanks. Can you start chopping while I put some water on to boil and get the oven heated up for some garlic bread?"

"Sure, I can do that." Allie got started cutting up vegetables, pepperoni, cheese, and ham, quickly joined by Cathy.

"If you're not doing anything this afternoon, maybe we should start getting your things together for this weekend," Cathy suggested.

"Yeah, we probably could. I'll just leave out things I'm going to use or wear the rest of this week." A few long seconds passed and Allie asked, "So, where'd you go this morning?"

Cathy went to the pantry for the rotini, olive oil, vinegar, spices and took a couple toes of garlic out of the fridge. "Downtown," she replied.

"The library?"

Cathy got a small bowl and a whisk out and started making the salad dressing. "If you must know, yes."

"Uh-oh, Mom. Better not let Dad know."

"I have a feeling he's already guessed I'd be going there today; but I'm not going to bring up the subject to him," Cathy said pointedly staring at Allie.

"Don't worry, Mom. I get it."

"I'm sure he wouldn't even care about this if he wasn't stressed out at work. Of course, he's feeling some stress with you leaving, too. He's showing it some, but he's going to miss you a lot more than he's letting on--you two are so alike." Cathy put the garlic bread in the oven, the pasta in the boiling water, and set the timer.

"Aw, Mom, don't make me feel guilty, now. You two know the chicks have got to fledge sometime, right?" Allie tossed Troy a piece of meat.

"I saw that," Cathy smiled and put the colander in the sink.

"Oh, just one piece won't hurt him."

"Just make sure it's only one. Troy knows how to work his cuteness already."

Allie laughed. "He sure does." Troy was resting his head on Allie's knee. "Well tell me. Have you found out anything interesting about the Anatoli clan?"

"Quite a bit, actually. I don't think I told you I found a picture of the whole family in one of the issues of the paper."

"Really? That's pretty cool. I bet you were excited to see that."

"I printed out a copy of it." Cathy went over to the kitchen desk and took a folder she'd labeled "Anatolis" out of the drawer. "Here they are," she said taking the copy of the ad from the folder.

Allie's eyes got wide. "Isn't that something." After a few seconds of scrutinizing the picture, she said, "Mom! The one boy's name is Troy. You named our Troy after him?"

"Yes, Troy is the name of one of the missing boys and no, I did not name our Troy after him. Troy found us before I saw this photo. I didn't even know there was a Troy Anatoli until I saw their ad." Cathy opened a can of olives and poured them into the colander to drain.

"That's pretty weird."

"I thought so, too. Of course since Troy Anatoli had an Australian Shepherd, it's kind of appropriate to name our Aussie Shepherd, Troy, don't you think?"

"How do you know he had an Australian Shepherd?" Allie looked at Cathy skeptically.

Cathy stopped bouncing the olives in the colander and thought a moment. She didn't want to tell Allie about all of her dreams, let alone admit she was believing them. She laughed a little. "Oh, I guess I don't. I just surmised that they must have had a dog. Farmers typically have dogs, and people certainly would have needed them in those days, particularly if they had livestock."

Allie squinted her eyes trying to peer into her mother. "Well, Troy's a good name for him, anyway." Allie snuck a piece of cheese to Troy.

This time, Cathy did not catch Allie. She was trying to sort out what she dreamt from what she had found to be fact. Somewhat distracted, she carried the drained olives in the colander to combine with the rest of the chopped ingredients. "Yes, I like the name, too. Not sure why it just occurred to me like it did, but it did."

The doorbell rang. Troy barked excitely and ran to the door. "Oh, that's Sharon," Cathy said looking at the timer. She wiped her hands on a dishtowel and started toward the front door with Allie.

"Come on in," Cathy said opening the door. She put her hand in front of Troy and told him firmly, "Sit, stay." Troy's behind quivered trying to obey her.

"Thanks for inviting me for lunch." Sharon smiled and she and Cathy hugged. "Hi, Allie. Not too long for you now, is it." Sharon reached out and she and Allie also hugged.

"No--just four more days," Allie said.

"Don't remind me," said Cathy with a wink. "Almost got lunch ready. I was a little longer at the library than I intended, but I did find out something interesting." The three walked into the kitchen and Cathy opened her Anatoli folder that was on the kitchen table. "First, here are the articles I found about Ernest Rosetti." Cathy handed the articles to Sharon.

"Who?" asked Allie.

"Oh, Ernest Rosetti is a younger brother of Lavinia Anatoli. Do you remember Tony coming back from the cemetery and saying he found a couple of graves among Lavinia's family plot but couldn't read the markers? Well, Sharon found out that one of them belonged to one of Lavinia's brothers, Ernest, and he, according to the articles here, was shot by Virgilio."

"Wow," Allie said with a little chuckle. "I guess you definitely are finding some skeletons in the Anatoli closet." Sharon gave the articles to Allie to read.

"But look at what I found today! I thought it would be in a September issue, but it didn't appear until November seventh." Cathy handed the copy of the article she found that morning to Sharon.

The timer rang and Cathy took the garlic bread out of the oven, and took care of putting the final touches on the pasta salad. "Although it's possible that Lavinia ran away with a traveling salesman taking Troy with her as Virgilio contended, I think it more likely that Virgilio had something to do with their disappearance. After all, he was abusive, no one heard from her after she allegedly left, and no bodies were ever recovered."

"How do you know that, Mom?" Allie asked. "You don't know if she was abused. If she did go to Hagerstown, Maryland with someone, maybe she's buried there. Maybe she lived happily ever after in Hagerstown and she didn't want to contact anyone back here because she knew her family would reject her for having left Virgilio for another man."

"Just from what Ernest said to Virgilio when they argued in the street. He and his family apparently never heard from Lavinia and Troy since their disappearance. He was demanding to know what Virgilio had done with them. He wanted to know where their bodies were so, apparently, they still were missing on her fiftieth birthday."

Allie and Sharon looked at each other, confused. "Did you uncover something other than these articles, Cathy?" Sharon asked.

"No, not yet." Cathy took the bowl of pasta to the table. "But it says it right there in the articles."

"No," Sharon said hesitantly. "It doesn't spell out what they argued about specifically. It just says, opprobrious epithets, defamatory accusations, and libelous obscenities were exchanged."

"Let me see that," Cathy said. Allie handed the article to her. Cathy's eyes opened wide and her eyebrows rose in surprise. She looked at Allie and Sharon and her hand rose to her mouth. "I, uh, don't know. I guess my imagination . . ." Cathy walked slowly to the counter to retrieve the basket of garlic bread, which she placed on the table. "What do you two want to drink?"

"I'll get it," said Allie. After finding out what Sharon and her mother wanted, Allie got the drinks. "Mom, like Dad said, maybe you're getting too involved in this. At least take a break."

"Did you have another dream after finding out about Ernest Rosetti?" asked Sharon as the women sat down at the dining table.

Cathy nodded. "I've had dreams almost every night about Lavinia, Troy, and their family. It's becoming almost a second reality to me, but I'm just an observer. I'm just watching what's going on and can't do anything about it. And I'd write it off if it weren't for the fact that there's evidence that things I've dreamt are actually true. It's kind of disturbing."

"What made you think to start looking at September 1862 for an article about Lavinia and Troy disappearing? Another dream?" asked Sharon.

"It was from the same dream about Ernest. In my dream Virgilio said that the war made it too dangerous to travel to Maryland, but she went anyway, so I looked up information about the Civil War and battles in Hagerstown, Maryland. I saw that Antietam occurred on September 17, 1862, so I looked for an article around that time, and, lo and behold, it led to something."

"That's really weird, Mom. Maybe you're psychic and you never knew it before," Allie speculated.

"I don't know, dear, but these coincidences are rattling me a little bit. And now that I can't seem to separate what I've dreamt from what I've read or seen from records. I don't know. Maybe I ought to take a break from this for a while."

"Well you're going to have to take a break this weekend. We'll be in Pittsburgh for orientation," said Allie. "I definitely think you need a little getaway."

"What other things have you dreamt, Cathy? Maybe if you talk about them, it'll help you sort things out. Besides, I'm interested," said Sharon.

Cathy wasn't quite sure if it was a good idea to divulge all the details of her dreams to Allie, but spoke freely hoping that Sharon was right. Perhaps the fact that she felt unable to talk about her dreams, she internalized everything too much and, thus, her dreams were remembered as actual experiences.

Allie listened, fascinated and concerned. "Gee, Mom. It sounds like one dream led to another each night."

"Yes, it's as if I'm looking through a window into a room in which their lives are locked and, unless I release their truth, they'll be destined to replay these scenes over and over, like they're in Limbo," replied Cathy.

"I think it's a combination of what you've learned and your intuition mixed with imagination. We don't know exactly what happened but we know what the family looked like, and we've learned about Virgilio shooting Ernest. It's certainly possible their argument happened as you dreamt it, but who knows?" Sharon offered.

"One thing for sure, I want to find out how I can get records from Hagerstown, Maryland and Saint James School. I have no idea if the school records will go way back to the eighteen hundreds, but they might." Cathy stated.

"Well, I better get back to the office," Sharon said getting up from her chair. "Thanks so much for having me over. Don't forget, I'll run down to the library again on Saturday while you're away and see if I can find out anything else."

"That'd be great," Cathy said as she and Allie got up and stepped away from the table disturbing Troy who had fallen asleep under it. Startled, he barked and limped after them to the door.

"I certainly wish you luck at school, Allie," Sharon said kissing her goodbye on the cheek. "I think you're going to do great!"

"Thanks Sharon. I'm sure Mom will tell you all about how I'm doing."

Cathy laughed. "You know I will, so don't get into any trouble so I can brag about you."

"Oh, I don't think Allie's going to get into trouble, are you Allie."

"Going to try not to," said Allie, "But I make no guarantees."

"You're lucky your Dad didn't hear you say that," laughed Cathy.

"You're lucky he isn't here right now, too, Mom," Allie replied.

Paul arrived home as Allie and Cathy were cleaning up the kitchen. "You're just in time," said Cathy, going over and giving Paul a kiss hello.

"Hi Dad," Allie greeted.

"Hi, kid," he said giving her a kiss on the top of her head.

"So, I guess everything went pretty well since Harry let you off early," Cathy surmised.

Paul was all smiles. "Yeah. The client loved it and didn't suggest any changes, thank God! So, we're all set to go. Tomorrow, we'll be setting up a strategy and specific timetable for TV ads, newspapers, magazines, and, of course, internet. It's a relief to have the afternoon off after working through the weekend."

"There's plenty of pasta salad and garlic bread left, dear. What do you want to drink?"

"Guess I'll have a beer to celebrate," said Paul walking to the refrigerator and getting himself a beer. "Why'd you make such a big bowl of salad? Expecting someone?"

"Oh, I had Sharon over for lunch today," Cathy told him as she scooped out a large serving of salad.

Paul raised an eyebrow. "Mm, and I can guess the topic of discussion during lunch," he said with a tone of disapproval and looked at Allie.

Allie looked down, and Cathy said, "Of course we talked about it. I've certainly spent enough time on it."

"That you have," Paul stated with seriousness.

"There's nothing wrong with speculating about things. We just talked about possibilities, really."

"I'm going to start sorting through my things upstairs, okay?" Allie said walking out of the kitchen to escape being caught in the middle. She didn't feel right that her mother was stretching the truth to her father, but, all the same, correcting her would start a big ugly discussion and put everyone in a bad mood.

"I'll be up in a little while to see if you need any help," said Cathy.

"Okay," Allie shouted. Right now she really didn't want to look her mother in the eye and was glad to have something to do.

"I've got a great idea," Paul said to Cathy. "I can't think of a better place to unwind than Presque Isle. You and I haven't gone there in I don't know how long. Since Allie loves it there, maybe we should all go, take Troy with us, and grab supper on the way home. What do you think?"

"That's a great idea, hon. I think I could use a beach day, too, since school's right around the corner." Cathy was thrilled realizing this would be just what she needed to get her mind off of her investigation.

There was just a bit of a breeze supplying waves large enough to enjoy, but not so large that they would be dangerous. The air off the lake was refreshing, cooling their bodies from the steamy August heat. Cathy saw first-hand how Troy took to the water. She and Allie played Frisbee with Troy who, despite his lame back leg, enthusiastically jumped for the toy. At one point, Troy took off with the Frisbee, running circles around their blanket. Paul was sitting in his beach chair reading a magazine and getting some sun. Troy ran up to Paul dousing him with a splash of sand when he stopped and deposited the Frisbee on his belly, then barked as if telling him to get up and play. Paul complied and when everyone was hot, sweaty, and sandy from the game, Paul picked Cathy up, carried her out into the water and threw her in. Allie took Troy into the water and threw a water toy for him to fetch. In addition to being active on the beach, they all did a great deal of sun worshiping until the sky was glowing pink, yellow, and red as it began to set.

"I'm so glad you thought of doing this today, Paul," Cathy said on the way home. She realized she had been right. She hadn't once thought about the Anatolis, and returning to her project almost seemed like a loathsome chore "It's been a long time since we've had a good time as a family."

"Yeah, Troy and I really enjoyed it, too, Dad," Allie said. "Didn't we boy." She patted Troy and noticed the sand going onto the back seat. "Ooh, you're a mess," she laughed. "It was nice going out with you guys today. I took lots of photos. I can't wait to go through them. I'd look now, but my phone's in my beach bag."

Cathy's and Paul's hearts warmed with Allie's comment. "Maybe we'll have to make it a yearly tradition to go to the beach as a family before school starts. Next year, we'll do it when your brother can come. We could have an end of summer picnic at Presque Isle. What do you think?" asked Cathy.

"That'd be fine with me," Allie said.

"Sounds like a good idea," said Paul.

As planned, they took some fast food home for dinner. As they were eating, Allie looked through the photos she'd taken. "Aww," she moaned in disappointment. "My phone didn't adjust the exposure very well. I hope nothing's wrong with it. In every shot there's a glare or something that ruins the picture and it always seems to be ruining my pictures of Troy. Of course, he's in most of the shots. I don't think I was facing the sun the same way every time." Allie continued reviewing her photos. "It's screwed up pictures of you guys, too. Here, look."

Cathy flipped through the pictures of their day at the beach. "Tch, that's too bad, hon. It would've been nice to print a couple good shots out to remember the day." Cathy handed the phone back to Allie. "Maybe you could ask Kelsea if she might be able to adjust or fix the pictures somehow."

"Maybe," Allie said hopefully. "That's a good idea. I'll ask her."

Cathy spent the rest of the night watching television and reading. With her mind clear, Cathy was sure she wouldn't have any disturbing dreams for a while, especially if she gave herself a break.

13

SIGNS

Cathy refused to allow any thoughts about the Anatolis to invade her peace of mind for the remainder of the night. Unfortunately, although rested and relaxed, when she tried to release her mind to the bliss of sleep, thoughts of Ernest, Virgilio, Lavinia, Troy, and the secrets buried with them spun and wove into plots and possibilities. For three hours, she tried one sleeping posture, then another, and employed all the falling asleep tricks she could recall, but the luxury of sleep evaded her. Finally, it occurred to her, considering her dwelling on the deceased, it would be appropriate to assume the yoga position, corpse pose, while doing deep relaxation breathing. Since she couldn't escape thinking about Lavinia and Troy, she decided her mantra would be, *you will be found,* which phrase she repeated over and over, feeling she was somehow calming their spirits as she was calming her own, until she floated off into dreamland.

Unfortunately, the dreamland in which she found herself was even more disturbing and frightening than her previous dreams. She was not merely an observer this time. She was lying immobile on her back, with something heavy and oppressive holding her down. She felt an itchiness, tiny piercing pinches, needle-like pinpricks, and tiny bites all over her body. Through tiny slivers of light that pierced down from irregular holes in the heaviness upon her, she could see huge fat black beetles and large mutant bicolored, red and black ants biting with large jagged mandibles. There were tiny brown ants, red fire ants, blowflies, and maggots on her, going in and out of the orifices of her body and squeezing out of the corners of her eyes. She felt long, slimy earthworms slithering over her arms, legs and chest. As much as she tried, she could not move even a joint of a finger to try to rid herself of the vermin. She couldn't scream for fear something would crawl into her mouth.

Then she heard the thunder, and blinding flashes of lightning intermittently brightened the laser lines of light illuminating her confinement. Rain started to slowly splatter down, a quick increase in intensity, then the downpour came. The rainwater started to puddle under her, rising slowly until it was tickling her ears. Bugs and worms that washed off were trying desperately to gain a foothold on her face and getting tangled in her hair. Bugs fought other bugs for the dry ground and meat that was her face.

She heard something. Someone was there. A dog was scratching, tearing away at her cumbersome cover, letting in more light as he scratched, making the insects and crawling creatures flee in terror. The dog was barking, feverishly digging, and he broke through, licking away all the itchiness and stinging wounds from her abominable captivity. She was free in her dream and from her dream. She awoke to Troy licking her face.

Cathy was breathing hard and sweating. She sat up and hugged Troy. "Thank you, Sweetie. You saved me, you good boy," she whispered, then she kissed the top of his head. She heard a loud clap of thunder and rapid pelts of rain beat on the roof, windows and the side of the house.

"You don't have to whisper," Paul said in a gravelly voice. "I've been awake. With you thrashing around the way you were, I wouldn't be surprised if I've got a couple bruises from you. What in the world were you dreaming?"

"Ugh. It was horrible. I was all covered with bugs and worms and I couldn't move. Yuch," Cathy said revolted. She shuddered and rubbed her arms.

Paul laughed. "I wonder what prompted that. You think we've got some creepy crawlies in our bed?" He stuck his head under the covers and started pinching Cathy's legs.

She laughed and slapped his hands, and then they wrestled in bed a little with Troy joining in the fray, barking. The alarm went off and although the mood seemed right for a little romance, Paul got out of bed to get ready for work.

Cathy was pleased that Paul's good mood carried over to this morning. "Listen to that rain! Wonder how long this is going to last." She stepped out of bed, into her slippers and put on a short, silky robe.

"Don't know. We'll have to listen to the weather. Sure glad it didn't hit yesterday."

"Mm-hm. Guess we were blessed," Cathy smiled from the inside out." She looked at Troy who was standing next to the bed looking at her intently. "You might have gotten out of a bath again, little boy. It was too late last night, and if this rain keeps up all day, we'll have to wait until tomorrow." Troy made a little whine and cocked his head. Cathy snorted a small laugh. "You think he understands?" she asked Paul.

"I don't think the whole thing, but he might have an idea what the word bath is," Paul said. Troy whined again. Both Paul and Cathy laughed.

They got their day underway and by the time Paul left for work, the rain was letting up. The forecast called for variable clouds for most of the day, hot, humid and thunderstorms late afternoon or early evening. "Too bad," she told Troy, crouching down and scratching both sides of his head. "We're going to get all that beach sand and dirt out of you. And then, since you'll be all handsome, we'll go show you off to Jessi today."

As predicted, the skies started clearing around nine in the morning. Cathy had just gotten comfortable on the couch with her computer when Allie came downstairs. "Morning, Mom. What're you up to already? Thought you were going to give it a rest."

"I really don't think I have much I can do, to tell you the truth. I'm just going to make a couple phone calls today, that's all. I've already found the phone number here for Vital Records in Hagerstown. After I get a number for St. James, I'm going to exhaust all possibilities through Find-A-Grave for Troy and Lavinia."

"Then what?"

"That's all, today. I've got lots to do around here. Speaking of which, what do you want for breakfast?"

"Oh, I'll just get myself some cereal and fruit. Then, I'll get to work on packing my clothes, etc. If you can get me some suitcases, boxes, whatever you want me to put my clothes and stuff in . . ."

"Okay, that's a good idea. You can get yourself started and I'll take care of Troy's bath."

"Have any more dreams?"

"Yes and no. I had a dream that was upsetting, but it had nothing to do with Lavinia and Troy for a change. I was immobile covered with bugs and creepy-crawlies." Cathy's face contorted into a mask of repulsion. "I think I'd rather dream about my adopted deceased family."

"Yuch. I guess I would, too." Allie stuck out her tongue and shuddered. "Since when are you thinking of them as your adopted family? Are you planning to invite the Anatoli's to holiday dinners from now on?"

Cathy laughed. "No, just Lavinia and Troy. They're sort of part of my life now."

Allie raised her eyebrows. "I think you've got that right, Mom," she said and headed upstairs. As soon as she was alone in her room, Allie texted Tony and Julia. "Really worried about Mom. Obsessed with Anatoli clan. She's dreaming about them almost every night and when she talks about them, she can't seem to remember if she read something somewhere or she just had a dream about it. Now saying they're her adopted family!"

Tony texted back, "Don't worry. She's just super interested. Nothing to worry about."

Julia responded, "She's stressed. Next week she'll be fine. She'll be driving again and you'll be settled in your dorm room. Anita will be back and I'll be back to my old schedule. I'll be able to come over and make sure she's not getting lost in dreamland. Have you talked to Dad?"

"No," replied Allie. "Not sure I should."

"I wouldn't," Tony advised. "It'd just create friction between them. There's nothing at all to worry about. I think it's really interesting. If I can help her with this somehow, I'm going to."

"I just keep wondering how I'd feel if I found out one of my ancestors killed one, maybe two or three other ancestors, and then my mind was concocting dreams about them? It's a little unsettling. I'd be wondering if someone in the family is stifling murderous tendencies--maybe even me!" Allie replied.

"Oh, sis - don't worry. You'll soon be too far away to murder or be murdered."

"Ha, ha - real funny, Tony. I just don't want to see Mom going off the deep end is all."

Julia texted, "Who's going off the deep end now?"

Tony texted a laughing emoji. "I've got to get to class. I'll call Mom and ask her if I can do anything. The quicker this is done, the quicker you'll stop worrying about nothing."

"Okay, just don't tell her what I said!" Allie wrote.

"I won't, but if Mom starts to chase you around with an axe, call 911. Mercyhurst is too far away for me to come to the rescue."

Allie sent him a middle finger emoji.

Julia and Tony signed off with laughing emojis.

Cathy made her phone calls and was disappointed but not surprised that no records were found for Lavinia or Troy. She did some additional searching on Find-A-Grave and several ancestor and genealogy websites finding nothing.

She closed her laptop and went up to the attic to get suitcases and boxes for Allie. After several trips back and forth between the attic and Allie's room, she said to Allie, "This ought to give you a good start. We've got more boxes upstairs, too. Now remember, there's only so much storage space in your dorm room, so you don't have to take every single thing you own. Be selective."

"It's going to be hard to know what clothes I'm going to want and need."

"It's not like you won't be coming home for a visit now and then and we'll be coming down there once in a while. So, if you find you left something here you really want, it'll be easy enough to get it to you. Do you want me to help you go through your things?"

"No, that's all right. I should probably be making the decision about what to take and what to leave."

"If you change your mind, let me know," Cathy said. "I'm going to give your fur brother here a bath while you're doing that."

"Sounds like a lot more fun than this."

"Want to switch?"

"No thanks. You don't want me blaming you if I don't have something I want when I'm at school, do you?"

"No, dear. I certainly don't." Cathy smiled and turned to go downstairs. "Come on, Troy. We're going to have some fun outside."

A couple hours later, Troy was all clean, fluffy, and smelling much better than he did after playing in the lake water. "Okay, my handsome boy. Are you ready to show yourself off at the bus garage?"

Cathy went upstairs to Allie's room, Troy trailing her. "How you coming, hon?"

"Oh, pretty good I think," Allie sighed and stood up looking at her handiwork. Her closet was thinned out some, clothes were laying on the bed, books were off bookshelves, her desk was cleared, and some wall art was off the walls. She'd labeled the boxes with their contents, folded up her art easel and her drawing desk, and had two suitcases closed and ready to go.

"I think so, too!" Cathy said, impressed. "Now you don't have to do it all today, you know," she chuckled. "You've got two more days."

"I know. I just want to get a handle on it. Probably better to get done what I can when I've got the time."

"Good thinking," said Cathy. "I'm going to take Troy over to the bus garage to show Jessi and whoever happens to be there. We shouldn't be long."

"Okay, Mom."

"Phew it's getting pretty sticky out, isn't it, boy," Cathy said to Troy as they left the house. The car had been sitting in the driveway, so when she opened the door, it felt like the inside of a hot oven. She opened the windows to let the heat out before they got in the car. With his weak back leg, Troy had trouble hopping into the back seat, so Cathy helped him up and strapped him into his car harness. She left the windows down to blow out the heat since it was only a five to ten minute drive. Troy stuck his nose out the window taking in all the smells that whizzed through the car as they drove along.

There were a number of cars in the parking lot, a bus being fueled, and a bus leaving when Cathy parked. Not having stood beside a bus before, Troy backed away from it as it was being fueled when they got near. Cathy introduced Troy to Michelle, who was doing the fueling. "Better not let him get too close to you right now, Michelle. He's a jumper. We're going to be inside for a few minutes if you'd like a few dog kisses."

"Who wouldn't be up for a doggie kiss," Michelle said with a laugh.

Fellow drivers, Denny, Bob, and Fred were sitting at one of the tables and chatting when Troy and Cathy made their entrance. Troy yanked at the leash to run over to their table. "Calm down, Troy," Cathy said, jerking the leash to get Troy's attention. Having a pocket full of excellent stinky dog treats to motivate best behavior, Troy decided that Cathy was much more interesting and came back to her side. "Behave yourself now," she told him and gave him a nibble of the salmon jerky and walked over to say hello.

"Lookee who you've got here," Denny said petting Troy. Troy put his front paws on Denny's thigh.

"So you got yourself another dog," Fred said.

"Yep. He actually found us and we've adopted him," Cathy replied and told them about Troy coming out of the woods behind her house.

Jessi came away from her desk around the corner to the break room and Cathy unclipped Troy's leash to let him run to her. "Aw, He's darling," Jessi cooed. "And so soft."

"We had him at the beach yesterday and he didn't look or smell too good after that. With all the white on him, he can look pretty grubby, pretty quick. So he's just had a bath. He'll be clean for another couple hours," Cathy laughed.

Just then, the driver of Bus 28, Jeanne, was radioing in to the office. "28 to base."

Jessi walked back into the office with Troy following her. "This is base, come in," Jessi responded.

The radio crackled. Bits and pieces of words could be made out amidst crackling and static, ▓▓▓ ▓▓▓ ▓ ▓▓▓▓ Stalled ▓▓ ▓▓▓ ▓▓▓▓ Road ▓▓▓ ▓▓▓ ▓▓▓▓ reds and ▓▓▓ ▓▓ ▓▓▓ ▓▓▓▓ ▓▓▓ ▓▓ died ▓▓▓ ▓▓▓ ▓▓ restart ▓▓ ▓▓▓ ▓▓ Scott ▓low ▓▓▓

"This is base, come again," Jessi radioed.

Cathy came into the office, scowling to sort out what Jeanne was trying to say, and clipped Troy's leash back on him. More crackling, a distortion squeal, and more static caused Troy to start barking. Cathy led him out of the office and back to the table where the three men sat.

The radio interference cleared and Jeanne reported Bus 28 had also stalled on Station Road by Scott Hollow. Cathy laughed, surprised. "That's weird," she told Denny, Bob and Fred.

"Sounds like Jeanne stalled exactly where I stalled. That reminds me. I wanted to know if Luke figured out what was wrong with 35."

"Oh, I saw 35 in there and asked Luke what was wrong," said Denny. "Last I knew, all the busses had gotten a clean bill of health. He told me what happened to you, but he couldn't find a damn thing wrong. He checked the tranny, the fuel filter, checked for electrical shorts. He said everything's in tip top condition-- perfect."

"Hmph," Cathy muttered. "I just hope it doesn't happen again."

Jessi came out of the office dangling a set of keys. "Denny, can you get 64 ready in case Jeanne can't get 28 started again?"

"Yes I can," Denny said, getting up from the table.

"I guess I better be going," Cathy said. "I just wanted you to see our new kid."

"Thanks for stopping by," said Jessi. "He's darling. See you next week."

Cathy came in the front door and looked to the top of the staircase when she heard Allie say, "I've done all I want to do today."

Allie was coming down the stairs, but it wasn't Allie. Her black hair was piled loosely on top of her head, a few loose ends framing her rosy-cheeked face. Bright blue eyes bore into Cathy's eyes. It was Lavinia's face she saw. Cathy sucked in her breath, her face and eyes showed shock and disbelief.

Stunned by Cathy's reaction, Allie hurried down the stairs. "Mom, what?"

Allie's eyes were now the dark brown they always had been. It was Allie, not Lavinia. "Oh, I'm sorry, honey. I guess you just startled me," Cathy laughed. "I wasn't expecting you to be coming down the stairs and I must've been daydreaming." Cathy noted Allie's look of disturbed concern. "Oh, I love your hair up like that, honey. You should wear it like that more often."

"Really, do you like it? It's just so hot and humid, I wanted to get it off my neck. What'd they think of Troy at the garage?"

"They thought he was real cute, of course. I didn't stay very long because things were a little busy. One of the busses had a problem--just like I did the other day." Cathy paused a moment. "I wonder if it could be bad gas."

"Don't you think they'd have checked that?"

"Probably. I just don't like to worry about it happening again."

"Yeah. That'd be miserable if you had a load of kids on the bus and you stalled."

"So what've you got planned for the rest of the day?"

"We're probably going to do some things inside today--stay in air conditioning. Maybe visit the Tom Ridge Center, then get something to eat. Probably hang out somewhere for a while and I'd like to go watch the sunset at the beach. Should be nice out by then."

"What time's Doug picking you up?"

"We planned on three-ish, but I think I'll call him and see if he wants to go out a little earlier. I thought I'd be working on my packing a lot longer. But . . ."

"It is a chore, isn't it. You made a big dent in it today. With two more days, we won't have any problem getting everything together."

"That's what I thought, too." Allie walked onto the back deck with her phone.

Cathy went upstairs to check out her daughter's progress and was quite pleased with how she'd tidied up her packing mess. The boxes and suitcases were making navigation in her room difficult, so Cathy took the suitcases and boxes into Tony's room to get them out of the way and went back into Allie's room. There weren't many things left hanging in Allie's closet, mostly very dressy dresses that Cathy assumed would be left at home. There were a great number of Allie's paintings filling up a large portion of her closet, which Cathy also assumed would be left behind. Cathy bent down to flip through and admire her daughter's work.

The third from the front was the street scene Allie had painted at the end of the year. Cathy had almost forgotten about this painting. She broke out in goosebumps as she focused on the woman in blue holding the hand of the blonde boy with the dog trailing behind, the large brown horse, and the buckboard wagon. She quickly flipped the first two paintings back to conceal the street scene and stood up quickly. She covered her mouth with her hand. 'What is happening?' she wondered.

The painting still in her head, Cathy walked downstairs to the kitchen almost without knowing how she got there. She poured herself a glass of wine and joined Allie and Troy on the deck.

Allie was on the phone with Doug working out their plans for the evening when Cathy sat down. Cathy visualized Troy showing up at the edge of the woods, remembered the pets in their cemetery, and visualized the path past her mother's grave to the Anatoli family plot. She thought of the ad for the Anatoli farm and the faces of all the boys, and Virgilio, and Lavinia and Troy. She pictured the photo in color, Troy's eyes blue, like her Troy's one blue eye.

Her fluffy, happy Troy was staring up at her, proud of himself after having chased a squirrel up their large maple tree and coming back to her to be praised. As she lovingly returned his stare, both his eyes looked blue and she felt unable to break their stare. When she finally managed to look away, slowly materializing to a glittery translucent mist, Cathy saw ten-year-old Troy Anatoli staring up at her with his bright blue eyes while stroking her Troy's head. Cathy closed her eyes and shook her head to shut out the image. When she opened them, her Troy was now laying down in the yard, panting, and staring vigilantly at the maple tree. Cathy took a long swig of her wine.

Allie hung up and, observing the glass of wine in her mother's hand, said, "A little early for you, isn't it?"

"I just feel a little nervous, that's all. Thought a nice glass of wine would take the edge off."

Allie's worry was rekindled. "Mom, you're going to be fine. You knew all of us would be leaving home one day, right?"

Cathy's eyes welled up. She hesitated looking at Allie for fear she would see Lavinia's face again. Cathy braced and forced herself to look at Allie. "I know, honey. I know things will be fine, but it's just so hard to think of all of you being gone."

When she finished her wine, Cathy got busy cleaning the house and cooking dinner, trying to occupy her hands and mind with the real and tangible, the here and now.

14

SYMPTOMS

Cathy poured herself another glass of wine before she retired for the evening. The wine earlier in the day had gotten her through the rest of the afternoon without experiencing any more logic-defying sights or sounds, so, she hoped another glass would provide a deep, dreamless sleep for her.

Unfortunately, the alcohol did not help. She found herself unable to escape from a chaotic dream of strobing images thrust before her. She was strapped in a seat of a rollercoaster being whipped around in complete darkness. Images from pieces of previous dreams flashed violently out of the blackness. Faces and scenes from her dreams assaulted her one after the other. She'd turn away from one horror and another would appear. She'd see Troy being whipped, then Lavinia's brother being shot, a horse rearing, Lavinia being raped. She saw the graves in the cemetery, the ad in the paper, her pup Troy with his bright blue eye, her Troy in the woods, then Troy Anatoli in the field. She'd see one face morph into another, into another. Faces melted into monsters, houses afire, all the time with loud dissonant music, crowds yelling in the background, the Anatoli brothers' and sisters' faces growing larger and larger, Lavinia, Troy, Leonardo and the girls disintegrating into dust, and faint plaintive voices whispering, "Help," "We're here," and "Find us." The distressing dream would not release her. Cathy would shift position, yet she could not force herself to awaken and the dream continued.

When she finally managed to pull herself from the grip of her nightmare, she felt exhausted and unsettled. She was surprised that Paul had already gone to work when she got out of bed. She blamed the wine for having slept through the alarm and for the slight headache she now had. She felt depressed and somewhat in a fog. After taking a couple of aspirin, Cathy went downstairs and put on a pot of strong coffee. She tried to read the newspaper, but found her mind was still in overdrive and she could not concentrate. She re-read sentence after sentence until she gave up and went in the living room to find the answers to the plethora of questions plaguing her.

She opened the computer on her lap and turned it on with questions running through her head. 'Why am I having so many dreams? What do they mean? Are they visions into the past? Are they just imaginings? Am I actually seeing things, hearing things that aren't there? Can stress, worry, or depression cause hallucinations, delusions? Are they supernatural phenomenon? Are ghosts real?' She searched for "Causes of hallucinations and delusions," then clicked on "Psychosis: Symptoms, Causes and Risk Factors," to "Hallucinations," then "Depressive psychosis," to "Psychotic Depression."

Cathy was engrossed reading when Allie startled her out of her focus. "Mom! Did you forget?"

Troy barked his displeasure at being startled as well. "Forget? Forget what, dear?" Cathy asked.

"I thought you had a nine o'clock appointment with Jules today to get your hair done.

"Oh my gosh! You're right," Cathy said, frantically looking around for a clock.

Cathy looked at the corner of her computer for the time just as Allie informed her, "It's twenty minutes till and you're still in your nightclothes. You better get a move on if you still want to get there."

Cathy jumped up in a tizzy. "Oh my gosh, oh my gosh! Can you call there and tell her I'll be a few minutes late? It won't be long. I'll just throw on some shorts and a top." Troy got up, barking and following at Cathy's heels.

"Calm down, Mom. I'll call her. You might still get there on time if there's not much traffic." Allie quickly phoned the salon and left a message on their voice mail as Cathy flew by her.

"Not even going to wash my face," Cathy mumbled to herself as she ran upstairs, Troy still by her side barking. "She won't care. It's not like she hasn't seen me at my worst." Cathy laughed nervously. "Oh my, good God."

Allie shook her head and sat down on the couch to see what had so absorbed her mother's attention, and she almost wished she hadn't looked. If her mom was experiencing the things that were on the computer screen and in the search history, she was troubled far more than anyone realized. Allie quickly e-mailed a summary of what Cathy was reading to Julia and Tony, along with a couple articles Cathy had just read. "I'm going to have to tell Dad," Allie wrote. "She hasn't said a thing to me or Dad about these concerns. I'm worried she's having a nervous breakdown. If you'd have seen her yesterday, you'd know what I mean. She's upstairs now getting ready for her appointment with you, Jules. Maybe you can get something out of her, or at the very least calm her down."

After sending the email, Allie quickly texted Julia, "Just sent you an email. Make sure you read it before Mom gets there. Important!"

Allie heard Cathy bustling around upstairs and as soon as it sounded like she was nearing the staircase, she got up from the couch and went into the kitchen to feign getting a bite to eat.

Cathy ran through the kitchen with Troy still yelping and jumping at her. Allie grabbed Troy's collar as he trailed Cathy to the door. "Stop it, Troy. Mom's got to go out. You stay here with me." She received a short growl of frustration from the dog.

"You called Julia, didn't you?" Cathy asked as she opened the door to leave.

"Yes, Mom. Don't worry."

"Thanks, dear," and Cathy slammed the door and dashed to her car.

Allie released Troy who scurried to the door, stood on his good hind leg, assisted by the weak one, and barked and whined. "Troy come here," Allie instructed. Troy limped over and looked at her with that quizzical dog expression in his eyes and Allie told him, "You were supposed to keep Mom from becoming a spaz. But look at her! It's going to be your job, now. You're going to have to take much better care of Mom." Allie gave Troy a hug.

Cathy burst through the door of Trendy Tresses and saw Julia sitting in her chair conversing with the stylist next to her and that stylist's customer. Julia saw her mother checking in and went to the reception desk to greet her.

"You didn't have to break the speed barrier to get here, Mom. You know I'll always fit you in."

"I know, dear, but I didn't want to louse up your whole schedule, especially with Anita out."

"Mom, you worry too much. Now, come on over here and relax."

After Cathy sat down, Julia adjusted her styling chair and put a neck strip and cape around her mother's neck. "Come on to the sinks, Mom. I'll give you a nice scalp massage today with your shampoo." Cathy got up and walked with Julia to the shampoo area. "Now, we're just tidying up your cut today, right? You're not wanting a completely new look, or do you?"

"No, no. I think there are a enough changes going on at home right now." Cathy laughed nervously as she got comfortable in the shampoo chair.

As Julia shampooed her, she could feel the tension in her mother's scalp and at the base of her head. "Now you just forget about everything else while you're here, Mom. Pretend you're being pampered at a micro-spa for a while." Julia quit talking while she lathered Cathy's hair, massaging until she felt her mother's scalp loosening up.

"So, how's it going, Mom? I wish I could have come over to help out with Allie's packing and all that, but I've been jammed these past two weeks. Next week things'll be back to normal." Julia made a mental note to visit a few times next week. "Maybe we can go out to breakfast or lunch, then go shopping afterward on Monday, if you want."

Cathy's spirit brightened, knowing that Julia was trying to fill the void left by Allie. "That would be wonderful, honey, but that's the day I have to take Troy to Dr. Warner to be fixed. I probably won't want to shop. I'll be too nervous about him."

"You have to drop him off in the morning, don't you? How about I meet you at Dr. Warner's office and we go out for breakfast." Julia proceeded to rinse and apply conditioner to Cathy's hair.

"Okay, that sounds great. It will take my mind off of him for a while, anyway," Cathy said. "Oh, and speaking of Troy, you'll still be able to watch him for us this weekend, won't you? You can

either take him to your place or leave him home and just visit him--
walk and play with him a little. Whatever's best for you."

"Sure, that's no problem at all. It'll be fun for me. But there is
one downside to doing that," Julia said.

"What's that?"

"I know I'll have the urge to adopt a dog or cat after I dogsit.
Oh well, might just have to give in and do it afterwards." Julia
chuckled and gave Cathy's hair a final rinse.

"Just don't kidnap Troy, okay?"

"No, I wouldn't do that to you, Mom." Julia wrapped Cathy's
hair in a towel and put the shower chair into an upright position.
"He's your rescue angel--think you rescued each other." There was
silence between them as they walked back to Julia's styling chair,
then Julia tried again. "So, are you sleeping all right, Mom? I know
changes like this can wreak havoc on sleep patterns and lack of
sleep can lead to all kinds of problems, or exacerbate them."

"Oh, I'm fine, honey. I am having dreams almost every night
that are extremely vivid, but they're just dreams. Entertaining, in a
way. It's just . . ." Cathy paused. She wanted to say, 'I'm seeing
things that can't possibly be there when I'm awake, too,' and
instead said, "With Allie leaving, your father working so much,
Troy getting fixed, my work starting again, and wanting to finish
my little research project, I guess I'm feeling a little overwhelmed is
all. Things will fall into place soon, though. Once I'm back at
work and on a regular schedule, I'll feel much better."

"I think you're right, Mom. Being on a daily routine of work
can really ground you. You probably won't even have time to
dwell on things." There was another patch of silence while Julia
concentrated on her work, then it occurred to her. "You know,
Mom, I've been going to Yoga classes lately. I think they'd benefit
you a great deal. It's extremely relaxing. It helps flexibility and
how your body feels in general. Why don't you come with me
once in a while? Then we'd get together more, too."

"Oh, I don't know, honey. I can't get into all those pretzel
shapes."

Julia laughed. "Mom, they're not all pretzel shapes and you
only do what you can do. No one ever pushes you in Yoga and the
instructors adjust poses for students. Think about it."

Cathy rolled her eyes and smiled. "I will."

After Cathy left the salon, Julia called Allie. "Did she confide in you?" Allie asked Julia.

"No, not really. She just seemed a little more tightly wound than usual, nervous I guess. She did say she wasn't sleeping that well lately--having a ton of dreams. I don't know what to think. She seems pretty good considering her last chickadee is leaving her nest. I think she'll be fine."

"Aren't you worried about what she was searching on the computer?"

"I was until I saw her," admitted Julia. "But I think she's fine. Just because she was looking at disorders that might cause hallucinations, it doesn't mean she's having them. Maybe she was looking at one thing, she found it interesting and it led to another, and another. You know how that goes. She might be feeling anxious and depressed and started looking at coping strategies and ended up being intrigued in hallucinations and such. I can see that. Happens to me all the time. I'm reading one thing and it has an embedded link which I find interesting and I end up looking at something entirely different from what I originally searched. I wouldn't worry and I'd wait to tell Dad for now. I'll keep a close eye on her and if I think something's wrong I'll tell him and I'll get in touch with you and Tony. Oh, and can you tell Tony what I said. I probably won't have time to contact him today--fully booked again. Actually overly fully booked. Lucky me," Julia laughed.

"All I can say is ka-ching!" Allie laughed. "See ya, sis."

"See ya."

Julia had eased Cathy's mind that she was not sinking into a diagnosable mental illness. Perhaps she would begin taking Yoga with Julia. After all, she was already feeling the aches and pains of aging and she'd heard that Yoga helped alleviate muscle and joint pain, too.

As Cathy drove home, she contemplated how she would spend the rest of her day. She might try to find more information from Hagerstown, Maryland for one thing. Then she remembered. She'd left the computer open to the article about psychotic depression and had a tab open to causes of hallucinations and delusions. She was sure Allie would look at what was on the computer screen.

As Cathy drove over Route 20, stewing about what kind of questions Allie might ask and how she should answer, an Amber Alert alarm over the radio jolted Cathy from her worry. As always happened to Cathy's car radio in this area, the powerlines caused static making it difficult to hear the alert clearly. "   Ambe▒ Alert ▒▒ ▒▒▒ declare▒ ▒▒ ▒▒ ▒▒ ▒▒ parental abduc▒ ▒▒ PA. ▒▒▒▒ ▒▒▒ taken by his mother ▒▒▒ ▒▒▒. T▒▒ is ten ▒▒▒ ▒▒, four foot, ten inches tall, thin ▒▒▒, ▒▒▒ fifty-eight pounds, ▒▒▒ blonde ▒▒, blue eyes. ▒▒ ▒▒ seen wearing ▒▒ ▒▒▒▒ and ▒ overalls. ▒▒▒ia A▒▒▒▒▒ is 35 ▒▒▒ old and is ▒▒▒ as five foot, five ▒▒▒, weighs one hundred twenty pounds, with long dark ▒▒ ▒▒, ▒▒ eyes. ▒▒▒▒ ▒▒▒▒▒ ▒ driving a bl▒▒ ▒▒ey, 20▒▒ Infi▒▒▒▒, Pennsylva▒ ▒▒▒ DSH 1862. Last seen heading east on Buffalo Road ▒ ▒▒▒▒."

Cathy was nearing Harborcreek High School on Route 20 when a black Infinity whisked by and cut in front of her where the lanes merged into one. Cathy caught the license plate, DSH 1862, and as the Infinity slowed to make its right hand turn onto Depot Road, everything seemed to flow in slow motion. The woman driving and youngster in the front passenger seat turned and looked directly at her. The woman turned back to look at the road, but the boy continued staring at Cathy, his bright blue eyes, Troy's eyes, locked onto Cathy's. The Infinity sped up. Cathy accelerated and in her attempt to retrieve her phone from her handbag, knocked her purse down to the floor, emptying its contents in the process.

She continued following the Infinity south on Depot until it drove onto the eastbound ramp for I-90. Cathy pulled into the Travel Center, parking in the first space she could find. She shoved all the spilled contents of her purse back inside it, grabbed her phone, and opened her messages to read the Amber Alert to respond to it that she had seen the car in question. Seeing nothing, she refreshed her phone, but still no Alert appeared. She guessed the message was accidentally deleted when the phone fell or when she picked it up. She put the car in gear to head home. If Allie was still there, her phone would have received the Alert as well.

Cathy's heart was beating wildly as she left the Travel Center and sped onto Davison Road. She glanced at the pasture to see if her the big bay stallion was grazing. He was, as was the chestnut mare that had come over for a carrot. Cathy saw the stallion as the double of Lavinia's horse, Bruno, and she pictured Lavinia and Troy stopping their buckboard in front of their house with Virgilio coming from the barn. All of a sudden the car was vibrating and Cathy turned the wheel quickly to save herself from driving into the ditch. "Oh my God!" Cathy yelled.

Regaining her composure, Cathy slowed and noticed she was driving by the entrance to St. Margaret Cemetery just as John Mayer singing "I Will be Found" was playing on the radio. Cold shivers went through her. The song ended when she put her car in park in the garage. The lyrics echoed in her head sounding like they were being sung by a young boy. As she walked to the back door, she was compelled to look toward the Pantona Pet Cemetery where she swore she saw little blonde Troy singing at the edge of the tree line, his dog Toby standing obediently beside him, both staring at her, blue eyes wide and pleading.

Allie had intended to ease into a conversation with her mother, but as soon as she noted Cathy's agitated state, Allie blurted out, "Mom, are you all right? Did something happen?"

Troy was jumping up and down, barking, as if feeding on Cathy's nervousness. "Troy, settle down," Allie instructed, getting little to no positive response from him.

"No, no, honey, nothing happened really." Cathy ignored Troy who quit barking and followed the two women into the living room. "I just - I just heard an Amber Alert and then, all of a sudden the very car they described was right in front of me. I followed the car over Depot Road until it turned onto I-90, and I - I'm just a little shook up about it. I imagine you received the Amber Alert, too. Can I see your phone a minute so I can contact them?"

Allie frowned in concern. "Sure, Mom, but I didn't hear an Alert come in on my phone. I've had it next to me for most of the time you've been gone." Allie looked at the settings on her phone. "It looks like the sound and notifications are all right." Allie looked at her messages. Not seeing an Amber Alert, she looked up at her mother and said quietly and as calmly as she could, "Mom, there was no Amber Alert. Nothing came in on my phone."

"What?" The color drained from Cathy's face. "That's impossible! I heard the alarm and portions of the Alert. I couldn't hear the whole thing because my radio was breaking up, but I heard it! This is insane!"

"Mom, why don't you sit down. You can probably look it up online or call the State Police if you want to make sure, but if it never came in on my phone, I'm pretty confident there wasn't an Alert. If your radio had a lot of static, maybe you just heard wrong and the alarm for the Amber Alert might have just been a test of the emergency system. Let's just sit down and unwind on the couch, okay?" Allie was surprised she had to be the comforter, and was more surprised she was actually doing it. "Can I get you something to drink, Mom?"

Cathy looked at Allie and smiled fondly. "Oh, I'm all right. Thanks, dear. I'll get it," and she started to get up.

"No, really, Mom. I'm going to get myself some green ice tea. Do you want some? I want to talk to you a minute."

"Ok, sure. Thanks, honey." Cathy noticed that the laptop was closed, but it was still on the coffee table. She knew what Allie wanted to discuss.

Allie returned with two tumblers of ice tea and put them on coasters on the coffee table. "So, Mom, I, um, saw what you were looking at on the computer." Allie took her mother's hand and looked directly in her eyes. "Is everything all right with you? You're not, um, well, seeing things or anything like that, are you?"

"Oh, no, honey. I," Cathy hesitated trying to remember what she was planning to say. "I, uh, really was going to look up dream interpretation and for some reason, got sidetracked and then became interested in hallucinations and," Cathy laughed nervously. "I wondered if somehow they were related, like daydreams, whatever. And the depression thing, well, you know, I am a little depressed because you're leaving, but, I'm okay. Now that we've got Troy here." Cathy scratched Troy behind his ears.

"Well I just wondered because you seem a little shaky lately. Are you sure there's nothing more? If there is, you know you can tell me," Allie offered.

It did Cathy's heart good to see Allie being so solicitous after all the mother-daughter strain they'd both experienced through Allie's teen years. Cathy felt her eyes glisten with happy tears and hugged

Allie. "Oh, thanks honey. Everything is fine with me. Don't you worry."

"All right, Mom. But if you do get depressed, you know there's medication for that."

"I know, hon, but I'm fine. I'm fine." Cathy got up, receiving a grumble from Troy for being disturbed. Guess we better get our day going."

Cathy went upstairs and sat down on the edge of her bed and removed her phone from her pocketbook and pressed her doctor's number.

"Pine Avenue Family Practice, Erin speaking," the voice answered.

"Hello, this is Cathy Pantona. I'm one of Dr. Tidmore's patients. I'm wondering if she could call in a short term prescription for me to help me sleep a little more soundly for the next few days. Quite a bit is going on in our household lately, and this weekend is going to be quite hectic. We're going away and I always have trouble sleeping when I'm in a hotel room anyway. I just need it until Monday."

"So you just need the medication for a few days, Mrs. Pantona?"

"Yes. I'm going to be back to work on Wednesday, and, being a school bus driver, I can't be taking sleeping pills. There'd be too much of a chance I'd feel groggy in the morning."

"Yes, you're definitely right there. I'll get a note to Dr. Tidmore. If she has a problem with a short term prescription for you, we'll call you back. Now, what pharmacy do you use?"

"Giant Eagle on Buffalo Road."

"Okay. We'll get this taken care of for you."

"Thank you very much, Erin."

Since she had left the house without showering, without even washing her face, Cathy headed upstairs. She closed her bedroom door, went into the bathroom and began filling the tub for a nice soak. Julia had done such a nice job on her hair, she didn't want to ruin it in the shower. Besides, a bath would definitely be relaxing.

Allie knocked softly on the bedroom door and opened it a crack. "You okay, Mom?"

Cathy started to the door. "Oh, yes, honey. You can come in. I'm just running a bath."

"Oh, good. That'll be good for you," Allie said opening the door and stepping in. "I just wanted to tell you I'm going over to Kelsea's house."

"Okay, that's fine. Say hello to her and her folks for me, would you?"

"Oh, sure. Now, she asked me to have dinner with them, and, well, I - uh, didn't know quite what to say. I mean, I don't have to eat there. Will it bother you at all? Would you rather I stay home?"

Cathy was mortified she was causing such concern in her happy-go-lucky Allie. "Oh my gosh, Allie. No, it will not bother me. Go ahead and eat over there." Cathy came over and hugged her daughter. "I want to apologize to you if I'm acting a little off lately. Please don't worry about me. You're too young to have to fret about your mother. When I'm in my seventies or eighties, then you might have to," Cathy laughed. "Since you're eating there, I'll just pick up something simple for your father and me. You know how he loves Kentucky Fried Chicken and you hate it. I'll surprise him with that tonight."

"Okay then. Now you're sure you're okay?"

For the first time Cathy could remember, it was she who was rolling her eyes at Allie for hovering. "Yes dear. I'm sure. I'm just adjusting to empty nest syndrome and not hiding it very well. I suppose it's better than suppressing it." Cathy smiled.

"Okay, Mom." Allie kissed Cathy's cheek.

A couple of hours later, Cathy received a text that a prescription was ready for her at Giant Eagle Pharmacy. With Allie gone to Kelsea's and Paul not home from work yet, Cathy left to pick up her prescription right away without having to explain anything to anyone. Despite her morning, Cathy was still compelled to see her project through until she had some answers. Since she was out and about with a few hours left before Paul got home, Cathy headed to Blasco Library to look for a birth announcement for Troy. She grabbed a Snickers bar and poured coffee into a travel mug to tide her over until dinner.

She again pulled the reel of microfilm which contained the birth announcement for Michael and searched through October of 1856.

From the newspaper ad, Cathy knew Troy could not be more than two years younger than Michael, and if it turned out he was older, he couldn't be older by much. Not finding anything after two hours of scanning, Cathy stretched her legs and purchased a can of Coke from the vending machine and went outside to get some fresh air. She strolled toward the dock and refreshed her mind with the sights and sounds of the Bayfront--the water gently lapping against the docked boats and the seagulls calling.

Feeling renewed, she checked her watch and returned to her microfilm reader working backwards starting in January 1854 which would be nine months before Michael's birth. It was after four o'clock when she finally spied it, "Mr. and Mrs. Virgilio Anatoli of Harbour Creek, PA announce the birth of a son, March 13, 1852. The boy has been named Troy Pietro Anatoli. This is the seventh child born to Mr. and Mrs. Anatoli."

Cathy printed out the announcement and quickly texted Sharon about her find.

When Allie arrived at Kelsea's house, Kelsea greeted her at the door, exhilarated and animated. "Oh my God, Allie. Wait till you see!"

"What?" Allie asked, surprised. When they ended their phone conversation and arranged for Allie to visit, Kelsea hadn't expressed any excitement about anything.

"After we hung up, I started working on some photos." Kelsea grabbed Allie by the elbow and ushered her through the house to her makeshift office/studio. "I thought I'd surprise you with editing the photos I took with my phone when you and your mother were here the other day. I was actually only going to clean them up a little, center them better, remove glare, that kind of thing."

Kelsea just about shoved Allie in the room and Allie laughed. "Alright already! Show me. What's so all fired remarkable?"

"I left it up on the screen for you," Kelsea said walking over to the computer screen. "Look!"

Allie looked at the computer screen. "Oh my God!" she exclaimed. "What is that?"

"I'm really not sure, but it's definitely weird. Now I want you to know I haven't tampered with anything here. I just was playing with the contrast, brightness and all for clarity." Kelsea sat down at her desk. "At first I thought it was a cloud, and maybe it still could be a cloud, but it's sure strange that it's sort of encircling or emanating from the hawk."

"Yeah, and it looks like the head of a woman, with long flowing hair formed out of mist."

"Like a," Kelsea began.

"Ghost?" they both said together.

Both girls laughed and said, "Jinx," then laughed again.

"You know what else?" Kelsea asked and continued. "I looked for information about hawks and in various cultures the hawk, because of its keen vision, is associated with spiritual forces, with seeing the unseen. I think that's pretty cool--a little creepy, but cool, don't you think?"

"It sure is, maybe more creepy than cool to me," Allie said, unable to take her eyes off of the image on the screen. Allie slowly took her phone from her purse.

Take a look at these pictures I took when I went with Mom and Dad to the beach. I was going to ask you if you could fix them for me, but now . . ." She handed her phone to Kelsea.

"Wow! That's the same sort of haze or glare or whatever that is in my photo!" Kelsea said in amazement as she looked at the beach photos. "You're right, Allie. This makes it a little more on the creepy side, but still kind of cool."

Allie was more convinced now that her mother was having psychic rather than psychotic experiences.

15

ALLIE'S LAST NIGHT

After all the craziness of the day, Cathy decided to take a sleeping pill that night knowing her mind would be going non-stop trying to figure out what was happening to her. Besides, she wanted to test the medication's effectiveness, to see if she had any side effects, and to see how groggy she would be in the morning. She did fall asleep faster, but the medication did not ward off her dreams as she had hoped. However, the dreams did not flow like a movie. This evening intermittent still images appeared in her head as if she were watching a slide show presentation.

The birth announcement for Troy kept appearing in the slideshow followed by a flash of Lavinia lying on a blood-soaked bed giving birth to Troy, her daughters and a midwife assisting. The first time those images hit her subconscious, Cathy opened her eyes, disturbed, but she turned over and fell back to sleep.

The slide show would resume with an image of the midwife holding the wailing baby Troy out to Lavinia, whose arms were outstretched to receive the child. The Anatoli daughters were standing beside the bed, looking on in horror at the naked, purplish-red newborn, still having traces of vermix on him and umbilical cord still attached. The left leg of the baby was only half the length of his right and his left arm was twisted and shorter than his right.

Cathy awoke briefly again and rolled to her other side. Unfortunately, visions of Lavinia and Virgilio continued with an enraged Virgilio shouting at Lavinia while he was reaching to take

Troy from Lavinia's arms. Lavinia was cowering against the headboard holding Troy protectively. The older boys were trying to restrain their father, the daughters and midwife were looking on in horror.

Cathy awoke once again and although unrested she got out of bed. Even awake, images of the Anatolis continued to invade her thoughts. She hoped if she focused intensely on whatever she was doing during the day, she could control her thoughts. As she brushed her teeth, she concentrated on each individual tooth. While washing her face, she thoughtfully massaged it. She counted the number of steps as she walked downstairs She studied the position of the furniture in the living room, scrutinized the furniture for dust, studied the carpet deciding if she needed to vacuum, and changed anything she looked at to a chore so she would not have that minuscule time slot available for an upsetting image to pop in her head.

She took Troy out, chattering to him and taking note of any birds she heard, considered what type of bird it was, noted the cars going by, the position of the sun in the sky trying to guess the time, looking over the house for any maintenance needed, looking for weeds in the gardens, making sure Troy's poop didn't indicate he was ill. By the time she came back inside with Troy, she already felt as if she had worked hard all day long.

When Paul got downstairs, Cathy was making an elaborate breakfast of home fries, bacon, an omelet, toast, fruit cup, coffee, and juice. She set the table as if the kitchen were a restaurant. "What's all this? You know I don't usually eat a lot before work." Paul realized how ungrateful he sounded as soon as the words escaped his lips.

Cathy let his remark slide letting her cooking keep her mind occupied. "Oh, it's Allie's last day. I thought I'd try and make it special."

"Are you going to get her up to eat? You know she likes to sleep late and since this is her last day before Pittsburgh . . ."

"Oh, I know. I'm pretty sure she actually won't want much for breakfast. You know how she is. But, I'll just save some of it in a microwaveable dish and if she doesn't want it, you can have it tomorrow morning before we go. I have a feeling all she'll want is the fruit cup and some toast." Cathy started dishing out plates of food for Paul and herself.

"That sounds more like her, but this looks great to me." Paul said trying to make up for his untactful remark. "I was going to rush off to work, but since you went to all this trouble, and I have a little time, I might as well enjoy it."

Cathy turned on the news and started chattering about every report she heard.

"How much coffee have you had?" Paul said with a laugh.

"Huh? Just a couple cups, why?" Cathy asked.

"Oh, you just seem a little more energetic and talkative than usual this morning, that's all."

"Am I? Maybe. I guess it's just nervousness. Big change and all with Allie leaving."

Paul was trying not to think about his feelings. "I know, honey. Try not to dwell on it. Realize that this is great--she's pursuing her dreams, she's a great kid and all that. It happens. Kids grow up."

"I know. I'm trying, but it's hard so I'm just trying to keep myself occupied."

Troy, who had been sitting between their chairs and was not getting his proper share of attention and, most importantly, no tidbits from their breakfast, whined to inform them of his presence. Paul tore off a small piece of bacon and tossed it to him.

"Paul! That's horrible for him. Bacon's all fat and I don't want him getting sick," Cathy said crossly.

"Oh, it's not all fat and it's just a little piece. It's not going to kill him."

"He's on a special diet right now, too, remember? He's not even on regular dog food yet. We have to take it easy on his system."

Paul rolled his eyes, wiped his mouth, wadded up his napkin and put it in the middle of his empty plate. "That was good, hon. Thanks. I better get going."

"Now don't forget. I'll be making a nice dinner tonight for Allie's last night at home." Her words seemed to stick in her throat. Cathy swallowed hard. "So, please come home right after work. It'd be awful for her, and me, if you don't."

"Don't' worry, I'll be home. If the guys want to go out after work tonight, I'll just tell them I can't. It's not every day your youngest kid goes off to college." It struck Paul, too, that Allie might never live in their home again, might never even live in Erie

County again and his happy enthusiasm for the kickoff for the new advertising campaign drained from his face.

Cathy got up and went over to Paul and they hugged. Tears came to her eyes. "We'll be fine, just turning the page to a new chapter," Paul told her.

After Paul left for work, Cathy immediately picked up her phone to text Tony. "Hi, Son - Hope I caught you before you left for class."

Tony responded, "You did. At breakfast."

"Just wanted to remind you today's Allie's last day home."

"Will stop by later to wish her good luck." Tony responded. "How's it going with the Anatolis?"

"Found a few more interesting articles and have new ideas. Found birth announcement for Troy Anatoli. Have had lots of dreams about them, some things have turned out to be true! Very strange."

"Want you to tell me more when you get a chance."

"I will."

"See you tonight." Tony texted a heart to her.

Cathy sent a kiss emoji. She smiled and put her phone down, and cleaned up the kitchen. She got another cup of coffee and headed outside to do a little weeding. She retrieved her tools from the shed and got busy while letting Troy wander in the yard. Troy nosed around like a bloodhound, meandering closer and closer to the tree line behind the Pantona pet cemetery. Cathy hesitated looking, not wanting to picture young Troy Anatoli there again, but looked when she saw her Troy suddenly pounce on something. Troy galloped to Cathy depositing a filthy tennis ball in front of her.

"All right," she laughed. "I'm almost done with this little section." She tried to finish but found it impossible with Troy either helping her dig or dropping the tennis ball where she was digging.

She started playing fetch with Troy and noticed enormous, explosive-looking thunderclouds quickly moving in. Lightning flashed in the distance and eight to ten seconds later, a sharp clap of thunder scared Troy who then darted into the woods with Cathy in chase calling his name. He zoomed through the woods losing Cathy when she stopped to catch her breath. Cathy plodded along after Troy, guessing he might be heading to the Anatoli obelisk where he had become so excited the last time he was in the cemetery with her.

Close to the Anatoli family plot, she chuckled to herself seeing Troy's butt up in the air as he busied himself digging at the base of the obelisk, just as she had anticipated. Not wanting Troy to attempt to nip her again, she stood next to him, clapped loudly, and said sharply, "Hey mister! No! Leave it."

Troy looked at her, then continued digging.

"Nah-uh," she scolded, and quickly snapped on his leash. "Tch, tch, tch. You're going to get us in trouble, you little devil." Cathy quickly surveyed the area and caught just a glimpse of Luella and Grandma Anatoli entering the cemetery office. "Oh, Troy, I think they saw you. Hope they didn't see me." Cathy quickly kicked the dirt back into the hole Troy had excavated, tamped the dirt down with her foot, then hurried back home with him.

The rain started as soon as they got inside the house. It was a typical dramatic August thunderstorm that would stop soon and the whole area would turn into a sauna when the sun came out. Cathy poured herself another cup of coffee telling Troy, "You're quite a little trouble maker, you know that?"

Troy responded by looking up at her questioningly his head tilted to one side. Cathy felt a surge of love in her heart for him and chuckled. "Oh, well--come here, boy. What will be will be."

She sat down with Troy laying by her chair and began looking through the newspaper when the phone rang.

"Hi, Sharon," Cathy answered. "I can guess why you're calling. Luella and Grandma Anatoli caught Troy digging at the Anatoli monument, right?"

"Mm-hm. Where were you? They didn't say they saw you. They thought Troy was a stray and said they called Animal Enforcement. They requested we ban dogs from the cemetery grounds," Sharon laughed. "What happened? Is Troy back home with you now?"

"Yes, he's home safe and sound. Crazy dog got spooked by that loud clap of thunder and ran into the cemetery. I think there must be a rabbit nest at the base of Virgilio's obelisk that he found the other day. He didn't come when I called, and there's no way I can keep up with him, so I headed over there and found him there having a ball digging away. I'm really sorry. He didn't do any damage, though. I refilled the hole that he started. Planning to sign him up for obedience classes today. He's got a lot to learn."

"Well, it's back-to-school season," said Sharon. "At least he doesn't need school clothes, books, a computer, and all that." Both women laughed. "It's good they only saw Troy."

"Mm-hm. In this instance, I'm glad I couldn't keep up with him. What did you tell them?"

"I told them banning dogs wouldn't prevent stray dogs from entering the cemetery grounds. The only ones kept out would be those visiting the cemetery on leash with their owners, and since we haven't had any complaints about people not being responsible for their dogs while they are here, we probably wouldn't be doing that. And I said we'd watch out for the dog they described, too. Of course, from her description, I guessed it was Troy."

"And?"

"They walked out in a huff. Hope nothing comes of this."

"Me, too. I imagine, the worst that would happen would be getting fined for Troy getting loose, and, of course, I'd have to deal with Paul's reaction when he found out."

"Remember, until you get Troy fixed and a license for him, if he gets loose again and is picked up, that fine could be pretty high; so I'd watch him very closely until you get him in to see Dr. Warner," Sharon advised.

"Luckily, that's going to be Monday and Julia's going to be babysitting Master Troy until we get home Sunday. I think she'll probably be dogsitting at her house so he won't be getting into any trouble around here."

"That's good. You know, if there's ever a time you and Paul are going to be away and Julia can't watch him for one reason or another, I could always pop in and look in on him, give him a little exercise. I live near enough and, of course, I work so close to your home . . ."

"Thanks, Sharon. I'll keep that in mind. I appreciate it."

"I've been wondering, Cathy. How're things in your dream world?"

"Very active, I'm afraid. Just had a doozy again last night."

The combination of thunder and Cathy's phone ringing had awakened Allie who was eavesdropping in the doorway. "What's going on?" she asked.

"Oh, just a second, Sharon." Cathy said and looked at Allie to answer her question. "Nothing, dear. Just talking to Sharon," she responded, and then returned to her phone conversation with Sharon. "We're going to have to get together again soon and I can give you the rundown of all my nightly stories."

"Okay, Cath. I've got to get back to work. Just wanted to give you a heads-up and find out if Troy was lost."

"Thanks, Sharon. All's well over here. I've got to go, too. Got to pack a weekend bag for Paul and me, and get things organized around here. I'll give you a buzz Monday."

"Okay, Sweetie. I'm still planning to go to the library tomorrow. If I find out anything exciting, I'll text you."

"Perfect," said Cathy.

"Okay. Have a great weekend."

"Thanks, you too," Cathy responded and ended the call.

"So what happened, Mom? Did Troy get loose? Did you get fined by the dogcatcher?"

"No, no, honey. We were just talking about Troy and I told her that he had an appointment for Monday. We were saying that Animal Enforcement could fine us if they caught him off leash and it would cost more if he didn't have a license." Cathy studied Allie for signs of skepticism. "I was wondering if you'd like to take a drive to the mall today," Cathy said quickly to change the subject. "Can't do much outside until the rain stops."

"Sure. There may still be some things I might need."

"Great. After you eat and get ready, we'll go. On the way back, I want to stop by Urbaniak's to pick up some scallops if you want Coquilles St. Jacques for dinner tonight."

"You know what, Mom? Why don't we go out for dinner instead. Then you don't have to cook and there won't be a mess to clean up in the kitchen."

"That's fine with me. Where would you like to go?"

"Since we're going to be at the mall, and I kind of have a taste for seafood, how about Red Lobster?"

"Okay. Maybe Tony and Julia would want to meet us. I'll text them and your father."

"Great," said Allie with a smile. She opened the refrigerator to get something for her breakfast and saw the leftovers from the feast her mother had put together that morning. "What's all this? You must have been hungry this morning." She laughed.

"Oh, I was up early and had some extra energy so I decided to make a big breakfast today. Not sure if you want all that but there's also a fruit cup there if you want it."

"All I want right now is some juice, but I'll have the fruit cup and some toast with peanut butter in an hour or so." Allie watched her mother for any signs of irritation or disappointment, then poured herself a tumbler of orange juice.

"That's fine, honey. The leftovers will be a quick breakfast for your father tomorrow before we leave." It occurred to Cathy that she was successfully blocking the disturbing images from her consciousness and she felt herself relax a trifle. "Why don't you bring your juice upstairs. I want to finish getting you packed and put what we can in your car. When we get home after dinner tonight, we'll put all the big stuff and what's left in Dad's SUV."

Nervousness, excitement, apprehension, and the realization of just how much she would be missing and worrying about her mother hit Allie like a punch to her stomach and she spontaneously hugged Cathy and gave her a kiss on her cheek. "Sounds good, Mom," Allie said and she and Cathy headed upstairs followed by Troy.

Allie's closet was essentially the same as before, but there were fewer good dresses than were there the other night. Her paintings and drawings remained neatly stacked, which Cathy purposefully avoided remembering how shaken she had been looking at the street scene. She refused to think about it and grabbed some items to take to Allie's car. After they'd done all the packing they could, Cathy busied herself with household paperwork and other chores and Allie called her friends, watched television, and played with Troy until it was time to get themselves ready for dinner.

"Ready, Allie?" Cathy shouted upstairs as she made sure her purse was in order.

"Yeah, Mom, be right down," Allie shouted back as she quickly put on lip gloss. She tossed the tube into her small shoulder bag and hurried downstairs. "You know, I think I've got everything I need. We really don't have to go to the mall if you don't want to."

"No, I haven't gone shopping in a while. I'd like to take a look around and maybe pick up something new for myself for a change. There are plenty of back-to-school sales going on. We might find some good bargains. One place I definitely want to go is PetSmart. I want to register Troy and me for the next beginner class. I want to work on his obedience skills a little."

Allie laughed. "Yes, he's pretty good but he definitely could use a little work in the recall area."

"Yes, among other things." As soon as Cathy grabbed the car keys, Troy made a fuss making them feel guilty for leaving him behind.

"Sure going to miss Troy," Allie sad glumly. "Even though he's only been with us a week or so, I've really become attached to him."

"I understand, dear," Cathy said. "We all have."

"I just thought of something."

"Oh?"

"We're not allowed to have cats or dogs in the dorm--might not even be allowed birds, hamsters, or gerbils. But I bet I'd be allowed to have a fish or two. Maybe I could get a couple goldfish to keep me company."

"Oh, honey, really? I think you ought to see how much time you're going to have. There's still a lot of work involved in taking care of fish. You have to clean the water regularly and all that. Do you think you'll want to lug buckets of water from the shower room to your room, or take the aquarium in there? I have a feeling the other girls might not appreciate you cleaning a fish tank in their bathroom."

Allie's face twisted into disappointed resignation. "Guess you're right," she sighed. "Fish aren't quite as cuddly as a cat or dog, anyway."

Allie's mood improved as the two browsed in their favorite stores, picking up a few BOGO bargain tops and a pair of jeans. Cathy found herself a baby blue, sleeveless sundress adorned with white lace and a full skirt to wear for the family orientation program on Sunday. Cathy occasionally was distracted when something caught her attention in her peripheral vision that reminded her of Lavinia, Troy and her dreams, but for the most part she was absorbed in enjoying her time with Allie, shopping for good buys and taking a look at the winter wear already making its way onto the store racks. About forty-five minutes before they were to meet Paul and Julia, they headed to PetSmart. Cathy was pleased to see a new six-week class was starting right after Labor Day and she filled out the paperwork to sign up.

Cathy and Allie were seated and given menus at Red Lobster just before Paul and Julia walked into the restaurant. Just as the door closed, it opened again and Tony walked in carrying what was obviously a wrapped framed picture. "Hi son," Paul said, catching him out of the corner of his eye.

"That was pretty good timing," Cathy said as the hostess seated the three.

"Hi, baby sister. " Julia said giving Allie a peck on the cheek.

Tony handed Allie the wrapped package and greeted her with a hug. "Jules and I bought you a little something to keep you motivated."

"Little?" Allie laughed. "You guys are so sweet." She tore off the wrapping and discovered a matted, framed print of Vincent Van Gogh's 1889 self-portrait under non-glare acrylic. In the right hand corner of the print, just large enough and dark enough to be legible, but translucent enough not to obliterate the artwork underneath was Van Gogh's quote, *If you hear a voice within you say you cannot paint, then by all means paint, and that voice will be silenced.* "How perfect!" Allie said getting misty-eyed admiring the gift. "I'm going to hang it above my headboard."

"And if you get discouraged or frustrated, maybe want to quit, you can just talk to your old friend, Vincent, here," Julia told her.

"Of course, he did quit entirely," Allie said sadly.

"Yes he did, but he did leave a great body of work and could have done a great deal more. I think he'd advise against the path he took. And, like Vincent with his brother, Theo, you can rely on your family if you ever need a helping hand. We'll always be just a phone call away."

"Quite frankly, sis, if you start having a conversation with Vincent, you better call one of us right away, regardless," said Tony with a laugh.

"I'd say that's pretty good advice," Paul concurred and the group laughed.

"So you all set to go tomorrow?

"I think so. I'm starting to feel a little nervous all of a sudden, though."

"Oh, you'll do great, and don't forget, you've got Kelsea with you to share your freshman jitters."

"Yeah, I'm so glad we're rooming together. I can't imagine how nervous I'd be without knowing we were going to be together. It's more excitement nerves than apprehensive nerves. I just hope I can sleep tonight."

"If you can't, that's okay," Tony smirked. "It'll be good practice for when you're going to have those all-nighters studying or finishing your art projects."

"I'd suggest you try and manage your time, honey, so you don't have to pull any all-nighters," Cathy said pointedly. "Remember how you had to scramble around at the end of last year with your term paper." Cathy felt a little shiver in her back as the painting Allie did popped into her head.

"Yes, Mom. I remember," said Allie with a sour look on her face which turned into a smile. "But look, Mom, if it wasn't for me procrastinating on that project, you'd never have gotten interested in Find-A-Grave, and look how you're enjoying that."

Paul shot Allie a look. "And you think that was a good thing, do you?"

"Well, yeah. Mom enjoys it, and . . ." Allie started.

"And I think we should decide what we want to eat." Paul opened his menu.

Everyone took his lead and did the same. Above the din of the other patrons' conversations, a couple of voices could be heard more clearly. "It's not fair. When she doesn't show up like this it makes it harder for the rest of us. She's always taking off. Why do you keep her on?"

"She twisted her ankle. You can't expect her to wait tables when she can't walk."

Cathy nudged Paul and whispered, "Hear that?" Paul scowled, disgusted. Cathy scowled back and shook her head.

The first voice continued. "No, but it's always something with her. If she doesn't need the money, that's fine for her. But I do, and every time she's out, I lose money because I can't take care of my tables properly and my tips go way down. We need someone who actually wants to work around here."

"That's enough, Isabel. This is not your concern."

"The heck it's not. If you don't watch out you're going to end up losing the people who show up reliably and work."

"Sure wouldn't want to work with that girl," Allie said quietly across the table.

"Mm," Julia murmured. "I can somewhat understand how she feels. I'm filling in for Anita, but Anita made arrangements with me and the other girls beforehand. I don't mind because she's my friend, she's entitled to her vacation, and she'd do the same for me. It's not that she just doesn't show up every time you turn around. Sounds like the girl they're talking about does that quite often. When someone doesn't show up it does throw everyone into a bind so, really, it's up to management to address it. Everyone has an emergency once in a while, but when it happens a lot, it gets old for whoever you work with. Of course, we don't know the dynamics of what's happening here. It does surprise me that someone would speak up to their manager in this manner, though."

"Guess one of the waitresses are pretty sure of their job," said Cathy. "I wonder . . ."

Paul cut her off. "Oh my God, Cathy! Don't wonder. There you go again. Sticking your nose somewhere it doesn't belong."

Cathy gritted her teeth stifling the angry response she wanted to blurt out, but didn't for fear of ruining Allie's dinner. Their food arrived and the rest of the night conversation mostly centered around Allie and the new chapter of her life that would be starting Saturday.

Paul was already snoring while Cathy prepared herself for bed. She found she still felt resentful and angry for being scolded by him at dinner. She could see nothing wrong with speculating about the argument they overheard at Red Lobster and she bristled at his insinuation that she was a nosy, peevish, busybody. She got in bed carefully so as not to disturb him out of courtesy, but also to avoid arguing if he did wake up. Troy jumped up and bumped his way into her side. She turned so he could cuddle comfortably against her stomach.

Cathy's mind was a vortex of thoughts, images, and feelings of the past few days. The angry words of the waitress about her co-worker, her withheld response to Paul, her anger, the thought of Allie leaving, Troy running into the cemetery, Allie's painting, seeing Lavinia's face and other things that couldn't have been real, and all the things she'd found out about the Anatolis rolled about in her head, swirling around, overlapping and appearing one after another as if she were looking through a kaleidoscope. She finally fell asleep and was watching Troy and Toby playing in the field again as if she had restarted a movie that she had paused a long time ago. The dream started where one of her earlier dreams had ended with an angry male voice yelling, "Troy!" startling Troy and Toby in the field. She now recognized the angry man as Virgilio.

Virgilio grabbed Troy by his good arm, holding it at an awkwardly uncomfortable position above Troy's head, jerking and wrenching it, pulling him toward the house. Troy limped and lurched along, unable to keep up with his father's stride. Virgilio castigated Troy, complaining about him in his thick Italian accent as he dragged him. "Mannaggia! Piccolo bastardo![8] You come when I call you! You hide from work in the woods with that dog of yours. Both of you are worthless. The dog has work to do, too. You both lazy and good for nothing." Troy fell and cried out in pain. Toby growled and snapped at Virgilio. Virgilio kicked at Toby, but the dog was quick enough to miss the blow.

"You think you can just play all day, eh, and not have to earn your keep? Oh, I show you how you are going to pay." Virgilio never shortened his stride causing Troy to stumble all the way across the pasture to the woodshed behind the house. "Okay pigrone,[9] you know what to do," Virgilio said removing a leather strap hanging by its handle from a nail on the wall.

"No, Papa. Please. I'm sorry. I'll do better," Troy begged, tears streaming down his face.

"Quit that baby crying. You deformed but you learn to be a man. You think life is easy--all fun and games? You think you get off easy because you have problem? This is what you get if all you do is think you can have fun and games." Virgilio stood with his

---

[8] Damn! Little bastard!
[9] Lazy boy

right hand tightly holding the handle of his weapon, the left with the leather strap laying softly against his palm.

Troy slowly unbuttoned his overalls letting them fall around his ankles and bent over the wood chopping block.

"Ready?" Virgilio barked.

"Yes, sir," Troy whimpered.

"You no cry or I whip you till you stop."

Troy screamed out and cried with the first few whips, then he did all he could to remain quiet. He closed his eyes tight, trying to send his mind back to the woods playing with Toby. New welts appeared on his behind with each new strike of the strap and try as he might to stop them, the tears still escaped.

The beating stopped abruptly with the sound of a woman's voice. "Virgilio! What are you doing to that child? You stop that right now. You know our Troy is fragile."

Troy felt Lavinia's skirt brush against his bare legs and looked around to see his blood had stained the baby blue cotton of her dress. Lavinia stepped between Troy and his father.

"Woman, this is not your place. Go back inside. I must teach this one to work, to not be lazy, to be strong. This is a man's business."

"But this one can't be treated as harshly as our other boys. You know that. Leave him be."

"What good is he? Never pulls his weight. He doesn't even try. He's got to learn."

Lavinia turned from her husband. "Pull up your overalls, Troy," she instructed and buttoned one of the top straps as Troy buttoned the other. She took Troy's right hand and faced Virgilio again. "You should be ashamed of yourself, Virgilio," she scolded and walked into the house hand in hand with Troy leaving Virgilio boiling with anger.

16

DREAM SITTING

Because move-in time at Carnegie Mellon was from ten a.m. to three p.m., the Pantonas were up at six to be able to leave between eight and eight-thirty. Julia was there to pick Troy up around a quarter after seven and said a final goodbye to Allie. Troy was hesitant to leave with Julia, so Cathy walked him to Julia's car carrying Troy's care tote bag. Cathy boosted him into the back seat of Julia's Honda Accord and clicked his safety harness into the safety belt clip. When she stepped away from the car, he began pulling toward her and whining.

Julia petted him, trying to console him. "It's okay, Troy. You're going to be fine. It's just going to be a couple days and I'll make sure you have lots of fun."

Cathy offered Troy a treat which he gobbled down. "Don't worry, boy. Your Aunt Julia is going to take good care of you.," she said, giving him a hug and kiss, then closed the back passenger door. "Here, Julia, take these. I saved out a little bag of his favorite treats for you to give him on the way to your house. He'll be your best friend by the time you get there."

"I'm glad Dad dropped off the crate the other day. Troy's going to feel a lot more secure in his own little den rather than roaming around all alone in a brand new place while I'm at work. I wish I didn't have to work today, but with Anita still out . . ."

"Oh, he'll be okay, hon. You said you were going to stop in at lunch, right?"

"Yes, and my neighbor, Ruth, said she'd pop over a couple times to check on him, too."

"That's nice of her. Don't worry then. He'll be fine until you're home for the night."

"I suppose. After that, he'll be getting plenty of attention. Do you remember me telling you about Jeff?"

"Yes, I remember you said you went out with someone named Jeff once or twice."

"Well, he asked me out for tomorrow night, but since I had Troy, I told him no and he said he'd love to dogsit with me, so he's going to bring some steaks over. We'll take Troy for a walk somewhere and then probably watch a movie. When he heard I was dogsitting, he sounded more excited to see Troy than me," Julia laughed. "Apparently, he likes dogs."

Cathy laughed, too. "That's points for him."

Julia kissed and hugged her mother. "You have a good weekend and try to relax, Mom, and give me a call tonight to let me know how things are going. Tell my baby sis to give me a call later, too."

"Okay, hon. Thanks for taking care of Troy for us."

"That's no problem at all, Mom. You know I'm going to love it."

Watching Troy look at her through the back window as Julia drove away pulled at Cathy's heartstrings. She felt a horrrible sense of loss, an emptiness she didn't expect, that was unwarranted for a separation of only two days. Then, did she see it, or were her eyes merely blurry from her welled up tears? There was a hazy mistiness around Troy. 'Maybe Julia's car windows are dirty,' she thought. Cathy blinked a couple of times and the haziness was gone.

Paul, Cathy, and Allie hit the road as planned a few minutes after eight. Cathy rode with Allie to squeeze in as much mothering as possible before she had to kiss her baby goodbye in Pittsburgh.

As soon as they got on the road, Cathy busied herself looking over the orientation packet and all the other informational materials provided by Carnegie Mellon sharing advice, warnings, and points of interest from the brochures with Allie. Allie soon tired of the constant Carnegie Mellon advertisement coming from her mother and decided to change the subject. "Mom, what do you think about ESP and paranormal activity? Do you believe in that kind of stuff?"

Cathy closed the pamphlet she was looking at, surprised at the question. "I've never really looked into it in depth."

"You've got to have thought about it once in a while, though. You've seen TV shows about people investigating houses that are supposedly haunted, and books written about hauntings that were alleged to be true, so what do you think?"

"I guess, if those things do truly happen, I'm just glad they haven't happened to me. What are you getting at, hon?"

"I'm just getting back to what I saw you looking at on the computer the other day." Allie glanced at Cathy for a brief second before she turned back to the road.

Cathy's stomach did a flip-flop. "Oh, you mean when I was researching dreams?"

Allie smirked. "I mean the hallucination and delusion searches you were doing. Level with me, Mom. Are you seeing some weird stuff lately--things you know shouldn't be there, shouldn't be real?"

"Oh, honey. Sometimes I think I see something strange and then I find that I've just glanced at it too quickly to focus properly, you know, and then I give something a double take. After I look back and focus, whatever I've seen is just something normal. The searches were just things I got sidetracked into reading."

Allie knew her mother was lying and felt frustrated she was not willing to open up. "Mom, I wasn't sure if I should talk to you about this or not, but take a look at my phone--at the photos I took at the beach. Look at the strange misty glare in most of the photos."

"I remember, honey." Cathy picked up Allie's phone from the console and went to the photo gallery. "Did you ask Kelsea if she could fix the pictures?"

"I was going to, but when I got to Kelsea's house she took me into her little photo studio and showed me the photos she took when we were at Scott Hollow and the same defect was in her photos of the hawk. She said she found out that hawks are associated with spirituality and seeing the unseen. Maybe spirit photography is real and maybe these aren't simply flaws in the pictures. After all, you are pretty wrapped up in this Anatoli thing. Maybe you're connecting somehow to their spirits. Maybe you actually have ESP. Have you thought of that?"

Cathy was studying the photographs. "No, no, Allie," Cathy chuckled. "I remember how fascinating it was to think about the supernatural at your age. I had a Ouija Board and I took a couple trips to Lillydale, New York to talk to a spiritualist then. But I think ghost photography has been debunked and as for spiritualists, there may be some legitimate people out there who have some extra sensory perception, but I'm afraid I'm not one of them. Nothing like that is going on here. I think your camera's settings must have gotten messed up somehow and your photos are simply overexposed. As for Kelsea's photos, I suppose she'd know a lot more about why there was some misty blur in it, but I think you're both romanticizing about these blemished photos." Cathy put Allie's phone back in the console.

"But, Mom, you've got to admit that you're having an awful lot of freaky dreams and I know you haven't told me everything that's going on with you. At first I thought it was all in your head, but since I saw my pictures and Kelsea's, I truly think there's something strange going on and it's all tied up with you trying to find Lavinia and Troy Anatoli. Don't you think so?" Allie asked in frustration.

"Now, Allie. I'm sorry my obsession is affecting you. It's fun to wonder about these things, but you can't just jump to conclusions that are so far-fetched."

Allie sighed. "So what do you think happens to our spirits when we die? I know what religion tells us, but do you think our spirits just rise up, evaporate away from the earth? Or do they hang around here, or maybe reincarnation is what happens, or when we're dead, we're dead--the spirit dies, too?"

Cathy smiled, and snorted a small laugh. "I really don't know, dear. All I know is that one day we're all going to find out. I think the most comforting thought is that our spirits don't die, just like most religions tell us."

"Of course, then you wonder where do our spirits go--another planet in another galaxy? Are you forced to become a human again on Earth until you've reached a state of purity, or say, pure enough, or are you reincarnated into another animal, or do you go to the traditional heaven, hell, purgatory scenario?"

This time Cathy laughed out loud. "Honey, maybe you should have majored in philosophy or religion. Let's get off this topic. Death and life after death are a little too complicated for us to figure out. I'm trying to get away from my research about people who have died and their graves this weekend and you're in the prime of your life, actually the very beginning of your life as an artist. Let's focus on what's going on with you right now and your future and talk about that instead, okay?"

Allie smiled. "Yeah, I guess you're right. But, you know what? I like to think that spirits hang around us and watch over us, or sometimes just connect with us in some manner. I still feel connected with Grandma. I even feel connected to Sadie and our other pets that have passed away, and I still love them and feel that they love me. So, I don't know."

"I know, hon. It's a big mystery, but not all mysteries are meant to be solved."

As Julia drove away, she tried to get Troy's attention. "Troy - Troy," she said with excitement while awkwardly holding a treat out to him between the passenger and her driver seat. "Look, treat," she told him. She glanced in the rearview mirror to see if he was focusing on her rather than Cathy and his house but wasn't successful until the family home was out of sight. She looked in the rearview mirror again and it seemed to her Troy was looking back at her. His expression was sad, confused, and questioning. Julia promptly gave him another treat. Soon, he had his front paws on the console and was pushing at her right upper arm with his nose for another treat, looking quite content.

Julia was home with Troy by seven-thirty and took him for a walk around her neighborhood. She was not ready for his lack of leash walking skills. He was either trying to pull her along, smelling things along the way and not wanting to continue, or trying to dart off after any varmint he saw. She wasn't sure how much exercise Troy had received during their walk, but she was sure her arms had gotten a workout.

She thought she'd introduce Troy to Ruth before she left for work, so turned up Ruth's walkway. Ruth saw them and came outside. Ruth was a petite, athletic woman, just two years older than Julia and newly married. "Hi, Julia and hi to you, cutie pie!" she said, delighted with Troy who darted toward her, almost pulling Julia off her feet.

"Oh my god, Ruth. He's a wild one. I'd suggest you just let him out in my yard to play with him while I'm gone unless you want your shoulder dislocated. Maybe he was just excited, being at a new place and all, but it was an adventure walking with him," Julia laughed.

Ruth chuckled as she crouched down to get acquainted with Troy. "Thanks for the warning. I'll do that. Barry's going to be home so if I get a notion I want to take Troy for a walk, Barry can come and handle this bad boy." Ruth giggled as Troy licked her face. "His eyes are mesmerizing. I can't stop looking at them."

"I love that his eyes are two different colors, too," agreed Julia.

"I noticed him limping. Is something wrong with his leg?"

"He was limping from the time Mom found him. The vet couldn't find anything physically wrong and thinks it's a sprain or strain. No telling when it happened, so no telling how long it'll take to heal. He'll be going to see the vet again on Monday to get neutered, so Mom can ask about it again."

"Well he's very cute. It's going to be fun to play with him a little today."

"Thanks for helping me out. I'll be coming home for lunch around one, and I'll be working until four, so any time you want to look in on him, feel free. You've got my key, right?"

"Mm-hm, yes."

Julia jerked the leash a couple times. "Okay Troy, come on. You'll see Ruth a little later. I've got to get to work." Troy was still eating up the attention from Ruth so Julia produced a treat from her pocket to entice him to come with her. She turned to go to her house and waved to Ruth. "See you later and thanks again, Ruth."

Julia let Troy familiarize himself with her house for a few minutes before she confined him in his kennel. Recognizing the smell of his kennel, his toys, his bed, and his food, he had no trouble going in and settling down. Julia put on some quiet, soothing music for him and left for Trendy Tresses.

Julia's eleven o'clock customer, Marie, arrived and as Julia walked to the reception desk she noticed a slim, towhaired boy slowly wandering with a slight limp around the waiting area. Julia noted that he suffered from limb length discrepancy syndrome, wearing an orthopedic shoe on his left foot that had a four inch sole and his left arm was much shorter than his right. The boy turned from handling the magazines on an end table and looked directly at Julia. She marveled at the beauty of his bright sapphire blue eyes. She smiled at him and the boy went to the children's corner of the waiting area. She tried to figure out which client might be his mother, but her thoughts were interrupted by Marie saying, "Hi Julia. Are you ready for me?"

"Oh, yes. Hi Marie. You're just on time and I'm happy to say my schedule's on time, too. How are you doing today?"

The two women got involved in conversation while Julia also concentrated on cutting, coloring, and styling Marie's hair. With a haircut squeezed in while Marie's color was processing, Julia forgot all about the little blonde boy she saw in the waiting area until she went home to check on Troy.

Troy barked when he heard Julia at the door and when she entered, he was standing in his kennel, happy and relaxed, looking at her. His sapphire eye reminded her of the eyes of the little boy from the salon. She felt a chill and as she went to check the thermostat to see if she had set the air conditioning too low, she wondered why she hadn't seen which stylist had cut the blonde boy's hair, that is, if he had gotten a haircut; and she had missed seeing him leave, so she had no idea which customer was the boy's mother. From her chair, she had a direct line of sight to the reception area so she usually noticed who was in the salon and enjoyed seeing the clients when they left with their new do's. As she walked toward Troy, she could picture the frail blonde boy so vividly that she had to blink her eyes to assure herself he was not standing beside the kennel.

"Okay, sweetie. Time for a little fun." Julia opened the kennel door. Troy ran a quick circle around his crate, then jumped on her. "I guess you're ready," she laughed. "Did Ruthie visit you?" she asked, grabbing his favorite tennis ball and leading the way out the back door.

Hearing the commotion from Julia's yard, Ruth came over and Troy jumped on her, resulting in Julia reprimanding him. "That's okay," said Ruth as she petted Troy. "I like his exhuberant hello. I was watching for you," she said. "When I stopped by earlier, Troy was sound asleep. I expected to hear him bark like crazy when I opened the door, but he really didn't wake up until I started saying his name. Looked like he was having quite the doggie dream. His feet were moving a mile a minute."

"If he gets enough exercise now, maybe he'll sleep all afternoon." Julia smiled and threw the ball which Troy scrambled after, then brought back to her.

"Funny, I didn't expect him to be a dog that liked to sleep a lot."

"Me either. Maybe it was just too boring for him in his kennel and he's comfortable and secure in there and with the music I had on . . . but, look at him now," Julia laughed. "Doesn't seem to be anything wrong with his energy. All he needs is something to do." This time, Troy did not bring the ball back and was having a good time all by himself at the other side of the yard. The tinkling of Julia's windchimes made her think of a child's laughter.

"Just wanted you to know that I did get him out for a little bit. I'll probably pop in again mid-afternoon, if you want, just to give him a little company."

"I don't want you to feel you have to stay home all day to look in on Troy. I'm going to be done at four, so it'll only be a couple hours now. It's a beautiful day. I'm sure you might want to do something with Barry. Troy will be fine."

"Are you sure? Barry was talking about taking a ride out to the peninsula."

"Okay, then go. There aren't going to be too many great days left for the beach this year. Troy's had a heck of a lot of attention already today and all I've got left is from two to four."

"If we don't go out there, I'll stop over just to break up the day for him--and me, too," Ruth said as she started back to her house.

"Okay, Ruthie. Thanks so much and have fun whatever you do today."

After a solid forty-five minutes of romping in the yard, Troy was panting and happily tired. He ran to the water bowl by the door and lapped up some refreshment. "Okay, boy. Let's get inside. You deserve a good rest until I finish work."

Julia kenneled Troy, grabbed an apple to tide her over until dinner and hurried back to the salon. Claire, her two o'clock, was getting out of her car in the parking lot when Julia parked and the two walked in together. "I was worried I'd be late," Claire laughed."

"Frankly, I thought I might be, too," Julia smiled and started telling Claire about dogsitting for Troy. Julia held the door for Claire to enter and said hello to Nora, who greeted Claire and marked her in.

Julia grabbed one of the updo style books and brought it with her to her chair. "Now, before we get started, let's look through a few photos and you can let me know what appeals to you. Your hair is in beautiful condition and with your length, you have a lot of options."

"I have this for my hair, too," Claire said. "The florist made these haircombs for all the girls in the bridal party."

"Beautiful," Julia said admiring the haircomb adorned with small blue iris and babysbreath. "This will look beautiful against your dark hair. You're going to be the bell of the ball with the exception of the bride, of course," Julia laughed.

Around three o'clock Julia was done with her creation for Claire. She'd arranged Claire's hair in smooth cascading curls whirls looked loose but were fixed in place to remain beautiful from the wedding to the end of the reception. She left a couple of tendrils tickling Claire's temples and the comb topped off the design just below the crown of her head. Julia gave a handmirror to Claire and swirled her around for her approval.

"Perfect!" Claire exclaimed. "I love it. You do beautiful work, Julia."

Julia was proud of her achievement as well. "You're hair is wonderful to work with," she told Claire. As Julia turned her chair again, she glanced in the mirror and could have sworn she saw the reflection of the pale blonde boy staring wide-eyed and expressionless at her through the front window. When Julia broke his gaze to look at Claire, Claire's reflection looked like a different woman with the boy's face right beside her. Julia blinked hard, shook her head slightly, and the vision was gone. 'Of course, changing someone's hairstyle dramatically does change how they look,' she thought. "You wouldn't mind if I took a picture of you, would you?" Julia asked.

"Not at all. Please do. I don't often look this good," Claire laughed.

"I'll add you to our wall of fame," Julia said, referring to the area by the receptionist desk that Bonnie had set up for photos of her stylists' best work.

"Wow! I suppose that will be my five minutes of fame," Claire laughed again.

"We'll get this cape off of you and you can look over your shoulder at me. I'll get the back and a little of your profile."

"Hmm, first gig as a model," Claire smiled and posed.

Julia took a couple of pictures from different angles then checked her phone. "Hmm, a little bit of a glare from the sun off the mirror, but it actually enhances the pictures. What do you think?" She handed her phone to Claire.

"Wow. I like them. Can you send them to my phone? I want to forward my modeling debut to a couple people." Claire grinned and returned the phone to Julia.

"Sure," said Julia. "Done."

Sharon was eager to read some of the old issues of The Erie Dispatch, so made sure she arrived at the Blasco Library when it opened at nine. With the key year appearing to be 1862, Sharon started looking more closely for hints of anything that might corroborate Virgilio's story about Lavinia leaving with another man.

It was a quarter to one and Sharon had scoured the 1862 and 1863 issues and all she had come up with was advertisements for St. James School. She texted Cathy, "Have to leave library. Did find an ad for St. James School in four issues. Printed one out. Not sure if means anything. Just shows Lavinia could possibly have seen it and wanted Troy to go there. Sorry, nothing else."

Cathy responded, "That's still something. Thanks for helping out. We're just about done getting the girls set up. Then out to lunch. Things going fine. Talk to you Monday."

"One more thing, researched your property records. It once was part of the Anatoli property."

That news struck a nerve as Cathy remembered staring into Sadie's grave looking at a piece of wood darkened by varnish, soil, and moisture that Tony and Paul had uncovered."

As planned, Jeff brought over the fixings for a great steak dinner which he and Julia put together; Jeff grilling the steaks, potatoes, and corn; and Julia making a garden salad and Texas toast. After dinner, they took Troy for a long walk and had ice cream for dessert. They enjoyed a movie together with a couple glasses of wine, and by the time Jeff left, Julia was exhausted.

"Come on, Troy. Bedtime," Julia said arousing Troy from his sprawled out sleeping position in front of the coffee table. Troy opened his eyes and rolled onto his belly. Julia locked the doors, turned out the lights, and headed upstairs to her bedroom with Troy getting to his feet and following.

It took mere minutes for Julia to drift off to sleep with Troy making himself comfortable on the other side of her bed. Troy's sapphire eye loomed large in her thoughts as she released herself from the bonds of consciousness. The pupil of the large, amazingly blue eye grew even larger and pulled her forward, sucking her into it like a black hole in space. The color of the eye turned into striations of kaleidoscopic colors whirling counter-clockwise as she went through the black hole and then, there she was, invisible, observing a woman and a man who were wearing nineteenth century clothing arguing in an austere living room.

The woman shouted, "Virgilio, Troy can't work in the fields. He doesn't have the strength! He has to go to school." She was holding a newspaper in Virgilio's face, pointing at an ad. "He's smart. They'll be able to teach him to use his mind along with the abilities he has to earn a living, to be productive."

The boy Julia had seen at the salon was sitting quietly in the corner looking scared and sad. Virgilio swiftly snatched the newspaper from her hand and tossed it in the fire.

"Virgilio," she shrieked, rushing forward in an attempt to catch the paper before it reached the flames. Virgilio stopped her and shoved her to the ground. The boy rushed over to his mother.

"You and your worthless whelp. He already go to school here. I no wasta my money on any special school for him. He's justa lazy. He no wanta work. He just usa his deformity. You too stupida to see!"

Virgilio stomped over to the boy, grabbed his good arm, and pulled him to the door. He shoved him outside. "Finda your brothers in the field. They teach you to work." Virgilio slammed the door and approached the woman who still was sitting on the floor."

Julia woke up with a start, her heart beating fast, her eyes open wide, staring at the ceiling thinking about her mother's dreams about the Anatolis, and she drifted back to sleep.

17

CATHY'S PROMISE

Everything went smoothly in getting Allie set up in her dorm room. The family orientation programs ended mid-afternoon and after tearful goodbyes, Cathy and Paul were on the road around four-thirty. The farther they drove from campus, the further Cathy slipped into depression. Both Cathy and Paul did not speak to each other for quite some time.

Paul finally broke the silence. "Well, guess that's about it."

The lump in Cathy's throat felt so big she wasn't sure she could speak. "Yeah," she replied, barely above a whisper.

"Ah, hon, don't do this to yourself. Don't feel so bad." Paul put his hand on Cathy's knee. "You wouldn't want it any other way, would you?"

"I guess not. I'm just glad there's one kid still at home," she said softly.

"Don't you mean two? Both Julia and Tony are still in the Erie area anyway." Paul reminded her.

"I meant Troy. He's actually living with us. At least he'll bring some life into our household--some noise. I think what I dread the most with all the kids gone is the quiet."

"I have a feeling after a while that's something we will grow to appreciate. Plus, you and I will have time for each other--just the two of us."

"Not with your work schedule. I don't see time for each other for a long while," Cathy said without thinking.

Paul stiffened with defensiveness. "Cathy, what do you want from me. We just went through this the other day. One of the reasons I work so much has just been deposited at Carnegie Mellon."

"All right already. I'm sorry. I know. And Allie and Tony are the reason I'm working part time, too."

"Speaking of which, maybe it would be a good idea if you found something full time--share the load now that you don't have to be home for the kids anymore."

"Maybe," Cathy said half-heartedly.

"It'll be good for you, too, Cath. That way you won't be coming home to an empty house after your morning run."

"I guess, but it won't be completely empty--there'll be Troy."

"Do you really think he'll completely fill the loss you're feeling right now?" Paul glanced at Cathy. "Just look at you. You look as if you've lost all reason for living." Cathy's eyes met Paul's, the desperate sadness within her unmistakable. "Of course it's understandable. You've raised and taken care of our kids for over twenty years. But now it's a new chapter in your life--in our lives. You've got to figure out what you want to do, how to move on."

Paul's words gave her some strength. "You're right," she sighed. "And it will make it easier for us financially. Guess I'm grieving the end of an era for us. I felt bad when the kids started Kindergarten, but this is so much worse. They were so young then and came home every day."

Paul and Cathy drove in silence again while Cathy forced herself to look to the future, to think about where she might like to work full time. "I will have to wait until the end of this year, you know. They're counting on me to drive."

"You can start looking, though. It takes a while to go through an application process and get hired. And, if someone wants to hire you for good money and you think you'd like the job, as long as you give STA enough notice so they can replace you, I'm sure they'd understand."

"I suppose. I just don't want to let them down." The thought of looking for and learning another job did not appeal to Cathy. "Besides, I like what I'm doing. I like the kids, and I like the fact that I have time to myself. I really can work as much as I want if I want to sign up for trips and I'm up to a pay rate that pays more than many entry level jobs, so . . ."

"There's no harm in looking, though."

"No, probably not."

For the rest of the drive, conversation focused on safe subjects such as the scenery outside, the upcoming week, Troy's surgery on Monday, and Harborcreek High School's first day of school on Wednesday. When they were a little over an hour from home, Cathy phoned Julia to tell her they were on their way and what time they expected to be home.

"Okay, Mom," Julia replied. "I know you two are tired. Instead of running to my house first, just go home. I'll take Troy over there soon and see you when you get home." Julia gathered all of Troy's belongings and headed to her parents' house.

Troy was jubilant about being home and scampered around the yard, then sniffed everywhere to determine who and/or what had encroached upon his domain in his absence. Julia followed him around, then took out his tennis ball to play fetch with him. When Troy appeared to be tired, Julia called, "Come here, Troy. Let's go inside." He followed her in, tennis ball in his mouth.

Julia refreshed Troy's water and glanced at the clock. She had about twenty minutes until Cathy and Paul would be home. In the meantime, she thought she'd look at the newspaper while she waited. Cathy's Anatoli folder lying on the kitchen desk caught Julia's eye. When she picked it up and opened it, her eyes grew wide at the printout of the Anatoli farm produce ad that lay on top. An icy chill went through her when she recognized the three characters from her dream that night in the ad. Stunned, she walked slowly into the living room, thumbing through the other papers in the folder with Troy trailing behind her.

When Cathy and Paul walked in the back door, Julia was still absorbed in the contents of the folder while sitting on the couch in the living room. Troy lurched from his napping spot at Julia's feet to greet Cathy and Paul, barking all the way. Julia got up and hugged her parents with the folder still in her hand.

"What've you got there?" Paul asked.

"Oh, it's Mom's information about Lavinia and Troy. It was on the kitchen desk. It's pretty interesting," Julia said, then looked at Cathy. "I've got to tell you something that's very strange. I had a dream about them last night and . . ."

"Oh, not you, too," Paul shook his head, made a face of disgust and walked brusquely to the kitchen.

Julia scowled in confusion. Cathy put her hand on Julia's arm and whispered "I really do want to talk to you about it, but maybe we should talk tomorrow morning when we take Troy in to the vet."

"What's with Dad?"

"He still has misgivings about me looking into this, but there's no way I want to stop. I almost feel it's my duty to find them and somehow I feel as if they're pleading with me to help them."

"I know what you mean," Julia replied. When they looked at each other, they knew they were on the same wavelength.

"Did you have to be so pissy when Julia obviously was eager to tell me something?" Cathy asked Paul after Julia left.

"You know my opinion and I'm just sick of this. I thought we agreed. You're done with this nonsense," Paul fired back.

"Just because you call it nonsense, doesn't make it so," Cathy stormed to the front door and took a leash off the hook. "Come on Troy. Let's go for a walk," she said.

"Where do you think you're going? It'll be dark soon." Paul spoke as if he were talking to a foolish child.

Julia turned to face Paul and asked with exaggerated sarcasm, "Where does it look like I'm going? I'm taking Troy here for a walk. Is that all right with you?"

"Yes, and I can just bet where you're going to take him."

"What difference does it make where I'm going to take him? And, I really wasn't asking your permission. In case you haven't noticed, I'm not your child, I'm your wife, and I don't have to ask your permission to do a damn thing." As Cathy's voice grew louder, Troy began barking, and continued barking as Cathy's and Paul's voices escalated.

"You're certainly acting like a child--a rebellious one at that, in which case, maybe you should ask permission to do something just so you don't get yourself into trouble. Just like this so-called hobby of yours. You're being nosy, interfering, and selfish and I don't think you should be doing it."

"Selfish? How is it selfish?"

"It's selfish in that you don't care what the Anatolis think about what you're doing. You don't care what I think about it, or anyone else; and you're doing this against my wishes, wasting your time when you could be adding some funds to our paltry coffers."

"Oh, don't you worry. I'll be bringing in some extra income this year. I'll be signing up to drive for as many school trips as I can so I can bring some money home, since that's all you seem to think I'm good for."

"I didn't say that!"

"You didn't have to. You've said it in so many ways that I'm sick at heart about it. I'm not stupid, even though I'm useless to you with the exception of bringing money into this house." Cathy bent over to clip the leash she had in her hand onto Troy's collar. Troy, all hyped up from the shouting and intense emotions was jumping and barking, not wanting to stand still. When she got hold of the ring on his collar, he snarled at her. Cathy ignored him and quickly clipped his leash to his collar.

Paul closed his eyes, took a deep breath and said in a controlled voice, moving his hands in a downward motion. "Let's just drop it, okay? We're both a little overtired and overemotional right now. Let's just calm down."

Cathy gave him a dirty look. "Come on Troy," she said to the dog in a civil tone, then walked out, slamming the door behind her.

Troy began meandering about the front yard, Cathy allowing him go wherever he pleased while the fight she had with Paul played over and over in her head. Like kindling on a fire, echoes of all the times Paul had expressed his disapproval of things she did continued to fuel her anger. She was so absorbed in her thoughts, she didn't see a black BMW SUV coming down the road that slowed as it approached, then stopped opposite her.

A car horn blared, startling Cathy and causing Troy to bark and lunge at the black BMW. Cathy squinted to see who was in the car and recognized Luella Anatoli in the front passenger seat, Great Grandmother Anatoli in the back seat with two preteen boys, and a middle-aged gentleman driving, who she surmised was Gino Anatoli.

With a ferocious scowl on his face, Gino pointed at Cathy and shouted, "Your dog was digging at one of our family graves. You better keep that animal under control. If I ever see him loose in there again, he's going to get picked up by and taken to the pound or I'm going to take care of him myself. And you--you've been snooping around those graves. You just stay away from them and mind your own business."

Still fired up from arguing with Paul, Cathy yelled back, "Everyone's allowed to look at any graves they want in the cemetery. There's no law or rule against it." Cathy approached the Anatoli car, with Troy pulling and barking all the way. "And I wasn't snooping. I was simply looking at graves one day and I noticed that there is no Mrs. buried in the plot for Virgilio Anatoli. Now that you've stopped by and are making such a fuss, maybe you can satisfy my curiosity. Where is the rest of the family? Why isn't Virgiliio's wife and Troy buried with him?" Cathy stood at the side of the BMW with her one hand on her hip, Troy being held on a short lead to prevent him from jumping on the car and scratching it.

"See, you are snooping! What makes that any of your concern? You're either trying to find some dirt for blackmail or to slander the Anatoli name. We'll put a stop to that right away." Gino put the car in gear and sped off.

Cathy yelled after them, "Where are they? What did Virgilio do to them? What're you trying to hide?" Cathy glanced at the house to see Paul glaring at her through the front screen door. She turned away from him. "Come on Troy. Let's get a little exercise," she said, and haughtily walked down the street holding her head up.

At first she felt full of self-righteous anger but as her adrenalin leveled off, her anger dissipated and worry took over. How would the Anatolis attempt to prevent her from looking into the whereabouts of Lavinia and Troy? Is there anything they could do legally? And what was Paul going to say later tonight? Was her marriage starting to fall apart? Wanting to talk to someone about all of this made Cathy feel depressed and alone. Then she began to think about Allie. What was Allie up to right now? Would she take proper care of herself? Would Allie start partying and forget about her ambitions, maybe become a drug addict, maybe even die from an overdose? Would Allie stay in touch, or would she be too busy with her own life that she wouldn't have time to even call home? Perhaps she would move so far away once she graduated it would be almost impossible to see her again.

Cathy looked down at Troy limping along beside her and said, "You're the only thing holding me together right now sweet boy." He looked up at her with, what Cathy felt, was compassion and empathy.

She walked slowly, letting Troy stop to sniff as often as he wished while she let her emotions and unrealistic worries churn within her blending into one ugly concoction that made her nauseous. She wished she could purge everything from her system. Every few moments one emotion would emerge stronger than another, then that emotion would be replaced by another, over and over again, causing her to feel dizzy, until she found herself standing before the entrance to St. Margaret Cemetery.

The security lights for the office, the equipment garage, and the crematorium created small oases of light within the darkness of the cemetery grounds highlighting grave markers and creating long shadows. Pale yellow lights on the outside of mausoleums dotted the darkness. The statue of St. Margaret whose outstretched arms seemed a promise of consolation was lit brightly with five floodlights. Cathy rested on the seating wall surrounding St. Margaret and the flower garden at the statue's feet feeling embraced and comforted by a loving presence. She became aware of the stillness save for the songs of tree frogs and crickets as she admired the well-tended flowers with Troy at her feet.

Cathy looked in the direction of the Rosetti graves and her eyes rested upon the head of the angel statue peeking above the headstones catching some light from St. Margaret's floodlights. The lightstream to the angels was diffused by the moisture in the air and seemed to glitter. Compelled to follow the glow, Cathy got up and walked to the Rosetti graves. As she neared, she was delighted to see hundreds of fireflies flickering like tiny stars, further illuminating the statue and giving it the appearance of life and a hypnotic, mystical quality. The stone angel faces softened to the flesh faces of Lavinia and Troy which turned and looked directly at her. She could not look away and felt a sense of communication, an understanding within her. In her thoughts she made a promise to Lavinia and Troy that no matter what, she would not stop searching, she would find out and reveal what had happened to them so they could rest in peace. Cathy's eyes drifted down to the foot of the statue and the hyacinths appeared to be black. Her spine shivered and as her gaze left the hyacinths and focussed on the statue, it was simply cold marble again.

Cathy remained for a few minutes admiring the angel statue, its beauty enhanced by the surrounding sparkling mist and fireflies. The calmness and sense of peace that came over her confirmed the virtue of her vow. She smiled at Troy and said, "Come on, Bud. Let's go home."

Paul was holed up in his office with the door closed. To avoid another argument, Cathy did not let him know she was home and got ready for bed wondering what kind of dream she'd have that night.

It was two a.m. when Cathy woke from a sound sleep and sat straight up staring at fire that was consuming the opposite wall of their bedroom. From the center, a black dot exploded into a phantomlike figure cloaked in black whose arms and gnarly hands were reaching for her neck. Cathy screamed, jolting Paul from sleep and causing a bark explosion from Troy.

"What - What? What's wrong? Are you all right?" Paul asked frantically, wiping the sleep from his eyes.

"I'm sorry, Paul. It was just a nightmare, that's all."

"That's all? I think that's plenty. Just relax and go back to sleep, would you? I've got to go to work tomorrow." Paul punched his pillow and lay back down.

Cathy hoped that everything that had happened between them from the time they got home would be buried and forgotten under the new events of the coming day.

18

TONY'S PROJECT

When Troy barked at the alarm on Monday morning, Cathy merely mumbled for him to be quiet and feigned falling back to sleep. If she got up with Paul today, it would inevitably perpetuate the argument of the night before. He surely would not be able to avoid mentioning her confrontation with the Anatolis that he had observed from the doorway. Mondays were always bad enough without starting on an ugly note. Paul, feeling the same way, hurriedly got ready for work and left early, deciding to buy a cup of coffee on the way to the office.

As soon as Cathy heard Paul leave, she scurried around to get out of the house with Troy. She was relieved to see Julia waiting for her in Dr. Warner's parking lot when she arrived. After getting Troy checked in, Vicki took his leash to lead him away to the surgical area of the office. It pained Cathy to see Troy strain against the leash while Vicki softly urged Troy to follow.

Julia put her hand on her mother's shoulder. "Mom, he's going to be fine."

"We'll call you when the procedure's over to let you know how he's doing, Cathy," Maureen told her. "Now don't you worry. We'll take good care of him. There's nothing at all to worry about."

Julia gently took Cathy by the arm and as they turned to leave, they could hear Troy whining and his nails scratching on the tile floor while Vicki tried to guide him through the doors. Cathy forced herself not to look back at him.

"Mom, you know he'll be fine, don't you?" Julia asked as they walked to their cars.

"Yes, I guess so, but . . ."

"No buts. This is the most common procedure veterinarians perform. Dr. Warner and her team could do this in their sleep, so just forget about it until they call you later."

"I just hate to leave him when he doesn't understand what's happening and why I've left him."

"He'll forgive you. Now, where do you want to eat?"

"I'm wondering if I'll be able to eat."

"Sure you will. How about Perkins? You follow me," Julia said in the most authoritative tone she could muster.

They parked next to each other at Perkins and as soon as they joined to walk into the restaurant, Julia siad, "Let's decide what we want to eat as soon as we are seated before we start talking. I've been eager to talk to you since last night and I want you to open up to me more about what you've been experiencing lately."

Cathy had been dwelling on Troy so intensely all morning, she hadn't thought once about what Julia had wanted to tell her Sunday night. "Oh my gosh, yes! I'm sorry about last night. Your father doesn't understand."

"To tell you the truth, I don't think any of us did and we've all been worried about you--especially Allie. I talked to her last night and even her attitude has changed. She told me about the photos and all. Of course Tony was interested in this from the start, but considering he likes looking into things that are dead and gone, that's no surprise."

Cathy chuckled. "Yes, for a while he was my only ally in the family. I wish he was living with us right now, he'd be a buffer against your father's negativity about this. Of course, even if Paul was all in about me investigating the missing Anatolis, he'd never believe a word of what I'm going to tell you. He'd be sending me to a shrink right away. Sharon's been a help, though, although I haven't told her everything. So much is off the wall, I didn't want her to think I was going nuts."

"You must have felt a little isolated within the family. I think you're right about Dad. I get the impression he doesn't want to hear the name Anatoli in the house at all anymore."

"Yes, I'm afraid you're right, dear. Whatever I do about this little mystery of mine, I'm not going to tell him anything until I have my answers. And if I discover I'll never have the answers, I've avoided a lot of arguments with him in the meantime."

After they were greeted and seated, and they ordered their food they shared their stories over coffee. Once Cathy had unburdened herself of all the extraordinary occurrences in her life lately and knowing Julia believed her, she felt she could finally breathe again and was able to convince herself she was not going mad.

Julia's eyes grew wide as she listened to her mother and the hair on the back of her neck stood on end. She filled Cathy in about her weekend with Troy, her dream, and her similar visions which, had she not heard her mother's stories, would have caused her to question her own sanity, too. Although distressed for Julia, Cathy was relieved that Julia had experienced sightings of Troy and Toby.

"You know, Mom, I can't help but think that Troy's a link to all of this. Didn't everything start happening when Troy appeared from behind our pet cemetery?"

"Yes, so I'm convinced you're right, hon," Cathy broke out into goosebumps, "And I think it's odd that I just happened to think to name him Troy out of the blue like that."

"Mm-hm. I agree. Now that he's going to be anaesthetized for a while and then at Dr. Warner's all night, I wonder if you're going to be free from any unusual phenomenon."

"We'll see, won't we."

They lingered at Perkins for over two hours and when they left, Cathy did not want to go home to a quiet, empty house. Instead, she detoured to St. Margaret Cemetery to pay Sharon a visit.

"Hey, how'd it go?" Sharon asked when Cathy entered the office.

"Very well, thanks," Cathy replied with a small smile. "Of course, I'm having a little separation anxiety."

Sharon smiled, understanding. "I imagine you would. It's not easy when the youngest one leaves. But, you'll survive. We all do."

Cathy laughed out loud. "Oh my gosh, Sharon. I just dropped Troy off at the vet's to get fixed. I thought you were talking about him."

Sharon burst out laughing. "Oh boy. You are a little attached to Troy already aren't you."

"Afraid so. I realize now, more than I thought." Cathy laughed again. "Of course, I am having separation anxiety from Allie being gone, too."

"Uh-huh," Sharon replied with a big smile as she took a folder out of the bottom of her three-tiered mail tray on the corner of her desk and walked over to the counter. "Here's something to refocus your attention."

Cathy looked at the copy of the advertisement for St. James School Sharon handed her. "So, it is a distinct possibility that Lavinia did enroll Troy in St. James School and left town."

"Yes. And if it's the case she did leave with someone, maybe there's a record of some traveling salesman or itinerant worker of some sort that might have taken Lavinia and Troy with him. Maybe there's a writeup or an ad for him or whatever his business is in the paper."

"Which would, in turn, give us a new surname to check out. Of course, if they were concealing their identity, they might have changed their given names, too, but this gives us something to look into."

"Definitely. If Lavinia did run away with another man, I'm sure in those days she certainly would want to be known as that man's wife."

A large crack of thunder and flash of lightning caused Cathy and Sharon to look out the windows. "I didn't know it was going to rain today," Cathy remarked. "Of course, I didn't have the television on this morning to catch the forecast."

"I did," Sharon said. "We're supposed to have intermittent storms all day today."

"I better not keep you from your work--just wanted to say hello. Oh, before I go I also wanted to tell you something. Julia and Allie both have been experiencing some strange things, too, so they're no longer thinking I'm going off my rocker. And, I'm not thinking I am, either." Cathy briefly described Julia's and Allie's recent experiences.

Sharon laughed. "Oh good. Now all you've got to deal with are ghosts and poltergeists."

Cathy laughed out loud. "Yep, that's all--and Paul, of course. He's oblivious to all of this, so far. Oh, and the Anatolis know it was Troy and me at the gravesite. They paid me a short and sweet visit yesterday."

"At least you won't have to worry about them finding you out."

"Mm-hm. There is that." Cathy patted the counter. "I better get going. Maybe I still can miss the rain. Thanks again, Sharon. Have a good one."

Thunder was announcing an approaching storm while the sky quickly darkened. Cathy hustled inside so she could close the windows before the storm hit. The wind was whistling through the rooms, sending drapes fluttering; one of which knocked over a lamp in the living room. As Cathy darted around, the television suddenly turned on. There was no reception. The only thing on the screen was snow and the only thing coming from the speakers was static. However, through the static Cathy told herself she didn't hear an angry raspy male voice uttering syllables or possibly words that were unintelligible, and she tried not to picture the phantom-like figure of the night before. She scowled as she darted from window to window and attempted to block these impressions from her consciousness.

After closing the downstairs windows, she turned on the air conditioner and ran upstairs to take care of the bedroom windows. As soon as she got in Allie's room, the door slammed closed causing her heart to jump. It felt like the air had been sucked out of the room. The curtains were flying straight out parallel to the floor with the forceful wind. As Cathy fought her way across the room to shut the windows, Allie's closet door flung open and crashed against the wall. Cathy jumped and the top two of Allie's paintings fell forward against the front of the closet revealing Allie's street scene painting. Cathy's heart started beating stronger and faster. Her eyes became riveted on the woman and boy walking toward the store. Cathy forced herself to look away and ran to the window. In her peripheral vision she saw something black reflected in Allie's dresser mirror. When she looked directly at the mirror, nothing was reflected. Another explosion of thunder and simultaneous lightning struck right behind the Pantona Pet Cemetery which was in direct sight of Allie's back window. As Cathy closed the window, she swore she saw little blonde Troy in the brilliant flash of lightning standing at the edge of the woods behind the pet graves looking up at her. She squinted at the boy and shivered when she saw him raise his hand in greeting. She raised her hand in return, the clouds let loose of their water, and the vision disappeared. Cathy didn't know why, but she felt like crying. She sat on the side of Allie's bed, put her head in her hands, and let her tears flow.

She sat there for quite a while, just listening to the rain with her eyes closed, concentrating on her breathing to try to calm herself down. She wished she could communicate with these visions she was having. She wished they could do more to help her in her quest to learn what had happened to them and to find them. As the minutes ticked by, Cathy became more convinced that the answers were not going to be found in newspapers. She felt positive Lavinia and Troy never left the Harborcreek area. Something had happened to them here and they would be found here. Virgilio was responsible. She had no idea how long she had been sitting on Allie's bed, but the rain let up and the sun broke through the sky, glittering off the grass and leaves.

Cathy was just ready to get up when her phone rang. It was Dr. Warner's office reporting that Troy had done very well in surgery and he was coming out of his anesthesia. After a night at the hospital, Cathy could pick him up any time after six-thirty the next morning.

The house was silent again. She now was aware of the sound of her breath, her footsteps on the carpet, the sound as she swallowed, and she was aware the television was no longer on as she walked downstairs. She wondered if she was actually hearing her heart beat--she certainly could feel it. She was not sure if there would be more thunderstorms, so decided to leave the windows closed. In the meantime, the ground having been softened by the rain made it a perfect time to catch up on yardwork and weeding. Cathy changed into work clothes, gathered up her gardening tools and went outside.

As soon as she walked outdoors she felt she was escaping something. She realized she had felt a heavy pressure bearing down on her when she was inside and remembered the glimpse of something in the mirror and the raspy voice coming from the television set. This was an ominous presence in the house, not the presence of Troy and Lavinia. It was dark and foreboding--the dark reflection in the mirror, the phantom from the burning wall. She hoped once Paul came home she would not feel this way since he seemed impervious to everything going on. For now, she was comfortable being outdoors.

Carrying her weeding tools, bucket, and clippers, she remembered that she wanted to tend to her mother's grave and felt she would gather strength by paying respects to her mother and her beloved deceased pets. As she tidied up the pets' graves, sending them her love, picturing them, and missing them, she could not rid herself of the question of what lay beneath Sadie in her grave. She tried to stifle the urge to grab a shovel and start digging to answer her question.

A soft rustling at the edge of the woods, no doubt a rabbit, squirrel or chipmunk caught her attention along with a fleeting glimpse of movement. She thought of how Sadie, Suzie, and Big Sammy used to enjoy chasing the animals in the woods and how Troy did as well. How she missed Troy right now. If he were with her, she'd feel much more at ease.

She began her walk through the woods listening to the songs of the sparrows, cardinals, and robins, trying to spot the birds in the trees. She caught the bright yellow of a goldfinch out of the corner of her eye and heard the laugh-like call of a white-breasted nuthatch, one of her favorite birds to watch. It sounded quite near and she stopped to spot it. She felt a gentle touch to her free hand and guessed she brushed the leaves of the weeds lining the path.

When she reached her mother's grave, she knelt down and proceeded to clear the weeds away from her stone. "Hi, Mom. Sorry it's taken me this long to come back to take care of your place here in the cemetery. I'm sure you know what's going on, don't you?"

"I'm looking for little Troy Anatoli, his brothers and sisters, and their mother Lavinia who disappeared a long time ago. Troy and Lavinia are the ones I'm most concerned about. You know, I think they're reaching out to me to find them. But I'm frightened now because I think Virgilio Anatoli might have killed Troy and Lavinia and Virgiliio's spirit is trying to scare me so I'll stop looking for them. I know it sounds crazy but very unusual things seem to be happening around me."

Cathy heard the nuthatch calling again. "And I don't know if I'm reading into things, or if what I hear or see is real, or if I'm twisting it into something strange. I just hope that if their spirits can reach out to me, then yours can, too, and you'll give me a little bit of motherly support." Just then, a black-capped chickadee called, "Hey sweetie; Hey sweetie."

Cathy shook her head and laughed. "What's happening is truly crazy, but, you know, I'm pretty sure I'm not," she said quietly to herself.

Cathy felt productive and satisfied. She'd cleaned up her mom's gravesite, the pet cemetery, and all of her flower gardens so she'd be able to sit and enjoy them for a few days before more weeds reared their ugly heads and teased her to come yank them out. She put her tools away, washed her hands, got herself a tall glass of lemonade and sat in her favorite chair on the deck with her feet propped on the railing with her phone beside her as she admired her handiwork.

About ten minutes into her unwinding, her phone rang. She was pleased to see it was Tony calling. "Hi, son. How are things going for you today?"

"Fine, Mom. Done with classes and I'll be heading out to eat pretty soon. How is Troy doing?"

"Dr. Warner said everything went fine. I'll be picking him up tomorrow."

"Tomorrow? If everything's all right, shouldn't he be able to come home today?"

"I'd like to, and if I insisted, I know Dr. Warner would let me take him home, but she likes to be extra careful with any surgery. She said in the unlikely event a complication arises, it's best the patients stay in the hospital. Plus, it's important to keep animals as quiet as possible after a surgery and it's sometimes easier if they're kept there. So, I'd rather be safe than sorry and we'll have him back tomorrow."

"That's good. I'm glad he did okay. So what have you been up to today, Mom? Anything new about the missing Anatoli ancestors?"

Cathy filled Tony in on everything. "I've been wanting to tell you all of this but not in front of your father. I didn't want to get him all riled up."

"I've got something I've wanted to tell you, too," Tony said with some excitement. "I talked to Professor Duncan about your project and she found it very interesting. She suggested I help you out and do a paper detailing what is being done to locate their graves. Actually finding and identifying them would be icing on the cake and an excellent project for the entire class."

"Really?"

"Yes. The Forensic Science Department encourages hands on projects. Professor Duncan thought this would be a valuable experience. So, how about that, Mom? You'll have an actual forensic archaeologic investigation into this."

"That's fantastic, son, but right now I don't know what I can tell you to do and I doubt your professor wants to hear about my dreams or visions or whatever you want to call them."

"No, I think it's better that your dreams remain between us, but you won't have to worry about telling us what to do. That's Professor Duncan's job and I've got some ideas where to start. Ever since I saw that angel statue, I've been wondering if it is actually a grave marker for Lavinia and Troy. Record keeping in those days was not very good. Just because the computer doesn't show someone is buried there, doesn't necessarily mean that's so. There are techniques to determine if remains are buried somewhere. I'm not talking about getting a backhoe in there and digging it all up. Some techniques are as simple as using a physical probe. But new technology is available now--like ground penetrating radar. Of course, there are permissions to obtain and all that, but I think we should give it a try. I'm pretty stoked about this."

"That would be wonderful, Tony. As for permissions, I can give a heads-up to Sharon about your project. In addition to the families, I'm sure you'll have to talk to her and her boss, Mr. Burns, at some point."

"Great. That'll be helpful. And I want to provide some background information for writing my paper, so if you could make copies of any documents you've got, that'd be wonderful."

"That's no problem, honey. And I have another place you might want to look," Cathy told him.

"Really? Where?"

"Our back yard. Remember thinking something might be buried under Sadie's grave? Our property used to be part of the original Anatoli farm."

"Oh my gosh! Yes, definitely! I'd forgotten all about that."

"I had, too, until I was reminded when Sharon told me she'd researched our property records and what she found."

"It certainly would be something if they were found right on our property!" Tony exclaimed. "Well, I'll be over during the week to pick up the document copies and we can talk some more about everything. For obvious reasons, I'm not going to tell Dad specifically what my project's all about right now. If I want to talk to you about the Anatolis, I'll try to do it when Dad's not around."

"Thanks, son. Once we've come to some conclusion, Dad will get over it, especially when he finds out everything was done legally and under the guidance of your Professor Duncan."

"Won't he be surprised! Especially if we find the missing Anatolis." Tony chuckled. "Well, I'm going to get something to eat. I'm starved. Just wanted to let you know. Thought it might make your day."

"It certainly does, son. Thanks. Love you."

"Love you, too, Mom."

Cathy was smiling from the inside out and knew Tony was, too. In a happy daze, she went inside and took a long, hot shower. The tension and loneliness she'd been feeling seemed to wash off of her and go down the drain along with the gardening dirt.

19

RESTLESS SPIRITS

It was going on six o'clock when Paul got home. He had no intention of bringing up Sunday night's discussion unless Cathy pushed the issue. Cathy heard him pull into the driveway and met him at the door. There was a brief awkward moment when both braced for the other to restart their argument.

Cathy broke the silence. "Hi dear. Your day go all right?" then she kissed him hello.

"It went," he sighed, relieved Cathy preferred to move on. "Pretty much the usual B.S. How about you?" Paul put his briefcase next to the coffee table, his tie draped over it. "Where's our Troy?"

"Don't you remember? He's having his masculinity removed." Cathy laughed. "I thought that would be something that would strike a nerve and you'd remember."

Pat smiled as they sat down beside each other on the couch, Paul's arm over Cathy's shoulders. "There you are wrong, my dear," he said. "That's something I surely don't want to remember--or think about. Our poor boy. So, how's he doing?"

Cathy felt good hearing Paul refer to Troy as 'our Troy' and 'our boy.' "Everything went fine. I'll be picking him up tomorrow morning."

"Speaking of boys, I've seen a boy I don't recognize running around in the woods behind our house. He's a skinny little blonde kid. Do you know if a new family's moved in the neighborhood?"

Cathy's heart fluttered, sure Paul had seen Troy. "Not that I know of. But, there are some new students on my bus route.

Maybe he'll be one of them. I can't remember any houses having been sold near our house recently, though."

"Hmm. He could be visiting someone , too. I just thought he looked pretty young to be roaming around in the woods by himself. If I see him again, maybe I'll call him over and talk to him."

"If he'll come to you when you call him, that is," Cathy replied.

"Why wouldn't he?"

"He might be shy or timid. I don't know. He might think you're going to yell at him. You can try, though."

Paul turned the television set on. "You were right about one thing," Paul paused looking at Cathy and she looked back inquisitively. "It's definitely quiet with Allie gone."

Cathy was reminded about the empty house and her stomach turned. "Yes. I'll be glad to have Troy back home."

"Did you have a good breakfast with Julia?"

"Mm-hm. We had a real nice visit."

"Anything new with her?"

"Not really. She was basically babysitting me, trying to keep me from worrying, which I needed."

"Your job as a mom." Paul gave Cathy a squeeze. "And you're definitely good at it."

"What, worrying or being a mom in general?"

"Both," Paul laughed. "How about Allie or Tony? Hear from them?"

"I just talked to Tony before you came home. He's doing fine. He was wondering about Troy and just wanted to say hello. I didn't expect to hear from Allie. Judging by her orientation program, she's going to be in and out and busy all week. She'll probably call when she gets a chance. If we don't hear from her I'll text her or maybe I'll call her myself tonight."

"Doesn't look like you planned anything for dinner tonight."

"Oh, sorry. I was weeding and lost track of time." Cathy moved to stand up. "I can throw something together quick, though."

"Why don't we just go to The Fiddle Inn for dinner tonight?"

"That's fine with me. It'll break up the evening for us a little, too."

"We better get going. We'll be lucky if we find a parking spot at this hour," Paul said getting up from the couch.

As expected, the parking lot was packed and he waited to take the place being vacated by someone leaving. "Let's hope we're as lucky getting a table," Paul said.

After a minimal wait, the hostess led them to their table. "You'll notice, we have a new menu," she said. "The owner's daughter did the artwork on the outside and we've added some information about The Fiddle Inn, too. The menu items are still the same, with the exception of adding a couple of new appetizers, so you'll still find your favorites listed. LuAnn will be around in a moment to take care of you."

"How nice these new menus are," Cathy said. "Oh my, have you looked at the write-up about The Fiddle? I had no idea the building dated back to 1803. And it wasn't always The Fiddle Inn-- it used to be called the Humes Hotel. So, it actually was an inn. And the bar was called the Keystone Tavern. Hm, interesting." Cathy began picturing Virgilio coming into the bar after working in the fields, sometimes just having a couple drinks, and other times drinking himself into a stupor, getting in fights, and going home to Lavinia to give her hell after a night of drinking.

Paul was reading the write-up as well. "And look at the names of some of the visitors: Abraham Lincoln, President McKinley, Thomas Edison, Oliver Hazard Perry. I'd have never imagined they'd have stopped here, but then this was a railroad stop and it's between Erie and Buffalo, so, I guess it makes sense."

Paul's comments did not register in Cathy's head and he laughed. "And Dracula and Frankenstein stayed here on their way back to Transylvania, too."

Cathy looked up from the menu. "What?"

"What?" Paul laughed again. "I was just commenting on the rest of the write-up here. Where was your mind? You didn't hear a word I said, did you."

Cathy quickly glanced through the article. "I heard you. I was just reading, too."

"Mm-hm," Paul responded.

"And I am a little preoccupied thinking about how Troy is doing. It's going to feel strange with him not at home tonight."

Paul recognized the deflection tactic, his left eyebrow raised in skepticism. "Well, let's decide what we're going to eat before our waitress returns."

"Think I'll get the marinated strip and sweet potato fries like always," Cathy said closing her menu and looking at Paul. "How about you?"

"You're so predictable," Paul laughed, "Guess I am, too. That sounds good to me, but I think I'll have regular fries, instead," he responded. As he reached for her menu to put with his, the entire Anatoli family entered the dining room to be seated. Paul's and Gino's eyes locked.

Noting the hardening of Paul's features, Cathy asked, "What?" and turned to see what Paul was looking at and flushed with embarrassment. "Oh boy," she whispered softly under her breath.

"Yep, oh boy is right," Paul said quietly looking directly, coldly at Cathy, then whispered, "I think it's time you apologize and smooth things over with them. I'll go with you."

Cathy's back stiffened. "Apologize?" she whispered back, feeling affronted. "I have nothing to apologize for."

Paul's countenance hardened. "Come on, Cath. If you're nice to them, maybe they'll even help you. Maybe they'll answer some of your questions."

Cathy took a deep breath and tried to believe that was a possibility and stood up with Paul. Her palms were sweaty and she wiped them quickly on her napkin. Approaching the Anatolis felt like walking through a tunnel of fire with daggers being thrown at her from Gino's and Grandma Celia's eyes who stood in front of the others, an impenetrable wall, shielding Luella and the children from Paul and Cathy.

Cathy swallowed hard and extended her hand. "Um, I - uh, guess we've never introduced ourselves. I'm, uh, Cathy Pantona and this is my husband, Paul, and I do want to apologize if my interest in your ancestors is something you don't, uh, welcome, um, but I really don't mean any disrespect." She glanced quickly at Paul, hoping for an assist, but his crossed arm stance told her she was on her own. "And I'm sorry I shouted at you yesterday. I was a little out of sorts."

LuAnn, seeing Cathy and Paul talking with the Anatolis, started over to the group and was ready to ask if they all wanted to sit together, when Gino, instead of shaking Cathy's hand, bent over slightly, pointed in her face, and said angrily, "I have no idea why you are so all-fired concerned about our family history. Virgilio and his family are none of your business. And that dog of yours! I don't ever want to see him digging at those graves again. It's illegal to have dogs off leash, you know. If I see him off leash again, I'll make sure they pick him up and you'll never see him again!"

Cathy was boiling mad at his inflammatory tone but controlled her voice forcing herself not to respond in kind in the hope he might one day consider supplying her with some information. "I apologize, Mr. Anatoli, and believe me, you won't see our dog at the graves again."

"I'm warning you, Mrs. Pantona, keep your nose out of our business."

Paul uncrossed his arms and rested his hand in the middle of Cathy's back. "Don't worry, Mr. Anatoli. Cathy won't be bothering you again, will you dear."

Cathy clenched her teeth knowing she could not keep Paul's promise and said, "Again, I apologize if my interest disturbed you."

LuAnn intervened. "Come with me, please," she said to the Anatoli's. "I've got a table ready in the other dining area." The Anatolis followed LuAnn toward the back room, the children's stares lingering on Paul and Cathy as the two families separated.

On the way back to their table, her forehead scrunched in a ferocious scowl, Cathy said to Paul as they sat down, "That was a great idea."

"Now, just calm down. You apologized. You did your part and they acted like assholes. You can't say you didn't try and make peace. The ball's in their court now. Let's just order our food and forget they're even here."

The beeping of a phone timer sounded and Marci, Dr. Warner's overnight vet tech, marked the place in the text she was studying and shut off the alarm. There were nine overnight patients, including Troy, to be monitored and attended to, and Marci was thankful none of her charges that night were critically ill. She made her rounds, looking in on her patients, most of whom were resting peacefully.

Troy's kennel was the last to check and a shadow swept across the floor in front of it when Marci approached. Troy was sitting up in his kennel, his head encircled by his translucent cone of shame. Troy did not look at her when she got to his pen. He was focused on the emergency exit door. Marci looked out the small window at the top of the door and noticed, backlit by a parking lot light, a branch of the tree just beyond the door moving slightly in the breeze. 'Oh, that's it,' she thought to herself, 'That branch caused the shadow.'

"Come here, Troy," she said softly. "Let me look at you."

Troy came over to her, still a little wobbly from the anesthesia.

Marci opened the kennel door and examined him. "Hey, you're doing fine big boy," she said petting him before she closed the door again. "Tomorrow you'll get to go home and be with your mommy and daddy." Marci squinted, thinking she heard a child laughing. Troy started barking and whining. "You heard it too, didn't you Troy." Marci knew that once in a while children came around and tried to catch a glimpse of the patients at the clinic. Sometimes, a child was a family member of the pet held overnight and was so attached he/she was desperate to see that their dog or cat was okay.

Marci walked back to the office, took a flashlight out of the closet and walked outside. If she saw a youngster hanging around and they were concerned about a particular pet, she would reassure him or her that their pet was doing fine. Of course, they might think she was out to scold them and hide from her, but she had to see who might be lurking around the building.

Not finding anyone outside, Marci went back to her studies. Five to ten minutes later, she heard a soft uneven clomping on the tile floor, followed by Troy's nails clicking on the floor, the cone hitting the wall and front of the kennel, and little yips and barks from him. It was imperative that he rest after his operation, so she walked over to him and looked at his chart to see if Dr. Warner had noted what to administer if he became fidgety.

"What's the matter, boy? Can't sleep?" Marci guessed it was withdrawal from anesthesia and finding himself in unfamiliar surroundings without his family. "How about if I sit over here with you?" she asked him. She brought a chair and her book over to Troy's kennel. Troy settled down near the kennel entrance. Marci forgot about the clomping noise she'd heard until she heard it outside on the cement followed by a wailing sound. Marci wondered if the child she thought she had heard earlier might have gotten hurt in the dark when he or she hid from her. Of course, it could be caterwauling of a cat that came around attracted to the smells of the clinic. Marci returned her attention to her book.

Troy dozed off quickly and Marci, pleased her presence had relaxed him, smiled. Hearing whispering outside, she got up from her chair quietly to once again scope out the grounds around the clinic. She was ready to exit the front door when she noticed the silhouette of a woman wearing a dress that went to her ankles and an old-fashioned bonnet walking on the sidewalk away from the clinic holding the hand of a thin boy with light blonde hair who was limping beside her. Marci watched them as they melted into the darkness.

It was three in the morning when Luella Anatoli abruptly awakened from slumber. Confused about what had disturbed her, she lay still, hoping to doze off again. A damp mustiness wafted through her nostrils and she had the uneasy sense of being watched. Thinking one of the children might have entered the bedroom, she sat up to see who it was. Her heart skipped a beat when she saw a foggy vision of a woman in nineteenth century clothing staring down at her. At the same moment, she heard Nico screaming. The vision evaporated before her eyes and she ran to Nico's room.

Gino simply stirred in bed and trusted that Luella would comfort Nico from his nightmare. Luella's blood-curdling scream compelled Gino to see what was going on. He stopped abruptly and stood by Luella in the doorway to Nico's room. They stared in shocked, terrified silence, both seeing a misty female figure dressed in a blue flowered dress wearing a cream-colored bonnet tied with blue ribbon next to Nico's bed. Her left hand rested on Nico's shoulder extending the mistiness to envelop Nico in his bed. With both parents transfixed on the scene, Nico sat up abruptly and stiffly as if he were folding up at his hip joints. His eyes were wide open with only the whites showing, his irises having rolled back in his head. Nico's dark hair was replaced with a glowing blonde brilliance and his face appeared thinner and paler. Nico's right arm slowly lifted to point at Gino, energy emanating from his eyes, finger, his open mouth releasing a hissing, growling, guttural, demanding roar. The force of the energy pushed Luella and Gino backwards. Nico's bedroom door slammed shut.

"Oh my God, Gino!" Luella screamed, her hands covering her mouth. Tears spilled from her eyes. "What's going on? What's going on?" she shrieked.

Gino was just as terrified as Luella, but he mustered his strength and took her by the shoulders. "It'll be all right. Just wait right here."

"Don't go in there!" cried Luella.

Gino reached for the doorknob that was red hot and yanked his hand back after feeling its searing heat.

Suddenly, the doorknob lost its red color and the door slowly swung open. Luella held her breath, peering inside as Gino burst in. The room was still and silent. Nico appeared to be asleep. Tentatively, Luella stepped over the threshold and went to her son's side. Nico was covered in sweat but seemed to be sleeping peacefully.

Nico stirred when Luella placed her hand on his forehead to check for fever. "Mom?" he asked groggily, wiping his eyes.

"Are you feeling all right?" Luella asked, her voice shaking.

"Yes, I guess so," Nico mumbled as he struggled to open his eyes.

"We're sorry, son. Go back to sleep. We heard something and we just wanted to make sure you were all right, but everything's fine. Just go back to sleep." Luella bent over and kissed his forehead.

Luella and Gino walked back to their room, confused and terrified. Gino took a deep breath and scowled, rationalizing aloud for Luella's benefit as well as his own. "Was just an optical illusion. Maybe some heat lightning, the moonlight, and wind. We'll just get some darker drapes and a doorstop for the door. We don't need windows open in the house anyway."

Luella, however, was not convinced and found it impossible to get back to sleep. The frightening scene from Nico's room replayed over and over in her head making her tremble each time it did. She held onto Gino all night and was grateful when the alarm went off to start the day. She rousted the kids out of their beds to provide some noise and to try to forget about the evening.

20

AN UNEXPECTED ALLIANCE

No one mentioned the overnight horror show in the Anatoli household and Gino, now satisfied with his optical illusion explanation, dismissed the subject. Gino left for a meeting at Welch's in North East, and Amelia and Adam left for classes at Behrend as usual. Luella tried to put the episode out of her mind and carry on like normal, too. "While I clean up the kitchen, you two go wash your faces, brush your teeth, and change your clothes," she told Vincent and Nico. "We'll take Grandma to the cemetery together today and then finish school shopping."

The two hopped out of their chairs and began scrambling to the staircase. They stopped and faced their mother spoke again. "And when you've gotten ready, will you go get Grandma up, please?"

"Aw, ma," they groaned.

"Now go on," she instructed.

"But her breath will stink and she'll want to kiss us," whined Nico.

"Nico! Please! She's your grandmother and I won't have you being disrespectful. Shame on you. You do as I say," Luella scowled with disapproval from the kitchen doorway, her hands on her hips.

Irritated, Nico turned and walked slowly to the stairs.

About fifteen minutes later, Luella heard the boys running in the upstairs hallway toward the top of the stairs, yelling, "Mom! Mom!"

"Something's wrong, Mom!" Vincent shouted.

Luella hurried to the stairs. "What is it?" she yelled back.

"We can't wake Grandma up!" Nico screamed looking down at her.

"And it doesn't look like she's breathing," Vincent said breathlessly. Then, in a quieter, hesitant voice, he said, "She might be . . ."

"What?" Luella flew up the steps to Grandma Anatoli's room to find her dead, lying on her back, a look of horror on her face; her eyes and mouth wide open as if she were screaming.

Immediately after Paul left for work, Cathy went to pick up Troy from Dr. Warner's office. As she was making the turn to Route 20, a fire station paramedic truck was turning onto Depot Road with its siren blaring. After she turned, an ambulance speeding toward her turned onto Depot Road to follow the paramedics.

It didn't take long to fetch a happy Troy from the doctor's office and to receive instructions and pain medication for him. During the ride home, Troy clearly became frustrated with the cone on his neck. He was banging it on the car seats, windows, and doors as he traveled from one side of the back seat of the car to the other looking out of the windows. After a few minutes of this aggravation, he began barking and yelping his displeasure.

Cathy was contemplating how she would keep Troy relatively quiet as he healed from his surgery when her thoughts were interrupted by seeing a conglomeration of vehicles including a State police car, an ambulance, a fire station rescue vehicle, and a white mini-van in front of a home further south on Depot Road, which appeared to be the Anatoli residence. Curious, instead of taking the turn to go home, Cathy drove toward the house and confirmed her speculation. Two policemen were exiting the residence, followed by two men in dark suits rolling a gurney on which lay a filled body bag. Cathy slowed as she passed and Luella appeared at the door with her two young boys. Luella's and Cathy's eyes connected.

Troy began whining and barking. "Quiet Troy," Cathy demanded. Cathy's compassion and curiosity compelled her to pull off the road and park. She had no idea what she would say to

Luella to express her concern and to offer help, or what reception she would get, but Luella looked like she could use a friend right now. Cathy rolled the windows down, intending to leave Troy in the car for just a few moments, but when his whining escalated, she unhitched him from his seatbelt harness and started walking toward Luella.

One of the police officers stopped her. "Can we help you, ma'am?" he asked.

"Not really, officer. I just stopped to see if there was anything I could do. I live a few streets away," Cathy told him.

"Are you close friends with the family?" he inquired. "They might want their privacy right now."

"I - I guess I'm not exactly . . ." Cathy began and stopped when she heard Luella's distressed voice.

"It's okay, officer. She - she's one of my neighbors." Luella was hurrying toward Cathy with Nico and Vincent, who immediately started making a fuss over Troy.

Stunned by Luella's intervention, Cathy asked, "Are you okay, Luella? Can I help you with anything?"

"Just - I just need to talk to someone - to you, that's all. I'm really shook up. Can you come in for a second?"

"Yes, of course. But we might want to stay outside since I've got him with me," Cathy said looking down at Troy.

"Oh, that's okay. He's fine. I just need to talk to you-- especially you." Luella held out her hand. "Please."

In her peripheral vision, Cathy saw the gurney disappear in the back of the white van. "Sure. I'm glad to be here for you." One of the dark-suited men closed the van's back door, took his place on the passenger seat of the van and the other man entered the driver's side. As Luella led Cathy to the house, the van and the other vehicles drove away.

Through chokes and attempts to stifle her tears, Luella said, "Celia died last night. The paramedics said it was a heart attack. We had no idea she had a problem with her heart but, of course, she was getting on in years, and then last night..."

Cathy looked inquisitively at Luella.

"Last night was really strange. Frightening, in fact. I need to tell someone about it and I know Gino will never acknowledge the reality of what happened, even though he was right there! He saw it, too!"

Cathy's face scrunched, wondering what Luella was about to tell her. Then it occurred to her that she hadn't seen Gino. "Where is Gino, by the way? Is he home? Maybe right now wouldn't be the best time for us to talk."

"No, it's fine. Gino is at an important meeting regarding his contract with Welch's right now. He knows what happened to his grandmother, though. I phoned over there and let him know." Luella sniffed and wiped some tears away. "There was nothing he could have done anyway. She was gone. So I told him I'd take care of everything. And I have. So, don't worry. He won't be home for a little while now." Luella opened the front door and let Cathy and Troy in.

As soon as Cathy entered, she began having flashes of the original home as she had seen it in her dreams. Of course, the modern accouterments disguised the room, but she could see the original footprint of the space. She could picture where walls between living and bedrooms had been knocked down to make the living room larger. She could see how the staircase had been added to access the new second floor, and how the kitchen remained in the same spot it had been when Lavinia lived there. The only difference today was that walls had been removed to create a clear sightline to the kitchen. Cathy's heart sped up as she saw Lavinia looking out at her from over the counter that separated the living area from the kitchen. Cathy blinked several times trying to clear her vision.

Troy was whining and crying at Cathy's side. All of a sudden, he let out a low, long howl that ended with barks as if he were trying to say something. He charged to the kitchen tearing the leash from her hand. "Oh my gosh! I'm sorry," Cathy said as she chased after him. "Troy! Troy!" Nico and Vincent giggled and ran to the kitchen as well.

"What did you call him?" gasped Luella.

Cathy looked quickly at Luella and grimaced. "Um, yes, Troy is his name, but I actually named him before I even knew about Troy. Really! But that's another story."

Cathy managed to get ahold of Troy's leash. He was barking frantically in the kitchen, pulling against the leash and looking toward the sink. Cathy looked back at Luella again, while doing her best to try and calm Troy. "You know, Luella. I think it might be better if we sit outside."

"Yes, maybe you're right." Luella led Cathy and Troy through the back door to the flagstone paved backyard patio. The boys began following. "Now, you two go and play, but stay where I can see you."

"Can't we play with the dog while you talk?" asked Nico who looked from his mother to Cathy.

"I'd love to let you play with him, kids," Cathy told them, "but I just picked him up from the doctor's. He had an operation and isn't allowed to play for a while. That's why he's got the cone on his head."

"So you two just go on and find something to do for a few minutes, please. I won't be long," Luella instructed. Troy made a failed move to follow the boys to the open area of the back yard.

"You know, ever since I first saw you in the cemetery I've felt a connection to you," Luella told Cathy.

"Maybe that's because of my daughter, Julia. I believe she's your hair stylist," Cathy said.

"Oh my gosh. What a small world," Luella said studying Cathy's face. "I can see the resemblance. Your daughter's a dear. You've done a great job raising her."

Cathy beamed. "We're very proud of our children."

"I'm so glad you were driving by and decided to stop. I was at my wits end with, well, you know, and then with Gino not being here. And I want you to know I'm sorry he was so nasty to you when we passed you in the car and the other day at The Fiddle Inn. He's such a private man."

"That's okay, hon. I wasn't very nice to him when I first saw him either. That was a bad day for me."

Luella shook her head. "He's so proud and protective of his family and family name. When someone asks questions, he considers it prying. It might be hard to believe, but even I have only hints of what some of his ancestors were like and what happened to them. I've heard rumblings and rumors about Lavinia and Troy going missing a long time ago, and that's about it. I don't know the whole story." Luella looked questioningly in Cathy's eyes. "Gino and his grandmother have always been pretty closed-mouthed about the affairs of the Anatoli family."

"I truly wasn't meaning any disrespect to anyone. It started out as mere curiosity, but it's become something much more than that." Cathy looked directly into Luella's eyes that were shiny from tears.

Luella stared back hoping for an open mind to listen, to believe, and to not think she was crazy. "When Grandma and I came home from the cemetery the day I saw you, she immediately told Gino. She said she needed to talk to him. I knew they didn't want me to be part of their conversation. They came out here but I still could hear them through the open kitchen window. I heard them mentioning Troy and Lavinia. Something ugly must have happened that they know about and they obviously want to keep buried. It couldn't be simply a disappearance or it wouldn't be such a secret. And if they know about it, there must be other family members that know about it, too." Luella paused and shook her head. "I can't help thinking Grandma's death last night has something to do with Troy and Lavinia. I don't know how, but what happened last night wasn't a natural event. It was awful and Gino saw it with his own eyes, but he's denying it and making excuses. But it happened. It really did. It was real, and I'm not positive it had anything to do with Grandma's passing, but it could have, I don't know. I don't know." Luella started sobbing.

"What happened, Luella? Tell me. I'll believe you. I'll try to help you," Cathy said taking both of Luella's hands in hers.

Cathy felt as if she had been standing beside Luella and Gino the previous night as Luella described in graphic detail her horrific experience. "Oh my God! You poor dear." Cathy put her arms around Luella and held her. She contemplated whether she should share her own unbelievable experiences but decided it might frighten Luella even more. This was not the time. "I do believe you, Luella, and I'm sure it is about Troy and Lavinia. I've been going through some crazy things myself lately, but you've got enough to deal with right now. When things calm down for you, I will share everything with you, and I definitely believe you. What I will tell you is that I've come to the conclusion that Troy and Lavinia are wanting to be found and they want what happened to them to be known. They want to be laid to rest properly with their family and for some reason, I've been elected to help them and you've been recruited to help."

"But I'm scared--terrified! I wonder if these," Luella paused, feeling silly to be believing it herself, "ghosts are responsible for Grandma's death, and if they are, we're all in danger."

"I don't think so, Luella."

"But what about Nico and . . ."

"Nico's okay, isn't he? You, Gino, and your other children are fine. I think we just have to find Lavinia and Troy and everything will get back to normal."

"I will do all I can to help," Luella said. "I'm not sure how much Gino actually knows about what happened so long ago, or if I can get him to open up to me, but I'm going to try. If not, there'll be quite a few relatives here for Celia's funeral. Someone's got to know something."

"I'll give you my phone number, Luella," Cathy said, getting a pen and piece of paper from her purse. "I think we really need to work together on this. Please call me anytime, even if it's just to talk. I want to tell you all I've found out so we can put our heads together. So please call me."

Cathy got up. "I'd better go before Gino gets home. If he finds me here, it might complicate things all the more, plus I've got to get my Troy home to rest. Take care Luella. Remember, I'm just a phone call away."

Luella walked with Cathy and Troy to their car and watched them disappear down Depot Road, the slip of paper with Cathy's phone number in her hand.

21

VINCENT AND NICO

When Cathy left, Vincent and Nico ran to their mother who was slowly walking back to their house.

"Who was that lady?" asked Nico.

"Just one of our neighbors, honey," Luella replied, smoothing her hand over his shiny dark hair.

"What did she want?" Nico asked.

"Wasn't she the lady Daddy yelled at?" Vincent added.

"Yeah," Nico spoke up. "We saw her at the restaurant, too. Daddy doesn't like her."

"Why did she come here, Mom?" Vincent prodded.

"She was just concerned, boys. She saw the ambulance and police cars, so she wanted to see if she could help us."

"Why doesn't Daddy like her?" Nico asked.

"Your Daddy was mad at her because her dog got loose and was digging at your great-great grandpa's grave. Since Grandma died, Daddy might get mad pretty easy for a while. I don't think he'll like it if he knows she was here. You don't want Daddy to be mad and in a bad mood, do you?" Luella asked them..

Both boys shook their heads and said, "No."

"Okay, then, let's not tell Daddy about her visit until he's not mad at her anymore, all right?"

"Okay, Mommy. We won't tell him," Vincent said, then looked at his brother, "Will we Nico."

Nico shook his head rapidly side-to-side.

"Now, Daddy will probably be home any minute, so you two can stay out and play, but stay close to the house. We'll probably be going somewhere soon."

The kids ran off to the backyard again and Luella continued into the house. She sank into the couch, looked at Cathy's note and then closed her eyes, letting her head ease into the soft back pillow of the couch. She could picture Celia's terror-filled death mask and wondered if she had seen something that had frightened her to death and, if so, what she had seen.

Cathy felt a buzzing in her head after talking to Luella. She was stunned and shaken by Luella's story, but also excited that Luella was joining the alliance to find Lavinia and Troy. Not only would Luella be in a position to ask questions of pertinent people, but she could be instrumental in getting permission for Tony to do some investigating in the cemetery. Cathy was feeling more optimistic than ever.

As soon as she got home and got Troy settled in his crate, she phoned Tony. "Hi son. Do you have a minute?"

"I'm just going into class, but I can talk for a second. What's up?"

"I've got some important news. Grandma Anatoli, Celia, died last night."

"Wow, I'm sorry to hear that. How did you find out?"

"I saw the EMT and police vehicles at the house on the way home from picking Troy up from the vet's and I stopped to find out if there was anything I could do to help."

"Mom! Why'd you do that for god's sake! They're not exactly your best buddies."

"I know but I saw Luella at the door and she looked so lost. She saw me going by and she looked right at me. She seemed to be pleading for me to stop, so I had to, and I'm glad I did. We had quite a conversation."

"You did? I can't imagine Mr. Anatoli being very welcoming."

"He wasn't home. No one realized Celia was dead until he was already at a meeting this morning so I didn't see him at all."

"That's good."

"That's for sure. You know, I didn't even think about him when I pulled in, Luella looked so desperate."

"So, Grandma Anatoli died in her sleep? Do you know if she'd been ill?"

"I don't think so. I guess she was doing fine for her age. Luella said it was a heart attack, but she hadn't had a history of heart problems. I guess some people tolerate pain much better than others and never know they're having problems. Celia seemed to be a tough lady. Maybe she never acknowledged having any symptoms. As far as I know, they're not going to probe any further. Luella didn't mention an autopsy, although, who knows what Gino might want to do."

"Hmm, I would think not if the EMT's said it was a heart attack," Tony said. "I guess, we might have to postpone our investigation of the Rosetti angel a little until Celia's laid to rest. Do you have any idea when the funeral will take place?"

"No. Luella had enough on her mind, so I didn't ask. She had a terribly frightening night. She saw a vision of Lavinia and she thought her son Nico became possessed by Troy's spirit. Luella felt as if she was going crazy just like I'd felt. So she wants to end this as soon as possible and will try and get some information from Gino and any relatives that come here for the funeral. She's bound and determined to help us find Lavinia and Troy."

"That's fantastic, Mom. Just don't get carried away with and rely on this paranormal and ESP stuff. I believe in intuition, and I believe there are things that science can't explain, but you've got to keep your feet on the ground, okay?"

Cathy had to smile seeing some of Paul's influence in Tony's remark. "I know, son. It's just hard not to try to read into these things."

"I guess since I haven't had a visit yet from Lavinia, Troy, or, heaven forbid, Virgilio, I can't relate completely with what you've experienced. So many things are so coincidental it's hard to deny there's a paranormal element to all of this. So, I'm going to keep an open mind and believe you're seeing what you're seeing and will see this thing through with you."

"You're a good boy, son."

"I do try, Mom," Tony chuckled. "Got to go. Class is ready to start. Thanks for calling me. I'm more intrigued now than ever. I'll let you know how things are going on my end."

"Great, son. I love you."

"Love you, too."

After ending their conversation, Cathy got the laptop out. Although she felt certain Lavinia and Troy died and were buried in Harborcreek, she wanted to put to rest the nagging notion that they traveled to Hagerstown, Maryland in 1862 and their lives had

217

ended there. To pursue this line of inquiry, Cathy logged in on Find-A-Grave and began a discussion on the forum about cemeteries in Frederick County, Maryland.

A few hours later, her question remained unanswered. She could not discard the possibility that Lavinia and Troy were buried in Maryland after reading that some Union and Confederate soldiers were buried en masse in trenches during the Civil War and to this day many bodies remained unidentified, perhaps likely never to be identified. Some trenches were found from the battles of Antietam, South Mountain, Monocacy, and other points in Washington and Frederick Counties where Lavinia and Troy could have been civilian casualties. Many bodies were exhumed from their trench graves followed by attempts to identify the remains, but all were not. The exhumed bodies were reburied in cemeteries, some with markers, many not. In two cemeteries alone, Antietam National Cemetery and Washington Confederate Cemetery, which is part of Rose Hill Cemetery in Cumberland, Maryland, she read that the bodies of 2,481 people are resting, still unidentified. Cathy sighed. If no trace of Lavinia and Troy was found around Harborcreek, she may have to accept the fact that they very likely may be among the unknown in Maryland.

Luella was still sitting on the couch when Gino arrived home. When he entered, she got up and they greeted each other with an embrace.

"I'm so sorry, dear," Luella told him, becoming teary again.

Gino squeezed her, then broke their embrace and walked to his favorite chair, perching on the edge of the seat, his elbows on his knees, hands clasped. "Guess we better get to the funeral home and take care of everything. Have you called anyone yet?"

"No. The paramedics and everybody just left a few minutes ago."

Gino stood up and raised his voice, "For God's sake? How long did they stay? You called me almost two hours ago. You, at least, called the kids, didn't you?"

Luella cringed. "No, I'm sorry. I'll call them now. There's nothing they could have done anyway." Luella sprung up from the couch to get her phone that was laying on the dining room table.

"How about the funeral parlor? They know we'll be over this morning, don't they?" He asked accusingly.

"Yes, dear," Luella said, as she called Amelia.

Gino was pacing back and forth in the living room. When he noticed Nico and Vincent running around outside, he opened the front door and shouted, "Nico, Vincent, get in here."

Gino stood in the entryway holding the door waiting for them. The kids came tearing around the corner. "Go get yourselves cleaned up. We're going out in a few minutes."

"Amelia wants to know if she should come home to watch the boys," Luella said to Gino.

"No. They can come with us. We're not spending money on college and having her miss class."

As soon as Luella got off the phone, Gino told her, "I'm ready. I want to get this taken care of. Go throw on something decent and bring the clothes Mom wanted to be buried in."

Luella hustled and the family was out of the house in fifteen minutes. "Where are we going?" Nico asked.

"To the funeral parlor," Gino told him, taking Celia's lacey black dress and the bag of clothing accessories from Luella then motioning the boys to get in the back seat. As he hung the dress on the coat hook and put the bag on the back seat, he added, "And the both of you better behave and be quiet while we're there." The two boys looked at each other quizzically, but sensed Gino's tension and asked no further questions. All four were silent for the ride to the Abiding Faith Funeral Home and Crematorium.

When they arrived, there were only two cars in the parking lot. Gino took Celia's burial clothes from the back. "Okay, boys, out. Take your mother's hand."

Luella held Nico's hand on her right and Vincent on her left and followed Gino who forged ahead, his long stride bringing him to the door much sooner than Luella and the boys. Gino held the door for his family to enter and a slightly overweight gentleman with thinning hair, wire-rimmed glasses, and clothed in a dark suit met them at the door. "Mr. and Mrs. Anatoli?" he asked.

"Yes," Gino replied accepting the hand extended to him. "I'm Gino and this is my wife Luella and two of my sons, Nico and Vincent."

"Robert Faith. Pleased to meet all of you and I'm very sorry for your loss," Mr. Faith said, taking Luella's hand, looking the boys in the eyes and acknowledging them with a nod. "I assure you we will help you through this difficult time and make it as easy as possible for you."

"Thank you," Luella said enjoying a faint hint of nutmeg and vanilla fragrance in the air. The bright atmosphere uplifted her spirits somewhat. The walls were divided in half by a chair rail; painted antique white on the bottom and wallpapered on the upper half in a pattern of blue forget-me-not flowers against an antique white background.

Mr. Faith reached for the black garment and bag in Gino's hands. "I take it these are Celia's burial clothes?"

"Yes," Gino replied.

"That's excellent. If you'll come with me to my office, we can get started." Mr. Faith stood slightly behind Gino and Luella guiding them to the right.

The boys were looking over the formal furnishings and decorations. The furniture was both heavy and substantial and at the same time feminine with graceful carvings in the wood. Nico traced his finger around the rounded swirl carved in the end of an especially ornate Edwardian armchair that he was leaning against. The chair was upholstered in a predominantly blue tapestry which matched the blue of the thickly padded plush blue carpeting. In addition to the antique pieces, comfortable cushioned traditional chairs and couches dotted the reception area and down the hall between doorways. An entrance to an office was on the right side of the reception area and a wide circular staircase was on the left.

Gino turned to see Vincent and Nico gawking down the hall and up the staircase. "Boys!" They turned their heads quickly and caught up to the grownups.

Mr. Faith's office was furnished with more modern and comfortable furniture. A sleek white credenza sat against the right wall with a large, colorful skyscape centered over it, a salt lamp and some sleek modern decorations sat on top of it. A window allowed a view of a colorful garden sitting area that was complete with a small waterfall, pond, and ducks. "You'll notice how bright my office is. All of our visitation rooms have windows to let in natural light like this."

"Yes, we've attended funerals here before and appreciate that feature of your funeral home," Gino said.

"I agree, and your gardens are lovely," Luella said.

"Thank you. Please, have a seat." There were three chairs facing the window in front of an unusual white polished desk that looked more like a table shaped in a half-moon. A folder and a shallow drawer marked the spot where Mr. Faith sat down.

"Boys," Gino said firmly, pointing to a couch by the door. "Sit there while we talk with Mr. Faith."

Nico and Vincent dutifully hopped up on the couch, Vincent sitting on the side closest to the door. Because of the depth of the seat cushion, the bottom of Nico's shoes were visible as his legs lay straight out on the couch. Vincent, in an effort to show how much bigger he was than Nico, slouched on the sofa so the back of his knees were on the edge of the seat and his legs could bend down.

"Sit up straight, Vincent," Gino scolded.

Vincent scooted forward and sat as straight as he could, refusing to sit back in the chair.

"As you're aware, Celia had made prearrangements," Mr. Faith began, "So we merely have to go over her wishes and take care of notices, and for you to pick out various items such as thank you cards, etc."

Gino reached in the inside pocket of his jacket and took out a thick white business-size envelope. "Yes. I've brought our copies of her plans. There are a few enhancements I'd like to make."

"Certainly. We'll go over everything together and I'll show you various options."

As Vincent and Nico quietly sat on the couch they tried to amuse themselves by looking out the window and around the room. The salt lamp caught their attention a moment, then a metal sculpture of a bird flying over a dazzling crystal orb, and a twisted metal sculpture of an infinity symbol that seemed to change slightly depending on the way one looked at it. There was a small water wall which supplied a soothing trickling water noise one craved when looking out the window at the outside waterfall, which captured the boy's attention for a little while. But, after several minutes of sitting still, boredom set in. Vincent gently elbowed Nico and motioned with his head to the door. Vincent took Nico's hand and the two slipped silently off the sofa while the grownups were immersed in discussions about Celia's funeral.

In the reception area the two stopped and stared down the hall then up the staircase deciding which way to go. Vincent started toward the staircase, but Nico tugged at Vincent's arm. "No," he whispered.

Vincent made a face of disappointment, but, because he wanted a willing partner to his mischief, whispered, "Come on," to his brother and they started down the hall.

Antique brass plaques were affixed to the wall to the right of each doorway indicating the room number. Each plaque had grooves under the room number to allow insertion of a name. They stared in the first two empty rooms opposite each other. The room on the east was brightened by the sun entering through a long arching cut glass window high on the wall. On the floor centered below the window was a white platform carved ornately with grapevines across the top and angels at the corners reaching up for grapes on the vines. As it was still morning, the empty room on the west side of the hall was dimmer. Otherwise, it was a mirror image of the first room.

The boys crept farther down the hallway. Vincent noticed a name inserted in the brass plate of the third room on the east side. "There's someone in there," he whispered to Nico.

The scent of flowers was drifting down the hall. The boys could see chairs and end tables with flower arrangements coming into view. The light streaming in cast a sparkly pattern on the carpet. As they crept closer, they saw an abundance of large floral displays. The corner of a shiny mahogany casket with gold handles and ornamentation came into view. The tufted interior of the casket revealed itself, then a bump in the blanket could be seen indicating where the gentleman's feet were. Finally the boys were in the doorway staring straight into the room, the full open casket sitting atop the white platform flanked by large colorful flower arrangements. The heady sweet smell of lilies filled the room. They noticed an easel displaying pictures of the man who lay in the casket in life on the far left side of the flower arrangements, and a computer monitor sat on a table on the right. Vincent's and Nico's eyes were transfixed on the elderly gentleman who seemed to be sleeping peacefully in his plush, cream-colored bed.

"Is he dead?" Nico whispered.

"Yes, Nico. Ssh." Vincent replied as the two walked closer.

"He looks happier than Gradma. Wasn't he scared to die like she was?"

"I don't know," Vincent replied with a bit of impatience.

"Maybe he's not really dead. What if they bury him and he's not dead?" Nico asked in horror.

"No, Nico. He's dead. Now, ssh."

Maybe we should check." Nico tore his hand from Vincent and made a bee-line to the casket.

Vincent dashed after him. "Nico, stop," he whispered loudly.

It was too late. Nico was on the kneeler standing on his tiptoes reaching out to the body. He touched the man's face and arm, then backed off of the kneeler. He looked at Vincent wide-eyed. "He's not real, Vinny! He's made of wood or something!"

Vincent scowled. "Of course he's real. Come on, Nico. We've got to get out of here."

They both turned to hurry out, but Nico stopped abruptly, staring at the doorway. "Nico, hurry up before they know we're gone," Vincent urged and reached for Nico's hand.

Nico's face drained of color and he pointed at the doorway. "It's Grandma, Vincent!"

"What are you talking about? Come on!"

Nico continued staring, unable to speak, unable to move. Just outside the doorway in a sparkly mist he saw Grandma Celia hand two purple hyacinths to a small blonde boy and a woman wearing a long blue flowered dress.

Vincent grabbed Nico's hand and jerked him from his stupor. The two ran back to the reception area where they caught their breath. The grownups, still engrossed in their papers and conversation, didn't notice the boys silently reenter and slip back onto the couch.

As they left the funeral parlor, once again, rather than walking beside his family to the car, Gino took long strides and got there well before Luella, Vincent, and Nico who were barely out of the building.

Nico hesitated and tugged at his mother's hand as the door to the funeral home closed. "Mommy, is Grandma really dead?"

Taken aback by his question, Luella stopped. "Yes, honey," she assured him in a sympathetic voice. "She is. But she's waiting for us in heaven."

"Nico!" Vincent reprimanded.

"But I saw her, Mommy," Nico insisted.

"Now, Nico. You shouldn't fib," Luella said and started walking again.

"But I'm not, Mommy. I'm not! I saw her at the funeral home."

"Tch, tch, tch, Nico. You know that's not true. You were sitting in the room the whole time. Did you fall asleep and dream about her?"

"No, I was awake. I . . ."

"No, Nico," Vincent warned Nico again.

Luella looked suspiciously at Vincent. "What do you know about this, Vincent?"

Before Vincent could answer, Nico said, "I saw her in the hall. She was handing flowers to a lady in a blue dress and a blonde boy."

Luella gasped and stopped to stare at Nico with frightened eyes. "Well, honey," she said haltingly, "Maybe she wanted you to know she's going to have friends and will be all right in heaven so she let you see her."

"Do you know who her friend and the little boy are, Mommy?"

"Not for sure, dear, but they could be relatives."

Gino had the car running waiting for them. He honked and motioned for them to hurry up.

The threesome began walking again. "Now, honey," Luella said to Nico. "Let's keep your seeing Grandma just between you, me, and Vincent. Daddy and our relatives that will be here for the funeral will feel bad that they didn't see her, too, and all of them will be sad already."

"Maybe it will make them happy if I tell them," Nico reasoned.

"No, honey. I know they won't and Daddy will get mad."

"Okay, Mommy. But if I see her again, can I tell you?"

Luella put her hand on the car door handle to let the boys in the car. "Yes, dear. You tell me if you see her again."

"What in the hell were you doing dawdling like that?" Gino barked at Luella. "I don't have all day. My morning's shot with the meeting and all this. The three of you, get in."

22

THE HAWK

It was difficult for Cathy to avoid telling Paul about the death of Celia Anatoli and about her newfound friendship with Luella, but she managed to keep these newsy items to herself. To avoid the subject, she talked about anything and everything else. She phoned Alexandra, then busied herself around the house until Paul fell asleep on the couch. After watching a little television, Cathy woke Paul and they went to bed.

Having suppressed what was at the front of her mind all day, Cathy knew her thoughts would present themselves in her dreams, and she was right. When she dozed off, the memory of walking up to and entering Luella's house began to scroll in slow-motion through her head along with bits and pieces of her conversation with Luella ringing in her ears. Suddenly, the memories stopped and Cathy was watching a drama unfold in the Anatoli kitchen.

"You whore!," Virgilio screamed in Lavinia's face, his right hand clutched some papers and his left hand was clenched so hard over her head it was white as if the blood had been squeezed out of it.

Lavinia was bending backwards, one arm in the air and the other bent over her face to protect herself from Virgilio's hammer-like fist. "No!" she screamed. "It wasn't your money, it was a gift from my family!"

The dog, Toby, barked viciously and lunged at Virgilio. Virgilio turned and kicked the dog violently, then backhanded Luella, who cracked her head on the coal-burning stove. Her head was bleeding profusely and little Troy screeched like a wild animal charging his father, his tiny fists pummeling him. Virgilio grabbed Troy wrapping both of his large hands around Troy's neck, squeezing, squeezing, lifting the small, frail boy who was kicking and struggling, off of the ground, until Troy's skin had a cast of blue, his blood vessels burst in his eyes, and his body finally hung limp like an under-stuffed ragdoll in his father's muscular, work-dirtied hands. Virgilio dropped Troy's body next to his bleeding mother who was making gurgling sounds and breathing shallowly.

With a ferocious, snarling bark, saliva dripping from his mouth, Toby lurched at Virgilio again, but Virgilio grabbed a cast iron pan and swung as hard as he could, meeting the dog's head as he lunged toward him.

Cathy screamed and sat up in bed. Troy, who was also sleeping restlessly at Cathy's side sat up as well, then growled and barked fiercely. Cathy put her arms around Troy's neck and held him tightly as she cried into his soft fur.

Paul, now accustomed to Cathy's outbursts from nightmares, groaned and threw himself to his other side.

That morning, Cathy was up, showered, and ready for work before Paul so she could arrive bright and early to transport her students for their first day back to school. She performed her morning ritual with Troy, and as soon as she had the morning news in her hands, she immediately opened it to the Death Notices. There it was--Celia Anatoli. Visiting hours were listed to be between 2:00 p.m. to 4:00 p.m. and 7:00 p.m. to 9:00 p.m. on Thursday at the Abiding Faith Funeral Home and Crematorium. The following morning at 9:00 a.m. friends and family were invited to a small service at the funeral parlor to be followed by a committal service at St. Margaret Cemetery.

As Cathy ate a light breakfast with coffee, she reread the Notice and looked over the rest of the paper while keeping alert for sounds of Paul getting up and getting ready for work. When she heard him coming down the stairs, she grabbed her purse and stood at the back door, her hand on the door knob, waiting patiently for him to enter the kitchen.

"Take a look at the paper, Paul. Grandma Anatoli died yesterday," she said as soon as she saw him, then immediately slipped out of the house closing the door behind her.

She heard Paul's incredulous, "What?" from the kitchen followed by the sound of the door opening and Paul yelling, "Wait!"

"I've got to get going, Paul. There's a lot to do on the first day of school. I'll talk to you later," she shouted back to him as she got in her car. She looked at him long enough to see the frustration on his face just before he slammed the door.

Cathy was pleased that she had successfully gotten out of the house without becoming embroiled in a conversation about Celia Anatoli's death which would have inevitably led her to telling Paul about her visit with Luella. Paul would be annoyed about her hasty departure for a while, but he'd get over it after the hours of the day became filled with other matters. Later, Paul would have far fewer questions about Celia's death and she would feel less compelled to elaborate.

Once at work, Cathy was able to release her mind from everything involving the Anatolis while performing her pre-trip inspection and talking with her co-workers. She looked over her route prior to leaving, paying particular attention to the new stops she had to make and the names of the new students. She was sure she wouldn't forget Alya Adler's home next to St. Margaret Cemetery with the driveway lined with maple trees.

Cathy's route was going well until she was passing St. Margaret Cemetery. Bus 12 was attempting to radio the number of students that would be transferring to 35 at the high school, but static and feedback made 12's transmission indiscernible. Cathy asked Bus 12 to repeat while she slowly approached Alya's driveway. The static and feedback reached an earsplitting pitch when a petite girl with a shock of platinum blonde hair, a glittering nose stud, and wearing several earrings stepped from behind the maple tree closest to the street. When Cathy came to a full stop Alya was already standing at the edge of the road.

The passenger door almost bumped Alya in the face when Cathy opened it. "Good morning, Alya," Cathy greeted cheerily as Alya stepped into the bus.

Alya murmured a, "Mornin," in return without looking at Cathy.

"Before you sit down, Alya, I want to remind you that you have to stand back at least ten feet from the edge of the road while you wait. That's at least five giant steps back. And, make sure I can see you, please. So, you need to stand away from the trees. I couldn't see you until I was right at your driveway. Then, you have to wait until I stop and the doors are open before coming up to the bus. It's very dangerous for you to approach the bus before I stop completely and the doors are open. Okay?"

Alya twisted her mouth into a surly pout. "Kay," she responded and hurried toward the back of the bus.

"Also, Alya, you're assigned seat is 6A."

Alya provided an audible, "Tch," and a sigh in response then turned back and took her assigned seat.

Pulling away from Alya's house, the interference on the radio ceased and Cathy finally successfully communicated with Bus 12. Other than the static on the radio, everything was going perfectly and Cathy thought how nice it would be if the whole year went this smoothly.

While she waited to make her left turn from Depot Road to Station Road, she remembered her dry run and the bus stalling on the incline at Scott Hollow. She turned onto Station Road, navigated the curves and the downhill preceding Scott Hollow, then she held her breath as Bus 35 began to struggle slightly ascending the hill. She glanced to check on her riders and saw a flash of platinum blonde hair in the back seat. She reached for her inside microphone to tell Alya to get back in her assigned seat, but then saw that Alya was in seat 6A looking out the window. Cathy's concern was refocused on Bus 35's protestation about climbing the hill. Thirty-five was struggling to attain a speed of ten miles per hour until it finally topped the hill and then cruised smoothly on its way.

Cathy breathed easy again. She smiled as she enjoyed the pastures and fields glowing in the early morning light. Overhead, she noticed a red-tailed hawk circling.

At the sight of Cathy unlocking the front door Troy began barking. Her phone started ringing as she walked in causing further excitement from Troy who sang to her in whines and barks while moving from side to side, clumsily banging his cone on the sides of the crate. As she unlocked Troy's kennel she saw it was Paul calling and braced for his questions about Celia. "Hi, Hon,"

Cathy answered, trying to talk above the din of Troy's greeting. "That was good timing. I just got in the door. How're things going today?"

"Oh, fine. Just taking a break and thought I'd call," Paul said.

Troy burst clumsily out of his kennel and jumped on Cathy, bumping her chin with his cone. "Ouch," she laughed. "Troy seems pretty happy I'm home. Can you hear him barking?" she laughed.

"Mm-hm. Hope he's not going to be a dog with separation anxiety."

"Nah, I think he'll be fine once he settles in, gets used to the routine, and feels more secure here."

"Yeah, I guess," Paul said, then paused a second. "So, been wondering, why'd you run out of the house like that this morning?"

"You know, first day, lots to do. I didn't want to rush through anything."

"Sure, but you tell me about Celia Anatoli dying and off you go. Just seemed kind of strange. Why wouldn't you want to talk to me about it?"

"It's not that I didn't want to talk to you about it. I was in a hurry, that's all. I just wanted to bring it to your attention."

"I guess it is kind of surprising with all you've been up to lately. But then, she was ninety-seven years old. She had a long life. It is a shame, though," Paul said somberly. "Have you talked to Julia yet? I wonder if she knows."

"No, I haven't called her yet, but I expect she knows. Bonnie has a couple issues of the paper delivered to the Salon every day for the customers, so I'm sure someone will notice the announcement. Luella may have already called to make an appointment to have her hair done before the funeral, too. I'll probably call or text Julia before I go back for the afternoon run."

"Now, I want to remind you, just because you feel somewhat involved with the Anatolis, I don't think it would be a good idea if you went to their house, or to visiting hours, or anything, Cathy," Paul said, trying not to sound overbearing.

Cathy's back still stiffened. "I agree, but I'm planning to write a note of sympathy in the funeral home's online condolence book."

"Do you really . . ."

"Paul, I'm doing it. They're our neighbors and despite the fact that we're not buddy-buddy with them, I want to express our sympathy for their loss."

Paul sighed, "I guess there's nothing wrong with that."

"No, of course there's nothing wrong with that!" Cathy tried to hold in her anger. "It might even help smooth things over with them. Who knows?"

"Mm-hm, yep. Who knows?" Paul said, not truly believing. "So how did your morning run go?"

"Fine. The kids seem pretty good and no big problem with the bus."

"What do you mean, no big problem? Did something go wrong?"

"Oh, a little static on the radio and the bus still seems sluggish going up big hills. I wrote it up again. They'll look at it."

"I hope so. You don't want to get stalled on that section of Station Road."

"That's for sure. It was bad enough when it happened on my dry run."

There were a few moments of silence which Cathy broke. "Think I better get Troy outside and start getting him used to this as his pee time. Since he's a little rambunctious today, I think I'll give him a little pain medication to settle him down in his kennel before I leave this afternoon."

"Yeah, you probably should," Paul agreed. "I better get back to work. Glad all went well for you this morning. See you later tonight."

"Okay, love you."

"Love you, too."

Troy followed Cathy to the back door. She clipped his leash onto him before leading him into the yard. Troy seemed content to meander around the yard sniffing his way to his favorite spot, Sadie's grave. As usual, he tried to start digging but, being on leash, Cathy was able to stop him immediately. "Good heavens, Troy," Cathy told him. "Let poor Sadie rest in peace. I'm sure she'd love to play with you, but you're going to have to wait awhile before you can meet her. And right now, you're in no condition to play, period," she chuckled.

Cathy scowled away the thought about what might lie underneath Sadie's coffin and led Troy away from his mischief to check on the condition of her flowers. She noted, then ignored, some new weeds already taunting her and closed her eyes to smell the intoxicating fragrance of her double delight roses. "You know what, little boy?" she asked Troy who looked at her with excited readiness. "I think we should cut a couple of these pretty roses and take them to your grandma's grave. What do you think?" Cathy led Troy to the shed, gathered her pruning shears, a weed digger and a bucket just in case weeds were rearing their ugly heads by her mother's grave, and a small vase that she filled with water from the hose, then started toward the cemetery.

The sky was becoming grey and overcast but it didn't seem buggy, so Cathy felt optimistic that the clouds would break up. Troy was settling down and happily sniffing the smells along the path, every now and then bumping into a tree with his protective head cone.

"Sorry, boy. Your headgear will come off soon," Cathy told him with a pat on his behind.

When they arrived at Grace's grave, Cathy transferred the double delight roses to Grace's pop-up vase. "Thought you'd appreciate these today, Mom," Cathy said softly and knelt down to tidy up her mother's marker. Troy lay down next to her. "Don't know if you've found out anything about the Anatoli's for me, Mom, but one of the Anatolis, Celia, is moving in here." Cathy shook her head. "It's so incredible. Celia died the same night that Luella said she had a visit from Lavinia and Troy."

Troy picked up his head and looked at Cathy. "Not you, boy," Cathy laughed. "The other Troy."

"It's so bizarre and confusing, Mom. I sure wish you were here to help me sort all of this out. If you could just give me a hint to point me in the right direction." Cathy caught a whiff of the roses and bent over, cupping the flowers in her hands, and inhaled deeply with her eyes closed. She pictured her Troy running across a field with the blue-eyed boy, Troy Anatoli, doing his best to follow. She saw her Troy look back as if checking on his follower, the dog's blue eye as bright as the young boy's eyes. They were running toward Lavinia who stood at the edge of the field against a rocky backdrop.

"Can't stay too long, Mom. It's the first day back to school for the Harborcreek kids." Cathy kissed the palm of her hand, then placed her hand on her mother's stone. "Come on, Troy," she said standing up. "We better go. I want to get in touch with Julia, Tony, and Allie before I head back this afternoon."

She heard the sound of machinery toward the middle of the cemetery and, instead of walking toward her house, Cathy walked toward the noise. Nearing the Rosetti and Anatoli plots in Section A where Cathy first encountered Luella and Celia, Cathy saw a backhoe at work and a dump truck by its side. She shivered as she could see Celia wearing black mourning clothes standing by the hole being dug, watching her and Troy with a dead stare. The harsh screech of a hawk overhead caught Cathy's attention. She turned to see the hawk flying south as the sky brightened, the sun sending streams of light through breaks in the clouds.

Back home after their outing, Cathy threw the ingredients for beef stew in her crockpot and sent a text to Allie telling her about Celia's death and a text to Julia asking if she'd heard about Celia. Julia texted back that she had seen the Death Notice in the paper and that she had made room in her schedule for Luella the morning of the funeral. Then she texted Tony that Celia was to be buried on Friday. Tony thanked her in a return text and said he'd make arrangements for the use of the GPR equipment.

Cathy was pleasantly surprised to hear Allie's voice shortly after texting her. "Hi dear. How are things going?" Cathy answered.

"Fine. I just got back to my room after morning classes. That's something about Grandma Anatoli! I thought I'd call you now while Dad's at work. I imagine she died of natural causes, didn't she?"

"Yes, apparently it was her heart. But I have a strange story to tell you about that, so I'm glad you called now." Cathy related her encounter with Luella the morning she picked Troy up from the veterinarian. "So now she's very motivated to learn more about Lavinia and Troy."

"That's good news. Have you discovered anything new?"

"Nothing concrete. Tony's going to employ some techniques from his forensic anthropology and archeology studies to see if there's anything buried under the angel statue in the Rosetti plot and under our Sadie."

"Wow. I hope he doesn't find them buried in the back yard. It's a little too ghoulish. Who knows how many other bodies might be buried there if that's the case."

"I have my doubts about our yard, but it's worth checking. Tony keeps insisting he wasn't hitting a rock or tree roots when he and Dad dug the grave."

"Are you still having disturbing dreams, Mom? Or seeing things--phantom images or anything still?"

"I don't know if I'm expecting to see things now, which makes me open to it, but off and on lately something strange will catch my eye. And I am still having dreams about Lavinia and Troy. I'm convinced Virgilio killed them and the dog, too. In my last dream I actually envisioned what happened. I don't know if it's true or not, but it makes perfect sense. I don't want to go into detail about it because I don't want to put gruesome images into your head, but if my dreams are actually a window into the past, Virgilio killed them."

"I believe you, Mom. Nightmares have been waking me up in the middle of the night, too. I thought it was a result of being homesick and the change in routine and all, but last night I dreamt about the street scene I painted. Do you remember the one I painted to accompany my history project?"

Cathy shuddered involuntarily remembering the storm and the painting seemingly showing itself to her. "Yes, I do."

"Well, it does remarkably resemble Troy and Lavinia from that ad you showed me and I've been dreaming different things involving that painting. Last night I dreamt they were charging home in a driving rainstorm. The road was muddy and slippery and they were driving their horse to go faster and faster. When they got home they found their house completely consumed by fire, and they just walked in! I heard their screams as they were burning to death. It was awful. I woke Kelsea up with my screaming."

"I'm so sorry you've gotten caught up in this, too, honey."

"It's not your fault, Mom. You didn't exactly ask for this. It's like you opened a door and were sucked inside. Besides, I think it has actually helped by opening my mind. It's helped my imagination and creativity."

"Imagination is great, but not so great if all of your imaginings are frightening."

"Oh, they're not. This whole thing has helped me open my mind to ideas that I might not have considered before, to listen to others. I think it's actually helped me in school. Oh, I wanted you to know, Kelsea and I will be driving home the weekend after this one. One of Kelsea's photography professors is very interested in her photos of the hawk. You know, the one we saw at Scott Hollow? She showed him my pictures from the beach, too. Remember? The one's with the light distortion."

"Oh yes. I remember them very well."

"He's wondering if she can recreate the anomaly with filters and he wants to see the other pictures she's taken of Scott Hollow and the hawk. She's going to be doing a paper on the history of paranormal photography and spiritualism. So far, all she's found out is that most purported photos of ghosts are cons, but she still can't explain the images from our pictures."

"I'll be interested in reading her paper."

"I'll let her know. I'm sure she'll be glad to show it to you."

When they ended their conversation Cathy only had a few minutes left to grab something to eat and to write her condolence note to the Anatoli family. She noted with surprise the last entry was from Raphael and Rachel Rosetti of Brecksville, Ohio.

Although Cathy had informed the students that their seat assignments were the same on the way home as the way to school, Alya hurried toward the back of the bus and had to be reminded of her seat assignment. As Cathy approached Alya's house, the radio again squealed from feedback as two busses attempted to communicate with each other. Cathy wondered if there was a ham radio operator living in the neighborhood causing the interference and looked quickly at the properties opposite the cemetery for an antenna, but didn't notice one. The kids, a bit noisy after their first day back to school, reacted overdramatically to the unpleasant radio feedback, requiring a reprimand from Cathy. She glanced at her riders in her rearview mirror and thought she caught Alya having snuck to the back seat of the bus. When she stopped to let Alya off, Cathy saw Alya get up from her correct seat and there was no vacant spot in the back.

Cathy had dropped off all but seven students by the time she was turning onto Station Road. Once again, the bus stuttered up the hill and, like that morning, after topping the crest it picked up speed and ran smoothly. She noticed a red-tailed hawk circling in the sky and suddenly, the bird was swooping toward her windshield screeching, wings fully spread and talons outstretched, causing Cathy to instinctively make a quick swerve to the right to avoid the bird. She corrected instantly and the hawk disappeared as swiftly as it had appeared and now was soaring on the air currents above.

She looked back to see her students sitting stiffly in stunned silence for a moment, then everyone began talking at once. "What was that?" "What happened?" "Did we hit a bird?" Relieved to see that no one had been jostled from their seat and all of the children seemed okay, Cathy got on her interior microphone. "Settle down, please. A bird just flew toward the windshield, but we didn't hit it. Everything's okay."

As Cathy drove Bus 35 past the Anatoli house on the way back to the bus garage, she noticed a car bearing an Ohio license plate in the Anatoli driveway.

23

THE PAPERS

"You can box up Grandma's clothes for charity while I'm working, Luella," Gino instructed. "But, don't touch anything else."

"Okay, honey," Luella replied, knowing full well she was going to peek into Celia's writing desk, cedar chest, and the antique trunk in the attic.where secrets might be hidden.

After the kids were off to school and Gino was busy outside, Luella found several large cardboard boxes and headed to Celia's bedroom which had been closed off since stripping the bed and disposing of the mattress Monday night. Luella felt like a trespasser as she slowly opened the door. Its creaking noise made her whole body shiver. The mattress-less bed was the first reminder that Celia had died there. The sun was glaring through the window, reflecting on the dresser mirror, causing dust particles hanging in the air to twinkle, and making the entire room appear to be engulfed in a white haze. Luella felt as if she were suffocating in the stillness and mustiness, so she opened the windows for fresh air and to allow the comforting hum of life to fill the room.

She first tackled the closet and removed Celia's blouses, black dresses, skirts, and jackets from their hangers, folded them carefully, and placed them in one of the boxes. As she tended to this task, she felt a deep sadness and a great sense of loss. Ever since Gino's grandfather, Salvatore, had passed away seven years ago, Celia had been a constant presence in the house. Despite Celia's occasional sharp tongue, Luella had enjoyed her spunky personality. Surprisingly, Celia had been very supportive of Luella and a softening influence on Gino, and she was always happy to help with the children. As Luella removed the last garment from its hanger, she pictured Celia, and felt a reciprocated warmth as if Celia was right there keeping her company.

Luella removed Celia's shoes, slippers, and canes to another box. She opened the stepstool leaning against the closet wall to retrieve the couple of handbags from the shelf above the hanger clothing. She made sure the purses were empty, removed a little spare change, bobby pins, and scraps of paper from them and placed them in the box with the shoes. The fragrance of lavender from Celia's favorite bath salts, lotion, and powder still clung to the robe that hung on a hook in the closet. Luella deposited the robe in the laundry hamper.

Before folding the stepstool, Luella removed two photo albums from the closet shelf to page through. She'd seen the photos before, but, feeling nostalgic, took the time to look at them again. She loved the black and white, and sepia-toned photos from the turn of the century with the subjects so stiffly posed they almost appeared to be manikins. She flipped through and found wedding photos of Celia and Salvatore. Celia looked a fairy princess in her tea-length tulle gown adorned with lace and a wide satin bandage bow. Remembering Gino's instructions to not pay attention to anything but Celia's clothes, Luella closed the albums. As she put them back onto the closet shelf, an envelope slipped to the floor from one of the albums. Picking it up, she felt something hard within it and discovered an unusually heavy key with a ring on one end and a large foot notch on the other.

Celia's cedar chest was not locked, but in comparing the key to the lock, Luella could tell the key was too big. She removed Celia's sweaters and other winter wear from the cedar chest, but left an afghan and two extra blankets inside. Luella found Celia's desk to be unlocked, but it was obvious the desk lock was also too small for the key. A cursory look in the desk revealed writing paper, envelopes, stamps, Celia's address book, checkbook, and a few stray receipts.

Luella put the key in her pocket and quickly went through Celia's dresser and night stand so she could head to the antique barrel trunk in the attic. The attic was orderly but was stifling, dingy, and dusty. She was already sweating by the time she opened the few small windows and turned on the attic light. The trunk was not where she had remembered it to be. It was at the top of the staircase to the right. It was locked, but as she'd hoped, the key fit.

Luella was surprised to find no soft goods in the trunk. It had served as a filing cabinet. Luella began thumbing through the alphabetically organized folders labeled in Celia's handwriting. An empty folder marked "Pre-Arrangements" was sticking up above the rest of the folders.

The papers in the chest were a treasure trove of information regarding the history of the Anatoli property. There were copies of documents relating to the sale and transfer of parcels through the years, the oldest being the gifting of the parcel to St. Elizabeth Church for use as a cemetery on All Souls Day, November 2, 1862. The language on the yellowed and fragile Deed was simple but it clearly spelled out the boundaries of the property and was executed by the authorities of the time. She shuddered seeing Virgilio's name and his signature on the piece of paper. Luella set the Deed aside to show to Cathy.

A folder marked "Homestead" attracted Luella's attention. She studied the document memorializing the original purchase of the Anatoli property which Virgilio bought from General Callender Irvine in 1840. A copy of the newspaper ad showing the entire Anatoli family with July 1858 handwritten in ink at the top was also in the folder. Luella fixated on Lavinia recognizing her as the figure she saw standing at Nico's bedside. Luella kept the ad out with the Deed.

A blast of icy cold wind swept through the attic pushing the trunk over, the folders spilling away from Luella. The dusty heat of the attic returned just as suddenly as the coldness had swept through. She pushed the trunk to an upright position while doing the best she could to keep the folders in order and spied some loose crumpled papers at the bottom. She carefully rescued the delicate yellowed vellum papers and gingerly opened them. She noticed a few small dark brown spots on the front page of the document. When finally opened sufficiently, Luella read, "Enrollment of Troy Pietro Anatoli to Saint James School, Hagerstown, Maryland, Fall Term 1862." Although creased irregularly, Luella could easily read every beautifully scripted word of the enrollment document.

She began to feel dazed and drowsy from the heat. Her eyes felt heavy and she closed them. She heard a pounding on a door and a firm male voice shouted, "Virgilio Anatoli! Sheriff Swalley. Come to the door."

Virgilio was sitting at the dinner table with six of his children. He scowled, went to the door, opened it abruptly, and stared coldly at the Sheriff.

"Need to have a word with you, Virgilio," Sheriff Swalley said matter-of-factly. "I've had an inquiry about your wife. Seems no one's seen her in weeks. Is she all right? Is she around?"

"No," Virgilio replied gruffly. "She run away with someone and take Troy with her."

"What do you mean ran away? Where'd she go and who'd she go with?"

"I dunno his name. He's a salesman and he promise to take her and Troy to Maryland. She wanted my Troy to go to school. Stupida woman. I show you." Virgilio left the door open and Sheriff Swalley followed him to a roll top desk. "Here," Virgilio said handing Sheriff Swalley the enrollment papers that he'd flattened and saved to show anyone who was interested.

"Hmm, St. James School, Hagerstown, Maryland. That's quite a ways away to be traveling now with the war going on. When'd all this school idea come about?"

"I don't know. She did it behind my back."

"So, when's she returning? She just taking young Troy there to get him situated, ain't she?"

"No. I tell her when she leave, she dead to me now. I tell her to take all her things. I don't want to see her again. She's disgraced herself, me, and mi familia."

"You wouldn't mind if I take a look around, would you Virgilio?

Virgilio stepped aside and opened his arm up magnanimously to the rest of the house, then followed behind Sheriff Swalley as he slowly poked around. Virgilio cast a threatening glare at his children who remained sitting, staring wide-eyed, listening, and dreading being questioned by the Sheriff.

"Appears you're missing another boy, Virgilio. Where's Leo?"

"He run away, too. He no lika to work. How I raise these lazy good-for-nothings, I dunno." Virgilio motioned to the dining table where his children sat frozen in fear.

As Sheriff Swalley and Virgilio wandered around, the Sheriff picked up things, opened drawers, looked behind and under furniture, trying to get a rise out of Virgilio. Although fuming, Virgilio controlled himself. In Lavinia's and Virgilio's bedroom,

Sheriff Swalley's eyes fell on the barrel trunk that sat at the foot of their bed.

Luella came out of her daze sweating profusely, her head pounding. "I've got to get out of this heat," she said quietly to herself. She closed and locked the trunk and got up holding onto the enrollment papers, the ad, and the Deed. Feeling dizzy, she steadied herself on the top newel post of the stairway and held onto the handrail the rest of the way downstairs.

As she rushed to the master bathroom to relieve her thirst, she heard her phone ringing downstairs. She hurriedly tucked the documents from the trunk in her lingerie drawer and went downstairs to find out who had called her. Before she reached the bottom of the stairs her phone was ringing again. It was one of Gino's cousins inquiring about Celia's death. After talking with her cousin-in-law she began a marathon of receiving, returning, and making phone calls, and chatting with well-meaning people who popped in offering assistance and bringing food with their condolences. Luella did her best to perform her normal everyday chores as well as arrange for a luncheon after Celia's funeral at the Lakeview Country Club.

Luella had been carrying her phone around due to the plethora of phone calls she'd been receiving nd put it on top of the dryer. While adding a load of laundry to the washing machine, Luella, as a matter of course, was checking pockets to make sure they were empty before tossing items in the wash. She reached in the shorts she had worn yesterday and found the slip of paper on which Cathy had written her phone number. She picked up her phone and immediately dialed Cathy before another call came in. Cathy was driving her afternoon run, so Luella's call went to voicemail. "Hi Cathy. It's Luella. I've found some paperwork that's very interesting. I'm thinking Troy and Lavinia went to Hagerstown, Maryland and never came back. I'd like to get together with you this coming Monday, if possible. Maybe for coffee at the Giant Eagle café' area? Let me know. Thanks."

Having finished the first part of her run, Cathy had about a half hour before she had to pick up the St. Boniface elementary students and checked her phone. She responded to Luella by text. "Monday around 9:30 is good. Will bring info I have."

Luella responded with a thumbs-up and the doorbell rang. She looked through the window before she opened the door and saw a man about six foot tall with prematurely thinning dark hair and an attractive, athletic-looking, brunette woman, almost as tall as the man, with a healthy bronze complexion. The man was carrying a box decorated with mauve roses.

Not recognizing either of them, Luella opened the door only wide enough for her to find out what this couple wanted and to quickly close it if she found it necessary. "Yes? Can I help you?" she asked.

"Hello. Excuse us for coming unannounced. I tried calling you earlier but you must have missed my call. Are you Mrs. Gino Anatoli?"

"I - I, um, yes, I'm Mrs. Anatoli. What can I do for you?"

"Well, my name is Raphael Rosetti. This is my wife, Rachel, and I've recently found through genealogical research that I'm related to your husband and I was hoping to have a word with him."

Taken aback, Luella bit her lip and said, "Gino isn't here right now." Luella pictured Celia placing flowers at the base of the angel statue in the Rosetti plot, making more sense of it now.

"Actually, I had hoped to talk with his great grandmother, Celia, as well, but . . ."

"Yes, I'm afraid Celia passed away yesterday."

"We know. Rachel and I saw the Notice in the paper and we'd like to express our sympathy. Obviously, this is an especially busy, stressful time for you both, but after the funeral is over, I was hoping to learn more about the history of my family. Do you think your husband might have some time, well you and your husband might have time, to talk to us?"

"I - I - I don't know. My husband is very touchy about his family. He doesn't like to talk much about his ancestors and things that happened a long time ago. He hasn't even opened up much to me, so . . ."

"Really? It's just that I've got these letters . . ."

"Letters?"

"Well, yes. They're letters dated from 1863 onwards, mostly between Leonardo Rosetti and his sister, Lydia, but there are others between other members of the family, too. I've been curious about my ancestors ever since I first read them. I'm a direct descendent of Leonardo Anatoli who ran away from home in late 1862 or early 1863 at the age of sixteen. He ended up in Brecksville, Ohio where he decided to take his mother's last name, Rosetti. Therefore, my surname is Rosetti rather than Anatoli."

"One thing I've learned from their correspondence, is that their father, Virgilio, was hated and feared by his children for his cruelty and abusiveness, but there was one horrible incident that must have occurred that the children deemed unforgiveable. On occasion they refer to "the atrocity" and "the horror they cannot forget" in their letters. It appears they were sworn to secrecy by their father who may have threatened harm to the siblings who remained under his roof. They were too frightened to even write it out in their correspondence to each other. It was my hope that Celia or your husband could shed some light on what awful thing happened in the family. Apparently, Leonardo never confided in anyone in Ohio, so no info was passed down."

Luella's eyes grew wide in excitement. "Oh my gosh. I don't know what to say. I actually would love to sit down and talk to you. Were you planning to be here long?"

"We were going to be here for two weeks. Planning to head home the weekend after this one. We decided this would be a great place to spend our vacation this year. Maybe try to satisfy my curiosity and also enjoy Presque Isle State Park. We saw that Celia's funeral will be this Friday. Do you think your husband might be willing to talk to us before we leave? Any time next week?"

Luella's heart began beating fast. "I, um, know my husband wouldn't welcome talking to you about this, but, as a matter of fact, I may have some information to share with you and I'm sure I will have more later. I'm actually sort of investigating all of this with a friend of mine, too, and your letters would be extremely helpful. Do you think you'd be able to make copies of the letters for me and my friend to read? Gino will be home soon and I know he won't take kindly to your interest in this."

"I'll trust you with the letters if you would like to make a plan to compare notes and return them to me before we leave. I've read them so many times, I can almost recite what's in them." Raphael held the box out to Luella.

When Luella's hands touched the box, her body shivered. "I will definitely safeguard these. Step in a moment, won't you? We can exchange phone numbers."

"Oh, you actually should have my number since I did try to call you earlier, so . . ." Raphael said.

"Oh, here honey. Let me write it down in case she can't find our call." Rachel reached into her pocketbook for a pen and a piece of paper on which she wrote down their names and numbers and handed the note to Luella. "Raphael has your number in his phone."

"Thank you, Rachel. I'll call you to make a plan to meet once I see how things wind down after the funeral. I might not be able to call until early next week."

"Oh, we understand."

"I'm going to ask my friend, Cathy Pantona, to join us, if you don't mind. She's actually the one who started looking into things around here so she'll have a lot of information to share and will be extremely excited to meet you."

"That would be wonderful. I'm so glad we decided to stop by," Raphael said.

"Yes, we weren't sure how busy you'd be because of the funeral, but thought we'd try anyway. We really appreciate your hospitality," Rachel said.

"I'm so glad you did come by, dear" Luella said feeling so optimistic she spontaneously reached out and hugged both of them. Without thinking, she blurted out, "You're welcome to come to the funeral and luncheon afterward if you wish."

"Why thank you," Raphael said. "Maybe someone at the funeral will have a little information they can share with me."

Luella regretted her invitation. "Please be discrete, though. You know, my husband . . ."

"Oh, of course. We feel honored that you're permitting us to be there at all. We'll be very tactful." Raphael and Rachel turned to walk to their car saying, "Thank you again, Mrs. Anatoli."

"Please, call me Luella," she said and noticed a school bus approaching. It was about time for Nico and Vincent to arrive home and she hoped they would not see the Rosettis leaving. She hurried in the house to stash the box of letters in the closet where she kept her vacuum cleaner and cleaning equipment. When she got back to the door Nico and Vincent were getting off the bus.

24

THE COLD SPOT

As Cathy drove by the Anatoli house on her morning run, she wondered how much more information Luella was likely to gather when mingling with relatives during visiting hours. As happened every day so far this year, the radio crackled with static while passing St. Margaret Cemetery. In addition to the noise, today of its own accord Bus 35 slowed, the ambers began blinking, it came to a stop in front of the lichgate, the reds started flashing, the bus arm extended, and the passenger door opened. Cathy was panicking inside. She had no control over the bus but she needed to remain calm.

The children started laughing and yelling various bits of wisdom to Cathy. "This isn't a stop!" "Alya doesn't live in the cemetery." "Did a zombie start at Harborcreek?"

"Quiet please," Cathy instructed using her interior microphone. She was able to close the door and continue on her route with an annoying murmuring static buzz emanating from the radio. Cathy stressed over what electrical malfunction was going on with the bus as she pulled in front of Alya's house with the students still snickering..

"Oh, no. The walking dead," Cathy heard from the back of the bus as Alya walked to her seat. More laughter ensued and Cathy hoped her mistake would not cause Alya to become the object of ridicule.

"Alya," a mocking voice was heard. "You better start waiting at your real home, the cemetery."

"Shut up you asshole," Alya shouted back.

Cathy pulled the bus over. She took her microphone, stood up next to her driver seat and stared at her students. "I want everyone in this bus to settle down. If I hear any more negative remarks to

Alya or anyone else for that matter, I will be writing you up. And Alya, I'm warning you right now that we do not tolerate vulgar language on the bus. I'm only giving you a warning because you were provoked, but after this, if anyone swears on this bus, I will write you up, despite the provocation. Now I want everyone to be quiet, considerate, and well-mannered for the rest of the ride to school."

Cathy tried to keep a careful eye on her students as she drove, knowing they were now keyed up and had mischief on their minds. She knew they thought she had not been paying attention and had made a stupid blunder, and they loved it.

Despite wearing sunglasses, the sun streaming in the windshield made visibility difficult, obscuring vision directly in front of her to a certain degree. Consequently, the necessity to watch the road extra-vigilantly hampered her efforts to keep checking on her passengers. When she did glance back, she saw bright yellow spots and couldn't look long enough to make out the faces of the students clearly. She thought she saw movement in the back once or twice and thought she noticed a very small student with pale blonde hair on the back seat. Cathy wondered if Alya was back there sitting in a slouch. However, a few minutes later she saw Alya in her assigned seat. Cathy wracked her brains for any other student with light blonde hair that might have snuck to the back. She picked up her microphone and warned the students, "I would like to remind you that you must remain in your assigned seat while you are on the bus. Anyone who moves from their seat at any time will get written up."

The radio's murmuring buzz continued, sounding like a raspy third voice talking in the background for the entire route. It was a relief to park out of the sun when she got to the high school. She looked back to check on her passengers and was startled to see the last three rows of the bus were empty of students. Instead, a pale haze seemed to permeate that whole area. As she eased to a stop, she grabbed her microphone. "Stay seated and quiet a moment please," she announced. After shutting down the bus completely, she named the seven students who had moved from the back and told them they were to stay on the bus so she could have a word with them after everyone else left.

When everyone else had exited, Cathy asked the seven students to sit down in the seats behind her. When she looked back, the haze was gone and the noise from the radio stopped. She turned around in her seat. "Could you explain why you chose to move from your assigned seats? You know I'll have to write each and every one of you up."

The kids responded with, "Ah, c'mon," moans, and protestations. "We couldn't stay back there," one girl spoke up, with affirmative support from her fellow reprobates.

Perturbed, Cathy got up, crossed her arms and faced her students. "Oh, and why is that? I noticed a haze in the back. Was someone spraying something back there? Am I going to have to check your bags?"

"No, no. No one sprayed anything," they argued.

"It just got so icy cold," one of the students explained. "I was in the back seat and it felt like all of a sudden we were in a freezer."

"Yeah," they agreed with one another, some rubbing their upper arms.

"I couldn't stand it," one of the girls remarked, "And it felt creepy back there. It felt like someone was touching me, but no one was."

"And I felt spacy, dizzy. It was just weird and cold."

Cathy shook her head. Now I know we had a problem on the bus today and I don't appreciate you causing more problems and making up stories like this."

All seven protested, and began talking at once about what they had experienced. "We're not lying," they said.

"Now, why would it get ice cold in only three rows of the bus on an August morning when the temperature is 83°?" Cathy looked at them with disapproval. "If there was some inexplicable blast of cold air, everyone on the bus would have felt it, including me. I would suggest you think of a better excuse. I'm sorry, but I'm going to have to write all of you up, and I dislike doing it for your sake, but also for mine. It's a lot of time and paperwork for me, plus time and follow up for other people."

"So don't do it," one young man shouted.

"What choice do I have?"

"You can just forget about it. We won't do it again," another said.

"I would consider that, but I told everyone before you did this to stay in your assigned seats and you totally ignored me. Also, must I remind you that there are cameras on the bus and I'd be shirking my duty if I did not report this. But, I will note that I discussed the matter with you and that you assured me that it would not happen again."

She heard a few groans from her captive audience.

"Don't worry. I doubt if any punishment will come from this as it is a first incident. So, have a good day. I will see you after school."

When she returned to the garage, Cathy wrote up the bus for having a mind of its own in stopping at the cemetery and for the interference on the radio, suggesting there might be an electric problem. Then she wrote up the children for not staying in their seats during the ride to school. Completing her last tasks before going home; i.e. double checking that the windows were closed and locked, that no one remained on the bus, placing the *Bus Empty - Checked for Children* sign in the back window, and sweeping the bus; she noticed an unusual yellowish brown piece of paper on the floor by the back emergency door. The scrap of paper appeared to be discolored by time and was dry and brittle. Cathy smiled as she remembered artificially antiquing paper for a replica of the Declaration of Independence that she made for an extra-credit history project in middle school.

Bus 35 was taken off the road for service to determine the cause of its autopilot issue and the problem with the radio. Cathy was given Bus S21 to drive while 35 was in the garage. Her pre-trip inspection for the spare showed everything in working order.

It was hot, humid, and cloudy heralding a rainstorm that was predicted for that afternoon. Cathy opened the windows to at least provide some air movement when she was on the road. Although this was one of the newest busses on the lot, Cathy preferred good old 35 because of her familiarity with the controls; therefore, she took extra time rehearsing the routine of turning on the ambers, reds, and opening the passenger doors on S21. This new bus was very clean, so if any marks were found on the seats or refuse was left on the bus it would be easy to identify the guilty party.

All was fine when she pulled in line to wait for the exodus of the children from school. When Cathy shut down S21 and opened the entry door, she became chilled by an icy blast of air which disappeared immediately. The radio began to crackle with intermittent static and when she glanced in the back she saw the same pale grey haze again shrouded the last seat.

Cathy walked to the back to take down her *Bus Empty - Checked for Children* sign and noticed a distinct chill in the air when she got to the third to last row. The sign was ice cold and the air was so frigid Cathy wondered if Jack Frost himself had sat down there. She touched the seats, the metal around the windows, the bus walls, and found everything to be as cold as ice.

The whispering Cathy heard from the radio seemed louder, but she could not make out any words and she walked back to her driver's seat. She knew the bus was not equipped with air conditioning, but glanced at the dash anyway to make sure. She did a radio check with the office and, although the transmission was difficult to hear over the interference, Cathy could understand Jessi adequately and vice versa.

As she replaced her radio microphone in its holder, the students began pouring out of school and into their respective busses. A stream of kids got on Cathy's bus and took their seats amped up as usual. When the first student assigned to one of the back seats arrived, Cathy watched her intently. The girl stopped as if hitting a wall when she got to the third to the last row. She hesitantly continued to her seat, sat down slowly sending sapphire blue dagger eyes to meet Cathy's eyes. Cathy blinked away the image of Troy being superimposed over the girl's face like a translucent mask.

The next student that belonged in the back entered with a buddy of his. The two were talking loudly and continued their conversation even though their seats were separated by several rows. Their conversation stopped abruptly by the boy assigned to the back. "Hey, it's cold back here!" he exclaimed.

The friend that was seated in row five shouted, "What? You're crazy."

"No! It's frigging cold back here. I ain't lyin'. Come back and see." The young man turned to the girl already seated who was holding her upper arms and had thrown a gym towel over her shoulders. "Aren't you cold?" he asked.

"Ya, but we aren't allowed to move," she said in a mocking voice sending another hostile glare Cathy's way.

"Hey, she's cold and I am too! What's the matter with this bus?" the boy shouted to Cathy.

"Watch your tone, young man," Cathy said on her interior microphone. "I'm not sure what is causing the cold back there. It's nothing dangerous, I assure you. Taryn, you move to 3B and Zachary, take 6B." The two dutifully took their new seats and Cathy preempted any further problems by assigning new seats for those who would normally sit in back as they got on the bus.

Cathy drove away from the school feeling as if she'd already had a challenging afternoon. As she pulled onto Depot Road, she saw dark thunderheads building to the south and west. Wind was picking up and she thought, 'The way today is going it's going to pour before I get everyone home.'

The radio continued its cacophony of discordant noises mixed with static, sometimes squealing with feedback causing groaning complaints from the students. Cathy had delivered half of her students safely to their homes and the cemetery came into sight as she turned the corner onto Davison Road. Apparently some of the students had prepared some remarks to badger Alya and to get a dig into Cathy at the same time. "Get ready Alya," a boy said in a sing-song voice. "Your stop is coming." Laughter ensued with other snide comments likening Alya to a zombie which required Cathy to deliver a sharp reprimand to the students. Cathy prayed they would get by the cemetery with no incident.

Unfortunately, the bus slowed as it did in the morning. A small murmur and tittering could be heard from the students. Cathy pressed harder on the gas, but the bus continued to slow down. She took her microphone and advised the children, "I don't want to hear a word from anyone. Not one word!" The ambers started as they slowed to a stop at the lichgate. As had happened that morning, the reds flashed, the arm extended, and the passenger door opened as if allowing a student to exit. Cathy saw the students trying to stifle their laughter, some with their hands over their mouths with the exception of Alya who started to get up from her seat.

"Alya, please sit down. This is not your stop," Cathy told her.

"That's okay. I'll get off here. I can walk." Alya said as she tried to hurry off the bus.

"No, that is not permitted. Please take your seat." Cathy now truly felt the meaning of, *if looks could kill.*

A gust of cold air whished through the bus from back to front and a bolt of lightning flashed in the cemetery causing screams and startled gasps from the kids. The door slammed closed and Cathy began slowly driving to Alya's house. Cathy could see smoke in the center of the cemetery, but could not see where the lightning hit as the cemetery office building was in the way.

The heavy, low-hanging clouds were the color of fireplace ashes and blanketed out the daylight so, although it was only three o'clock, it was as dark as it might be at dusk. Thunder rumbled as the tempest approached heading north. Cathy was traveling southwest, sure to meet it head-on. She could see lightning flashing in the distance but so far, the storm was holding off.

Cathy finally reached the intersection where she made her left turn from Depot Road to Station Road when the first huge drops of rain pelted her windshield. Cathy groaned inside. "Please close your windows," she instructed. "The rain is starting."

She made her turn and the rain spattered down harder. Thunder crashed overhead and gusts of cold air blew through the bus. Hail pounding the roof sounded like someone feverishly playing a snare drum. The clouds let loose and Cathy turned her windshield wipers to high, but it still was almost impossible to see through the sheets of rain. Lightning was flashing very close and Cathy prayed that none of the trees on the hill to the right side of the road would be struck. The bus began to struggle toward the top of the hill just past Kelsea's house.

Cathy's eyes were wide open making sure the bus stayed on the road centered in her lane of traffic when an explosion to her left caught her attention. A tree had been struck by lightning very close to where she, Allie, and Kelsea had sat just a few weeks ago. Flames were shooting up into the sky. She heard a crackling, and the flaming tree tilted away. The flames struggled to survive but were doused by the rain. There was another large crash as the tree disappeared, followed by a rumble that shook the bus.

Cathy discharged her remaining students and continued to her turnaround at the Greenfield Township Volunteer Fire Department. She parked the bus, closed the windows, and wiped down the seats while she waited for the storm to wind down. The rain let up and the day brightened to a soft gray gloom as the most violent part of the storm headed out over Lake Erie. She powered up the bus and waited to pull back onto Station Road to head to

Saint Boniface for her grade-schoolers. To the south the sun pierced through the clouds creating a full double rainbow.

25

THE LETTERS

From the time the children got home to the time she went to bed, Luella was unable to begin looking at the letters Raphael had left with her. Frustration rendering her unable to sleep, she lay beside Gino, listening to his rhythmic snoring, the bathroom clock ticking, and the air conditioning going on and off, until she had to satisfy her curiosity. At one o'clock, she eased herself carefully out of bed and quietly made her way downstairs.

She removed the various and sundry bottles and spray cans of cleaning fluids in front of the decorative box containing the letters then lifted the box from its hiding place. She filled her cleaning tote with cleaning products and rags and carried it and the box of letters into the living room making herself comfortable in a chair where she could clearly see the top of the stairs.

Her heart was fluttering and the hair on her forearms and the back of her neck stood on end as she removed the top of the box to reveal several packets of yellowed envelopes with tattered edges tied together with ribbon. Some envelopes were smudged or stained. Some were torn on the side or had the flap missing, and some had no envelope at all.

As tenderly as she might handle a baby bird, Luella took the top packet from the box, laid it in her lap and untied the ribbon. She gently lifted each letter one by one and observed that they were arranged in chronological order. Then she began to read.

The earliest letter dated June 21, 1863 was from Leonardo addressed to his sister, Lydia. It was difficult to decipher Leonardo's letter due to his poor penmanship, misspellings, and badly formed sentences, a testament to the fact that school was not a high priority when he was growing up. The letter was just one page long apologizing for his having left home but stated he

252

couldn't stand living under his father's roof anymore after what he referred to as *the atrocity*. He expressed his hope that Lydia's beau, Samuel, had gotten his letter to her without their father finding out. He said he shed the Anatoli name and was now going by the name Leonardo Rosetti and was working on a farm for a kind-hearted, honest gentleman named Emil Chadwick, who had been left alone after his entire family was taken by smallpox. Only Emil survived to bury his wife and nine children. Because Emil was rendered blind by the disease, he was in desperate need for someone to help him with his farm and when Leonardo happened by, he took him in.

Luella struggled through the letter, the last few lines confusing her and increasing her curiosity.

> . . . My hands still burn from my deeds of that fateful night. Our secret festers inside me and I fear it will poison my very soul. May the good and understanding Lord forgive us. Prayers for your safety and the safety of Christina and our brothers.
>
> Your loving brother,
> Leo.

The next letter was artistically written in flourishing calligraphy by Lydia. Each character of every word drawn expertly with a fountain pen seemed a piece of artwork in itself with its embellishment of swirls, swoops, and swishes. To Luella's dismay the extra scrolls and flags which made the letters beautiful, also made Lydia's correspondence as difficult to read as Leonardo's.

Her first response to Leonardo was dated July 12, 1863.

> Dearest Brother,
>
> It was so great a relief to receive your kind letter which put my worries over you to rest. With the exception of Father, we have all fretted about your disposition and have missed your smile and support. Father has not uttered your name since your departure and has forbidden us to mention you in his presence.
>
> Rumors and suspicion are circulating about Father murdering our poor Mother and little Troy. The newspaper having even published articles to that effect.

Indeed, the Sheriff unexpectedly came by to make inquiry into the matter whereupon he became aware of your absence and thus asked Father about you as well. We children trembled in fear that Father would react to the Sheriff's bold questioning with violence. You could verily see the blood boiling within Father so we sat in frightened silence as the two men tensely walked around the house keeping a respectful distance from one another. Father told the Sheriff that you had run off shortly after Mother and Troy left for Maryland and he, therefore, has disowned you.

I am happy that you were fortunate to find work and decent living arrangements at the Chadwick farm. I hope Mr. Chadwick will prove to be as good a man as you believe. In time under his tutelage, you may be able to rid your mind of the hateful, brutal treatment at the hands of our father and of the horror we endured. I, too, am plagued by memories for doing Father's bidding, so much so I could not eat for many months and I looked to be wasting away perhaps to soon join Mother and Troy.

I would like to share my good news with you, my dear brother. I am betrothed to be married to Samuel and will be living with him in Erie following our nuptials. The prospect of escaping from Father has brought me from my melancholic state to one of hope and now that I have heard from you, and know that you are alive and well, I feel blessed.

Christina showed happiness for me at my announcement but her joy seemed restrained and I was later to find out why. That same night I awoke in the early morning hours to find Christina not in her bed. My search for her resulted in finding her in a distraught state crying in the barn, curled up next to Bruno's stall. As I held her weeping in my arms, she confessed her joy was tempered by her fear at being the only woman left in the household with Father. Not even the presence of our brothers was assuring to her. I, therefore, pledged to her that she would come to live with Samuel and myself in Erie where she said she will plan to find work as a seamstress.

I do wish you could be here for my wedding, but even if it were possible for you to travel here, I am certain Father would not let you step foot at the affair. Please keep me informed of your well-being and I shall do the same.

Your loving sister,
Lydia

Leonardo responded on August 3rd.

My Dear Sister,

My congratulations to you and Samuel. I hope for both of you a happy life together. Samuel has always shown himself to be a good and honorable fellow and I trust he will be a good husband to you. I also wish I could be there to share your joyous occasion. My heart is put at ease knowing both you and Christina will no longer dwell in fear in Father's house and can escape all of the terrifying memories stored there.

We are getting much news of the dreadful war tearing this country apart. The call for volunteers for President Lincoln's army has come to our small community and drafting will commence soon. Terrible reports of riots in New York City against conscription have caused over one hundred deaths there by brutal inhumane acts. As I will be turning seventeen on the eighteenth of this month, I informed my benefactor, Mr. Chadwick, that I will be answering the call to duty on that date. Mr. Chadwick, being unable to support and care for himself and feeling providence has given me to him as a son, has provided the $300.00 necessary to pay for a substitute to exempt me from service so that I may stay with him and continue to help him with his small farm.

Much love to you, Christina, Samuel, and my brothers.

Leo

Lydia's next letter dated September 20, 1863 informed Leonardo about her marriage and the firestorm that erupted with their father when Christina left home to reside with Lydia and Samuel in Erie.

> . . . Communications between us and our brothers have all but ceased with the exception of the rare occasion when Virgil is able to come to Erie without Father. He is then able to stop for a brief moment to inform us of our brothers' health and to see to ours as well.
>
> We, too, have received the news of the riots in New York City and enforcement of the Civil War Military Draft Act. I am comforted to know you will be spared from going off to war. I fear for Samuel who will be of age when the second draft will be held in Erie County in October. I regret to tell you that your brother, Virgil, has volunteered and will be leaving for Pittsburgh with the conscripts in October. It would be more fitting and a just penance if it were our Father offering up his life for our country and perhaps attaining some forgiveness by performing some heroic act. He, however, having attained the age of forty-six is exempt from service and, being his nature, is not capable of a selfless act.
>
> When Virgil informed me of his plans, he had young Josiah with him. Virgil was in the process of instructing Josiah what will be expected of him once Josiah is left as the eldest of our three brothers left with Father. I am much concerned about Josiah. His deportment is distant and detached. I fear a crushing melancholia has set upon him at the prospect of Virgil leaving. With no one to uplift him and he being left to bear the brunt and burden of our Father's volatile temperament, I fear for his future.
>
> Christina, too, I know, continues to suffer from our shared past suffering, as at night I sometimes hear her weeping and she occasionally wakes up in a fright with dreadful shrieks. Despite this, she is doing well and has begun taking in sewing work for her upkeep and has otherwise been a ray of sunshine and a great help to me in our home.
>
> With love,

Lydia

The third week of October Lydia wrote to Leonardo distressed that Samuel also volunteered for the Union forces in the hopes he could serve alongside Virgil. Both Virgil and Samuel took advantage of the $302.00 bounty for volunteering offered by Governor Curtin who was trying to meet a quota of thirty-eight thousand volunteers in 1863. In addition to that money, they received $300.00 from the County, and $50.00 from the district. Although Samuel left his bounty money with Lydia to support her and Christina while he was at war, Lydia was at her wits end worrying how long Samuel and Virgil would be away, if he and Virgil would survive, and if she and Christina would be all right while Samuel was away. .

Interspersed within the letters between Lydia and Leonardo, there were letters between Samuel and Lydia, Virgil and Lydia, a couple penned by Christina to Virgil, Leonardo, and Samuel, and a couple back to her. Most of the letters were quite short reporting news of the war, local news, and of personal and family matters. They discussed how they were getting through the winter and expressed their worry about their loved ones away from home fighting.

In a letter dated March 21, 1864, Samuel wrote to Lydia while recovering from wounds he suffered on March 2nd in Virginia under Brigadier General Hugh Kirkpatrick. Fighting beside Virgil, both were injured, but Virgil was struck twice in his upper thigh which necessitated an amputation a mere four inches from his torso. After lying comatose next to Samuel, Virgil finally succumbed to sepsis. Samuel related their harrowing experience and miraculous escape from capture and lamented the loss of Virgil. In heart-wrenching detail he acclaimed the courage of Virgil who had fought by his side and attributed his survival to his brother-in-law. He informed Lydia that Virgil's body was being transported back home for burial.

When Virgil's remains arrived home, a massive turnout came to honor him and bid him farewell at his funeral. Although barring Lydia and Christina from his home, Virgilio was unable to prevent them from being present at St. Elizabeth Church and Cemetery for Virgil's services.

Lydia forwarded this sad news to Leonardo as it occurred and continued to express her concerns about Josiah, which fears were realized in April when Josiah's broken body was found on the banks of Six Mile Creek off of the new Station Road after having thrown himself into the gorge from a sheer rock cliff.

Instead of having services in the church, Virgilio arranged for Josiah's funeral at his home followed by burial at St. Elizabeth Cemetery. The sisters again found their way to the cemetery. Staying far away from the other mourners, they cried and prayed for their deceased brother, now being laid to rest next to Virgil.

Luella, now emotionally spent, put away the letters, her cleaning supplies, and returned to bed.

26

THE FUNERAL

Cathy, having finished her morning run, was waiting to pull onto Depot Road to go home. The cars traveling on Depot were spaced just close enough to make it unsafe to enter the flow of traffic. She stared to her left wondering why, at this hour of the morning, there should be so much traffic. A spasm of dread went through her when the black hearse carrying Celia's body came toward her like a specter, its headlights glaring, grill grim and foreboding. Her eyes were glued on the hearse as it seemed to glide along dragging its followers along in a veil of dark gloom. When the last car in the procession passed, Cathy was able to turn onto Depot Road. She felt the veil envelop her car and she followed the funeral cortege to the cemetery, breaking off and parking near the Rosetti family plot.

Cathy made her way to a sturdy maple tree, her concentration riveted on the tent in the Anatoli plot and those gathering there. Gino, Luella, and their children were already seated by the gravesite while mourners dressed nicely in dark, muted colors joined them.

Gradually, her vision blurred. She blinked hard and squinted at the mourners at Celia's grave. Every individual there looked now to be in black. The women wore black dresses to their ankles, the men dressed in black tails holding black top hats. Celia's ivory casket adorned with gold handles was now a small plain pine coffin.

In her peripheral vision to the left, Cathy noticed a shadow and turned to see two young women dressed in long black garments wearing black bonnets keeping their distance from the graveside service. Both girls were crying, the older of the two had her arm over the shoulder of the younger girl. Cathy blinked and looked

259

back toward those gathered at the committal rites. Her vision now clear, she saw Luella, Gino, their children, and the rest of the mourners as she'd seen them when she had arrived at the cemetery.

Cathy was mystified as to the meaning of this twist to her incomprehensible visualizations. She'd become accustomed to phantom appearances of Troy and Lavinia, but who were these two young women and whose burial were they watching? As she contemplated the answers to her questions, she could hear the priest's baritone voice, but she could not make out what he was saying. His voice was merely a comforting hum combining with the sound of the occasional bird chirping and the leaves rustling in the soft breeze overhead. She saw the priest close his Bible and a few of the mourners in the back began to peel off to their cars. Cathy did the same and drove home.

Luella and her family solemnly left Celia's burial site. Luella was holding Nico's hand and everyone was walking slowly with downcast eyes not saying a word. On the drive to Lakeview Country Club, Nico spoke up softly from the back seat, "Do we have to go?" Immediately Vincent elbowed him.

Gino scowled at Luella who turned around to look at the youngster. "Yes, Nico, and you're going to be good while you're there. No running around, no being noisy, and no pouting. You're going to be a little gentleman while you're there," she instructed.

"But why? We already did a bunch of stuff for the funeral. Wasn't that enough?" Nico asked causing Amelia to giggle and everyone with the exception of Gino to smile.

"Nico!" Gino said gruffly.

Luella was about to reprimand Nico when Amelia turned around to look at her brother. "Honey, this is only a lunch. This is what happens after a funeral. People get together. They talk. Go over old times and just remind themselves that they're carrying on and they're happy to be alive and have each other. You just hang out with me today. Okay?"

Luella was stunned wondering where that came from. She glanced at Gino who was looking straight ahead. Luella caught a quick flash of surprise in his eyes, too. Whether it was college, or

Celia's death, or the combination of both, Luella was glad to see this sign of maturity in her daughter.

Gino took a parking place near the front entrance that was being vacated by someone leaving and, as he maneuvered into the spot, Luella noticed the Rosettis walking toward them. She fortified herself for the unavoidable introductions.

Raphael and Rachel smiled warmly at Luella as she exited the car and slowly angled toward her. "Hello, Luella. Very nice service."

Gino closed his door, locked the car, and stared at them, trying to remember who this couple was.

Luella herded the children to Raphael and Rachel with Gino bringing up the rear. "It's good to see you. I'm glad you were able to come. This is Amelia, Adam, Vincent, and Nico. And this is my husband Gino." Gino came around the children to shake hands with Raphael and Rachel.

Luella watched Gino's face carefully as she said, "This is Raphael and Rachel Rosetti. They've been vacationing in Erie and researching Raphael's ancestry and, do you know what?" By Gino's face, Luella knew that Gino knew what. "They're distant relatives of the Anatoli family. I had always wondered why Celia left flowers at the statue in the Rosetti family plot. Raphael and Rachel stopped by the other day when you were out and we chatted a few moments. I told them they were welcome to come to Celia's service and luncheon, if they wished."

"Hmph," Gino grunted. "Yes, Grandma had mentioned the Rosetti family was somehow related. Glad to meet you." Gino looked at Luella with steely eyes and took hold of her upper arm. "We better get in there," he said and began walking quickly to the entrance of the country club, moving Luella along, the children trailing behind. "I'll talk to you about this later," he whispered harshly to Luella.

Raphael and Rachel looked at each other in shared discomfort and slowed their walk to fall behind the Anatolis. "I think you can forget about talking with Mr. Anatoli, hon," Rachel said softly. "I'm sorry."

"Me, too," Raphael replied. "Especially because I think he does know about the family history."

"Mm-hm. Maybe someone else will, too, and perhaps be willing to talk about it." Rachel took Raphael's hand. "If nothing else, we'll have a nice lunch and meet some of your distant relatives."

A small buffet of luncheon meats, cheeses, rolls and breads, salads, sweets, and coffee was set up. A waitress was working the room taking orders for other beverages from the bar. The guests were milling about talking in low voices, meeting and mingling with seldom seen relatives and friends. A number of people were already seated and eating.

"Go ahead and get yourselves something to eat, kids," Luella told her children. As the kids walked away from her she studied them for any resemblance to Virgilio's children with whom she now felt an intimacy after reading their letters. Her eyes were feeling heavy from her late night reading and she asked Gino, "Would you like a cup of coffee, dear?"

Still angry, in a rough whisper he replied as if he hadn't heard her question. "What right did you think you had to invite complete strangers to a family funeral? And the Rosettis, no less. They're just trying to find out some dirt about us."

"What dirt? We don't have any dirty secret to hide. You weren't there when they came. I'm sorry, I felt I had to invite them."

"Had to, shit. I know you. No backbone. I can see you now. Hey, but that's all right. Have our reputation torn to shreds all over this town."

Luella tried to control her exasperation. "Gino, even if there is some horrible skeleton in the closet from long ago, it doesn't affect us. We didn't do anything wrong. And it's not going to be plastered all over the papers."

"Oh, you're so naïve. You just wait. You'll see." Gino stormed off toward the waitress.

Luella noticed the Rosettis standing awkwardly by themselves, each holding a drink. Feeling responsible for their awkwardness, and for Gino's anger, she decided she could at least be a good hostess and joined them. "I'm sorry about Gino coming off a bit rude. I'm afraid I warned you."

"Oh, don't worry about it, Luella. We're fine," Rachel said.

"Why don't you put down your drinks and get yourselves something to eat. I might as well, too. I definitely want some coffee. I spent a good part of the night reading many of the letters from the box. The last one I read was about Josiah."

Raphael shook his head. "Such a tragedy. It's hard to imagine a young man doing that, and for what reason?"

"Yes. I'd noticed from his gravestone that he'd died young and I always thought he probably had died from disease. I never imagined he committed suicide," Luella said as they walked to the buffet table.

"Yes, you'd think that. Whenever I see the grave of a child or someone very young, I always wonder about them, how and why they died so young," Rachel said.

"I do, too. I think everyone probably does," Luella agreed. As she took a plate and utensils she noticed Gino staring at her from across the room standing with three other men. "I imagine you visited St. Elizabeth Cemetery prior to today, didn't you?"

"Yes, it was one of the first things we did when we got here," Rachel replied.

"It was quite heart-stirring to see the names of the people I'd known through their letters, and who have seemed so alive to me all these years, engraved on headstones," Raphael added. "And the obelisk for Virgilio, so stark and stained right in the middle, looks downright menacing."

"Yes, it looks malevolent. One thing that struck us, too, we saw no markers for Lavinia and Troy," said Rachel.

"We looked in both the Rosetti and the Anatoli plots," said Raphael. "No matter what had happened, you'd think they'd still be buried with their family."

"Their absence is actually what started my friend from doing her, I guess you'd call it, investigation." Luella looked at them and laughed a little. "She tells me she's found out some interesting things and I have as well. So it will be nice when all of us can sit down and put our heads together. I've got to tell you," she sighed and shook her head. "All this speculation is wreaking havoc on my sanity."

"The Rosettis laughed. "You don't appear to have anything to worry about in that regard, Luella," Rachel assured her.

"No, really. I've had disturbing dreams and queer things seem to be occurring, I perceive things that absolutely can't be real." Luella did not notice that Gino had left his conversation and come over to the food table.

263

"I've had dreams all my life about the family," Raphael told her. "But dreams are only your mind working on a problem. Don't worry about it. You're as sane as anyone else."

Gino touched Luella on the shoulder. "The kids are over there eating," he said pointing. "I'm getting a plate and will join you in a minute." He left the three and walked to the beginning of the food line without looking at the Rosettis.

When they arrived home, Luella was dreading being left alone with Gino. However, when the kids dispersed to their own activities, she was surprised she did not get reamed out for asking the Rosettis to Celia's funeral and wake. Instead, Gino retreated behind an icy, impenetrable wall of silence.

After such a long day with only a couple hours of rest the previous night, Luella felt exhausted and alone. The stress of Gino's silent treatment built up until she approached him in tears. "Gino, I'm not merely your housekeeper, child bearer and nanny. I'm your wife. I'm supposed to be your partner. We're supposed to be sharing our lives with each other--combining our lives. Why can't you tell me about your family history so I can understand why you don't want anyone to know about it? You can at least tell me. I'm your wife."

Gino had just finished drinking another gin and tonic and was watching the news in his favorite chair. Gino's eyes lasered in on Luella, getting smaller with his scowl. His lips disappeared as his mouth straightened into a hard line. "There's nothing to tell." Feeling the effects of the alcohol he had consumed, he got up from his chair and unsteadily headed toward the kitchen carrying an empty glass.

Luella followed him pausing in the kitchen entryway. "My God, if something happened way back in the 1800's, there's nothing for you to be ashamed of."

Gino turned abruptly and glared at her. "So why are you so all fired concerned about it?" He turned to put his glass in the sink but he was too close and shattered it on the bullnose of the counter.

"Here, let me," Luella said as she brushed by Gino to get her whisk broom and dustpan. "You seem to forget what happened the other night, or you don't want to remember. There's some unfinished business, don't you see? I want to do what I can to make things right, to settle matters." Luella didn't realize that when she knelt down, she'd cut her knee on a fine piece of glass and it began bleeding. "Part of your distant family is not resting in peace and they want to be found and to be properly laid to rest."

"You're out of your fucking mind," Gino said in disgust. "I'm going to get the kids in. It's getting late."

Luella finished picking up the shards of glass and when she got up, noticed the puddle of blood from her knee and felt woozy looking at it. After wiping it up, she went to the powder room to tend to her wound and heard Nico and Vincent clamor into the house.

All Luella could think about was getting to bed. When she walked into the living room to go upstairs, Gino was back in his chair and Vincent and Nico were on the floor watching television. "I'm exhausted. I'm going to bed. You kids should get ready for bed, too."

"Aw, Mom. It's Friday and it's only eight o'clock," Vincent whined.

Luella took a deep breath and was about to argue the point, but Gino uncharacteristically announced, "I'll get them to bed."

The boys looked gleefully at their heroic father and Luella was too tired to care that Gino did not back her up. "Okay, good night."

"Night, Mom," the children chimed together. Gino said nothing.

Her body craved sleep, but, all the same, Luella wanted to read more of the letters. She told herself she'd read more if she woke up in the middle of the night, felt rested, and everyone else was asleep. Minutes after she laid her head on her pillow, she was out and REM sleep began.

She was standing in the middle of her kitchen lit with blindingly bright fluorescent lights that hurt her eyes, making her squint. A profusely bleeding slash crossed her torso from her left collar bone to her right hip creating an ever expanding puddle of blood at her feet. Gino, standing two feet away from her, was glowering and holding a large, triangular shaped piece of glass, blood dripping off the razor sharp edge. His hand, too, was dripping blood from clenching the cut glass. Luella opened a cabinet door from which spilled thick, white towels into the puddle of blood. She knelt down, the front of her was saturated with blood which continued to leak from her wound. She tried to soak up the blood with the white towels which slowly turned crimson as they absorbed the blood.

The glaring, white-light fluorescence of the room began to dim until it was a shady murkiness, lit only by flickering oil lamps. Luella was watching two young women in long dresses wiping blood off of her kitchen floor with rags. But it wasn't her kitchen floor, it was a wooden floor that was now stained a dark Indian red from the blood of a woman, boy, and dog lying behind them. Looming over the girls was a large gnarly ogre with red glowing eyes. Five boys stood in the doorway staring at the scene in shock.

"Berto, Michael, help your sisters clean up this mess," the red-eyed fiend commanded. "Virgil, Leo, Josiah, get the wagon ready. Lay some hay down in the back. Presto."

The monstrosity followed the boys out the door and left it open to monitor both them and the work being done in the kitchen. Through the quiet night, he could hear Bruno snorting and being taken from his stall, the boys handling tack, and finally the wagon being moved to the front of the house.

Virgil, every cell of his being hating the brute that was his father, stomped in the house with Josiah and Leonardo behind him. "Wagon's in front," he said with disdain.

"You watcha you mouth or you join your Mama. Now put them on the wagon." The ghastly ghoul flung his hand toward the kitchen.

Anger emanated from their eyes as the boys filed past their master. An unseen force seemed to control them which prevented them from thrashing out against their tormentor. As they walked out, Virgil carrying his mother, Josiah carrying Troy, and Leo cradling the dog, Toby, the souls of the three boys were consumed by horror, grief, remorse for not protecting their loved ones, hate for the killer, and lust for revenge.

"You're not done," the ugly goon commanded, directing his instruction to the four in the kitchen who immediately scooted to the area, wet with blood, previously occupied by the three corpses.

"We gonna be a little bit. After you done here, you get alla Mama's and Troy's things and put 'em in grain sacks. And don' you thinka runnin' off an' talkin' to no one about this. You have

266

all this done when we get back. You understand?" His red eyes bathed the kitchen in red.

The demonic humanoid took his seat beside Virgil in the wagon. Josiah and Leonardo rode in the back, leaning backwards against the driver's area. The ogre that was Virgilio motioned its head to get going. Virgil cracked the reins hard on Bruno's rump, yelling, "Hya!" Bruno lurched forward.

Restless from her dream, Luella moaned and rolled while she slept but did not wake up until her hand knocked over her water glass from her night stand. The cracking of the glass on the bedside table jarred Luella from slumber. She stumbled, not quite awake, to the bathroom, grabbed some towels and soaked up the spilled water. If she had more dreams that night, she did not remember them. However, the kitchen scene came back to her vividly when she awoke and saw her thick white bath towels on the night stand and carpet, wet from having soaked up her spilled water.

27

PIECES OF THE PUZZLE

Gino was already downstairs when Luella woke up for the day. She could not be sure if he had even come to bed that night or he had fallen asleep in his chair. She picked up the damp towels from her nightstand and the floor and hung them back on the towel bars where, in her semi-awake state, she had gotten them during the night. The details of her dream were so graphic it felt more like a memory of a life experience than a dream. Her heart thumped wildly as she yearned to talk to Cathy. They just had to resolve this.

She put a robe on over her nightgown and went downstairs trying to escape from the grasp of her nightmare. "Good morning," she greeted Gino when she walked into the living room.

"Mornin'," he responded, barely looking at her, an edge still in his voice but his anger had definitely subsided.

"Do you want breakfast?" she asked.

Gino looked at her, his face softening, "Ham, eggs, toast sounds good before I go out into the fields. Harvest time you know, so I'll be busy out there a good part of the day."

Hearing Gino was going to be occupied all day, lifted Luella's heart. The kids filtered through the kitchen one by one as she was cooking. While accommodating their requests for breakfast, she learned of their plans for the day. Nico and Vincent wanted to ride on the picker with their dad, Amelia had plans to go to a girlfriend's house, and Adam was going to get some schoolwork out of the way so he could enjoy his evening and Sunday. As soon as she had a moment to herself, she called Cathy.

"Luella! I'm surprised to hear from you. Is everything all right?"

"Oh, yes. Everything is fine. I just have so much to talk to you about and, luckily, I've got some time right now."

"That's great. I've been itching to talk to you, too. What's been going on?"

"Oh my, I've learned so much since we've spoken to each other. You'll be amazed to hear who came by the house and attended the service at the cemetery and the wake. It's unreal. And combined with the dreams I've had lately, my mind is spinning. I'm just glad I have you to talk to about all this."

"I totally understand, Luella. So who came to the funeral?"

"A descendant of Leonardo Anatoli who goes by the last name, Rosetti."

"Really!"

"Yes, his name is Raphael Rosetti. It turns out that in 1862-ish Leonardo ran off, ended up in Ohio, and changed his last name to Rosetti. Raphael lives in Ohio with his wife Rachel and they came to Erie for vacation this year because he's been researching his family tree. He wanted to see the family graves and hoped he might get information from any of the Anatolis or Rosettis that still lived in the Erie area. They saw Celia's obituary in the paper and stopped by our house, hoping to talk to Gino. Gino wasn't home, but you know how he is. He wouldn't have talked to them anyway. I only spoke to them briefly but they brought a treasure trove of letters that you're going to want to see. They're letters written between Virgilio's kids!"

"Holy crap!"

"I know! I've read a number of the letters and I tell you, I almost feel like I know Leo, Lydia, Christina and the rest of the kids personally now. They feel real to me."

"Oh my goodness! I'd love to read them."

"And I'd love for you to see them plus I need to hear all that you've wanted to tell me. I don't know if you're doing anything right now, but Gino's gone for who knows how long out in the field and he took Nico and Vincent with him. Amelia and Adam are busy, so I was wondering if I could stop over for a while and we could talk."

"No, I'm not busy at all. Please, come right over. You don't know how intrigued I am."

"Actually, I think I do. I'll be over in a few minutes." They ended their call and Luella rushed upstairs to throw on some clothes and put the box of letters in a grocery bag along with the papers she'd found in the attic.

"Adam, I'm going to be gone for a little bit," she yelled. "I'll probably pick up some groceries and lunch. Think you'll be here when I get home?"

"I don't know," Adam shouted from his room. "Don't worry about me for lunch. I can throw a sandwich together if I get hungry."

With that, Luella felt free to spend as much time as needed with Cathy.

Cathy stood holding her phone feeling her heart pounding in her chest, her nerve ends making her skin prickle with excitement.

"Who was that?" Paul asked.

Cathy hesitated. "Luella Anatoli."

"What?" Paul exclaimed. "Since when did you get friendly with her?"

"I, uh, well, I ran into her one day and we started talking."

Paul raised an eyebrow and his mouth turned down in disapproval. "I'm done worrying about this. If I don't, I'm going to end up with high blood pressure."

"It's about time," Cathy told him.

He turned away from her and snapped his newspaper back in position before his face.

"It's about time," Cathy told him. "Come on, Troy. Let's get some snacks out and put some coffee on," she said and hurried to the kitchen with a smile on her face.

It wasn't very long before the doorbell rang and Troy ran barking to the door. Cathy greeted Luella with a hug. "How are you doing, hon?"

Luella embraced Cathy and smiled. "Okay. Everything's been so strange lately and my dreams. . . Well, I'll have to tell you about the dreams I've been having."

"Come on in. This is my husband, Paul," Cathy said as Paul got up from his chair.

"Yes, I remember you from the restaurant. I apologize for Gino. He can be a difficult man at times, but he actually means well. He can come off confrontational like he did that day, but he's actually trying to be protective of his family."

"No need to explain. It's a pleasure to meet you," Paul said.

"Pleasure's mine," Luella shook Paul's hand. "Cathy here has been a Godsend for me. I'm so glad she didn't take Gino's rudeness to heart."

Paul looked as if someone had popped a balloon in front of his face and Cathy smiled smugly in self-satisfaction. Perhaps Luella's words would end Paul's worries about the Anatolis objections to her inquiry.

"Come on into the kitchen, Luella. I just put on a pot of coffee."

Luella put the grocery bag on the table next to Cathy's Anatoli folder and removed the box and her documents. Troy put his paws on the table and began sniffing the letter box and whining. He sat down and stared at Luella who felt compelled to pet him. She looked into Troy's eyes and had difficulty breaking his stare. An overwhelming sense of grief came over her and she teared up. Cathy grabbed a box of Kleenex for Luella.

As she dabbed at her eyes, Luella said softly, "I really didn't cry at Celia's funeral. I suppose I'm just starting to relax after all that's happened, so I'm crying now." She laughed nervously.

Cathy rubbed Luella's shoulder. "You've been through a lot." She poured both of them mugs of coffee, and put creamer, sugar, and a plate of cookies on the table. "May I?" she asked reaching for the box containing the letters.

"Certainly. I have a feeling you're going to be just as taken by their words as I have been. I can picture the people behind the letters and I feel they're part of me now." Luella paused. "They've given me a glimpse into the past."

Cathy looked straight at Luella. "You're exactly right." Cathy started looking at the first letter and became absorbed. "I think, before I get engrossed here, I'll show you what I've got." Cathy proceeded to fill Luella in on everything she'd experienced from the time Troy came into her life until that day, that moment, showing her various documents that went along with what she was saying.

271

Luella then reciprocated as Cathy studied the letters. "I've been seeing things, perceiving things, that I know are impossible to be real. I just want to put all of this to rest--put Lavinia and Troy to rest. And now, I'm convinced how horribly they died, and how carelessly their remains were treated, I have to find them and give them a proper burial. Because, as crazy as it sounds, I believe my dreams. And I know they died here and their bodies were hidden somewhere in Harborcreek."

"I believe our dreams, too," Cathy assured her. "Now, I told you my son is going to get permission to use the GPR equipment from the forensic science department at Mercyhurst. His whole class might get in on this as a learning project, who knows. But, I'll find out how he's coming along with getting the equipment. With both your and the Rosettis' permission, he should be able to survey both the Rosetti and the Anatoli plots for any unmarked graves. Also, he's going to investigate what may be under our personal pet cemetery."

Luella glanced at the clock. "Good heavens! Look at the time. We've been talking for almost four hours! I think I'll run to the IGA, get some subs, a few groceries, and get on home. If Gino and the boys aren't in the house, I'll take the ATV out to deliver their lunch to them, and no one will be the wiser about where I went."

Luella started packing away the info she'd brought over. "You know, I don't think we'll have to get together on Monday now that we've caught each other up. Why don't I just contact the Rosettis and we can get together with them next week. You do want to meet them, don't you?"

"Yes, I certainly do. We can meet at my house again, if you like. I think it would be less likely that Gino would notice you and the Rosettis being at my house rather than yours." Cathy and Troy walked with Luella to the front door.

"I agree. I'll get in touch with them."

"Ten o-clock-ish would be best for me after my morning run. Just send me a text as to what day would be best. Any day's fine."

"Okay, I'll let you know," Luella said in parting.

As soon as Cathy closed the door, Paul asked, "Well?"

"Well, she filled in some gaps for me and I hope I did the same for her. I gave her some background with what I've learned from my research and," Cathy stopped herself from saying, 'my dreams,' instead said, "gave her moral support by letting her know she's not alone."

"That's good, hon. You're going to have at least one friend in the loony bin."

"Very funny," Cathy smirked. "I did observe that you took note that she seemed quite thankful for my efforts."

"Yes, dear. I did."

"Ok, then . . ."

"Okay then, you have my blessing to carry on with your snooping."

"Anything else?"

"Oh, I see. You're looking for an apology, aren't you?"

Cathy folded her arms and raised her eyebrows waiting.

"Okay, then. I'm sorry for giving you such a hard time about this. But, I doubt you're ever going to win Gino over."

"Probably not, but he's not the one that's having the nightmares."

Cathy picked her phone up and walked to the deck where she called Tony and updated him on everything.

"That's great, Mom. All we need to do now is pick a day."

Dawn was breaking on Thursday when the caretaker at St. Elizabeth Cemetery unlocked the gate to allow Tony and Professor Duncan's graduate assistant, Max Pulaski, to enter. They parked at the corner of Lot 1 of Section A and rolled the GPR unit onto the ground and sat down on a nearby bench to drink the coffee they bought on the way and wait for the other students and the Rosettis to arrive.

"I haven't had as much opportunity to use the GPR equipment as I would like, so I've been looking forward to this," Max told Tony.

Tony went into detail about his mother's project. "I'm hoping we can come up with something for her."

"I hope we come up with answers rather than more questions. You never know what you'll find in the old sections of cemeteries," Max replied.

"Yes, I've been reading about GPR use today. More and more cemeteries are using GPR mapping to find unmarked graves and to more accurately mark graves that may have shifted due to ground movement. My gut tells me, we're going to find something today."

"It's amazing what GPR can uncover. It's been instrumental in finding mass graves of slaves, especially in the plantations of the south. The bodies are sometimes not even buried in a cemetery. In 2013, the bodies of almost one thousand people were discovered at a Shell refinery in Ascension Parish, Louisiana alone. And that's not the only case. More and more burial grounds are being uncovered--one hundred bodies here, one hundred there. Even Mount Vernon had a slave burial ground, all with unmarked graves with the exception of George Washington's favorites." Max shook his head and made a sour face.

"GPR's certainly been helpful in revealing the awful truth. The good 'ol days were not so good." Tony took a sip of his coffee thinking, 'If the souls of Lavinia and Troy had been crying out for justice and acknowledgement, the cries from the souls of all those slaves whose bodies were discarded so callously must be deafening, if we would only hear them.'

Around seven o'clock the rest of the students began joining Tony and Max. The Rosettis showed up shortly after seven with the last student and introduced themselves. Tony and the Rosettis discussed their interest in the area around the angel statue which, because they were mapping the lots in numerical order, Lot 4 being the second to last in Section A, it would be a little while before their curiosity would be satisfied. Tony had made sure that he would be the individual running the GPR unit in Lot 4.

Max gave a small lecture about GPR equipment, its applications in industry, building, forensics, and archaeology, how it works, procedures to follow, etc., then they began their mapping. They had already begun work on Lot 2, when Luella joined everyone, but they had not yet gotten to Virgilio's, Virgil's, Josiah's, Alberto's, and Michael's graves.

"How is everything going?" she asked the Rosettis.

"Fine, but nothing unusual has been found yet," Raphael told her.

"We had a little education this morning about ground penetrating radar," Rachel said. "It was pretty interesting."

"It would be so nice if they were found here in unmarked graves," Luella said with hope. "Then, perhaps, we'd know they were at least buried in an appropriate place, even if they'd had a terrible life with Virgilio and he hid their bodies here."

Another fifteen minutes and the GPS was being rolled in the vicinity of Virgilio's family graves. Their findings indicated that the markers were not precisely at the head of the graves, but no graves were found without markers and the group moved on to Lot 3 with the same result.

Tony took over handling the GPS machine as planned for Lot 4 when Cathy and Troy joined everyone. She noted the markings on the ground. "Looks like you're making progress," she said to Tony.

"As to covering area, we are," Tony replied, somewhat discouraged. "We've actually come across one questionable spot. See where they're probing? It doesn't look promising, however."

"At least you're eliminating possibilities," Cathy told him and walked over to where the Rosettis and Luella were seated. Troy sought attention from them, then settled down."

"We're waiting for a Eureka," Raphael said.

"Have you been here all morning?" Cathy asked.

"Mm-hm, we have," Rachel said. "After they finish this lot, we were thinking of going to lunch. Care to join us?"

"I've got my sidekick here that I have to give some attention to, so I'll probably just grab something at home. Anything else new?"

"The dream I had over the weekend has reocurred, actually a couple times." Luella said. Troy went over to her, licked her hand, then lay down on her feet.

"Troy, don't bother Luella. Get back over here."

"Oh, he's okay. He's actually a comfort." Luella bent over to pet Troy. "I haven't dreamt the whole dream over again in its entirety. Just parts of it come back. And one night, it picked up where it left off." Luella looked past Cathy as if in a trance. "As soon as they got on their way, Josiah began sobbing in the back of the wagon. Then Virgilio turned around and cracked him on the side of his head so hard he fell against the side of the wagon opening a gash above his ear. Virgilio was yelling at him to be a man. I can just picture it when I'm talking to you. Virgil was sitting by his father with such hate in his eyes. I could hear Bruno's hooves pounding, taste the misty air, and smell Virgilio's grapes as they thrashed through the vineyard. It's as if I were there. It was a chilly, dank, dreary night." Luella shivered, then she seemed to focus on Cathy again. "They seemed to be going on and on, driving for a great distance. I could see the bodies being jostled around in the back. It was awful!"

"Did you have any idea where they were headed? Did they arrive anywhere?"

"No, they were just racing along. Virgilio pushing the horse, whipping it to go forward."

"Did it seem like they might have been traveling farther than here from your house? It wouldn't take a long time to get here even in those days."

"That's what I'm feeling, too." Luella scrunched her forehead trying to search for any other clues from her dreams. "I don't think we're going to have any answers today. They buried them someplace else," Luella said dejectedly, her eyes tearing up.

Rachel rubbed Luella's back. "Don't worry, Luella. I think we're close."

"Come on, Troy," Cathy said. "Let's go talk to Tony. He's just getting to the angel statue.

When Tony made no exclamation after he had moved past the statue, Cathy knew. "Nothing?" she asked.

"No. Sorry, Mom."

"Are you still going to take a look at our pet cemetery?"

"Mm-hm. If we don't find what we're looking for, at least we'll learn what small graves and remains look like compared to larger ones with the GPR," Tony rationalized. "Good experience anyway."

"I'm going to finish giving Troy his exercise," Cathy told him. "If you don't get to the house before I leave for the afternoon run, text me what you find, okay?"

"I will."

Cathy was fixing herself a quick lunch when she saw Tony and the others going to the Pantona Pet Cemetery. Troy barked frantically at the noise in his yard. They were finishing up when Cathy left the house for work. She looked at Tony who shook his head, "No."

Before she shut her phone off to leave on her bus run, she saw Tony's text. "There is something under Sadie's grave, but it's too small to be human remains."

28

THE FINAL PIECE

Cathy was disappointed and frustrated. She tried to resign herself to the fact that she may never learn what Virgilio did with Lavinia's and Troy's bodies. She found herself hoping to have some unexplained interference on the radio, malfunction of the bus controls, or some fantastic phantom vision that might give her some clue or at least let her know she still had a connection. She'd then have some hope, but the afternoon was uneventful.

Looking at the pet cemetery when she walked into the house that night, she sighed. On the one hand, she was glad they hadn't been found there. She didn't want to have to disturb any of the graves, but if they had been there, everything would have been resolved.

Troy's exuberant greeting cheered her, but his bright blue eye reminded her of the little boy forever lost to the world. Cathy took Troy's face in her hands and kissed the top of his head. "Do you think you could find them, boy?"

Troy cocked his head trying to understand her words.

"Come on. Time to go out."

While Troy took care of his business, she walked around the yard trying to concentrate on what to make for dinner that night rather than brood over her unresolved quandary. She brought Troy in and was ready to start cooking when her phone rang.

"Allie! What a nice surprise. How are you honey?"

"I'm fine, Mom. How are you doing?"

"We're doing okay. We miss you, of course."

"Well you won't have to wait to see me much longer. Kelsea and I are getting ready to come home this weekend, remember? Kelsea's all excited about her photography project and has made a list of some of the places said to be haunted in Erie--The Erie Cemetery, Axe Murder Hollow, the Gudgeonville Covered Bridge, and Wintergreen Gorge, just to see if she can capture any metaphysical ghostly types on film. And, she wants me to bring Troy along with us, if we could, because of the aura that showed up on the photos I took. She thinks he might attract spirits, says he'd be called an animal PSI, sort of an animal medium. Would it be okay to take him along?"

"Sure, if you have to promise to watch him very closely. He won't be familiar with those areas and he still limps, you know."

"Don't worry. We'll take good care of him." Allie paused a moment. "Hmm, I wonder if I could find us a couple of Ghost Buster T-Shirts before we come home. That'd be kind of cute to wear them, don't you think?" Both she and Cathy laughed. "Speaking of spirits, Mom, what's been happening with your search for Lavinia and Troy?"

"A lot has happened, but we haven't found them. Your brother was out with his class and they mapped out part of the cemetery and our pet cemetery with their GPR equipment. Unfortunately, they came up with nothing."

"Tch, oh, I'm sorry, Mom. So are you going to keep looking?"

"I don't know. I don't even know where to begin anymore."

"If it gives you any hope, I had a dream about Troy Anatoli playing hide and seek in the field with his dog, Toby, just last night."

"You did?" The first dream Cathy had about Troy replayed in her head.

"Yes. It was a rather pleasant dream. I was at the edge of a wheat field, at least I think it was wheat. The wheat, or whatever it was, was straw colored, and an Australian Shepherd was jumping and sniffing around. Then all of a sudden a little towheaded boy with bright blue eyes peeked out of the hay. He was somewhat camouflaged because his light hair blended in so well with the wheat. The dog jumped on him and they tussled. The boy was giggling and the dog was yipping and barking. It was a nice dream. But when I woke up, I was kind of bummed, because I know the story."

Chills went through Cathy. "I've got to keep looking," she said.

"Wish I could help you, but I'm down here."

"Oh, you have already, dear."

"I've got to get going, Mom. I'll see you tomorrow afternoon. Kisses to Dad and Troy."

"All right, dear. You two drive carefully."

As Cathy continued dinner preparations, with Troy following her about hoping for scraps of food to be dropped, all the dreams she'd had about Lavinia and Troy whirled through her head mixed with the information she'd gathered, the letters, the documents, and what she knew about Luella's dreams. She was convinced that their dreams were a peephole into a past reality. She could almost hear, see, and feel the wagon clacking along through the vineyard path in the dark night, as Luella had described. But where were they going? Where did they end up if not in the cemetery?

She got Troy's attention with a piece of cheese and he sat down obediently staring back at her with his happy dog smile, the end of his tongue out. "Do you know something little boy?" she asked. "Can you find your namesake?"

Paul, although glad this nonsense would be coming to an end, was sympathetic when, during dinner, Cathy told him the results of Tony's GPR study.

"I am sorry, dear," he told her with sincerity. "You put a lot of work into this. You did all that you could. I'm afraid you'll have to just let this one go." He noted her look of defeat. "It wasn't all for nothing, don't forget. You have made sure Lavinia and Troy were not forgotten. You kind of resurrected them by looking into it and talking about them."

"Yes, but they're still laying somewhere discarded like trash, like they didn't matter. That's not right."

"All I can say is you did what you could. You couldn't have done any more." Paul said but Cathy still looked glum. "I know one thing you could possibly do."

"Oh?" a flicker of hope crossed Cathy's face.

"Perhaps you, the Rosettis, and Luella could possibly get small stones for each of them made, even have one made for Toby. I'd be willing to design them if you want." Paul smiled. "And you could place the stones by the angel statue. At least they'd have a small memorial. I'm thinking the Rosetti family put that statue there for Lavinia and Troy anyway."

"That's a wonderful idea, Paul." Cathy got up to get her phone.

"Aren't you going to finish eating?"

"Yes. This will only take a second. I'm going to text Luella to call me."

Paul smiled feeling like a hero. Now, surely, this would be the end of it.

Allie arrived home when Cathy was walking to the house after work. After a hug and a kiss, they walked in together causing a manic eruption of confused happiness from Troy who ran back and forth between the two, barking, jumping, and giving wild, wet kisses.

"Okay, okay," Allie laughed. "I missed you, too." She turned to her mother. "Feels nice to be home."

"You're happy there, aren't you? Is everything all right?"

"Oh, yeah, Mom," Allie smiled. "School's great. I'm loving it, actually. It just feels so layback coming home. Just a nice little break."

"Well, I'm glad you feel that way. We'll always be your Zen oasis when you need it."

They smiled at each other. "That's good. I will probably need it. College life is proving to be pretty hectic and demanding."

"How're you doing with your schedule?" Cathy asked, picking up Allie's overnight bag and placing it at the foot of the stairs.

"Oh, I'm getting used to it. You know. I'm not the best at time management, but so far, so good. I downloaded a schedule planner app and it seems to be working for me so far. But there is one thing about the app that I don't like."

"What's that?"

"I'm beginning to resent it. I find myself telling it to shut up once in a while."

Cathy laughed. "Somehow, that doesn't surprise me. Speaking of schedules, do you know when you're going to be doing your running around with Kelsea--if and when you're going to be home for dinner tomorrow?"

"We're going to start out early because she wants to go as many places as possible. We might even go to Presque Isle where they found the body of Janine Kirk years ago. Her murder has never been solved. But I'll be home for supper. I'm not sure if Kelsea wants to go out again on Sunday morning, but I want to make some time to see Julia and Tony while I'm home."

"I'll see if they'd want to come for dinner tomorrow night, then."

As planned, Allie was up early and went to pick up Kelsea. Allie had expected her to be sitting on the porch with her equipment waiting, but Kelsea was not there. Allie hated to ring the bell for fear of waking the entire household and decided to text her and wait on the porch. As soon as Allie opened the car door, Troy forced his way past her and bolted out, heading for Kelsea's back yard.

Allie was panicked and felt sick. She berated herself for allowing Troy to sit loose in the front seat rather than securing him in the back with his harness. "Troy!" she yelled, running after him. "Come. Come back here. Now!"

Troy continued racing toward the path where she, her mother, and Kelsea had walked together last month.

Kelsea rushed out the back door of her house and chased after them. Allie continued yelling for Troy until she was too short of breath to call him anymore. Both girls were struggling for breath when they reached the top of the hill.

"Oh my God," Allie gasped. "Do you see him?" They heard some loose rocks and dirt tumble into the ravine.

"He's found his path," Kelsea said, pointing to the right.

"Oh no," Allie groaned. "Here Troy! Come here, boy," she cried out loudly, then put on an authoritative voice. "Come now!" she shouted to no avail.

Troy was whining, barking, and making grumbling noises as he continued on the path that was more deteriorated than Allie remembered.

The sound of the front door closing when Allie left woke Cathy. She sat up, wide awake, realizing she knew where Lavinia and Troy were.

In her sleep, she'd seen Virgilio driving Bruno hard. He'd turned off the vineyard path and traveled south on a dirt road that she knew was Depot Road. Virgilio took it all the way around the treacherous curves running across the top of the cliffs. She heard the sound of Six Mile Creek gushing and gurgling below. Virgilio turned left onto a wider dirt road which was the newly created Station Road. He whipped Bruno to the top of the hill, the exact spot Bus 35 had stopped during her dry run, the same spot the hawk bombarded her bus window, the same spot she'd observed the tree being hit by lightning and going up in flames, and the same spot she felt the ground rumble as the tree toppled over the cliff.

Virgilio unhitched Bruno.

"Put them on the horse," Bruno instructed his sons.

The boys did as they were told and followed their father through the trees until they reached a plateau that had a wide path leading to the right.

Allie started on the treacherous path after Troy.

"Allie, that path has gotten much worse. Be careful. My folks said there were some bad thunderstorms and even more of it has collapsed and eroded. They said a tree got hit by lightning and it must've been the old white oak that had been there. It's gone and looks like it took part of the cliff and rocks with it. I don't think you should go down there!"

"I have to get him!" Allie was scared for herself and for Troy who showed no sign of turning around. "If something happens to Troy, I won't want to go home anyway."

Allie picked her way slowly, carefully, trying to find hand-holds to help stabilize herself, watching and wondering how Troy, with his lame back leg was managing to stay on the path.

Cathy jumped out of bed and threw on some clothes.

"What are you doing?" Paul moaned groggily.

"Just getting up. Go back to sleep."

Paul started snoring again.

Cathy put on her hiking boots and got in her car. When she turned onto Depot Road she did not feel as if she was driving her car. She felt as if she were lying in the back of a buckboard wagon being bounced around on a dark, damp night. .

When she reached Kelsea's home, she ran up the same path as Troy, Allie, and Kelsea had, ending up standing next to Kelsea, watching her daughter and Troy try to navigate their way to the outcropping of rock that now had an opening at the top where rocks had been displaced.

As she watched, in the back of her head Cathy felt she was being carried through a narrow opening. Her arms and legs scraped on the rocky sides of a cave until she finally was laid down on the cold clammy ground.

Her mind playing tricks on her, Cathy didn't realize she was following Allie and Troy. She couldn't hear Kelsea's and Allie's voices telling her not to go on the path, to stay where she was, Allie assuring her that she would get Troy. Mindlessly, Cathy continued on the path.

Troy finally reached the ledge on which the rocks were piled. The hawk was flying over, calling. Troy found his way to the opening and began digging, making it big enough for him to fit through.

Allie and Cathy reached the ledge safely and tested the rock and dirt pile for stability. They perched themselves on the rocks and looked in.

Cathy struggled to see into the darkness and an explosion echoed in her head, followed by the raining down of rocks, dirt, and debris that sealed off the entrance to the cave. Her eyes began adjusting to the dim light that entered the cave from the rising sun which highlighted three skeletons. Troy came bounding toward them, a human femur in his mouth.

DNA confirmed the identity of the remains to be that of Lavinia and Troy Anatoli and an Australian Shepherd dog. With Sharon's help, the Rosettis, Luella, and Cathy arranged for the burial of the remains. Because Lavinia, her son, and his beloved dog, Toby, had lain together undiscovered for so many years, their bones were placed side by side in a specially segmented box. Their bones would be interred at the base of the angel statue.

On September 17, 2017, the interment service was held at St. Elizabeth Cemetery. Everyone who had been involved in the search for Lavinia and Troy, or who knew about the search, was in attendance, including Raphael and Rachel Rosetti, Sharon, Cathy and Paul's children, Luella's children, even Karen from the research room at the Blasco Library, and Gino.

Cathy thought it only right that she bring Troy to the ceremony. As she walked with Paul over the cemetery grounds, Troy on leash slightly ahead of them, she remarked in surprise, "Paul! Look. Troy isn't limping."

"You're right. I wonder when that happened. We probably never even noticed it. Whatever was wrong with his leg is finally healed. That took quite a while, didn't it?"

Cathy didn't say anything, puzzling over whether Paul was right and she just hadn't noticed his limp was gone.

Troy lay obediently and quietly at Cathy's feet during the service. At the very end when the minister said, "May they rest in peace," and closed his prayer book, Cathy looked lovingly and thankfully at Troy. He looked back at her and before her eyes his bright blue eye turned brown to match his other eye.

ABOUT THE AUTHOR

Arleen McFadden Anderson resides in Woodbury, The Villages, Florida with her husband, Philip, and their Australian Cattle Dog, Maxine. For the majority of her life, Arleen worked as a secretary for a variety of businesses in Erie, Pennsylvania. When her parents became ill, she quit working full time and obtained a part time position as a school bus driver in Harborcreek, Pennsylvania where she worked for five years. Now, happily retired in the warmth of central Florida, she is free to pursue her lifetime passion for writing, enjoy some golf, and spend some quality time with Philip and Maxine.

OTHER BOOKS BY ARLEEN ANDERSON can be found at Amazon.com or obtained by special order through your favorite book store.

CLIODHNA'S WAVE - an emotionally charged tale of love, lust, domestic violence, madness and murder.

> This is by far the most intriguing book I have read in a long time. Arleen has found a way to bring about such an amazing spectrum of emotions. At times I loved, hated, sympathized with and wanted to slap both the protagonist and antagonist. I found myself thinking about this story throughout the day because of it's amazing depth and complexity. Arleen is a truly talented writer and did a magnificent job of creating a story that captivates her readers while taking them on an emotional roller coaster ride. I will be rereading this story for years to come. (Brooke Lewis 3/1/15)

TOURIST TRAP - College student, Marili McAdams, tires of the harsh winter weather in Erie, Pennsylvania, quits school, and pursues her dreams in Key West, Florida, but finds herself in the middle of a nightmare instead.

> Arlene [sic] Anderson has done it again. Tourist Trap is a page-turner with a protagonist that has you constantly thinking "Don't do it!" I enjoy the author's characters with such true to life mixture of good intentions and irresponsibility. I also highly recommend her first book Cliodhana's Wave. A year after reading it, those characters return to my mind surprisingly often. (Angela Stanford 3/2/17)

Made in the USA
Columbia, SC
05 December 2019